PRAISE

THE KIT PELHA

"Laugh-out-loud-on-the-bus funny."
Ben Aaronovitch, author of the Rivers of London series

"One of the funniest writers in Britain."
John Lawton, author of the Inspector Troy and Joe Wilderness series

"A dark, funny look at fandom from someone who really knows."
**Jenny Colgan, bestselling author of *Meet Me at
the Cupcake Café* and *Do You Remember the First
Time?*, and writer of six *Doctor Who* novels**

"This is a delight. Nev Fountain's genre savviness,
his sardonic humour and his skill at storytelling come
together in a perfect storm of crime-fiction fun."
**Andrew Cartmel, author of the Vinyl Detective
and Paperback Sleuth series**

"Funny, acerbic, ingenious. Nev Fountain's *The Fan Who Knew
Too Much* is a witty, twisty murder mystery set amid the egos and
eccentrics of sci-fi fandom. Podcasting, conventions, professional
fans and unprofessional stars… it's all here. Shrewdly observed,
it's at once very familiar and yet constantly surprising."
**Simon Guerrier, author of *David Whitaker in
an Exciting Adventure with Television***

"Nev Fountain… revels in sci-fi nerdism, spoofing it and
extolling it simultaneously, outrageously… Out of these
21st-century oddballs and freaks comes a murder classic."
John Lawton, author of the Inspector Troy and Joe Wilderness series

"I'm really annoyed with Nev Fountain for writing this book before I had the chance to think of it. People like him, who happen to be hugely talented and funny writers, think they can come up with original and clever ideas just because no one else has thought of them before. Yes, I admit it's a brilliant, genre-spanning novel that's hard to put down, but is that enough?"

Peter Davison, Doctor Who 1981-1984

"I loved this funny, intriguing, moving, bonkers story. It's a world I recognise and a must read for any fan of science fiction and beyond."

Sophie Aldred, Ace in Doctor Who, 1987-1989

"Nev Fountain is a very funny writer. *The Fan Who Knew Too Much* is a very funny book."

Simon Brett, author of the Mrs Pargeter, Fethering Village and The Decluttering mysteries

NEV FOUNTAIN

LIES AND DOLLS

A Kit Pelham Mystery

TITAN BOOKS

Also by Nev Fountain
and available from Titan Books

THE FAN WHO KNEW TOO MUCH

Lies and Dolls: a Kit Pelham Mystery
Print edition ISBN: 9781803365572
E-book edition ISBN: 9781803365596

Published by Titan Books
A division of Titan Publishing Group Ltd
144 Southwark Street, London SE1 0UP
www.titanbooks.com

First edition: July 2025
10 9 8 7 6 5 4 3 2 1

This is a work of fiction. All of the characters, organizations,
and events portrayed in this novel are either products
of the author's imagination or are used fictitiously. Any
resemblance to actual persons, living or dead (except
for satirical purposes), is entirely coincidental.

A CIP catalogue record for this title is
available from the British Library.

EU RP (for authorities only)
eucomply OÜ, Pärnu mnt. 139b-14, 11317 Tallinn, Estonia
hello@eucompliancepartner.com, +3375690241

Printed and bound by CPI Group (UK) Ltd, Croydon CR0 4YY.

Extract from the 'Vixens from the Void' Programme Guide, originally printed in 'Into the Void' Fanzine #28.

PRISON PLANET (Serial 4A)

Transmitted: 7 September 1989

Recorded: Studio 8: BBC Television Centre
16—17 May 1989
Location: Oldbury Nuclear Power Station,
Oldbury, 17—18 June 1989

Arkadia/Byzantia: Vanity Mycroft
Medula: Tara Miles
Professor Daxatar: Brian Crowbridge
Tania: Suzy Lu
Velhellan: Jennifer McLaird
Elysia: Samantha Carbury
Zerox: Petra De Villiers
Excelsior: Maggie Styles
Captain Talon: Patrick Finch
Production Design: Paula Marshall
Writer: Boris Shakespeare
Script Editor: Mervyn Stone
Director: Leslie Driscoll
Producer: Nicholas Everett

Synopsis:

After intercepting garbled space signals, TANIA and VELHELLAN lead a secret mission into STYRAX space to liberate prisoners held during the war. They arrive to find the prison planet mysteriously empty of all prisoners.

Tania and Velhellan find ARKADIA held on the planet – seemingly the only prisoner. They make good their escape, running the gauntlet of automated security systems and Styrax guards.

Arkadia insists on bringing a suitcase with her; but she doesn't tell the others what's inside.

Once back on VIXOS, the audience learns that 'Arkadia' is not Arkadia at all, but her missing twin sister BYZANTIA, who has been missing – presumed dead – for the past four years.

Inside the briefcase are all the missing prisoners, miniaturised for storage. Inside is the real Arkadia, who has also been reduced to the size of a doll...

Notes:

The much-heralded return of Vanity Mycroft after missing a season was keenly awaited by fans who considered Arkadia to be the very 'heart and soul' of 'Vixens from the Void'. However, this return was not to be a pain-free process.

Producer Nicholas Everett made a strategic mistake when hinting at Arkadia's return. He had been given verbal assurances from Vanity Mycroft that she would be prepared to rejoin the show but crucially she had not signed a contract at that point.

As soon as news of her return emerged in the press, she immediately made several demands, including (it was rumoured) the doubling of her salary, freedom to write her own scripts and the removal of any cast members she didn't like (which was pretty much all of them).

Meanwhile, while planning Arkadia's return, script editor Mervyn Stone decided that the character should not become Prime Mistress as expected. He concluded that it would restrict her role in the series. Instead, he would resurrect Byzantia, Arkadia's older sister, who was assumed killed in a shuttle crash (serial 1A: Coronation), to take over the hereditary title. Mycroft objected to the new character, and this too was a major obstacle in negotiations.

Everett decided in a moment of genius (or madness, according to Stone) to make Byzantia the slightly older twin of Arkadia, and to offer Vanity both roles – Arkadia AND Byzantia.

As expected, Vanity was intrigued by the idea, and agreed, dropping her other demands. She made only one further request: she claimed that, as she was now playing two characters, she should be given two dressing rooms to help her prepare for the dual role. The producer gladly acquiesced.

The enthusiasm for Vanity's return was not shared by the cast, as the atmosphere on the show had improved since her departure. Petra De Villiers, who played Vanity's android replica Zerox, had proved popular among the production team, and some saw no need to change the format. Most dreaded the inevitable tension between Vanity and Petra.

In the event, this tension was short-lived, as Petra elected to leave the show of her own volition, returning to her native France and marrying the owner of a chain of restaurants. She was torn apart by a pack of mutant crabs off-screen, and not seen again.

The return of Arkadia and the introduction of Byzantia brought the total of main cast members up to ten; Mervyn Stone freely admitted he'd added several characters in order to help secure a merchandising deal for action figures.

When rewriting 'Prison Planet' (the original writer having revealed he was a Russian agent and fleeing to Moscow after handing in a sketchy first draft), Stone incorporated a major sub-plot involving miniaturised prisoners held in a suitcase so that they could use the actual models on the show.

Lincolnshire company Braxtons Models outbid Sevans Kits and Dapol Figures and bought the licence to make a range of ten action figures. The company met with a series of misfortunes; firstly, it was sued by Vanity Mycroft, asserting that she hadn't cleared the finished sculpt as per her contract. She claimed that her action figure would have a detrimental impact on her acting career as the breasts were too small. Secondly, the BBC chose to end 'Vixens from the Void', causing demand to plummet. Shortly after, the Braxtons Models factory burned to the ground, killing the CEO, Jack Braxton, in the process.

Braxtons was developing the second wave of ten figures (the 'Ceremonial Range') at the time, and only five prototypes survived the inferno. The figures have since been highly prized by fans of 'Vixens' and collectors of antique toys.

PART ONE:

WHY DIDN'T THEY ASK SEVANS?

1

The severed torso and limbs were wrapped in cellophane, placed in a package and sealed up with heavy-duty masking tape. The package was taken to the post office, weighed and sent by first-class delivery. It travelled to the sorting office, where it landed in another bag. The bag was placed in a van, and the van started the long drive down to London. The body parts sat in Hammersmith sorting office for an afternoon and then were taken to Wormwood Scrubs prison.

After being opened and checked by prison warders, it was resealed and ended up in a cell in D Wing, on a table by a jug of strawberry milkshake and a plate of waffles. One waffle was covered in maple syrup, the other in chocolate sauce. Both were decorated with little pointy mountains of squirty cream.

The fat man sat down to eat the waffles at 9.52 a.m. He ate the waffles, drank a glass of milkshake, opened the jiffy bag, saw the contents and screamed his guts out.

2

"Leave the M25 at Junction 27, you will – and then take the M11 towards Cambridge, you must."

The satnav had the voice of Yoda. Of course it did.

Binfire leaned forward and squinted out of the windscreen like he was looking for enemy starships. "Okay, we're free of the asteroid belt now," he said. "Let's go up to warp seven."

The asteroid belt. What Binfire calls the M25.

Binfire flicked a broken switch on the dashboard that he had labelled 'warp drive' and slammed his foot on the accelerator, pushing the battered motorhome up to seventy miles per hour. He punctuated the acceleration by making the roaring sound of a TIE fighter.

Kit Pelham groaned too, but quietly, and pushed her earbuds deeper inside her ears.

At a casual glance, Kit and Binfire seemed like an odd pair of friends: he, a crazed-looking man in his fifties with shaved head, cargo pants and a sleeveless T-shirt, who looked like he had tunnelled out of a Vietnamese prisoner-of-war camp, and she, a gawky-looking woman just turned thirty, with bright orange hair, jaunty pink velvet cap, black velvet coat and tartan trousers, who looked like she'd flounced out of a Human League video. They seemed to have nothing in common but a penchant for wearing big clumpy boots.

But they *were* friends, and now they had become *even more* friends, after they had solved a murder in Brighton a few years ago, culminating in an incident where they were nearly killed by a maniac who tried to blow them both up with a gas cooker.

It was a shared experience like that which could create a bond between the oddest of couples.

Kit liked having Binfire as her best friend as he was the only individual in the universe whose presence didn't exhaust her. As Binfire's presence exhausted everybody *else* in the universe, it was a bit of a paradox. Kit thought long and hard about it and concluded that, as Binfire lived in his own special universe he didn't really impinge upon hers. On this occasion, however, Binfire's universe was breaking through. She just wanted to submerge herself in back-to-back Ultravox tracks, but Binfire insisted on producing a constant stream of loud chatter and even louder sound effects.

She pulled her earbuds out of her ears. "Can you stop doing that?"

"What?"

"Everything."

"Sorry, pilgrim, I'm just a bit nervous."

"What about?"

Binfire looked at her, surprised. "Loaning my action figure to this museum, of course. It's a bit of a big moment. I dunno – how to describe it? It's emotional, man. Like driving your only daughter to university."

Kit harrumphed. "I'm not sure what's emotional about driving your daughter to university. My parents gave me a lift to Bristol and they didn't even wait to have lunch. They were driving out of the car park before I found my room."

"Okay, well. Bad analogy in your case, pilgrim. But you get what I mean. It's nerve-racking. My hands are shaking here."

He took his hands off the wheel and showed them to Kit to demonstrate how they were shaking.

"YES! So I see. Can you put them back on the wheel please?"

Binfire looked at his hands as if he'd only just realised they belonged to him, then put them back on the steering wheel.

Kit exhaled with relief.

Why were they sitting in a battered motorhome, hurtling up the M11 towards Lincolnshire? It had all started with the Reverend Jerome Bell. He was a bona fide vicar, with his own parish, but more importantly he was a minor celebrity in the world of action-figure collectibles. He had a popular YouTube channel 'The Garden of Ebay', where he showed his 'flock' his latest charity shop finds, and if they were dirty, he'd 'baptise' them in his sink with some cotton wool and soapy water.

Reverend Bell had contacted Binfire and explained that he'd been tasked with putting together a toy museum at Furley House in Lincolnshire, and he would be thrilled if Binfire would, by any chance, be kind enough to loan them his rare *Vixens from the Void* action figure. No cash was offered, but there were several incentives: an invitation to the opening of the museum, a night at Furley House, a dinner with the Marquess of Furley in attendance and a chance to have a lesson in clay-pigeon shooting.

He was also allowed a Plus One.

This dovetailed nicely with Kit Pelham's job. Part of her work as a 'professional' fan of cult television meant Kit wrote articles for *Vixmag*, which covered the sci-fi series *Vixens from the Void*: both the classic series from the 1980s and the revived series streaming on Fliptop. She asked Binfire if she could come so she could write about the museum. It would make a great 'interesting' article. And Binfire agreed.

Kit hadn't told Binfire the *real* reason why she wanted to come. Furley House wasn't just the home of the toy museum. It was also home to the Marquess of Furley's older sister, Lady Tabitha Pendragon, or, as she was better known, the Cosplay Countess. She was a minor aristocrat who had gained a lot of attention with YouTube videos in which she posed in figure-hugging outfits to the delight of her fans.

There was hope in the back of Kit's mind that perhaps she would meet her during her visit? Or get an interview? Or just a glimpse of Lady Tabitha in her Princess Leia slave girl costume?

It made sense for Binfire to drive them to Furley House. The stately home was miles from the nearest train station. The only problem (as far as Kit was concerned) was it also meant that they were stuck sitting side by side in a dirty van for two and a half hours.

Kit's phone buzzed. It was a text which said:

I can see you've just got off the M25 and you're making good time. Well done you. Jackie xxx

Kit didn't want to send her girlfriend a heart and a smiley face. A fantasy flickered in her head, an image of herself sending a skull and an Edvard Munch scream, as if to say *Why are you tracking my every move?*

But she sent a heart and a smiley face anyway.

3

"Turn off the M11 and take Junction 14, you must. Follow the road for two miles, you will, and then the A428, you will take."

Yoda guided them into the countryside, where the Lego landscape of identical housing estates gave way to misty flatlands. They negotiated winding roads for miles until, at last, they reached the top of a hill where the fields were a patchwork quilt below them, squares of green and brown. Nestling in the middle, like an aged labrador having a nap, was Furley House.

They continued down the hill until they could see the stately home in better detail: the huge entrance framed by Doric columns, the stone walls peppered with tall, thin windows, the roof spiked with turrets and a single flagpole rising out of the roof.

"Reached your destination, you have," said Yoda.

A man was waiting at the entrance. He looked like he had been carved out of the same mossy limestone as the house. He wore a green tweed jacket, waistcoat, plus fours and thick socks stretching up to his knees. He had thick wavy brown hair that had been wrestled into a side parting.

This was Archibald Pendragon, the eighth Marquess of Furley. Even though he was only in his early thirties, he looked like he was preparing for acquiring the appendage 'old buffer'. He waved cheerfully as Kit disembarked from the motorhome and strode forward to shake her hand. His palm was warm and damp, and Kit resisted the urge to recoil from his grasp.

"Terribly good to see you!" the Marquess bubbled with enthusiasm. "Kit Pelham, I presume?"

"That's me."

"I hope your journey wasn't too irksome. We are a bit out of the way here."

It was awful.

"It was fine."

"Good, good. Now, I gather from my PR girl Melanie you want an interview. I don't have her here today as she doesn't do Fridays or weekends, so I'm happy to give you any access you require while you're here. As I said in the email thingy, if you want a chat, I'd be happy to oblige."

"Thank you, Marquess."

"Please, call me Archie. Everybody does. Apart from the servants of course. One has to have *some* boundaries."

"Thank you, Archie."

"I say, I like your hat. Very bohemian."

With an air of insouciance evolved from centuries of breeding, the Marquess of Furley seemed utterly unfazed by her appearance.

He's probably used to people wearing anachronistic clothes, Kit thought. *Given he's dressed like he's about to wave his servants off to fight the First World War.*

Archie's smile didn't flicker when Binfire poked his shaven head out of the driver's side of the motorhome and leapt onto the drive, heavy boots crunching on the gravel. He was holding his army kitbag on his shoulder like he was being posted to a warzone.

"Aha!" the Marquess barked with delight, glancing at a piece of paper in his hand. "And you must be Benjamin Ferry. Honoured to meet you, Mr Ferry."

Binfire stroked his chin and put on his best Alec Guinness impression. "Benjamin Ferry? Now there's a name I haven't heard in a loooooong time."

Kit explained. "No one calls him Ben Ferry anymore.

Everyone calls him Binfire. For lots and lots of reasons which quickly become evident the longer you know him."

The Marquess chuckled. "How splendid! I do love nicknames. The chaps at school used to call me Winky. Couldn't work out why. Finally found the courage to ask after a term or two. Turns out I looked a bit like *another* boy who once lost his shorts during rugger."

He directed his attention to their mode of transport. "Oh my." He gave out an appreciative whistle. "What a van! That *is* impressive. Such colours!"

Binfire's motorhome was in the classic style, like the one Walter White used as a lab to cook his meth (*Breaking Bad*, 2008–2013) but Binfire had 'pimped his ride'. Every inch was covered with murals. The side facing Furley House depicted a blaster-wielding man and a space princess surrounded by stars and galaxies.

"You like it?" Binfire winked. "I tracked down the guy who paints fairground rides and got him to do it. I frokking love that style." He pointed proudly at the figures. "You see that guy? You see his face? Half of it looks like Harrison Ford, the other half looks like Mark Hamill. It takes a special skill to achieve something that looks almost-but-not-quite like two different people at the same time."

Archie nodded. "Yes, gypsies are so creative, aren't they?" He clapped his hands. "Let me show you to your rooms."

They entered the massive hallway of Furley House, then Archie took a sharp right and led them into a corridor where the way was blocked by two silver stanchions supporting a thick red rope. He unclipped one end and ushered them through.

"Shortcut," he explained. "Saves us going the tourist route."

He led them briskly along wood-panelled corridors, past dark oil paintings and grim suits of armour.

He gave a sideways glance at Kit. "I'm given to understand I'm in the presence of an ace detective? Reverend Bell told me you were involved in a web of mystery and intrigue in Brighton? And apparently you solved a murder?"

"Aha. Sort of."

Binfire piped up, "Yeah, she solved it alright. I was honoured to be her loyal sidekick."

"Well, that sounds terribly exciting."

"Let me tell you, Marquess, man, it was frokking dynamite."

Archie was bubbling with excitement. "What actually happened? Do tell!"

"Well, it's a long story," said Kit gravely. "I'm sure we'll have time, and I'll happily recount to you 'The Case of The Fan Who Knew Too Much'."

"The Fan who…?"

"I catalogue my adventures in my casebook. That's the one I call 'The Case of The Fan Who Knew Too Much'."

"Goodness. And how many cases have you investigated thus far?"

"Just the one. But by cataloguing it now, it'll be a lot less work if any more cases come up."

Archie chuckled. "Well that puts a topper on an exciting day! I'm very excited, believe me. Not as excited as the Reverend, of course. But it's so nice to see such enthusiasm for *something* in this modern age, even though it's only a television programme. I expect you know my guilty secret." He tapped his nose. "I'm not really a fan of *Vixens of the Voids*."

Kit's pedant monster awoke and struggled to break free, urging her to correct the Marquess and say *Actually, it's* Vixens from the Void. To her own immense satisfaction, she managed to wrestle it to the ground and put it back in its box.

"No," continued Archie. "It was more a passion of my father's."

They were passing by a section of corridor that was covered in framed photos and clippings, most of them in black and white, all of them featuring a fat man dressed in a kaftan, wearing John Lennon glasses and sprouting an incredible set of mutton chop whiskers. It looked like scientists had taken the DNA from a scatter cushion and spliced it with a walrus. Kit recognised who it was, of course: it was Archie's dad, Roland Pendragon, the seventh Marquess of Furley, who had passed on three years ago.

One photo was of Roland in front of Furley House, standing by someone dressed as a giant crab. Another had Roland beaming with a young actress wearing Spandex and a cloak. Roland had snaked his arm across her shoulders and placed his hand shamelessly on her left bosom. The young actress was grinning, too, choosing not to register where his hand had parked itself.

"Father loved the show, as you can see."

"Yes," said Kit dryly. "I can see how much he loved it."

"Anyway, you'll find the museum just outside the east wing. Just walk around the house and you can't miss it. Pre-meal drinks and canapés are there at six, proper nosh-up at seven thirty in the main hall."

"Is Lady Tabitha at home?" asked Kit, in a way she hoped sounded like a casual question but suspected it came out like the gurgle of a hormonal teenager.

"Big sis?" Archie stroked his chin. "Oh, she's definitely about. She wouldn't miss it for the world. She owns one of the action figures, you know, bequeathed to her by Father. So, she's got a stake in the enterprise, albeit a small one. She'll definitely make an appearance at some point."

"I'd like to interview her too, if that's possible."

He chuckled. "Yes, I'm sure you would. She's quite the celebrity, I gather. She's known as the Cosplay Countess. Though

'Lady' is more the correct term than 'Countess'... Father was a bit of a showman and I think she got all those genes. Compared to the rest of my family, I'm a bit of a dull old cove."

"So could I?"

"Could you what?"

"Interview her?"

I'm being utterly ridiculous. What's the point of interviewing her? I already know everything about her. I know her favourite flavour is salted caramel. I know she's allergic to citrus. I know her favourite song is 'In the Year 2525' by Zager and Evans. I know she likes tidy men who buff their nails...

"Well, I can't promise anything. She is rather shy—"

"Stop ye curs! Go no further!"

He was interrupted by a shout from above. On a landing about forty feet above them was a slender woman dressed in an outrageous costume. She wore a silver tricorn hat, a big frilly white shirt over a black basque, huge flappy boots and a scrappy waistcoat. Her huge, bejewelled belt held two futuristic-looking guns which she unholstered and aimed at them.

As Lady Tabitha Pendragon walked to the edge of the balustrade, Kit could see her face was obscured with eye patches over *both* eyes. One was covered by a normal black patch, the other was covered by a rotating robot eye which swivelled and threw out a dazzling red light beam.

Kit wondered how on earth Lady Tabitha could see. *Probably got a tiny bit of gauze sewn into the black felt.*

There was something on her shoulder: a robot parrot. Its head bounced around on its neck as its beak opened and closed, and its wings flexed.

"Ahoy there," she boomed. "I spy strangers, me hearties!"

Archie smiled up at her like an indulgent father. "Very impressive, Tabby. I like the parrot."

"I do not take kind words from a lily-livered planet-dweller, like ye. Scum!"

Archie flashed a watery smile at Binfire and Kit. "You're in luck, Kit. Allow me to introduce my big sis. She's being a space pirate today."

Tabitha pointed her guns down at them. There was an electronic whine as they pretended to power up to 'kill mode'. "Go no further, Spaceforce vermin, or I'll fill ye full of laser bolts!"

Archie indicated Kit. "Tabs, this lady is a journalist for some space magazine. She'd like to interview you about – whatever it is you do. Would that be amenable to you, at all?"

Lady Tabitha looked down with disdain, examining Kit in her pink hat and black velvet coat. "Why, you're a thin-hipped excuse for a cabin boy. I'll wager I'll squash you like a space weevil when I get you between my juicy thighs!"

Kit blushed.

She pointed her gun to each of them in turn. "I feel it only fair to warn ye, that's *my* treasure in that museum. And if ye so much as think of making off with me gold, then I'll run you through with my laser cutlass and push you out of the nearest airlock!"

She gave a hearty laugh and disappeared inside the depths of Furley House.

"I think that might be a 'no'." Archie grinned.

"Oh well."

"Apologies. She's a bit of a character, but in our family, we do have a tradition of indulging eccentricities."

"Don't apologise," said Kit. "It was… quite a performance."

They walked on.

Binfire leaned into Kit's ear and whispered: "Robbie is going to be so bloody jealous."

4

"God, I'm so bloody jealous," said Robbie.

He gave a theatrical sigh and put his fist over his heart. "For a lot of gay men of my age, Lady Tabitha Pendragon is a *god*."

Binfire gave Kit a quick *told you so* look.

They had WhatsApped Robbie. He was on the screen of Binfire's phone, propped up on a table near a box of Kit's complimentary teas and coffees.

Robbie was sitting in the living room of 33 Hanover Parade in Brighton. It looked startlingly different. There was a new sofa. The walls had been given a fresh coat of paint. Videos were not piled on planks of wood propped up with bricks anymore, but neatly arranged on gleaming white shelves.

Robbie looked different too: his break-up with his last boyfriend Victor had been messy, to put it mildly. Kit understood that. The worst discovery anyone would usually make in a rocky relationship was finding your partner was having an affair. Robbie had discovered his partner was a psychopathic murderer who'd attempted to kill his friends, so he had a right to a period of rehabilitation. It had been a year since Robbie had decided to stop crying about it and set about reinventing himself with grim determination, camping out in the local gym and toning his pear-shaped form into something beach-body ready.

It's ironic, Kit thought. *He's finally regained his mental perspective at the cost of losing his physical perspective.* Robbie's harassed-looking bald head now looked tiny, sitting atop a triangular mass of muscle, and though she didn't like the look, Kit was glad Robbie was putting his ex behind him.

"I don't believe this! I'm stuck here and you've met *her*? What's she like?"

"Well, we didn't actually *meet* her, Robbie," said Kit. "She looked down on us dressed as a space pirate and pointed her space guns at us."

"Oh wow," gasped Robbie. "Oh wow! She did that? She must have been amazing!"

"Yes, she was." Binfire grinned. "She's even more impressive in real life, man."

Robbie's eyebrows crawled up his shiny head in disdain. "The Cosplay Countess is more than impressive, Binfire. She's got about ten million followers. There are only three ways you can get ten million followers on YouTube. Learn to cook, take your clothes off or say you love Hitler, and she's done none of them. All she does is go on expensive holidays and wear fantastic costumes. And *that*, in my world, is living your best damn life. And you've met her *and* you're going to see the opening of a new toy museum full of *Vixens from the Void* action figures. It's bad enough Binfire possessing one of *the* rarest action figures in the world. But the fact he's decided to take *you*…"

He tailed off. Obviously, it was too painful to put into words.

"Yes," said Kit.

"But I thought you'd be teaching at the college today, pilgrim," said Binfire. "It *is* term time, isn't it?"

Robbie flinched at the unwelcome reminder. "Yes, I am, yes, that's true. But I could have thrown a sickie for Friday. Those kids wouldn't notice… I should be there. *I'm* the action-figure guy. I know much more about them than Kit."

"I know," said Kit.

"That's *my* thing."

Kit felt obliged to say something to make him feel better. "It's just a room full of old toys."

It was the wrong thing to say.

Robbie's eyes flashed. "Exactly. That's all it is to you. A room full of old toys. You don't appreciate it like me. I bet you know nothing about the *Vixens from the Void* Ceremonial Range, do you?" he snapped. "I bet you don't even know who owns the other four figures."

"We don't, man." Binfire grinned. "We haven't a clue. Please tell us. Lay your *amazing* expertise on us."

Kit looked at Binfire quizzically. *We know all that stuff!* Binfire gave Kit the tiniest wink. And nodded to the phone. She understood the wink. *Let Robbie lecture us. It'll make him feel much better.*

Robbie harrumphed. "Oh. Right. Where to start? Well, let's start with the most obvious. The Arkadia figure is owned by Graham Goldingay, the biggest *Vixens* memorabilia collector in the country, in more ways than one. Obviously, *he's* not going to be there because he's in prison for blackmail and people-smuggling, thanks to Kit."

Binfire punched Kit on the shoulder as if to say *Well done.* Kit mouthed an *ow* as if to say *Ow.*

Robbie continued, "The Medula action figure – that's owned by Fenton Worth, the comic shop guy."

Kit knew about Fenton Worth. They all did. Fenton's sci-fi and fantasy shop, The Starshop Enterprise had started life in London, specifically Lewisham. Over the years, it had scuttled sideways like a crab, heading slowly eastwards where the rents were more reasonable. Kit imagined that Fenton, ever the optimist, was guiding his shop to a promised land where the rents were so low they'd pay him to stay open. Every time Kit visited the shop, it had moved somewhere else, always to an area a bit shabbier and nastier than the last time, like it was wandering the London streets spoiling for a fight. The last time she saw it, it was passing through Woolwich, presumably making a break for the countryside.

"Fenton probably won't be there either, because he also went to prison, for insurance fraud." Robbie frowned. "Oh wait. No! Tell a lie. He's out now. He closed The Starshop Enterprise after he finished his sentence, married some woman with a lot of money who owned a corner shop, and now he's set up in Peterborough. He opened up The Battlestore Galactica last year."

Robbie cleared his throat. "Now... The Velhellan action figure. That's owned by Matty Kearney. You know him, the anti-woke warrior, always complaining about *Star Wars* being stuffed with gays and lesbians and coloured people and trans people and the like. He reviews movies and TV shows on YouTube and goes on about not being able to offend anybody, while being offensive to everybody."

Robbie tapped his chin with his finger. "Now, where was I? Oh yes, well there's Excelsior, that's owned by Binfire, for whatever reason I cannot fathom in a *million years*."

Binfire grinned and held up his shopping bag. He gave it a little shake.

"Don't do that!" Robbie exploded. "That is mint-in-box and one-of-a-kind. You do *not* stick a piece of history in a Sainsbury's carrier bag!"

Kit's pedant monster woke up. "It's a *Tesco* carrier bag."

Robbie's voice dripped with sarcasm. "Yes, well that makes it all completely okay! Now, who do I have left? Oh my god, how could I have forgotten? The Byzantia action figure is owned by Lady Tabitha. She inherited it from her father, Roland Pendragon. She talks about it a lot on Instagram, saying it's her most treasured possession ever... And I can't believe you've bloody *met* her!"

"Thanks for telling us all this, Robbie, man," said Binfire. "You've proved a great help."

"You're just humouring me," he huffed.

"Yeah, we are, but you do appreciate the effort."

He sighed. "I suppose so."

"Hey, where's my little goth girl?" asked Binfire.

"Freya?" said Robbie. "No idea. I'm sure she's at the Hanover Community Centre with her odd friends." He pulled a disapproving scowl. "She does that a *lot* now."

Binfire and Robbie's housemate was Freya, a goth/hippy hybrid in her twenties. Like Robbie, she was struggling to get past a dead relationship, but in Freya's case her significant other was literally dead, murdered in the middle of his podcast by Robbie's ex-boyfriend Victor. She had spent the last two years ingratiating herself with the Krellevangelists, a dodgy quasi-religious group based on an obscure episode of *Vixens from the Void*. They enticed her in by saying they could put her in contact with her deceased boyfriend and ask him if he was happy, if he missed her and where he'd put that signed copy of *The Hitchhiker's Guide to the Galaxy*.

They ended the call and Binfire slipped his phone back in the pouch on his belt.

"Okay, I'm going to head to my room." He looked at his chunky survival watch. "Frokk, is that the time?"

He was just about to leave when Kit's phone flared into life with her signature ringtone, the opening bars of Eurythmics' 'Sweet Dreams (Are Made of This)'.

Kit could see that the phone said 'Jackie'. It was vibrating across the coffee table. Before Kit had time to react, Binfire pressed 'accept' and 'speakerphone'. Kit looked furiously at Binfire, but he just grinned, saluted, held a finger to his lips and pointed to the phone.

Jackie's voice said, "Hello? Kit?"

Kit leaned across and said, "I'm here."

"You sound funny."

"You're on speakerphone."

"Speakerphone? Are you alone?"

Kit was caught with two options, none of them desirable. She could admit that Binfire was in her room, which would lead to a long, well-trodden conversation later about how Jackie disapproved of Binfire, how she thought he was a crazed nutter, how she *knew* he was in love with Kit so she'd be wise to cut off all ties with him ASAP...

Or she could just lie.

"Yes. I'm alone." She gave a murderous glance at Binfire, who just stood there and held his thumbs aloft. "So how are you?"

"I'm fine. Are you busy?"

"No."

"Oh. That's odd."

"Why?"

"I just noticed on *Life360* you've been at Furley House for an hour now. I thought you would have texted me to tell me you got there safely."

Why would I need to text to tell you I've got here safely when you already know I've got here safely? she thought.

"It's been a bit hectic here. I've just unpacked and phoned the guys in 33 Hanover Parade."

"Right. So getting in touch with *them* was the priority."

Kit almost sighed. "I was tired, so I thought I'd get them out of the way first."

"You're tired? Poor darling."

"Yes."

"So, if you're tired, I guess you're not going to the dinner tonight. You can stay in your room and we can talk on the phone."

Binfire pulled a shocked face and mimed using a knife and fork, then he shook his head in disbelief. Then he swirled a finger next to his ear. Kit didn't need an explanation for what he was trying to say.

"I'm not *that* kind of tired. I just need a bit of time to myself, you know?"

"Too tired to talk to me, but not tired enough to go to dinner. I see."

"How about I phone you once I get in after the dinner? We could talk then."

"I might be asleep by then."

This conversation was rapidly becoming pointless. A lot of their conversations had become pointless lately. They weren't hostile, but they weren't friendly either; not peace as such, but an absence of war.

"Okay, I'll text you when I get to my room. If you're awake, we'll talk. If you're not, then we can talk tomorrow afternoon, before we get on the road."

"Won't you want to get back straight away? Beat the traffic? I've got something really important I really need to talk to you about."

"Well tell me."

"No, it's really important. We've got to talk face to face."

Kit could feel her jaws pressing together, threatening to grind her teeth into a powder.

She's done this before, she thought. *Just last year when I was away at that Devon convention In Space No One Can Eat Ice Cream, she rang me up and said she'd organised a commemoration ceremony for her friend Lily Sparkes on the occasion of Lily's birthday. She said it had been in the diary for months, but I knew I hadn't been told. Even so, I knew if I hadn't come home early to take part in the ceremony there would have been hell to pay.*

"Talk about what?"

"I'll tell you when I see you. Can you get back first thing?"

"It's the free lesson in clay-pigeon shooting tomorrow afternoon. I don't think Binfire would forgive me if we miss that."

"Well, as long as *he's* happy."

Kit felt her left eye start to twitch.

"I wasn't happy about you travelling up with him, let alone staying the night with him under the same roof."

Binfire pulled an indignant face and mimed performing a strangulation.

"Technically," said Kit, "we're not under the same roof. We're in reconditioned stables. He's in a different stable."

"Don't set your pedant monster on me, dear."

"I wasn't."

"You *were*."

"Okay, let's agree to differ. Let's talk tomorrow, and I'll let you know when we're on the road."

"Okay, I suppose it'll have to do."

"I'd better get on. The preview opens in…"

She looked at the pocket watch fastened to her velvet coat.

Fifteen minutes?

"It's in fifteen minutes."

"Fine. Goodbye then, sweetie. Have a good one."

From the way Jackie said it, she didn't mean it at all, but Kit took the words at face value. It was ironic; Kit had spent so many years learning to detect the undercurrents in people's voices, only to train herself to ignore the subtext in Jackie's.

"Thanks, Jackie."

"Love you."

"Love you too."

She ended the call.

Binfire exhaled.

"Don't start," said Kit. "Don't say *anything*! You just listened to a private conversation, so don't judge her. She's very protective of me, which is only to be expected, given we met in unusual circumstances."

"There's a fine line between protective and being controlled by a control-freak psycho."

"She's not a control-freak psycho. And I'm not being controlled."

Binfire continued, "It never feels like control freakery, from the inside. When you're in the relationship it all feels normal, but once you break out of the mind control you realise how mad it's got. Remember my old girlfriend Scary Sandra?"

"Of course I remember."

Binfire conducted his love life like a drowsy wasp, bumping against women at random. If Kit wasn't a more fastidious person, she would have lost track of his girlfriends years ago. But Kit was Kit; she had a file of them in her head and could recite them in order, length of duration and reason for their demise, as if they were Doctor Whos.

Kit downloaded the relevant data from her brain. "Sandra Gale, 2016 to 2018. Long blonde hair. Big fan of the *Twilight* movies. Didn't blink enough. Vegetarian. Worked at the Sea Life Centre. Her tenure as your girlfriend came to an end during a climactic confrontation in Somerset. She was the one who put a dog tracker chip in your arm, wasn't she?"

"Yeah, that's her. Remember I thought the chip was a good idea? It was cute, not to mention pretty groovy and sci-fi at the time. It was only when we split up and I went to Glastonbury and she turned up at my tent, locating me using a phone app, that I realised I had to get rid of it – and her – pronto."

He tapped his shoulder. Kit knew that underneath his jacket there was a rectangular scar, which had been covered over by a tattoo of R2-D2. "Have you ever tried to cauterise a wound with a joss stick? It's not the ideal way. But hey, it's a lovely smell. Surgical instrument and anaesthetic all in one."

"Jackie is *not* Scary Sandra, Binfire," said Kit coldly, with a conviction she did not feel. "We'd better get moving."

"Good thought, pilgrim. We've got to get there before those bastards eat all the canapés."

5

When Archie had shown them to their rooms, Kit had expected to be led up dusty corridors and into a room containing oil-lamps and a cobweb-strewn four-poster bed. Instead, he'd brought them outside and showed them a collection of reconditioned stables that had been converted into adorable apartments, like Bilbo Baggins' Hobbiton house (*The Lord of the Rings*, 2001–2003, *The Hobbit*, 2012–2014). They had kept the original stable doors and inserted little stained-glass portholes in the top section.

They emerged from Kit's particular hobbit house, walked around the perimeter of the courtyard and along the outside of the main house, their boots scrunching on the gravel.

"Lady Tabitha, right?" said Binfire at last.

"Yes," agreed Kit.

"Wow. She was frokking something."

"She was."

"She's got a lot of spirit. What do you think? Do you think a princess and a guy like me?"

"No," said Kit firmly. "No."

Having completed their traditional ritual upon meeting any attractive female, cribbing old dialogue from *Star Wars* (1977), they stayed silent until they reached the chapel. It was a beautiful building with tall stained-glass windows. The door had a cardboard cut-out fixed to it, artwork of a woman in *Vixens* costume. A bubble came out of her mouth, saying WELCOME TO THE **VIXENS FROM THE VOID** TOY MUSEUM!

As they walked towards the door, Kit could hear a murmur

of conversation coming from within. She instinctively tensed at the sound of the crowd.

I'm not ready for this.

Kit knew she probably had Asperger's, or autism, or ADHD. But she hadn't bothered to find out what particular colour on the neurodivergent chart she was because (ironically, for someone who liked to categorise everything within reach) Kit was very resistant to slap a label on herself. She didn't want to know. Life was complicated enough without having a Thing that she had to take tests for and talk to experts about. It sounded too exhausting. All she did know was she didn't like crowds, and she definitely didn't like parties.

She braced herself and followed Binfire inside.

It was a white octagonal room, framed with high beams that stretched into the ceiling. It was decorated with panels with facts and timelines printed on them. Glass display cabinets lined the walls, divided roughly into subcategories. There was a giant pyramid that jutted out of the middle of the room, displaying action figures.

Standing like sentries in the corners of the room were full-size mannequins, dressed like characters from *Vixens from the Void*. Kit recognised them instantly as the promotional figures Braxtons had constructed to stand outside toy shops back in the 1990s. She used to fantasise about owning one and having it in the corner of her bedroom. She was impressed that they'd found eight of them in such good condition.

The room was filled with people, dressed in various approximations of eveningwear.

The men were wandering around the place, examining everything with keen interest, while the women sat wearily on the chairs, clearly bored and waiting for the sweet release of death. It looked like the Bizarro version of a branch of John Lewis.

Archie Pendragon was there, in an immaculate dinner jacket, talking to a man with a drooping grey moustache and beard, wearing a clerical collar. Kit recognised him as Reverend Jerome Bell.

There was no carpet, just flagstones, so the buzz of conversation was deafening. Kit flinched from the sudden horror of it all. Her hand strayed to her lapel, where her panic badge was pinned, a yellow smiley face that she could spin upside down and signal to Binfire that she wanted to be taken somewhere – anywhere – else.

But Binfire was nowhere to be seen. She looked around and saw he had raced into the depths of the museum in pursuit of the canapés. Now, with his mouth full, he was attempting to talk to a shabby man dressed in an ill-fitting jacket. Fenton Worth. Even from this distance, she could see that Fenton had aged badly, which was only to be expected for comic shop owners who sat in dark spaces all day reading graphic novels and scowling at customers. His mousy hair had long since left the crown of his head and migrated to his ears and down his neck.

She thought about joining their conversation, but she didn't have the energy. She didn't want a drink, and she wasn't going to eat the canapés because she didn't know how many calories they contained. She was trapped, rooted to the spot and alone in a crowd. A situation she dreaded above all else.

She thought about silently slipping away and hiding in the main house, but then she saw the television set, fixed high on the ceiling.

Sanctuary.

She went over and stared up at it. The picture wobbled and crackled. It was an off-air video recording, of one of the 1990s television adverts promoting the *Vixens from the Void* Braxtons toy range. A boy and a girl, both about ten years old, were crouching over a *Vixens from the Void* playset, a docking bay dominated by a huge round platform.

The boy, a fresh-faced lad with a mop of blond hair and big teeth trapped behind shiny braces, was holding a spaceship in the air. He was slowly lowering it onto the platform. It emitted a tinny roar as it descended.

"*Hydra* spaceship coming in to land on the planet Vixos! No danger detected!"

The girl, also with a mop of blonde hair and big teeth, pushed forward an action figure of a woman in revealing black leather. Then she pushed forward a couple of robots until they flanked the woman.

"Not so fast," the girl hissed. "I, Medula, have been waiting for you! Me and the Styrax robots have sprung our trap!"

A fruity male voice erupted from nowhere. "The *Vixens from the Void* action playset is here, coming from a distant galaxy!"

There was a quick cut. The *Hydra* had been placed on the platform, the side hatch had been opened and a group of action figures placed outside, Arkadia, Elysia and Velhellan, all with right arms raised and pointing little plastic laser pistols. It was painfully obvious that the figures were not to scale, as the only way they would have fitted inside the spaceship was to melt them down and pour them in. The figures were arranged around a giant laser cannon centred on a circular trolley.

"Not so fast, Medula!" the boy said. "We have our laser cannon ready, and it can pulse with a death ray!"

The boy reached down, pressed a button, and the laser cannon's barrel pulsed with a red light, and made a *pew-pew* noise. The girl went "Aargh!" and knocked Medula and the Styrax over.

Another quick cut, and the boy was holding his arms above

his head, clasping his hands together in triumph. Then another cut, and the boy and the girl had changed teams, the girl whirling the spaceship around her head, the boy pushing the Styrax along the floor. The image changed to a shot of painted stars, and the *Hydra* and the playset appeared with a shimmer in the middle of the starscape.

The disembodied fruity voice spoke again: "The *Vixens from the Void* action playset! From Braxtons! All the action and thrills from the original television series, beamed into your own home! Action figures and spaceship sold separately!"

The screen went dark for a few seconds, then the advert started again. Kit calculated if she just watched the advert another one hundred and eighteen times, then the pre-dinner drinks would be over and she'd have achieved her goal of not talking to anybody.

It was a good plan, but it was immediately doomed to failure, as someone was talking to her.

"God, you look ridiculous. What have you come as? A woman from 1985 who's come to the twenty-first century in a time-travelling DeLorean?"

She turned. The voice came from a man holding a glass of champagne in his hand and an expression of disdain on his face. He was in his fifties and trying desperately not to be. His long hair was greased back on his head, and it was dyed black, as was his ridiculous goatee. He was wearing a dinner jacket over a grey T-shirt with 'Woman: Noun: Adult Human Female' written across it.

Matty Kearney. Anti-woke warrior.

He nudged his champagne glass against Kit's coat. "I'm not being rude. I'm just being honest."

A woman appeared at Matty's shoulder. She was tall, black and slim, in her early thirties with pretty eyes and a wide, friendly mouth. She looked very classy. Her head was covered in blonde dreadlocks, and she was wearing a white suit and cream shirt.

"Matty!" she said, outraged. "Sorry about Matty. He has to be obnoxious. It's his job." The woman had a husky voice, flavoured in a Midwest US accent. "That's actually his catchphrase: 'I'm not being rude. I'm just being honest'. I'm Saskia Shapiro. His producer."

Matty gave her an evil grin. "Not just his producer."

Saskia glared back at him. "*Just* his producer."

"Oh yes," said Kit. "Matty Kearney. I know you. I sometimes click on your YouTube videos."

Matty's eyebrows leapt up in interest. "Oh, do you now?"

"Yes."

Kit said nothing.

"So?"

Kit blinked. "Oh, do you want my opinion?"

Matty didn't want to admit it, but his ego dragged it out of him. "If you've got one. Not that I care either way."

Kit frowned, thinking. "Well, you do make good points occasionally, about homogeneity in modern sci-fi franchises, but it's so buried beneath all that repetitive stuff about 'woke messaging' that I've never actually watched one all the way to the end yet."

She gave a cold smile. "I'm not being rude; I'm just being honest."

Saskia hid a grin behind her hand.

Matty's face clouded in fury, but before he could say anything, a girl pushed her way into the group. She was mid-twenties, and short and plump, her face caked with white make-up and aggressive black lipstick. There was a ring through her left nostril. Her hair was dyed white and cut in a Harley Quinn style (*Suicide Squad*, 2016) and she had a black denim jacket with sew-on patches that depicted DC Superheroes on one shoulder and Marvel Superheroes on the other, worn over the top of a black cocktail dress.

"Hey, Kit Pelham amiright?" Her voice was that of a child's, a cross between Marilyn Monroe and a squeaky toy. "You're in the *Vixens from the Void* documentaries for the Blu-Rays? And you do that podcast, yeah? *The First Cult is the Deepest*?"

"Yes," said Kit.

"I love your podcast," she gushed. "It's dope. I'm Vixy. That's my proper name and everything. Changed it by deed poll." She gave another squeak. "Oh my god! I'm with Kit Pelham! This is so legit!"

"Oh yeah." Matty feigned disinterest. "I know who you are now. Kit Pelham. Right. I thought I recognised you." He pointed a finger into her face. "You're the *lesbian detective*. The one that thinks she's Miss Marple."

"I don't think I'm Miss Marple," said Kit. "I'm more part of the Marple Extended universe."

This time, Saskia gave a proper laugh, and Vixy emitted a high-pitched giggle.

Matty glared at Kit. He looked like he was a rumbling volcano about to explode, but instead of molten magma, he would gush forth with an invective-flecked diatribe.

"Haven't you got that spaceship, Matty?" Saskia asked, pointing into a nearby display case. It was obviously a ruse to distract him, and it worked.

Matty gave it a quick dismissive glance. "The *Hydra*? Of course I have. I've got three of 'em. The basic one, the one with battle-fatigue stickers, and the one with the realistic engine sounds and flashing laser blasts."

"I had it too," said Binfire, appearing on the other side of the cabinet. "Just the basic one. I had to make my own engine noises." Binfire proceeded to demonstrate, going "vrrrrooom".

Saskia laughed.

"Oh *there* you are." Kit's voice was edged with meaning, and the meaning was *Why did you abandon me to these people?* "Glad you could join us."

Binfire ignored her. He grinned at Saskia. "Yeah, I loved that spaceship."

Kit shook her head. "You tied a firework to it!"

"Correction. I activated its self-destruct sequence. It made a fantastic bang," said Binfire. "I regret nothing."

Fenton spoke to Matty. "This is Binfire," he said meaningfully. "He's the one with the doll."

Matty looked at Binfire. "Oh yeah. Right."

"The one with the *doll*. Who isn't *us*."

Matty scowled. "I got you, Fenton. I heard you the first time."

There seemed to be a hidden conversation bouncing between the two men, but for the life of her, Kit couldn't see the meaning behind it.

Binfire seemed oblivious to the atmosphere swirling around him. He raised his Tesco plastic bag. "Yep," he said cheerfully. "It's in here. Safe and sound."

"Ooh," said Vixy. "Can I look?"

"Best not, Vixy. Best let the professionals handle this," said Fenton gruffly.

"Oh yeah, well you know best, Fenton. You always know best," trilled Vixy. She grabbed his arm and held it tight.

Fenton gently disengaged from Vixy and cleared his throat. "Well it's good you brought it. Jerome is going to be pleased. He was getting worried." He peered around the museum. "He's got to be around somewhere."

"He's over there," Matty said, pointing.

Reverend Bell waved and headed over to them. He had a

very odd way of moving, twitchy, ill-at-ease. As if he was a puppet trying to act like a real boy.

"The Excelsior doll is here," said Fenton, gesturing to Binfire. "He's brought it."

Reverend Bell stared at Binfire intently. "Splendid! I've been waiting for you. I was worried you wouldn't get here."

Binfire proffered the bag. "Well I'm here. And here it is, safe and sound."

"Thank heavens." Bell took the bag gingerly and slid the doll out, and they all clustered around to get a good look. Matty feigned indifference, but it was obvious he was glancing covetously at it out of the corner of his eye.

It was a dark blue box with a transparent window in the front. The words said: THRILLING SPACE ADVENTURES WITH TV'S *VIXENS FROM THE VOID*! In the corner it said 'Braxtons Models'.

The box was decorated with moons and planets, with a spaceship whizzing between them leaving a trail of stardust in its wake. There was a tiny face staring out of the plastic window at the top, vacant and immobile, like a mummified pharaoh. The name underneath the window read: EXCELSIOR: HIGH PRIESTESS OF VIXOS

"Turn it around," breathed Fenton. "I want to see how mint-in-box it is."

Reverend Bell turned it over. The main photo was of little dolls dressed as characters from the classic *Vixens from the Void* series, smiling crazily. Little plastic hands held tiny exotic swords and ray guns. Little cloth capes hung around little plastic necks.

There were ten of them, of course, arranged in a neat little semi-circle, in poses designed to look combative, but they looked more like they were about to break into song.

The strapline read: TAKE ON THE UNIVERSE WITH THIS EXCITING NEW RANGE OF DOLLS FROM THE *VIXENS FROM THE VOID* BBC TV SERIES!!! And COLLECT ALL TEN FROM THE EXCITING CEREMONIAL RANGE!

"Wow," said Saskia. "I can never get over the packaging. It's so... *retro*."

Fenton beckoned at Binfire with waggling fingers. "I'll buy it off you. I'll give you a very good price."

Matty chortled. "He's asked me to sell mine too. Fenton can't see any piece of memorabilia without wanting to get his sweaty fingers on it."

Binfire shook his head vigorously. "No way. She's not for sale. She's the nearest thing to a steady girlfriend I've got."

Fenton popped his bottom lip out with obvious frustration but quickly recovered himself.

"Aren't you going to open it?" asked Vixy.

Everyone looked at her in horror.

"No we're not going to *fucking open it*," growled Matty.

"That would be sacrilege," hissed Bell.

"It's mint-in-box, Vixy," sighed Fenton. "We've had this discussion. 'Mint', meaning 'perfect condition' and 'in-box', meaning 'in-the-bloody-box'. If you take it out, it's not mint-in-box anymore, remember?"

Vixy was chastened. "Oh yes, sorry, Fenton."

"Next time, *ask* me before you decide to make up a window display for the shop."

The Reverend examined the packaging, turning it around and around in his bony fingers with unvarnished relief. "I must offer my congratulations, Binfire. This has been kept in exceptionally good condition."

"I put it inside a Quality Street tub, and buried it in our back garden," said Binfire proudly.

"Yes. Well. You've done well. You must tell me how you came by it. I can imagine it's *quite a story.*"

Binfire just gave him a wink. A shadow fell across the Reverend's face before he recovered and smiled once more. "Well, however you got it, it's in wonderful condition. As good as my other exhibits."

"They're not *your* exhibits," said Fenton automatically.

"Yeah," agreed Matty. "They're just on loan, Bell. Don't forget that. Never forget we can take them back at any time."

Reverend Bell forced a smile on his face. "Merely a figure of speech." He stared at Binfire with a strange intensity. "If you'll allow me, I'd like to add this to the display."

"Knock yourself out, pilgrim."

"Capital," Bell said. "Come, Binfire, let me show you where it will reside, in the place of honour." He put one arm around Binfire's shoulders and guided him to the glass pyramid. Matty, Fenton, Saskia and Vixy joined them.

Kit took one longing look at the exit, before following on behind.

Bell took a key from his belt and unlocked the cabinet. "As you are no doubt aware, I was given the honour of curating this particular collection for the Furley Estate. I consider this to be my passion project."

'Passion' was not a word that came to mind when looking at Reverend Jerome Bell. He looked like an unpainted action figure: completely grey. Grey skin, a grey moustache, grey linen suit and a grey fedora.

On the bottom shelf was a large collection of *Vixens from the Void* action figures, free from any packaging. There was a sign at their feet, telling the museum visitors that this was the entire range of dolls that Braxtons Models released from 1992 to

1995. On the shelf above were three figures from the Ceremonial Range, safe inside their blue boxes. Reverend Bell took Binfire's doll and added it to the top shelf, holding his breath as he did so.

"Voila," breathed Reverend Bell. "Excelsior."

"Nice," said Matty.

"There's a lot of money in that cabinet," added Fenton.

"Looks like the gang's all back together," Saskia muttered.

"Only they're not," Kit said.

"Not what?" asked Saskia.

"All back together."

Saskia looked mystified. "What do you mean?"

"The gang. There were five prototypes made for the Ceremonial Range before the Braxtons factory burned down. There are only four of them in here."

Reverend Bell scrutinised her, registering her for the first time. "Sorry, I don't believe I've had the pleasure?"

"She's Kit. She's my plus one," said Binfire proudly.

"She's the *lesbian detective*," said Matty brutally, ignoring Saskia's look of reproval.

"Of course!" said Reverend Bell. "How could I have not recognised you? I'm quite a fan of yours."

Kit didn't know what to say to that.

"Oh," she said. "Thanks," she added.

"I'm a bit of an aspiring detective myself! I love them all. Holmes, Poirot, Peter Wimsey, Father Brown… I wrote a thesis on Agatha Christie for my doctorate, don't you know? Anyway, I was delighted to hear of your exploits. We have so many types of amateur detective, gardener detectives, actor detectives, cat detectives…" he smiled apologetically, "vicar detectives… It's so nice to have a 'cult' detective join their ranks."

"That's very nice of you to say, but…" Kit's pedant monster woke up, "they're *fictional* detectives. I'm not fictional. I'm real."

Reverend Bell gave a crooked smile. "Well, we are all extensions of fiction to some degree. As I posited in my book, we are fed fictions from birth to create our own realities. Who's to say how much of us is fiction and how much is fact?"

He closed the cabinet.

"Well, your astute observation is correct. There were *supposed* to be ten in the range. But only five sculpts were made. The five figures are all in the hands of private collectors." Reverend Bell pointed into the cabinet. "The Byzantia figure was owned by the seventh Marquess. He left it to his daughter Lady Tabitha Pendragon when he passed on. She has kindly allowed it to be displayed." His finger travelled across the shelf. "And these three are owned by the three gentlemen present. The one that is missing…"

Kit supplied the name. "Arkadia."

"Yes, the Arkadia figure is missing. Well spotted. Would you like to deduce why that is?"

"Huh. Well, I'd deduce that it's in the possession of someone who's not as co-operative as the other collectors, Graham Goldingay. And he's refusing to give you permission to display his figure."

Reverend Bell's grey eyebrows leapt in surprise. "Goodness! That is quite a deduction. Worthy of Holmes himself."

"Not really. I just know the facts. I've done my research. I know who owns which doll. I know who owns Arkadia, and I know how annoying Graham Goldingay is."

"Aha. Well… well done, anyway. You're correct."

Matty laughed. "Graham won't let him have his figure. Jerome's been kissing the Great Gutsby's fat arse for months, haven't you? You'd think a guy who's stuck in prison for ten years wouldn't care who plays with his toys, but no dice. He wasn't interested. Fat fuck."

There was a gentle *ting-ting* noise. Archie Pendragon was standing at the middle of the floor, tapping a pen against a champagne glass.

"Can I have your attention, everybody? I hope you haven't filled up on nibbles because dinner is about to be served."

6

Once they had all vacated the museum, Kit noticed that a large man in a tuxedo locked the heavy wooden door of the museum with a sepulchral clunk.

"Thank you, Malcolm," Archie said to the man.

They crunched back across the gravel. Archie led them around the front of Furley House and up to the main entrance. He brought them into the hallway, past the staircase and through a large set of double doors. They all wandered in, *ooh*ing and *aah*ing at their surroundings like winners of the golden tickets in *Willy Wonka and the Chocolate Factory* (1971) and *Charlie and the Chocolate Factory* (2005).

Compared to the gloomy corridors, the ballroom of Furley House was incredibly bright, with huge windows framed by heavy burgundy curtains. There was a massive fireplace, a huge white block of marble surrounded by the heads of surprised-looking animals, and oil paintings of men on horses chasing after foxes.

There was a long table in the centre of the hall, covered in a forest of knives, forks and spoons. Kit had nightmares about these kinds of dinners, of being the last one to sit, wandering around looking for her seat in full view of everyone like she was the loser in a hellish game of musical chairs. With that in mind, she made a beeline straight for the table and scuttled around it, checking out the name cards.

The top of the table was their host, **Archibald Pendragon, eighth Marquess of Furley**. The other end was **Lady Tabitha Pendragon**.

It was arranged, according to etiquette, in the male-female pattern, with partners and significant others facing one another. One side had: **The Reverend Jerome Bell**, **Mrs Moni Worth**, **Mr Matthew Kearney** and **Ms Kit Pelham**. The other side had **Mrs Ruth Bell**, **Mr Fenton Worth**, **Ms Saskia Shapiro**, **Ben 'Binfire' Ferry** and **Ms Vixy**.

She sat opposite Vixy, who had shrugged off her denim jacket with the sew-on patches of the DC Superheroes on one shoulder and Marvel Superheroes on the other, and hung it on the back of her chair, revealing a sleeveless dress that showed off her pale upper arms. Amusingly, her shoulders displayed an array of tattoos that pretty much matched her sew-on patches: Batman and Co on the right, Iron Man and the other Avengers on the left.

Binfire had noticed her tattoos. He was prodding her bicep.

"Ben Affleck?"

"Yeah." She nodded. "Obviously it's a bit out of date now. Ideally it should be Robert Pattinson, amiright?"

Binfire nodded sadly. "That's the problem with Batman tattoos, as soon as you get one, they change the Batman." He rolled up his sleeve. "Look, I've got an original Michael Keaton."

"Woah! That's such a period piece."

"I had it done in 1995. You see there? Jack Nicholson on the elbow?" He shook his head regretfully. "If I'd just held off a decade, I could have got Heath Ledger. But I'm sure if I'd got him, I'd be sitting here saying if I'd held off a few more years I could have got Joaquin Phoenix."

Vixy rested her hand on his. "Jack Nicholson's a classic Joker. And Michael Keaton's back in the DC universe now. Your shoulder is trendy again."

A smile crept back on Binfire's face. "You're right."

"You should savour this moment, yeah?"

Binfire grinned at her. Vixy smiled too, but then her smile

slid off her face. She took her hand away from Binfire's.

Kit looked in the direction of Vixy's stare, and saw that Fenton was frowning at Vixy through his goldfish-bowl glasses and only broke his glare when he realised his wife, Moni, sitting opposite, was glaring at *him*.

A tall woman with short blonde hair, wearing a tuxedo, leaned over Binfire's shoulder. "Excuse me, Mr Binfire?"

"That's me."

"I'm Jane, your head waiter for tonight. I do apologise but we don't seem to have any of your details."

"I travel under the radar," Binfire said earnestly. "I'm usually off-grid."

"Do you have any dietary requirements?"

"Oh yeah," said Binfire. "I definitely have to eat. Otherwise I'd die." He scratched his head. "Though I haven't tested that hypothesis, so, you know, jury's still out."

"He's fine," said Kit smoothly. "He'll eat anything. Just don't get him wet and don't feed him after midnight."

Jane the head waiter smiled. "Thank you, Ms Pelham." She nodded to the occupants of this end of the table. "Enjoy your meals."

She started to leave. Kit waved her hand and said plaintively: "Um. Jane? You did get my form, didn't you?"

"Yes, Ms Pelham. Chef has been made aware. Your total calorie count for the meal should not exceed five hundred calories. That won't be a problem. You'll get a printout with each course. I hope that's acceptable?"

"Oh, yes. Thank you."

Jane flashed a dazzling smile at both of them and left.

"Frokk," muttered Binfire. "That was intense. These people do not mess about, do they?"

"Are you counting calories?" said the girl called Vixy. "Woah. I wish I had your discipline. I only have to look at food

51

and I put on weight."

"Well," said Kit. "You could just try looking at healthy food and stop looking at cakes."

The second it came out of Kit's mouth she felt it was the wrong thing to say. Fortunately, Binfire was on hand to make the save.

"You don't need to count calories, pilgrim. You need more meat on your arms. You need to make room for the Justice League."

"I don't really like the Justice League."

"Neither do I. But they make great tattoos."

The waiters entered, carrying large plates decorated with pheasants and men in hunting pink riding horses. Kit found herself staring at a huge round tomato stuffed with goat's cheese and chives. There was a menu tucked between the plate and her water glass, and it informed her this was her starter, and that it was two hundred calories.

The room drained of conversation and it was replaced with the clatter of cutlery. Kit could hear only one conversation, on her left. Matty was talking to Fenton, Reverend Bell and Archie at full volume.

Matty jabbed a fork into the air. "I had the pellet gun too. Now those bastards were brutal."

Fenton nodded; his head hunched over his plate. "I've got some of them in the shop – second-hand of course. I've actually got one in the boot of the car. You can't make them these days. I sell them on eBay, 'cos I'm not allowed to sell them over the counter in case a kid buys one, loses an eye and I get sued. Do you know, if I set up my shop in the US there'll be more rules about selling toy guns than real ones?"

Matty looked mildly irritated, as if Fenton had taken the words out of his mouth. "I made that exact point on my YouTube channel. You could lose an eye with one of those darts if you pointed it directly at your eye and pulled the trigger. And a few kids did as well. Everyone had a friend in school with an eye patch, didn't they? But in those days, if a kid did that it was their own bloody fault, and they had to live with the Long John Silver jokes. These days if a kid falls down in a soft-play area there's a lawsuit filed before he opens his mouth to go 'wah'. Kids are never allowed to grow up these days."

Archie gave a polite nod. "I quite agree. When I was seven, my father put a shotgun in my hand and took me out to shoot my first rabbit. I'm sure questions would be asked if I did the same with my heir, should I produce any offspring."

Reverend Bell put his knife and fork down and dabbed his beard with his napkin. "I have written about this at some length in my book, *Vixens from the Void: the Intertextual Paradox* published by Crazy Badger Press. I posit that modern children are incredibly infantilised to such an extent that their abilities to consume popular culture are circumscribed. They can't cope with the bolder narratives and subtle themes prevalent in *Vixens*, or indeed any cult television programme made pre-twenty-first century."

"Fuck yeah." Matty nodded vigorously. "Unless there's a fucking cartoon raccoon popping up at the end to tell them what to think, they can't cope with it."

"Did you *read* my book?"

"No. Why would I need to read a book telling me what I know already?"

"I've got your book in my shop, Jerome. Still." Fenton grinned. "I added to your word count. I put discount stickers on the front."

Matty sniggered.

"Leave him alone, Fenton." That comment came from Fenton's wife, Moni. "The joke's not on him, *dear*. He's been paid for writing his books. The joke's on *you* for filling our shop with useless stock that doesn't sell."

Fenton glowered at her but said nothing.

Ruth Bell looked up from carving her stuffed tomato. She was a slender woman with a thin face that carried a bit too much nose and a bit too little chin. She fixed her husband with an amused stare. "Darling, you don't think it's a little ironic?"

Reverend Bell frowned. "Ironic?"

"Writing a chapter of your book bemoaning the infantilisation of today's youth, when you've just spent months of your life putting together a museum for children, and the afternoon tussling with your friends about how many toys you own?"

Reverend Bell's cheeks blossomed with embarrassment. He didn't reply.

Fenton frowned. "They're not toys. You play with toys. You're not supposed to play with action figures."

Moni gave a mirthless laugh. "Perhaps if kids played with them, we might sell a few."

Fenton sighed. "There's still a market."

She snorted. "I don't call selling one a week 'a market'."

"Yeah, well, it was easier in the old days, before the new series came back. Back when I was in London, my shop was the only place you could buy *Vixens from the Void* toys, now every bloody toyshop in the country stocks them."

"So you keep saying, *dear*," snapped Moni. "It doesn't help us to sell any of the damn things, does it?"

Ruth smiled condescendingly at Fenton and her husband. "I'm sure the toys are for children. I've seen that advertisement from the 90s – the one playing on a loop in the museum? It definitely shows children playing with them."

"That was the 90s," grunted Fenton. "They didn't know any better back then. The ones we're displaying are antiques. Twentieth-century equivalents of your Chippendales and your Hepplewhites."

"I'd say more like pop art," added Matty. "They sit right alongside Andy Warhol's soup tins and Lichtenstein's screen prints."

"Exactly." Fenton nodded vigorously, throwing dandruff into his soup. "They're just for display purposes."

"Really?" Moni pursed her lips. "That little doll of yours? The one wearing leather straps, dressed like a trollop? You'd display that in our front room?"

"Well not to display in our *front* room, no."

"No. You just display your trollops to the world."

Her eyes flicked to Vixy and back to Fenton. Fenton's face bloomed with embarrassment but said nothing.

"My husband would display a doll like that if he had one." Ruth jerked a finger back at Reverend Bell. "It would be hanging above the mantelpiece, right next to the crucifix. I don't know what his parishioners would think."

"There are worse things to hang above a mantelpiece, dear," mumbled Reverend Bell, but not quite loud enough for his wife to hear.

Ruth leaned over to Archie. "Is Lady Tabitha not joining us, Lord Furley?"

The seat at the other end of the table was conspicuously vacant.

"Please, my dear, call me Archie, everybody does," said Archie. "My sister is a bit of a germophobe and is uncomfortable being in close proximity to people. She is averse to gatherings like this. I'm sure she'll be dining in her room."

So Tabitha's a lot like me, thought Kit. *Doesn't like gatherings. Not keen on human contact. We've got a lot in common...*

Unbidden fantasies threatened to send her into a daydream, so Kit shook them off with a huge effort, and focused on her calorie-conscious tomato.

7

Archie stood up and surveyed the table. The conversation drained away as nine pairs of eyes turned in his direction.

"Thank you, everyone, for coming. All of you, in ways big and small, helped to contribute to the Furley House toy museum, so I'll always be very grateful. I'm sure my father is also grateful. I'm sure he's up there somewhere..." His eyes flicked to the ceiling. "And by up there, I mean heaven, not in one of the maids' bedrooms."

There was a polite tinkle of laughter.

"Father had a love of the arts that I'm afraid I never inherited. He loved all sorts of culture: plays, films, paintings, opera, and he loved television, and he particularly loved that space television programme of yours. It was very much his 'thing' for some reason..."

There was another, louder rumble of mirth, and Kit knew why. Everyone was well aware of the reason why *Vixens from the Void* was the seventh Marquess's 'thing'. Roland Pendragon was known for his eccentricity, his belligerence, but above all he was known for his rampant libido. He was, to put it bluntly, a randy sod who kept a harem in the gamekeeper's cottage and replaced the peeing cherubs in the fountains with statues of naked ladies who gushed water from their nipples. *Vixens from the Void*, with its cast of young attractive women clad in Spandex, was a natural draw for all kinds of Dirty Old Men. And at the time the seventh Marquess was the most high-profile Dirty Old Man in the country.

"It was my dear father who, in 1990, solicited the BBC to

open the *Vixens from the Void* Experience."

He had to pause because spontaneous applause broke out, starting with Matty and joined by Fenton, Reverend Bell, Vixy and Saskia. Binfire banged on the table and gave a high-pitched whistle with fingers in his mouth. The two wives did not join in.

Archie waited for the applause to die down before continuing. "For thirty years, Furley House played host to that exhibition, housing monsters and costumes and props and all manner of weird things. I vividly remember wandering around it as a boy, marvelling at the creativity of those special-effects wizards. The exhibition continued until 2020 when the BBC, in its wisdom, chose to withdraw their permission and give it to the chaps behind the new version of the programme to do their own thing."

Matty cupped his hand around his mouth and shouted, "Boooo!" This time, the *boo* was just taken up by Reverend Bell and Fenton.

The others looked on in bemusement.

"Well that *is* their prerogative," said Archie chortling, after the jeering had dissipated. "Nevertheless, we keep buggering on, and this rather splendid toy museum is the result, and I like to think my father will look upon this new enterprise with wholehearted approval. And the BBC can't take this away from us, can they?"

"Actually, they can," said Kit.

The room fell silent.

Pairs of hostile eyes turned in her direction.

Kit realised she should have chained up her pedant monster and put it back in its cage.

Too late now.

"Sorry. I was just pointing out that as you're marketing this museum using the *Vixens from the Void* name, they have a right to close you down any time they want for breaching their copyright…"

The silence grew darker and colder.

"Not that I think they'd do that," she added. "At least I think they wouldn't…"

"So says the *spokesperson* for the new series," said Matty, seasoning the word 'spokesperson' with extra contempt.

"I'm not a spokesperson for anything," said Kit tartly.

"No?" snapped Matty. "You write glowing reviews for their shitty Pravda magazine, *Vixmag*, you appear on their crappy behind-the-scenes extras, like a nodding dog, or Lord Fucking Haw Haw…"

With a squeal of chair legs on polished floor, Binfire leapt to his feet. He pulled back his jacket to reveal a Nerf pistol in its holster. His fingers tickled the handle.

"I'm not the biggest cheerleader of the new series myself," he hissed. "But if you want to take your hate-watch out on Kit, we can take this outside, fan to fan."

Matty stood up. "Anytime."

Incredibly, Matty flipped the pocket of his jacket to one side, also revealing a Nerf pistol.

Fenton stood up, his chair squawking across the floor. "You'll need someone to hold your jackets."

"For god's sake, sit down, all of you," hissed Saskia. "You're embarrassing yourselves."

"And you're embarrassing *me*." Moni looked furious with her husband. "You are guests in someone else's house. At least pretend that you have some manners."

"Gentlemen." Archie beamed at each of them in turn. "A duel sounds frightfully exciting, and very much in keeping with the history of Furley House. But I would ask you to refrain on this occasion. Kit is indeed writing an article for her magazine, and I would prefer she write about the *museum*, rather than report about a fracas in the car park?"

Matty's brow furrowed. "Okay. Take your point. As you were."

They all grudgingly sat down and the main courses appeared in front of them.

Kit stared at the table, avoiding the faces around her.

This is not turning out to be fun, she thought. *It's obvious that some people in this room hate the new* Vixens *from the Void series, and they hate me for being associated with it, however tenuously.*

I'll write up my article tonight, have breakfast, get my interview with the Marquess first thing tomorrow, get in that motorhome and go straight home. I'll even let Binfire go up to warp factor ten.

Jane the head waiter glided up to Archie and whispered in his ear. Expressions flitted across his face in rapid succession: confusion, surprise… And was that anger?

Archie leaned across to Reverend Bell and whispered in *his* ear. A similar flurry of expressions crossed Bell's face. As they stood up to leave, Bell bent down and whispered something to Matty, and Archie whispered to Fenton. Matty and Fenton also sprang up and followed them out.

Kit looked around at the table. Binfire and Vixy were still chatting about tattoos, and Saskia was listening in on their conversation. Ruth Bell was chatting with Moni Worth, commiserating about the stupidity of their husbands.

She looked at her plate. Her main meal was roasted cauliflower (two hundred calories). She wasn't in the mood for it. When she got up and walked to the door, no heads turned. She followed the group of men along the corridor, into the hallway and walked cautiously out of the main entrance.

8

It was a pleasant summer evening. Even though it was nearly eight p.m., dusk had yet to smear itself across the sky. Kit could clearly see Archie, Matty, Fenton and Reverend Bell standing on the steps of Furley House, watching a shiny transit van park on the drive.

A young woman with ginger hair and freckles got out of the van. She was dressed immaculately, in a beautifully tailored lavender suit covered by a leather apron. She opened the big sliding door on the side of the van and dragged what looked like giant bits of Meccano out of the back, then laid them delicately on the gravel.

As if hypnotised, they watched her slowly construct some kind of vehicle. She took a wrench out of her toolbox and attached two sets of wheels encased in caterpillar treads together, as if she was constructing a toy tank. But it didn't stop there. She attached a squared-off chassis on a platform that stood waist-high, out of which protruded two claw-like arms, making it look like a bomb-disposal robot.

Curiosity overrode caution. Kit moved closer to the little group to see what was going on. No one noticed her. All eyes were fixed on the woman.

The woman fastened a computer screen on the top, giving the robot a 'head'. Finally, satisfied with her work, she stepped back into the van and re-emerged with a handheld remote control. She played with the levers and the robot juddered into life, rumbling towards the house. The caterpillar treads gripped the steps and it lurched upwards, climbing until it reached the top step. And it still kept coming. The group instinctively backed away because they had all been conditioned by their television habits to fear robots.

The woman guided the robot until it was about three feet from them, then brought it to a halt with a shuddering stop. The screen flickered into life to show a small grey room with a single window and a single chair: a prison cell. A man waddled into shot and sat on the chair. A very fat man with a big grey beard and a bald head. He was large, lumpy and grey, like an angry boulder.

"Greetings to you all," said Graham Goldingay.

9

Graham Goldingay. The self-proclaimed *Vixens from the Void* superfan. A pushy, arrogant know-all who had been annoying fans and stars of the show alike since the show started. A man too irritating to tolerate, yet too rich to ignore. Maker of documentaries, hoarder of props, and the owner of Arkadia, the fifth action figure in the Ceremonial Range.

How very typical of Graham, thought Kit. *That he didn't allow the inconvenience of being in prison prevent him from showing up to be the centre of attention.*

"Oh my god," groaned Matty. "When you said that he was here, I thought someone was taking the piss."

Fenton was admiring the robot. "This is some impressive kit. How much did it cost you?"

Reverend Bell stepped forward eagerly. "What do you want, Graham? Are you here to bring us your Arkadia figure?"

Graham glowered out of the screen, his enormous form surrounded by the exposed bricks of his prison cell, as if a fatberg had been stuck inside a sewer so long it had gained sentience.

"I presume that is some kind of joke," he growled. "I know you've taken your revenge on me for refusing to take part in your second-rate museum."

"I beg your pardon?"

On the screen, Graham Goldingay stood up and came close enough to the camera to see the spidery red lines that coalesced around his irises.

"Do NOT try to make a fool of me, Reverend Bell. I am

here to tell you that you will NOT get away with this. As I am...
indisposed... at present, pending the appeal to my incarceration,
I have tasked my personal assistant to present my ultimatum. I
demand recompense and I will not stop—"

There was a rattle of keys to Graham's left and the sound of
a heavy metal door opening. A voice came from off-screen.

"Come on, tubs, out you come. Exercise time."

Graham's face looked like he'd been called to go to the
electric chair. "I have to go now. My personal assistant will
continue to appraise you of the situation and deliver my
demands."

He leaned forward to press a button and the screen went
blank.

The young woman with ginger hair wasted no time. She
went into the van and emerged carrying a pile of plastic folders.
As she handed them out, she said, "Ladies and Gentlemen, as
Mr Goldingay just said, I am his personal assistant, Penny Lane.
And to answer your questions, no, I am not from Liverpool, and
yes, my parents were Beatles obsessives. Please open the files
and look at document A."

Kit leaned forward and took one. No one had noticed that
Kit had nosed her way into the group, or if they did, they hadn't
commented on it. They were all focusing on Penny.

Kit flipped open the loose-leaf folder. The first page was a
picture of a cavernous room full of objects kept under glass, not
unlike the Furley House exhibition.

"This is a photo of Mr Goldingay's personal collection,"
said Penny. "Props, costumes and merchandise. This is the
most extensive cache of *Vixens from the Void* collectibles in the
world."

There was resentful muttering from the other collectors, but
they couldn't deny it. It was a simple fact.

"They were displayed in Mr Goldingay's Holland Park house, all under lock and key with full security measures in place. Please go to document B."

Kit flipped the page. This was another picture. A doll in a box. A model of a blonde woman in tangerine Spandex and boots, wearing a legionnaire's helmet and a cloak. She was holding a jewelled staff.

"The object in the picture is NOT a Ceremonial Range figure, even though it looks like one. Last week, Mr Goldingay's figure was stolen from its packaging and replaced with an ordinary figure of Arkadia from the main range. Quite a common figure, as you all know, something that can be easily picked up from eBay for a few pounds. It had been customised to look like the rare figure with several homemade accessories."

She cleared her throat apologetically.

"As Mr Goldingay has been… indisposed of late… and he was not available to personally curate his collection, the substitution was not detected. Please turn to document C."

Kit flipped the page again. A hiss of horror escaped from the group of collectors. This photo showed the dismembered parts of an action figure, eight pieces scattered across a chipped table. A head, an upper arm, two lower arms with moulded grip-action hands, one bit of lower leg, two thighs and a torso.

A brown package was next to it, a ragged hole in its side.

"Unfortunately, the substitution was only detected when his Arkadia – Ceremonial Range – figure was posted to Mr Goldingay one week ago at his current residence. The action figure in question was dismembered, and the accessories and packaging missing."

"This is horrible," moaned Reverend Bell. "Unthinkable."

"My god," muttered Fenton.

Kit stared at the photo. A sad collection of eight painted

pieces of plastic and a few torn scraps of material. "Is this all there is? No note? No message?"

Kit realised she'd spoken out loud. Penny looked at her and she blushed.

"Good question Miss…"

"Um. Pelham. Kit Pelham."

Penny smiled. "Ah, of course you are."

What does that mean?

Penny continued, "There was a message of sorts. If you would like to turn to document D, you will see what was inside the package."

Kit flipped the page, and saw a photograph of a strip of paper, about the size and shape of a fortune cookie motto.

On it was written the words:

Ten little figures
Once all were mine.
One went to pieces
And then there were nine.

"Ten figures?" said Reverend Bell, his voice rising with excitement. "Goodness. I do believe this is a nod to the Christie novel with the rather controversial title, *Ten Little…* um, now known as *And Then There Were None*, though it was also released as *Ten Little Indians* before the publishers settled on the current title."

"Personally, I think Agatha should have kept the original name and not caved in to woke pressure," grumbled Matty.

Bell looked confused. "Woke pressure? In 1940?"

Kit was thinking about the rhyme. "Ten little figures?" she muttered. "Once all were mine? Did anyone own these figures before?"

Even though she spoke quietly, Matty and Fenton heard her. Once again, they exchanged glances.

"No one owned them before us," said Fenton at last.

"Everyone knows where they came from," said Matty. "Tell her, Fenton."

Fenton spluttered. "Me?"

"Yes," said Matty. "You tell her."

Fenton shrugged and said, "Roland Pendragon was poking around a charity shop, and he found four figures in a cardboard box. He bought them for twenty pounds. He kept one of the figures and kindly shared the others amongst his Furley Fanboys – me, Matty and Graham Goldingay – who he considered to be true *Vixens from the Void* fans. Fans who he knew would appreciate them."

"But what could it mean?" Kit asked. "Ten little figures once all were mine? There are only five in existence. Why say ten little figures?"

"To fit the rhyme, of course," said Reverend Bell testily. "Because of Agatha Christie."

"Mr Goldingay refused to allow his action figure to take part in your exhibition," said Penny. "Then it was stolen and sent back to him in pieces. Ergo the only logical reason for this to happen would be the result of a petty act of vengeance from the person who organised this museum: the Reverend Jerome Bell."

Reverend Bell was enraged. "That's a monstrous accusation! I've spent my life rescuing action figures and restoring them to factory quality. I could no more destroy a priceless piece of cultural history than I could murder one of my own children."

Nevertheless, all the other collectors backed away from Reverend Bell, staring at him suspiciously.

"Good lord, you really are a bunch of idiots!"

Lady Tabitha Pendragon had appeared around the corner of the house and was leaning on one of the Doric columns. She had changed into some steampunk highwayman gear, and in the dwindling light of the setting sun, she looked amazing in her copper-coloured goggles, copper flintlocks, tricorn hat and flappy leather boots.

Tabitha continued, "There's no way this old toot could break into a house and steal an action figure. I mean, look at him! One good gust of wind and he'll blow over!"

There was a lull in the conversation as they admired Lady Tabitha's costume and then all eyes travelled over to inspect Reverend Bell's spindly frame. The logic was inescapable.

Archie stepped forward and cleared his throat. "Look, I don't want any bad publicity for Furley House, particularly as this museum is about to open. I can assure Mr Goldingay that Reverend Bell had nothing to do with the destruction of your employer's merchandise."

Penny Lane fixed him with an impassive stare. "With respect, Lord Furley, you have no way of knowing that. You can't vouch for him. And the last thing my employer cares about is any bad publicity you might incur."

Archie chewed his bottom lip. "Would a certain amount of remuneration settle the matter?"

Tabitha snorted. "Brother! Don't be naïve. You can't throw money at a jailbird. He'll just come back for more."

Penny sniffed. "This is not about money. A priceless piece of Mr Goldingay's collection has been destroyed. An irreplaceable exhibit."

Lady Tabitha swaggered around the Doric column, her big flappy boots going *gal-umph gal-umph* on the flagstones. She disappeared from view for a good ten seconds, then poked her head around the other side.

"How about I give your boss *my* action figure?"

Archie spluttered. "What?"

"What?" echoed Penny.

"You heard. A trade. Those bits of mangled plastic for my one. He can end up with exactly the same number of priceless action figures he had before, and he can rumble out of Furley House with his TV screen held high."

Archie was waving his arms in agitation. "Tabitha, *no*! That figure was bequeathed to you by *Father*."

"Exactly, little brother, it was bequeathed to me. Ergo, I can do what I like with it. I think it's a small price to pay to get Mr Creosote off our backs. I really don't care what happens to mine. Speaking for *myself*, I would cheerfully blast mine into tiny little bits, just to see your stupid faces."

She aimed her futuristic flintlock at Reverend Bell and pulled the trigger. The end lit up and it made a *zap* noise.

"Ker-pow."

Archie's face was a picture of anguish. "Are you *sure*?"

"I never say anything I don't mean, and I don't mean anything unless I'm sure." She turned to Penny and waved her copper pistol. "So what say you, Pepper Potts. Does Iron Man here take my offer?"

For the first time since she arrived, Penny Lane looked uncertain. "I don't know. I'll have to ask Mr Goldingay when he's brought back to his… When he's no longer indisposed."

"Fine." Tabitha laughed. "You ask him when he's 'no longer indisposed', find a window in his schedule between lights out and slopping out time." She caught her brother's eye and held up her finger. "Oh, yes. One condition: it gets to stay in the museum until the exhibition closes, and then your boss can take it home."

"I'll put your proposal to him."

They all fell silent, staring awkwardly at one another. Finally, Archie said, "Well, splendid. Perhaps we should return to the great hall? My other guests will be wondering where we've got to." He turned to Penny. "Have you had dinner, my dear?"

"Now you come to mention it, no. I got the call and drove straight here."

"Well, you can come and dine with us."

"You can take my place at the table," added Tabitha. "I'm not going to sit and watch you lot eat." Her eyes flicked to Kit. "Well, maybe I'll make an exception for you, Sherlock."

Kit's ribcage suddenly felt too small for her heart.

10

All heads turned when the little group returned to the hall, this time accompanied by a mystery guest who happened to come with her own pet robot.

Fenton and Reverend Bell explained the presence of the robot to their wives, who both rolled their eyes as if to say *More of this nonsense*.

Lady Tabitha loitered around the edge of the room before sitting in a large leather-backed chair near the fireplace.

Penny guided her metal friend to the corner of the dining table and took the seat at the end reserved for Lady Tabitha. Kit explained the reason for the robot's presence to Binfire and Vixy.

"Who's Graham Goldingay?" asked Vixy.

"You don't know who Graham Goldingay is?" said Kit. "I thought everybody in *Vixens* fandom knew who Graham Goldingay is."

"Well… Sort of. I've heard his name come up on forum discussions and on Twitter, but when that happens I just pretend I know what everyone's talking about."

Kit loved imparting facts and was happy to oblige. "Okay, quick potted history of Graham Goldingay. He's a rich superfan who thinks he's God. Fourteen years ago, he got blackballed by the BBC for trying to sabotage the first attempt to relaunch *Vixens from the Void*, because he didn't like the cast."

Penny frowned. "Mr Goldingay would take issue with the events you described."

"The jury didn't take issue with the events," retorted Kit. "That's why he got a suspended sentence for trespass and vandalism. And then, last year he got sent to prison for helping sex-pest television celebrities escape a police investigation by smuggling them across the English Channel."

Penny tapped the side of her plate with a fish knife. "I repeat, my employer would also take issue with that interpretation of what happened. He was providing a service."

Kit smiled. "And that's why he's in prison, of course, for 'providing a service'."

"Frokk," cackled Binfire, peering into the robot's computer screen. "Graham's really in there?"

"As long as the Wi-Fi holds out," said Penny.

Binfire reached out to tweak a knob on the robot, but Penny slapped his hand away.

"Let's respect Mr Goldingay's personal space, shall we? You wouldn't want to get arrested for harassment."

"It's a robot. You can't harass a robot."

Penny gave a tight smile. "There are always test cases that form new legal precedents. Let's make sure you don't find out the hard way."

Just as the waiters finished handing out the desserts, the robot's computer screen blazed into life. Graham's face scowled out of the picture.

"I have returned. Report!" he barked.

The robot jerked, moving on its own axis. Kit noticed that Penny's black box was untouched, sitting by her plate.

So, the robot isn't just powered by that single device, thought Kit. *Graham obviously has his own remote. Dual control.*

The robot turned ninety degrees towards her. It advanced, as if she was a bomb and it was going to defuse her by ripping her head off.

"Kit Pelham," he said. "You are here. I thought you might be here."

"Hello, Graham."

"I am glad to see you here."

"Really?"

"I have a proposal for you. I wish to employ you in your capacity as a detective. I want you to investigate the destruction of my action figure. I will pay you two hundred pounds a day, plus expenses."

"What? No chance."

"You cannot say no," he grated. "No one says no to me."

"Come on, pilgrim." Binfire was holding his arms out imploringly, clasping his hands together in prayer. "We've got to do this! It's detective work! You and me, doing our thing!"

"Fine," sighed Kit. "I'll think about it."

The robot revolved so its screen was facing Penny.

"Report," Graham demanded.

Penny explained the situation and outlined Lady Tabitha's proposal. Goldingay's eyes narrowed. His huge hand reached up and scratched his shaggy grey beard.

Eventually, he said, "Nothing can replace my Arkadia figure. *Nothing!* But Lady Tabitha has the Byzantia action figure in her possession. As Byzantia is the twin sister of Arkadia, and thus those figures are identical save for a slightly different-coloured cloak, I find the substitution acceptable. I will accept the offer."

Penny called out to Lady Tabitha, slumped in her leather chair. "He accepts the offer."

Tabitha gave a thumbs up sign. "Fan-effing-tastic. Let's hope this is the end of the matter, yeah?"

She got up out of the chair, twirling her guns as she clumped across the polished floor. Kit watched her out of the corner of her eye, straining to see the last flap of her space highwayman's coat as she disappeared out of the door.

11

Coffee and biscuits were served, then Archie said a few more warm words, thanking them all for coming, thanking the kitchen staff and the servers for working on the weekend, and then the dinner was over.

The guests left the hall in dribs and drabs. Binfire fished out his night-vision goggles from his cargo pants, winked at Kit and disappeared into the night. Fenton, Matty and Saskia rushed outside too, for a quick smoke outside the stables before bed.

Moni and Ruth left, walking arm-in-arm to the stables. Reverend Bell looked lost, as if he didn't know where he wanted to be. Then he too disappeared in the direction of the stables.

Jane the head waiter trotted up to Penny, giving her a key attached to a large lump of wood. "This is your room for tonight, Miss Lane," Jane said. "Number twelve. It's the stable at the end, the one that used to accommodate dray horses. It's got a very wide door, that I think would allow your friend…" Her eyes flicked to the robot. "… To access the room."

"Thank you." Penny smiled. "That's very thoughtful of you."

She picked up the remote control and accompanied the robot to the exit.

So, everyone was gone, apart from Kit, and the catering staff clearing away the cutlery and the napkins. She sat in the big chair opposite the fireplace and waited for them to finish, and then allowed herself to soak up the silence.

She closed her eyes and breathed slowly and deeply. *With any luck I'll make it to my room without having to see anyone else today.*

She walked quietly to the front doors. No such luck. Archie was there, standing on the patio. He was leaning on a Doric column, a pipe clenched between his teeth.

"Hello there."

"Hello."

"Just having a quick puff on the old briar before bed." A thin stream of smoke curled its way out of the bowl of his pipe. "Rum do, isn't it?"

"Very rum."

"Never thought opening a toy museum would create so much of a kerfuffle. These little toys certainly generate a lot of passion amongst a certain type of chap."

"They certainly do."

"But, then again, wars have been fought over less. A thought, an idea…"

Archie stared out into the lawn. The lights of the house threw beams into the darkness, illuminating the midges and making them look like dancing stars. About forty feet of the drive and lawns were lit up, leaving the rest of the estate in blackness. It looked like the rest of the world had vanished and only the house and its guests existed.

"I often spend a few minutes here on my own at the end of the day."

"It's very pretty."

Archie's face was in shadows, but Kit could still see he was smiling. "I find it gives one a sense of perspective. Knowing that an ancestor of mine would have looked out onto this estate from this house over four hundred years ago, and a descendant of mine may well look out on this same vista a hundred years hence… Well, it makes one humble, you know?"

"Huh. I guess it would."

"So many have fought for this little tract of land. So much

blood spilled so that we can stand here tonight."

"Huh."

"But here's me yammering on. Better turn in. Big day tomorrow. Goodnight, Kit."

"Goodnight."

"Shall we find time for that interview tomorrow?"

"That would be fantastic."

"How about after breakfast? About ten thirty?"

"Great."

She trotted away from the house, trying not to look too eager to reach the safety of her room.

12

The moment she got in her room her phone lit up. A WhatsApp. Jackie Hillier.

Are you back in your room? Are you awake? Can you talk? xxx

Yes, she was back in her room; yes, she was awake; but, no, she didn't want to talk. She didn't click on it: if she did, Jackie would know she had seen the message. Let her think she had already gone to bed. She slid the 'power' sign off and watched the screen go dark.

During the drinks and the dinner, she'd felt exhausted, but now she was wide awake. And she knew why. Binfire was right. Being asked to be a detective again *was* exciting. She was definitely going to say yes to Graham but she didn't want to be seen to be *too* keen. Maybe she would do a bit more humming and hawing tomorrow at breakfast, before grudgingly accepting his offer.

But for now her brain was buzzing. She did what she always did when insomnia struck and groped for her laptop, preparing to watch an endless cycle of self-help YouTube videos. The last time she did it, she finally nodded off to a man instructing her how to replace a rubber seal on a washing machine.

She lay on her bed, opened her laptop and clicked on her YouTube icon, but instead of typing 'how to', she found her fingers tapping out the words 'Cosplay Countess'. The screen filled with Lady Tabitha's masked face in a variety of thumbnails.

She clicked on a video labelled 'Crazy Cat Lady'. Lady Tabitha appeared, encased from head to foot in a black leather catsuit, complete with mask. The look was a definite homage to Michelle Pfeiffer's original costume (*Batman Returns*, 1992), including ragged stitching across the body and mask.

One hand was on her hip, the other was holding a whip. It was recorded at night and she was outside, standing outside a hotel (presumably a convention venue). There was a sickly yellow glow seeping from the concourse lights, but the main source of illumination came from an arc light beside her. She grabbed the light, swivelling it around, showing a paper bat-signal sellotaped to the glass, then she swung around the stand, striking pole dancer poses and allowing the spotlight to bathe her in white light. She danced around to the tune of Zager and Evans' 'In the Year 2525' for a few seconds, then she sashayed towards the camera, filling the screen. She pulled off her mask, stared directly into the lens and went "*Meow.*"

It wasn't as if Kit hadn't seen this video before. She'd furtively watched them all (when Jackie wasn't around of course): Lady Marvel, Wonder Lady, Lady Galadriel, Slave Lady Princess Organa... She'd *even* watched the more recent, less interesting ones: Iron Ma'am, Ant Ma'am and Bat Ma'am. The ones where her body was less exposed, covered in chunky plastic exoskeletons. Kit guessed she was tired of using her body to sell her channel and was seeing how it would work if she hid her curves in muscle suits and robot costumes. It hadn't worked: the Lady series had tens of thousands of hits and the Ma'am range only had a few hundred.

Kit clicked on another, this one labelled 'Lady Deadpool'. The format was much the same, only it was in daylight, and the leather costume was red and black. This time, she danced around a flight of steps, hanging off the handrails. She strutted to the camera, pulled off her hood, revealing a tousled mop of blonde hair. She said: "*Do you like me breaking the fourth wall?*"

The video ended.

Kit was about to click on a third.

"She has a nice face."

Kit screamed.

The voice came from Binfire. He was leaning over her shoulder, looking at the screen.

"Shame we haven't seen much of her, with those goggles and eye patches? Maybe her next costume will be more… slave girl… If you know what I mean."

"Binfire! You n… nearly gave m… me a heart attack!"

Binfire looked surprised. "Sorry, pilgrim. I thought you knew I was here."

"W… why the f-fuck would I th… think that? What the efff… are you doing in my room?"

Binfire waggled a thermos in his hand. "Getting coffee. Your room has a better coffee machine than mine. It does loads of flavours, and frothy milk. It's like something… *from the future*!"

As he said 'from the future', he cupped the cup of the thermos over his mouth, making it echo. He grinned. "Got to keep warm. The Cosplay Countess is taking me badger-watching tonight."

"Wh… wh… You?"

"Yeah, she just saw me with my night-vision goggles and asked me if I wanted to see the badgers. There's a badger set down on the edge of the estate." He stared at Kit, then at her laptop and an idea staggered into his brain. "Hey, you want to come? I mean, I'm sure she'd say yes."

Kit was so tempted. So very tempted. But the dark. And the mud. And the cold. Could she do it? *Come on, Kit*, said the voice inside her. *This is an amazing opportunity. A chance of a lifetime. You'd be insane to turn it down, utterly ins*

"No thanks. I'm a bit tired. You go and have fun."

"Cheers, pilgrim." He bounced to the door and held up his phone. "If I see a badger, I'll send you a photo."

And he was gone.

Kit got into her pyjamas and lay on her bed, not feeling tired at all.

* * *

Kit opened her eyes and saw a figure standing at the end of her bed.

It was a sturdy-looking woman wearing a Puffa jacket. Kit had a strong suspicion who it was. There was a sudden lightning flash, illuminating Jackie Hillier's angry face, and leaving no room for doubt.

"You think you can just ignore my calls?" she snarled. "You think you can just run away from me and hide here?"

"I'm not running away."

"Don't kid yourself, sweetie. You're running away. And it's up to me to help you realise you can't do that to me."

Jackie picked up a heavy lump hammer and held it against her cheek, in a pose that instantly reminded Kit of Annie Wilkes (*Misery*, 1990).

"No. Jackie… Please don't. This isn't you…"

"How do you know who I am? How do you know?"

Jackie raised the lump hammer above her shoulder and aimed it towards Kit's left foot. Kit tried to roll across the bed but her duvet felt as heavy as lead. She was trapped. She opened her mouth to scream but no sound came out.

Jackie snorted. "You can't even scream properly, Kit. Pathetic. You want to know what a scream sounds like? This is what a scream sounds like."

Jackie opened her mouth, wider than she should have

been physically able to do, and emitted a horrific, high-pitched scream, a single note ripping through Kit's body and causing physical pain in her head.

And then Kit was awake.

Jackie had vanished along with the rest of the dream, and the only thing left was the high-pitched scream. The distant scream of a security alarm.

13

The *drrrrrrrrr* was ear-splitting, as if the museum was screaming its guts out into the courtyard. Then, as Kit approached, it cut off abruptly. If anything, the silence was even more deafening.

Kit dashed inside and skidded to a halt in stunned disbelief. The place was in ruins. The main window had been broken. Shards of glass and chunks of lead were on the floor, glittering in the harsh electric light like crazy paving.

The display in the centre of the room was shattered. The ordinary common-or-garden action figures on the bottom shelf were scattered, lying amidst fragments of pyramid. It looked gruesome, as if someone had taken a photo of a terrorist attack in a busy shopping centre at the precise moment the bomb had gone off.

Of the precious, priceless, mint-in-box, one-of-a-kind action figures, there was no sign.

Beside the door was a tangle of wreckage that had once been Graham Goldingay's robot. It had been wrenched out of shape, almost flattened, almost *smeared* across the floor, as if a giant hand had picked it up and hurled it back to earth.

Reverend Bell was swaddled in a dressing gown. Fenton was wearing jeans and a T-shirt, but also slippers and no socks, and his sparse hair was sticking out in all directions. Matty was wearing sweatpants and a T-shirt with 'Toxic Male' written across it.

Ruth Bell, Moni Worth, Saskia and Vixy had wisely thrown some clothes on before venturing out. Archie was still in his eveningwear. They were all staggering through the wreckage like shell-shocked survivors of a zombie apocalypse.

"Holy shit," whispered Matty, looking around at the debris. "They're gone. They've all been fucking nicked."

"I feel faint," moaned Reverend Bell. He was wandering around in a circle, holding his arms tightly around his shoulders like he was wearing an invisible straitjacket.

"What the actual fudge?" yelled Fenton. He was gripping his head, his eyes spinning around the room. He looked at his wife. "Was my action figure insured? Did we insure it?"

"Of course we did," snapped Moni. "And by 'we', I mean of course 'me', because it's me that sorts everything out."

"Good." Fenton gasped with relief. "Well done, love."

"It's insured. Of course it's insured. But only if anything happens to it on the premises of the shop. They won't pay out because you brought it here."

"What?" he screeched. "But…"

"Don't scream at me. *You* didn't tell me you were loaning it to Furley House. I didn't have time to change the policy." She gave him an icy glare. "Perhaps you should have discussed it with me?"

Vixy looped her arm around Fenton's and stared at her defiantly. "He discussed it with *me*."

"Well, this is all down to you then." She barked with sudden laughter. "I'm sure Fenton will forgive you."

"Don't worry about insurance," Archie said, his face grim. "The museum is insured for theft and breakages. You will be reimbursed for anything stolen."

Fenton deflated with relief. "Thank heavens."

"Well, that's some fucking consolation," growled Matty.

"Has anyone called the cops?" asked Saskia.

"Yes, my dear," said Archie. "I got my security chap to make a call. They should be here soon."

"This is terrible! Awful," muttered Archie. "Why would anyone do this?"

"Obsessive collectors," replied Reverend Bell grimly. "There are people out there who would do anything to get their hands on those figures."

"I thought you *were* the obsessive collectors," retorted Ruth.

Pink spots appeared on Reverend Bell's grey cheeks. "*Other* obsessive collectors, dear. Unscrupulous ones."

He looked at Fenton and Matty, and Fenton and Matty looked back at him, and then glanced at each other. Nothing was said, but it was obvious to Kit that each collector assumed the other two were just the right sort of maniac to try something like this.

Ruth shivered. "If we're going to have to wait for the police, I'm going to wait in my room. It's freezing in here."

"Good idea," said Moni. "Let's get a hot chocolate and warm up. Anyone else? Fenton?"

Ruth tried to get the attention of her husband. "Jerome?"

The two men didn't hear them. They were both staring at the place where the action figures used to be.

Ruth and Moni exchanged long-suffering glances and left the museum.

Kit had made a wide circle of the crime scene, searching the floor for evidence. She stopped at the wreckage. "What's Graham's robot doing here?"

Archie walked over and peered at the dismembered robot with obvious concern. "I haven't the faintest idea why this thing is in here. The museum was locked up tight."

"Where's Penny Lane?" asked Saskia.

As if on cue, Penny burst in, carrying her phone in front of her.

"Oh my god!" she gasped. She ran to the crumpled robot

and picked up some of the pieces helplessly, holding them up, as if she was about to start working on an impossible jigsaw puzzle.

Archie waved a hand at the wreckage. "What's the meaning of this, Ms Lane?"

Penny ignored him.

"Ms Lane!" repeated Archie, with a little more authority.

Penny held up her hand. "Wait! I'm calling Mr Goldingay!"

Archie simmered with rage as he watched her tap on her phone.

"Come on pick up!" she muttered. Eventually she looked up and said, "You were saying?"

"Can I just trouble you for an explanation?"

"What kind of explanation?"

"For this state of affairs?"

"State?"

Matty sighed and pointed to the mangled robot. "I think he's trying to ask you what the fuck Sir Killalot is doing here *inside* the museum, after it got locked up tight for the night."

"Oh, I *see*!" Penny put the phone in her pocket. "Mr Goldingay was concerned that what happened to *his* action figure would happen to the others. He wanted to protect his new acquisition, so he decided to position his robot in the museum overnight to guard the collection."

"Fat lot of good that did," scoffed Matty.

"But how did the robot get in the building?" asked Kit.

"Good question," muttered Archie.

"He had a key and the combination," said Penny simply. Her phone rang. "Sorry, I've got to take this." She ran outside, her phone pressed to her ear.

Archie looked surprised. "He had a key and a combination? Did I hear her right?"

Matty shrugged. "Sorry to say this, Archie mate, but in the

interests of full disclosure, all of us Furley Fanboys, me, Fenton and Graham, have got both keys *and* the combination to this place. Your dad gave them to us years ago."

"The combination is easy to remember. It's the date of the first broadcast of *Vixens from the Void*," added Fenton.

"I say!" said Archie. "That's bang out of order. It's hardly a decent security system if Father handed those things out willy-nilly."

"What can I say?" Matty held his arms up in surrender. "It just made it easier to go in and out of the old museum when we used to stay here for the weekends. Your dad trusted us not to mess about with the exhibits."

Kit looked at Archie. "Do you have any security cameras in the museum?"

Archie looked embarrassed. "Sadly, no. Father was adamant that there be no security cameras *inside* the buildings. He and his harem tended to run naked through the corridors, and he didn't want his – and their – privacy invaded. Since Father's death, we've discussed putting internal cameras in the corridors, but it's a tricky process, interfering with the structure of a Grade I listed building. We're still working it out."

"No cameras?" Fenton was aghast. "No cameras at all? You have all those antiques and priceless objects, and you put this museum together, and all the while there are no security cameras?"

"If I'd known Father was handing out the keys and security codes like sweets to any Tom, Dick or Harry, I might have made it more of a priority!" he snapped. Then he remembered his manners. "There are *many* security cameras as a matter of fact. They are around the grounds, on trees and the like, to keep a look out for thieves, vandals and poachers. We have cameras trained on this house, and a few pointing right at the museum.

I couldn't have got insurance if I didn't have a decent security system."

"Well that's something," said Matty. "We can at least see who might have broken in."

Vixy dropped her hand onto Fenton's shoulder.

"Don't worry, Fenton," she cooed. "The police will sort this out, you'll see. I'm sure they'll find the culprits and get your action figure back."

"I wish I had your faith," said Fenton gloomily. "In my experience, the police never take property crime that seriously. They'll just make a report, file it, and we'll never hear from them again."

"He's right," snapped Matty. "Fuck the police. We know that they're not going to do anything. We have to solve this ourselves."

Penny re-entered the building.

"I've talked to Mr Goldingay about the situation," Penny said. "And I'm organising a replacement automaton for delivery so he can help in the investigation."

"Fucking great," said Matty, yawning. "I'm sure that makes everyone feel a whole lot better."

Kit bent down to examine the mangled fragments. "The thieves really had it in for Graham's robot, didn't they? They smashed it into tiny pieces."

Penny agreed. "The force does look a bit disproportionate, I agree."

Kit rubbed her chin. "I guess when they broke in, they weren't expecting to find it waiting for them." She straightened up. "So, did Graham see what happened?"

Penny patted the phone in her pocket. "I was asking him that, but I'm afraid I got cut off. He might ring back when the warders move to another wing…"

As if on cue, the phone in Penny's pocket rang, and she answered it, propping the phone on a chair so they could all see him. He was sitting in his cell, this time wearing a large grey T-shirt and baggy sweatpants.

"Report!" he barked.

Matty barged his way into Graham's line of vision. "*You* report, you arsehole! Your robot was in the bloody museum! *Tell us what you saw!*"

Graham got up from his chair, with no small effort. He came close and pointed out of the screen, where a grey figure was slumped by the shattered cabinet.

"I saw *him*. I saw Reverend Bell," he growled, jabbing his engorged finger in the Reverend's direction. "I saw him enter the museum in the middle of the night and open up the cabinet!"

14

They all convened in the Furley House library. Kit approved of the place because it had rows of leather-bound books, all in complete sets. There were all six volumes of Churchill's *The Second World War* and encyclopaedias covering all the letters of the alphabet. Kit recalled many unpleasant hours in a hotel lounge staring at a bookshelf containing odd copies from larger sagas: *A Game of Thrones: A Song of Ice and Fire, Dune Messiah* and *The Lord of the Rings: Part Two*. Kit wondered what kind of sick individual would be inclined to pick them up and read a random book from the middle of a trilogy.

The library also had lots of lamps, one of which was being shone in Reverend Bell's face.

"Talk!" snarled Matty, who was sitting in a leather chair opposite Bell. He was the one holding the lamp.

Kit was already thinking that things were getting out of hand. She wasn't the only one. Saskia, Penny and Vixy all looked uncomfortable at the turn events had taken. Archie didn't look too happy either.

Reverend Bell's red-rimmed eyes blinked in the glare. He had his elbows pulled into his chest, and he was holding his clenched fists inches in front of his face, like a punch-drunk boxer waiting for the bell.

"I say, steady on," Archie piped up. "Isn't this against the Geneva Convention? Perhaps we should wait for the police?"

"Yes," sighed Kit.

"Put the damn light down, Matty," sighed Saskia.

"You keep out of this," he snapped. "You too, Kitty Kat. This is man's work."

"The police?" whimpered Bell. "Not the police! I have a reputation! I have a parish!"

Matty pushed the lamp closer into Reverend Bell's eyes, making him wince. "Admit it! You went into the museum last night!"

"I admit it!" whimpered Reverend Bell. "I did go into the museum!"

"And you *stole* our figures and trashed the place to cover it up!"

"No! I swear!"

"Liar!"

"So, what were you doing in the museum, Reverend?" Archie said. "It's a bit late to start checking on the exhibits."

Reverend Bell hesitated, clutching the arms of his chair as if to make a run for it.

"Answer!" snarled Matty.

"I just wanted to touch them!"

Fenton went pale. "Touch them? You mean…"

"I'm sorry!" he blurted. "I've never owned anything so wondrous as an action figure of that rarity! I've never had the pleasure of having one in my hands before. I couldn't help myself. I've been… opening the boxes."

Saskia was confused. "What?"

"You sick fuck," muttered Matty.

"I know! I'm sorry. I only opened the box lids! I just wanted to touch them! To reach inside and caress their little plastic bodies with the tips of my fingers. Just brush their unique head sculpts for a tiny moment."

Fenton was shaking his head in disbelief. "You had some mint-in-box, one-of-a-kind action figures left in your possession, *in your care*, and you peeled back the *original* sticky tape, destroying the stickiness in the process, and you... *opened the boxes*?"

"But you can replace the sticky tape?" said Vixy.

Fenton exchanged glances with Matty. "Sorry about her. She still doesn't get it."

Bell gave out a short, sobbing breath. "I know it was wrong but... I don't know what came over me. I couldn't help myself!"

Matty turned the lamp off. "That's what all you vicars say, after you get caught. You hide behind the dog collar, say you can't help yourself, when deep down you know you're an opportunistic sicko. You *molested* my little girl."

Reverend Bell whimpered.

This is getting ridiculous, Kit thought. "If only the dolls were here, they could show us on a human where he touched them," she muttered tartly.

"You were warned, you bitch," snapped Matty, whirling round and throwing the glare of the lamp into Kit's face. She winced.

"Matty!" Saskia was outraged. "Watch the language! Be a better man, for Chrissakes!"

"A better man," he scoffed, "is just a feminist code for a *new* man. No one's taking *my* bollocks."

Reverend Bell was no longer being cornered by the glare, and he took the opportunity to plead his case. He staggered to his feet. "I can only apologise a thousand times for what I did. But that's all I did. I went in, I opened the cabinet, touched Excelsior gently on the head, and I departed. That was all. I had nothing to do with the disappearance of the dolls or the destruction of the exhibit. Why would I do that? I've just spent months putting it all together."

"He has a point," muttered Kit.

"Shut up," snapped Matty.

Bell continued, "If Graham was there, hiding in the shadows, if he was watching me, then he can vouch for me."

He walked towards the phone, where Graham's face bobbed on the screen like a Halloween balloon. "Tell them exactly what you saw, Graham. You saw me open the cabinet, yes? But did you not see me then *close* the cabinet and leave without causing any damage?"

Graham reluctantly nodded. "He's telling the truth. That is what I saw. And as far as I could see, nothing else happened until my robot was destroyed and my screen was deactivated."

"And the screen stopped working at one a.m. Seconds before we heard the alarm," added Penny.

"Fuck," said Matty.

"Well, that was a goddamn waste of time," muttered Saskia.

A blanket of silence fell on the room, with the word 'gloom' crocheted on the edge.

"Kit Pelham, are you still here?" grated Graham.

Kit flinched at the mention of her name. She ignored it.

"Kit Pelham, are you still here?"

She wanted to go, but now she was trapped.

"Yes."

"Your task has become more complicated. I am now willing to increase your daily rate to three hundred pounds a day, so you can investigate, save the remaining figures and find the culprit."

"What?" said Fenton.

"What are you talking about?" added Matty.

"I have already hired Kit Pelham to investigate the destruction of my Arkadia action figure..."

"I haven't said yes yet," sighed Kit.

"... and I am now tasking her to investigate the disappearance of the whole Ceremonial Range. To retrieve the figures and catch the culprits."

Matty was not happy. "What? No way! Her? You can't be serious!"

"I am serious."

"You've got a room full of straight white males, and you cast her as the main protagonist? You're putting a 'strong independent female' in charge to show everyone you're down with 'the message'." He put up his hands and made sarcastic air quotes.

I don't feel like a strong independent female, thought Kit. *Quite the opposite. I feel like a very tired female in need of a good night's sleep.*

Matty continued, "How clichéd can you get, Graham? Why don't you go and work for fucking Disney and have done with it? How bloody woke can you get?"

"Nobody calls me woke, Matty Kearney."

"Well, what other reason is it, other than 'diversity'? A woman *and* a lesbian? She only has to be black and disabled and you've ticked *all* the boxes."

"Fuck off, Matty," sighed Saskia.

Matty ignored her. "How do we know that she will take the investigation of our *classic* series figures seriously? She represents the *new* series. She writes columns in *StarCrash* pointing out that the classic series looks cheap." He shuddered. "She'll probably only conduct the investigation in an *ironic* way. Winking at the fucking camera that no one should take the theft seriously, encouraging others to find the *humour*."

"Too right," agreed Fenton. "She does podcasts interviewing the *new* production team and the new actors, telling them they're wonderful. As far as I'm concerned, she's on *their* side."

Vixy looked bemused. She turned to Saskia. "What are they talking about?"

Saskia rolled her eyes. "They're talking complete horseshit, is what they're talking about." She furiously banged the table, causing the bickering to cease. "Listen to yourselves, guys! You're assessing a woman's ability to do a job, depending on how she feels about an old television show? You're all crazy!"

"Saskia, love." Matty shot a patronising look in her direction. "It's not crazy. It has a direct bearing on her ability to do the job. It's self-evident she won't take it seriously because she doesn't rate the classic series."

"I am a fan of the classic series," retorted Kit. "I've been a fan since I was young."

"Yeah, right," sniffed Matty. "Ever since the new series made *Vixens* popular again, everybody and his wife has *conveniently* revealed they were always fans, ever since they were babies. I don't believe Jonathan fucking Ross for a second, and I don't believe *you*."

Saskia stepped between him and Kit. "I'm sorry, Kit. I did tell you Matty's a professional asshole, didn't I? It's just a shame it happens to be his hobby too."

Matty stepped forward, put his arm around Saskia's shoulders and rested his hand on her hip. "I think you *know* what my hobby is, darling."

She shrugged him off. "Hands off the merchandise, Matty. You know very well everything you touch decreases in value."

Matty's face clouded in sudden fury, but he took his hand away.

"This is irrelevant," rumbled Goldingay. "All your protests are irrelevant. You've said yourselves that the police will be of no help, and I agree, so I've made an executive decision. It is her ability as a detective, yes, but it is also combined with my assessment that out of all of us present, she is *least* likely to have perpetrated this heinous crime."

Fenton, Reverend Bell and Matty exchanged glances, and

Kit was irresistibly reminded of the meme in which three identical Spider-Men were pointing accusingly at each other.

They were all thinking it. They all suspected each other of having a hand in stealing the action figures. They know the logic of Graham's words is inescapable.

"What are you all doing in here?"

That was Lady Tabitha.

She and Binfire were in the doorway of the library. Lady Tabitha was still dressed as a space highwayman. Binfire's face was smeared with camouflage make-up and he was wearing camouflage fatigues. His night-vision binoculars were dangling around his neck.

Tabitha stared around the room. "Well? Why are you all skulking around in here?"

Archie managed a watery grin. "Things have taken a bit of a turn, old sis. Have you seen the museum?"

"No, we saw the lights were on in the library and came straight here."

"I think you'd better accompany us. Prepare yourself for a bit of a shock."

15

Lady Tabitha strode into the museum. She stared into the broken cabinet and looked up with a cock-eyed grimace.

"Can't leave you alone for a moment, can I, little brother?" She pointed a flintlock in the direction of Fenton, Matty and Reverend Bell. "I take it from these hyperventilating nerds that all the action figures have gone?"

"What, they're gone?" said Binfire.

"They've all gone. Yes. Sorry," said Archie.

"Mine too?" said Binfire.

"Yours too. Sorry."

"Frokk. I only dug it up out of the garden last week. I take it out this one time and it gets stolen!"

"I'm terribly sorry."

"'I'm terribly sorry'," Tabitha drawled, mocking his hopeless tone. "What an utter shitshow. Daddy dies and you get the estate, and all I get is one plastic toy. That was all I get, and now you go and lose it."

"I'll make it up to you, Tabby," he sighed. "I'll find it and get it back."

"Hah. Really not the point is it, little bro? I was going to give it away anyway, because it was worthless to me. And you know why it was worthless? Because Daddy giving it to me was an insult."

She strode back to the doorway and holstered her guns. "I'm three years older than you, and I'm still treated like a teenager. You get the estate, and Daddy leaves me a plastic toy in his will! And here I am relying on *you* for an allowance! A bloody *allowance*!" She turned to the group. "Is that fair, in this day and age?"

"Never thought about it." Fenton shrugged.

"I'm sorry about that, but that's the way things are," said Archie to Tabitha. "I didn't come up with the law of primogeniture, did I?" He lowered his voice. "Perhaps this is a conversation for another time?"

"Perhaps this is the perfect time to have this conversation."

"We have an ongoing situation here."

"This situation is *gone*, little brother. You just have to collect the insurance and move on. Hopefully it will cover the damage." A thought occurred to her. "Hey, perhaps we could torch the whole place? That way you'll definitely get enough money to make this whole shitshow worthwhile."

To illustrate her point, she pulled the trigger on one of her flintlocks. A blue flame burst out of the nozzle, like an oxyacetylene welder.

Everyone backed away.

"Perhaps we should burn it to the ground? Anything to stop this boring conversation."

"That's enough!" barked Archie.

The flintlock's flame was extinguished. Lady Tabitha sashayed cat-like out of the museum, chuckling to herself. She paused to run the back of her gloved hand down Kit's face. Kit was too surprised to react.

"I'm sure you'll sort this out, little Kitty," she purred. "Binfire tells me you're a *brilliant* detective."

And she left.

"Christ," muttered Matty. "I bet she's great in bed."

Archie clasped his hands together, as if in prayer. "I... I'm sorry, everyone. I'm sorry for my sister's behaviour, and I'm sorry for all of this. I honestly don't know what's happening here." He stared at the shattered cabinet, as if willing the action figures to reappear by sheer force of will.

With a huge effort, Kit forced herself to stop thinking about Lady Tabitha.

"Does anyone have any idea who would do something like this?" she asked. "I mean… This rhyme that Graham got sent. It feels more vindictive than anything. More like an act of revenge. Is there anyone who holds a grudge against any of you?"

Fenton and Matty exchanged glances. It might have been her imagination, but it looked like *something* was being passed between them, like they were having a telepathic conversation. They stared at one another for a few seconds too long.

"No," said Fenton. "No one springs to mind."

Malcolm appeared in the doorway. "The police are here, sir."

16

Two police officers were standing in the hallway of Furley House. They were led by Archie to the scene of the crime, where there was much scratching of heads and impressed whistling as they surveyed the mess.

PC Kelly was young, barely past her teens, with blonde hair sprouting from dark roots. She had holes in her face, just under her eye and on the crests of her nostrils. Kit guessed she wore a lot of piercings on her days off. She was very short – barely five feet in her boots – and looked very aware of it. She stood so erect that she looked like she was about to topple over backwards.

PC Howard was much older with short grey hair, monstrous eyebrows and sideburns that tapered into points. He didn't look like he had piercings, but Kit thought he might have interesting tattoos, tucked away under his uniform. He had very twinkly green eyes, which made him look like he was slightly amused at everything.

Those eyes are probably very useful in his line of work, thought Kit. *Good at defusing awkward situations and the like. But maybe not in relationships. No woman would ever take what he said completely seriously.*

PCs Kelly and Howard listened politely to the events of the evening and made sympathetic noises as Reverend Bell and Archie outlined in great detail the incredible sentimental value of the action figures.

"Well, rest assured we'll keep an eye out," said PC Howard soothingly, his eyes a-twinkle.

"Keep an eye out?" Archie sounded aghast. "I sincerely

hope you can do better than that. Didn't my boffin send you the footage from all my security cameras?"

"Yes, I'm having a look at those right now," said PC Kelly. She raised her gloved hand, to show him her phone. On the screen was a blurred black-and-white image of the museum door, partially obscured by a branch of a tree. "It's a right old museum piece, your security system. Looks like it was put in when the house was built."

"Very amusing," said Archie dryly.

"She's very technical," said PC Howard. "She does really funny things on Instagram."

Kelly blushed. "I didn't know you saw my Instagram stuff."

"Oh yeah. I saw the video where you were at the Beerfest and you filled up that police helmet with IPA and put it on your head. I was tempted to show it to the chief. Damaging police property and all that."

"That was one of those kid's plastic ones, you 'nana! I was off duty!"

"Is any of this relevant?" sighed Archie.

"Yeah. Anyway. I can't see anything on the footage yet. Just you lot going in and out of the chapel, and that robot thing. No one carrying any objects that fit the description. And I had a quick whizz through the camera footage on the main gate. No movement at all, as far as I can see. No one going in or out, apart from the servants leaving around ten o'clock-ish."

"But there has to be!" spluttered Archie.

PC Kelly wrinkled her nose, making the holes in her nostrils turn scarlet. "Well, I could have missed something, but these motion-sensitive cameras are really easy to go through. No motion, no footage, you get me?"

PC Howard turned to Archie. "It's a bit of a puzzle this, isn't it?"

"It is indeed."

"Missing artefacts, place turned over in seconds… It's a bit like one of those panic rooms."

"Escape rooms," said Kit automatically.

"Exactly, like one of those escape rooms. Lots of odd clues everywhere." He grinned and twinkled. "You don't remember me, do you, my lord?"

Archie slapped a panicked grin on his face. "I'm… not sure. Your face doesn't ring a bell, but I do meet a lot of people in my line of work. No offence."

"None taken," PC Howard said cheerfully. "I got called out to Furley House last year, well mostly last year and a bit of this year. New Year's Eve. When you had that big, masked do."

"Oh yes. The Flannery Young Farmers' Ball."

"That's right. We were called up because one of the stone lions had gone missing from the gate. Really heavy it was. We were in the middle of taking witness statements from drunken revellers, some of whom swore blind they saw it come to life and walk off down the drive, when we got a call from the local cats' home, saying they'd found a giant statue outside their front gate."

"Oh yes."

"Yes. That was an evening and a half."

"Those Young Farmers are rascals, aren't they?"

PC Kelly chipped in, "Well, the Flannery group certainly are."

PC Howard grinned at PC Kelly, and PC Kelly smiled back. It was incredibly obvious, without actually saying it out loud, that they were treating the stolen dolls as seriously as the missing stone lion: a drunken prank committed by bored rich people in order to create a bit of commotion.

"Well." PC Kelly broke the silence. "I think we've just about got everything we need here."

"Aren't you going to dust for fingerprints?" said Fenton plaintively.

"No, I don't think we'll need to do that." PC Howard's voice was very soothing, almost on the right side of patronising. "This looks like the work of a professional. I don't think they'd leave anything. We'll run a PNC check to see if any gangs are working in the area, and if they pop up you'll be the first to know."

"Perhaps you can do a bit of digging yourselves," added PC Kelly. "After all, you probably know the market for these toys better than us."

"Our advice is to get in touch with your insurance company."

And with that, they were done. Archie was issued with a piece of paper telling him he was now in the system, but that and a few dirty tea mugs were the only evidence the police had ever been there.

17

They all went back into the library because it had the greatest number of chairs. Ruth Bell and Moni Worth grudgingly joined them.

"Well!" puffed Archie. "I'm not sure what to make of that."

Matty scowled. "They don't believe a word. They think we're just a bunch of overgrown kids playing silly buggers."

"Aren't we?"

Lady Tabitha was at the top of the gallery above them, standing under a sign that said FICTION (A–F). She was flicking through a dusty hardback. "Who's to say it's not one of us having a big joke at someone's expense?"

Matty glared up at her. "Is that a confession?"

"Hardly!" She laughed. "I don't think so. I haven't got the time to do something this moronic." She nodded at Bell. "My money's still on Reverend Bell. He went inside the museum last. And it was he who outed himself as an Agatha Christie obsessive, didn't he? I bet he only became a vicar so he could sound like a character in an Agatha Christie book." She laughed. "Looks like the type to do a Murder Mystery weekend. He's chief suspect material to me."

Reverend Bell looked indignant. "I've already explained what I—"

Ruth interrupted her husband. "Don't take the bait, Jerome. She's just trying to get a rise out of you."

Lady Tabitha leaned over the balustrade and smiled at Matty. "And what about you?"

"What about me?"

"Well, this whole ridiculous incident *does* seem to be inspired by one of the most politically incorrect book titles in English literature. You're the anti-woke bloke, aren't you? Perhaps this is your idea of an anti-woke joke."

"I wouldn't do that, would I?" Matty glanced at Saskia. "Tell her, Sas."

Saskia shrugged. "I don't know you well enough to say you wouldn't do it."

"Fuck you," he snapped.

"Right back atcha," she retorted.

Tabitha held the hardback book in front of her and dropped it. It landed with a deafening thud on a coffee table, throwing up a mushroom cloud of dust.

"Jesus Christ!" yelled Fenton, shaking his head and sending up a cloud of dandruff. "I nearly jumped out of my skin!"

Kit looked down at the book. It was old and dusty, with a faded green jacket flaking at the edges. The cover depicted a rather obscure illustration of three multi-coloured fish superimposed on each other.

The title was in big red capitals. It was the first edition of the Agatha Christie book, complete with the outrageously offensive word plastered across the cover.

Matty glowered at her. Lady Tabitha leaned on the balustrade and blew him a kiss.

Reverend Bell drew himself up to his full height and gripped his lapels. "I think we have to face the very real and sobering prospect that it may indeed be one of us who did this."

Matty laughed and folded his arms. "Thanks for that, Dr Obvious. Well, I for one know I didn't do it. Furthermore, I'm not leaving this place until whoever did admits it, apologises for it and gives me my fucking figure back."

"Me too," added Fenton.

Archie clapped his hands. "My dear fellows. As this took place on the premises, I cannot help but feel responsible. As a way to make amends, you can stay in your rooms in Furley House, free of charge, until this matter is resolved."

"That's a very generous gesture." Reverend Bell gave a bow. "I for one am happy to accept."

"Me too."

"We are not staying here!" Moni was not happy. "We were planning to visit my father tomorrow."

"Me neither," said Ruth. "Jerome, we have better things to do than wait around and hope for your toys to turn up. It's *Saturday.* You have a sermon to give tomorrow."

Fenton and Reverend Bell looked frozen, unable to go forward to their cars or back to the museum.

"Surely..." said Fenton slowly, "he *is* your dad, not mine, and given he's pretty gone with the Alzheimer's, he wouldn't *really* know if I came to visit him or not?"

Moni's expression could have started a forest fire. She advanced on her husband and it looked like she was going to physically attack him, but Vixy stepped in front of Fenton. She eyeballed Moni, her chin jutting out defiantly.

"Would your dad really know if he was there?" Vixy said.

Moni glared at her, then at Fenton. "You are going to be sorry, Fenton. Sorrier than you will ever have been, ever, in your sorry life."

She stomped out of the library. Seconds later, a car engine roared into life, and there was the sound of spluttering gravel as it accelerated down the drive. Fenton shrugged and tried to act as if nothing had happened.

Eyes turned to Ruth Bell.

"Fair enough, dear," she sighed, surrendering. "I know this museum is close to your heart. Heaven knows why. And I do

104

forget that Archie is *paying* you for your services. So, it's only fair you should at least be given a couple of days to help him rescue something from the wreckage. Why don't you ring Nigel and get him to take the service for you? I'll take the car. Let me know when you're ready to return."

She kissed Reverend Bell on the cheek and went to get her coat.

If anything, Bell looked *more* unnerved than Fenton by his wife's response. He touched his cheek like he had been marked for death.

Archie frowned and sidled up to him. "Did you tell her I was *paying* you for your services?"

"Ah," he spluttered. "Well, I had been spending a *lot* of time here, so I had to say *something*."

Archie looked around at the others. "Does anyone else need to leave, or are we all committed to staying?"

"I'm staying," said Saskia.

"Me too," agreed Vixy.

"I'm staying here as Mr Goldingay's representative," said Penny.

There was a rumble of assent from the men.

Archie smiled at Kit. "I presume our resident detective will be here for the duration?"

Kit nodded.

"Splendid!" Archie beamed.

18

One by one, they filed out of the library and returned to their rooms. Matty was still shaking his head and muttering, "Fuck."

Fenton and Reverend Bell looked dazed, though it wasn't clear if they were more shell-shocked about the missing figures or the reactions from their wives. Saskia and Vixy were chatting excitedly amongst themselves.

Archie and Tabitha left together. Archie was making reassuring noises to his sister, but Tabitha was having none of it. "Dad always said you weren't fit to fill his shoes, and now here's proof of it. You *knew* very well he always wanted me to take control of the estate."

"Don't you think I don't know that?"

"You could have—" Tabitha broke off as they passed Kit and Binfire. She gave Kit a slow wink, before carrying on with her point. "You could have renounced your title."

"Out of the question."

The sounds of their bickering grew soft and inaudible as they drifted along the corridor into the house.

Kit and Binfire left too, turning the other way, towards the front door and the stables. Soon they were back in the night air, the stars twinkling over their heads.

But was that the faint glow of dawn in the distance?

Kit snapped open her pocket watch and stared incredulously at the time.

"It can't be three o'clock!"

"Yep. It is. Oh-three hundred hours."

"I'm never going to get my eight hours tonight!"

"Not a chance."

"So, how were the badgers?" asked Kit.

"The cubs were really cute."

She grinned. "And how was Lady Tabitha?"

Binfire gave a grimace. "She spent most of the time asking questions about *you*."

"Me?"

"I know. I never took her for one of your lot, given her YouTube videos. She was always talking about that boyfriend of hers. Nate. Perhaps it was all just an image thing, you know? For clicks."

"Huh," said Kit. "Sorry about your action figure."

"Hey, easy come, easy go." Binfire grinned. "I may have lost my Excelsior, but *we* have gained a mystery to solve!" He punched Kit playfully on the shoulder, causing her to wince. "It's experiences that make life worthwhile, yeah? Not possessions. They're meaningless. When you die, you go in one landfill and they go in the other."

"Don't let Reverend Bell hear you say that. He looks like he was about to have a breakdown."

"Yeah… He did, didn't he?" Binfire's voice floated off into the darkness.

"Are you okay?"

Binfire blinked, suddenly back in reality. "Never better, pilgrim! Sharp as a tack and ready to embark on some serious detective work."

"Can I ask you a question? It's been nagging at me for a while."

"Fire away."

"Well, these action figures. The story goes that Roland Pendragon found four of them in a charity shop and he shared them with the Furley Fanboys. One for Fenton, one for Graham, one for Matty, and he kept one himself."

"Yep."

"So how did you get one?"

"Me? Just lucky I guess."

"Lucky? Finding a *fifth* doll, that was unique, one-of-a-kind and was presumed destroyed in a factory fire?"

"Do you know what?" said Binfire, suddenly loudly. "I think I went to that very charity shop just before Roland Pendragon got there and bought one."

"Bought one? Just one? There were five unique *Vixens from the Void* dolls in the shop, and you, a huge *Vixens from the Void* fan, just bought the one?"

"I dunno. I probably didn't have enough cash to buy them all."

Kit knew Binfire was lying, but she also knew she didn't have the courage to confront him about it. She waited for him to grin and say "Only kidding, pilgrim" and explain the real reason he had it. But he didn't. He didn't say anything. He just kicked at the gravel, dug his hands deep in his cargo pants like a bored schoolboy and started whistling a meandering tune.

They walked on in silence until they reached the stables. Dawn was spreading across the rooftops, turning everything into a dull, coppery orange. Birds were breaking the silence with their songs.

Despite her tiredness, Kit was glad she was up to see it.

They paused awkwardly at Kit's door. As she was wary of the usual friendship rituals: handshakes, hugging, kissing, etc., and Binfire tried to respect that, their goodbyes were particularly awkward.

"Well…" said Kit.

"Yeah," said Binfire.

"It's been quite a day."

"Yeah."

"A day of surprises."

"You can say that again. Well, the day's not over yet."

Kit looked up at the sky. "Binfire. It's three thirty in the morning. I think the day's pretty much over."

"You should live on Binfire time, pilgrim."

"I'll pass, thanks."

Kit wrestled the huge lump of wood out of her pocket and inserted the attached key into the front door.

"Have I ever told you why my parents called me Kit?"

"I don't believe you have."

"I haven't thought about it for ages, until tonight. It's because—"

The door was barely open an inch before someone squealed: "Guys! I've just seen a ghost!"

The door swung open to reveal a woman in her twenties, sitting on the bed, her arms curled around her knees. Her pretty face was milk-white; partly from make-up, partly from shock. She was dressed like a goth/hippy hybrid, with a black lace top with long sleeves, a multi-coloured skirt with black leggings, skull earrings and a tie-dyed head band.

"Freya?" said Kit.

19

It took them a while to calm Freya down. Binfire made her a hot chocolate from Kit's swanky coffee machine and passed it to her. She took it gratefully but didn't drink. She held it for a while, teeth chattering on the edge of the mug. When she finally took a sip, Kit knew the chocolate was going to be tepid, but it didn't seem to matter. Freya drank it greedily.

Binfire and Kit made themselves a couple of coffees in the tiny en suite kitchen. They looked at each other, aghast.

"What's she doing here?" Kit hissed.

"I dunno," whispered Binfire. "What makes a goth girl suddenly appear from nowhere? Did someone say 'Winona Ryder' three times?"

"Be serious."

"Let's go and ask her."

"We need to go gently. She looks pretty shook up."

Kit and Binfire returned to the sitting room/bedroom, all smiles. Freya offered Kit her empty mug. The edge was stained with black lipstick.

"I'm sooo sorry. I really am. I hope I didn't startle you by being in your room. I did Binfire's credit card trick. Pushed my card into the side of the door and it opened."

Binfire patted her shoulder. "Nice one, girlie."

"And, may I ask, if I may, what are you *doing* here?" said Kit gently.

Freya looked embarrassed. "Binfire has been talking about this museum for ages. You made it sound like such an *amazing* thing."

"I was only doing that to annoy Robbie."

"I know that, but I just sooo wanted to come with you guys… But I wasn't invited… So I did the stowaway thing, in the back of your van? I thought I could sleep in there and creep out tomorrow morning, and surprise you. I'm sooo sorry!"

Binfire patted her arm again. "Don't be sorry. I'm really glad to see you, goth girl."

Freya glowed at the sentiment. "Thank you for saying that."

Kit folded her arms. "So, you crept out of the motorhome, and…?"

"Oh yes." She made a determined face. "I always go out at night and stare at my particular star? My hypno-spiritualist shaman from the Krellevangelist group tells me it's very important to keep in contact with it… I went around the back of the chapel to find a good view and it was sooo dark. And I saw the window and I thought, 'Now's the time I can have a little look,' but the window was really high up. I thought about climbing it to see in. And while I was staring at it… the window shattered. Just shattered! Completely on its own!"

"No one was about?"

"No. No one! Just me. And I was nowhere near!" She shook her head. "It just shattered! Like an invisible hand from outside the museum *punched it in*! It was sooo scary! And no one climbed in or out of the window, *at all*! And then the alarm went!"

She widened her eyes and put her mug down. "It was definitely a ghost! It has to be a supernatural phenomenon or something! A ghost that has stalked the corridors of Furley House for hundreds of years!"

"A ghost who collects action figures?" said Kit. She was trying to go gently with Freya and trying *really hard* to keep the scorn out of her voice. She almost managed it.

"No, a ghost that's *angry* that the chapel is being used as a toy museum," replied Freya tartly. "Maybe a priest who used to work here centuries ago and died when a cross fell on him or something, and he thinks having toys in the chapel is blasphemous."

Kit folded her arms. "May I point out that the chapel hasn't been used as a chapel since the Second World War. There was another exhibition in there for thirty years, displaying kinky *Vixens from the Void* costumes. Why didn't the ghost get angry about that?"

I can't believe I'm debating this, thought Kit. *I had this golden rule, didn't I? Never get into an argument with anyone about the existence of ghosts, UFOs or Doctor Who missing episodes.*

Binfire couldn't resist joining in. He leaned forward and slapped the table. "I know who the ghost is! Roland Pendragon, the seventh Marquess of frokking Furley! He only died three years ago!" He snapped his fingers. "He loved *Vixens from the Void*. I bet he regrets giving his figures away, and now he's decided to take them back!"

"Exactly," sighed Freya.

"Do they have shelves in heaven to put the figures on?" Binfire grinned, playing along. "I guess he's in heaven, because if he was in hell the action figures would just melt in the heat."

"Freya, I think your hypno-spiritualist shaman has a lot to answer for."

"Don't diss Madeline. She is sooo amazing. She regressed me through my earlier incarnations. It turns out in a past life, I..." She paused for dramatic effect. "I was Princess Amidala."

"Princess Amidala?"

"Yes."

"From…"

"Naboo. Yes."

"Right."

"Now, I *know* what you're thinking."

"I don't think you need to be a telepath to know what I'm thinking."

"You're thinking that Princess Amidala happened in the future. Well, it says at the start of *Star Wars* that it was set a long time ago in a galaxy far far away. So, in terms of time…"

"Can I just throw in something here at this point? Like the fact that Princess Amidala is *fictional*?"

Freya shook her head in sadness. "Oh, Kit. You're sooo wrong."

"Um. No. I think you'll find I'm right."

"Madeline explained it all to me. The Krellevangelists believe everything is real, even the things we take as fiction. All the things we know to be 'fiction' are telepathic waves from other galaxies that hit this planet and impregnate the brains of our most receptive humans, like George Lucas."

Kit sighed and turned to Binfire. "Help me out here."

"No, I think she's got a point." Binfire's eyes were twinkling. "I've always thought I was a reincarnation of Greedo in the cantina on Tatooine. I can't believe Han Solo shot first. But when I got reincarnated again, I was ready for him next time. Fool me once… Second time around, *I* shot first."

Kit rolled her eyes wearily. She just wanted both of them out of her room so she could go to sleep.

"This is very interesting, both of you, but what you've said tells me that this is probably an inside job. Someone you didn't see in the dark, Freya, someone with an air rifle, or even a pellet gun, shot out the window from the *outside*, to create the impression that someone was breaking in, when in *reality*, someone was already *inside* taking the figures and trashing the place."

"But the cameras didn't see anyone leave with the action figures, pilgrim."

Kit shook her head wearily. "I know. I don't know how that happened. But I'm working on it."

"It has to be a ghost," sighed Freya.

Kit was so very, very tired.

"Okay, Freya," she said wearily. "That's a theory. Why don't you do some research in the Furley House library? That's your job in this investigation, to research every ghost this place has ever had in its history and work out which one did it."

Freya glowed with a sense of purpose, and Kit knew she'd said the right thing.

"Okay," said Freya. "I'm sorry to keep you guys up. I'll go back to the motorhome."

"You're not doing that," erupted Binfire. "Those mattresses in my van are like cardboard. You can sleep in my room. You take the bed, I'll have the floor."

"I couldn't do that."

"I was going to sleep on the floor anyway. I don't do beds. Take it, no one else is gonna use it."

"Thanks, Binfire."

"Have fun, you two," said Kit. "Don't tell each other ghost stories until the morning." She opened the door to let them out and winced at the daylight. "What am I saying? It *is* the morning."

20

Kit slept long and soundly. She swept the covers back, groped for her pocket watch on the bedside table and snapped it open.

Eleven o'clock!

So much for the free breakfast.

She turned on her phone. There were a number of missed calls from Jackie. She was wondering how to answer them when the phone erupted. Jackie was calling. She wearily pressed 'accept'.

"Hi."

"Hi," said Jackie. "You've not been picking up."

"Bit of a rough night."

"Poor darling. So, you'll be on the road this afternoon after the clay-pigeon shooting?"

"Oh."

"What do you mean 'oh'?"

"Not exactly…"

"Why not?"

"Hum. Here's the thing…"

"You need to come back. I want to talk to you."

"Fine. Let's talk."

"Not over the phone. I want to talk to you face to face. This is *important*."

The guilt. Here it comes. Jackie always had a guilt trip to spring on her. Kit wanted to scream, *Why is it always important? Why do I have to come running to you because things are important? They never turn out to be important! It's all about control!*

"I can't come home today."

"Why not?"

"There's been a bit of a thing going on here. The toy museum has had a burglary. A load of action figures has been stolen. And… I've been asked to investigate."

There was no answer. Kit could hear Jackie breathing down the line.

"You've been asked to investigate? You?"

"Yes."

"Who by?"

Kit closed her eyes and forced her lips to form the words. "Graham Goldingay."

"Oh, right. I see. Graham Goldingay."

"Yes."

"The fat guy."

"Yes."

"The man you put in prison has asked you to play detective. He asked you and you just said yes."

"He's offered me a lot of money—"

But Jackie carried on. "And of course you said yes. Because you're obviously a great detective. Because we know what happened the last time you played detective."

"I did catch a murderer."

"You *helped* a murderer. And thanks to you the murderer stuffed me in a car boot, scared me half to death and left me in the middle of nowhere. And someone died. That's what you did."

Kit could have taken issue with the details of that statement, but she had learned over the past six months that it would only make things worse. She stayed silent.

"Fine," Jackie huffed. "Fine, if that's what you want then who am I to get in your way? You take your own sweet time. I'll wait here like a good little wifey for your return."

Jackie ended the call without saying goodbye.

Kit stared at the phone, not quite understanding why a relationship that seemed so promising at the outset would get so toxic so quickly, but Kit was never very good at seeing those kinds of patterns.

21

Kit wearily trudged from the stables and into the house. It was deserted. No staff or guests. She was painfully aware of the sound of her boots as she clumped along the hallway.

Where is everybody?

She tried ringing Binfire and Freya. No response. It was like waking up to find the rest of the world preoccupied with a major catastrophe (*The Walking Dead*, 2010–2022).

"Hello?"

No answer.

Stately homes are like schools. When they don't have anyone inside them, they feel that bit more empty than other empty buildings.

To her relief, she saw someone right at the other end of the main corridor. It was Malcolm, the security-man-stroke-butler, hurrying on his way (she guessed) to the chapel.

"Hi! Excuse me? Malcolm?"

Her voice sounded terrifyingly loud in the emptiness.

Malcolm's head whipped around and he walked towards her.

"Yes, miss?"

"Hi. I was just wondering... Where is everybody?"

"The Marquess is in his study on the east wing. Lady Tabitha is, I believe, still in bed."

"But what about everybody else?"

"They all left in rather a hurry."

"All of them?"

"Yes, I think so." He counted them off on his fingers. "Reverend Bell, Mr Kearney, Mr Worth... Mr Binfire was driving his colourful van... Aaaand Miss Lane, Miss Shapiro and Miss Vixy. And there was another lady who I believe is a friend of yours? Miss Freya Grant? She told the Marquess she was helping you with your investigations and used the library this morning for her research."

"Is she *in* the library?"

"No, miss, she went to breakfast and then, as I said, they all left together."

"Okay, thanks."

"You're welcome."

Kit walked to the main staircase, half-expecting Malcolm to stand in her way and say *"Where do you think you're going?"* but he looked at her and smiled politely as she ascended the stairs.

Well, I am a detective, and this is me doing some detecting. Here we go. First day on the job.

She walked deeper into the interior.

The police said they didn't find anything on the cameras at the main gate. No one came and went that night.

"So, I have to conclude that the action figures are still on the premises," she muttered, startling herself at the volume of her voice in the cavernous corridor.

With most people off who-knows-where, it seemed like an ideal time to look for them. She *ker-lumped* along the corridor and tried a few doors. Most were unlocked and were just dusty offices. Table and chairs, and shelves full of folders. She opened a few box files but found nothing interesting.

She walked on, to the rear of the house. The corridor forked into two and she decided to go left, as that direction looked slightly more lived-in. Carpets took over from bare wooden floors, and the sound of her boots were muffled – thank goodness.

Another row of doors. She opened the nearest and revealed a mad-looking room, containing an opulent four-poster bed with drapes and an exotic patchwork quilt, pulpy paperbacks on shelves, a huge hookah in the corner, curly slippers on the mat, bean bags and bronze statues of Buddhas sharing space with bronze statues of naked women with huge breasts.

Not exactly the bedroom of someone like Archie, or Tabitha for that matter. I'm willing to bet that this is the seventh Marquess's old room.

Kit pulled open some drawers and just found socks, faded underpants, and a few gaudy kaftans. Nothing under the bed.

The room next door was definitely Archie's. It had a cheery, childish look to it. Spitfires hung from the ceiling. Rosettes (for shooting) were pinned to the headboard of the bed, and rowing trophies gleamed from little wooden shelves. There were faded photos of smiling children: him and his sister; him and his father. And a large recent photo of Archie with a woman Kit didn't recognise. She had dark hair cut into bangs and square glasses, a bit like Velma from *Scooby-Doo* (1969–present).

A quick search revealed nothing. The action figures stayed stubbornly absent.

She went back into the corridor and was about to turn towards the staircase when she heard a tiny rhythmic bleeping. Following the sound along the passageway, she found herself outside a door with a heavy padlock on it. Pressing her ear against the door, she confirmed the bleeping was definitely coming from the room inside.

She pulled on the shackle to make sure it was definitely locked, then clicked a tumbler back and forth to see if someone had just twitched the numbers slightly when he or she locked it. No such luck. The padlock was very substantial: a copper-coloured monstrosity the size of a giant's fist.

No chance of cutting through that without attracting attention.

It was a combination padlock: four numbers needed to release it. Kit thought about trying a number of combinations, but she felt very exposed, standing in an empty corridor trying to break into a room that was obviously not intended for tourists.

She dropped the lock gently back into place.

Okay. Let's pretend this padlock belongs to Lady Tabitha. What four-digit number would she use? How about her favourite song? The one she uses for all her videos?

"In the Year 2525..."

She tried it and was astonished when the shackle moved and dropped open.

She entered the room and was even more astonished.

Another bedroom. Anonymous oil paintings were on the wall. There was a desk at the window. There was a bed made up with pristine white sheets, and beside was a tiny table upon which was a lamp and a heavy Rolex watch, which was making the bleeping noise. She pressed a button at random and the bleeping stopped.

She opened the wardrobe door and found a selection of men's clothes, suits, trousers, ties, waistcoats. All looked brand new. Most were enveloped in clear plastic. They weren't Archie's clothes, that was certain. There wasn't a tweed pattern in sight. It was all light and elegant. Silks and cottons and linens.

The en suite bathroom had ablutions, a razor, toothbrush, toothpaste, soap, shampoo and a small jar. She picked it up and there was a torn label on the side. Most of it had been ripped off, leaving a smear of glue, but what remained was the word NATE printed on it.

She put the jar in her pocket.

Apart from that torn label, everything in the room was unused. Everything was new and immaculate. *It has the anonymity of a hotel room*, thought Kit.

No, not a hotel room. Not quite. At least hotel rooms look a bit lived-in. There would be scratches on the skirting board, a television remote with the numbers worn off the keys, a carpet with the faintest of marks. This is something completely different.

Oh, yes. I know what this reminds me of.

A bedroom in a doll's house.

This could be a room designed for an action figure.

She tried the desk by the window. It was just as pristine as the rest of the room. Just pens and a blank notebook. She reached into the back of the desk drawer and felt something soft. She pulled out a shiny leather wallet. There was an inscription etched on it, in golden italics:

George Jamieson Pendragon

Kit had researched the history of the Pendragon family thoroughly before embarking on this assignment (of course she had) and George Jamieson Pendragon wasn't a name she had come across. She looked more closely at the contents of the drawer and noticed that all of the pens were inscribed with 'George Jamieson Pendragon'.

She closed the drawer and took photos of the room on her phone, taking in every detail. Then she left, closing the door quietly behind her and refastening the padlock.

She opened the door next to it.

This room couldn't have been more different from the others. It was enormous (two rooms knocked into one?) and had obviously been completely refitted at great expense with soft creams and browns. A modernist chandelier, fashioned like a crown of thorns, was poised over the huge oval bed, which was covered with coffee-coloured throw pillows. It was unmade, suggesting the occupant had just got up.

The only elements that reminded Kit she was in a stately home were the arched windows composed of leaded glass looking out onto the grounds, but even they were altered to appeal to the Lady of the House, as they were framed by huge velvet curtains in teal.

Any doubt that this was Lady Tabitha's room was extinguished by the tall canvases hanging above the bed. Artful photos of her in black and white, dressed as Katharine Hepburn, Lauren Bacall and Audrey Hepburn, striking poses that had made those movie stars famous in decades past.

In the middle of them was a photo of another woman, smiling gracefully, also looking a bit like Audrey Hepburn in a big floppy hat. Kit didn't recognise the woman, but she certainly looked intriguing.

She opened drawers and found them full of lacy knickers and garters.

There are many people who might see me doing this and think I'm just being a bit pervy. But I'm not a peeping Tom, she told herself. *I'm just being a detective.*

No action figures.

"Good morning!"

She turned. Archie was in the doorway of the bedroom.

Oops!

"Oh. Yes. Hah. Good morning."

"I take it you're looking for me?"

"Um… Yes."

"Well, I promised you an interview, so a promise is a promise, even in these circumstances." He looked around. "I think we'd better get out of my big sis's room, though, don't you? She is a rather *private* person. She'd scream the whole place down when we were kids, if she found me standing where you're standing now."

"Yes. I'm sorry."

"Oh, don't apologise. This place is like a rabbit warren. I'm always doing it, finding myself standing in a room I don't even recognise! Let's go over to my study, shall we?"

22

Archie led her to a poky office filled with dusty box files. The only hint that it belonged to someone important was a picture of the seventh Marquess on the wall – a black-and-white photo of him standing in front of Furley House holding a glass of champagne.

"Welcome to my little grotto! Come in!"

He gestured to a swivel chair that was pointed at the desk. The chair wobbled alarmingly when she held the arms, but somehow she managed to pivot her bottom onto it without it collapsing.

"Hello! Are you Kit Pelham?"

There was a tinny little voice that floated up from nowhere. Kit looked around and realised it came from the laptop on the desk. Kit peered at the screen. It was the woman from the photo in Archie's room, a mousy little thing with short brown hair cut into a sensible bob, large heavy glasses and a T-shirt with 'Dogs Make Me Happy' written on it. She was sitting in a little room with a single bed. There were posters on the walls, artistic renditions of a wolf, a tiger and a husky.

"Yes I am."

"Pleased to meet you."

Archie gave an apologetic smile. "Sorry, I'm actually in the middle of a Zoom meeting. Just updating my better half on the tumultuous events of the past twelve hours. Kit, this is Angelina, my fiancée. Angelina, this is Kit. Our resident sleuth."

Angelina waved out of the screen. "Gosh. Wow. You're the sleuth! Pleased to meet you. Do you have any suspects yet?"

Kit had seen enough crime drama to know the answer to that one. "At this stage, *everyone* is a suspect."

"Gosh. I suppose you're right."

Archie looked at his fiancée with obvious adoration. "Angelina is studying in Guildford. She wants to be a vet." He shook his head in wonderment, as if amazed at the idea of training for a job.

"That's great," said Kit.

Angelina simpered. "I do love animals. Do you love animals?"

"I do. I have a dog. He's called Milo."

"Gosh, how wonderful!" She clapped her hands. "What breed?"

"A dachshund."

"Oh, they're my favourite! So cute! And so intelligent as well! I bet Milo is so clever!"

"He is."

"Do you have a photo? I just *have* to see a photo!"

Kit fished in her coat pocket, got her wallet out, unfolded it and produced a photo of Milo looking particularly cute, lying on his back in his dog bed. She aimed it at the computer screen and Angelina gasped with delight.

"Oh, he's *wonderful*! Just *adorable*! It's just the *perfect* dog for a detective! Did you get him before you became a sleuth, or after?"

"Before."

"Oh, it's kismet, then. The universe provided you with the perfect little pooch..."

Archie broke into her flow. "Sorry, Angel, I've got to go. Got to do my interview with Kit now."

"Okay, can we speak tomorrow, Archiepops? You know I get the frowny face if I don't speak to you for more than a day."

"Of course, button. Same time tomorrow, I promise. I'll send you a link."

"Okay, I'd better go."

"You say goodbye now."

"No, you say goodbye."

"No you."

"No you!"

"Let's say goodbye together," suggested Archie. "On a count of three?"

They sang the word 'goodbye' in perfect harmony, and Archie pressed 'leave meeting'. He turned back to Kit with an embarrassed grin. "Sorry about that. We can get a bit nauseating when we get together. Young love and all that."

"It's fine. It's lovely to see."

"We're hoping to get married next year. We've been putting it off for a while because of Tabitha. You know she doesn't approve?"

Kit shook her head.

"Well, she has already made her displeasure known about me inheriting the estate instead of her. Lots of tirades about male privilege and the like. And she gets particularly vocal whenever I dip my toe in the world they call 'dating'. I think Tabby assumed that I would do the decent thing, and stay single and celibate for the rest of my life, so I would, um, so to speak…"

"Die without an heir?"

"Precisely. Though, of late, I do think she's coming around. Tabitha may grumble about it a bit, as you've witnessed today, but I do believe she's mellowing. We've had a chat about it, and she hasn't posted anything horrible about me for months. So, here's hoping."

He allowed himself a quick stoical grin. "Anyway, I hope you've got your questions ready, so fire away! Leave no stone unturned!"

Kit pressed 'record' on her phone and took out her notepad and pen. All the questions in her notepad seemed rather out of date, so she decided to wing it.

"Well, first off, I have to ask, how are you feeling? The whole thing must come as a bit of a shock."

"Gosh, shock? That's not the half of it. I'm feeling. Dismay. Frustration. Outrage. All this work for nothing! And the damage! That stained-glass window was three hundred years old – it was as old as the chapel. It survived the *Blitz*, for goodness' sake! It's going to cost a fortune to repair."

"But you've said you've got insurance?"

"Oh yes, but as I say, it's terribly disappointing. I was hoping the museum was going to become a major attraction but now, sadly, it's come to naught. And no amount of insurance can mitigate against terrible publicity like this. When this gets to the press – and it will – I won't be able to have any more exhibitions. Can you imagine any collector or curator allowing me to have anything of *real* value on the estate?"

He flashed an embarrassed smile. "When I mean real value, I *know* those dolls had value – but they were hardly priceless."

"Who do you think committed the burglary?"

Archie threw up his hands. "You tell me, Kit. I defer to our resident experts. Some fan with a grudge… Some toy collector who's gone a bit ga-ga… Everything seems plausible to me."

Kit continued with her prepared questions. *"Whose idea was it to have the toy museum? How do you think your father would react to what's happened? Do you have fond memories of the last* Vixens from the Void *exhibition? What's your favourite—"*

"Christ. I've had another message."

Lady Tabitha was in the doorway. This time she was wearing the costume of a steampunk explorer: huge brass goggles over her eyes, a Nehru jacket edged in gold braid, a pith helmet decorated with brass gadgets, plus fours, stockings and sturdy shoes. She was slightly out of breath.

"I was just in the west wing choosing my costume for the day, and I realised I hadn't switched my phone on after my shower. I've been sent photos of one of the action figures. And a rhyme like the one left for Graham."

"Oh god," sighed Archie. "Not more trouble."

"Can I see?" said Kit.

"Be my guest." She tossed her phone over to Kit, who fumbled and nearly dropped it. The screen was on WhatsApp and showed a photo of an action figure dressed a bit like a dominatrix, which Kit recognised as the character of Medula. It was taped to the inside of a refill bottle for an office watercooler, as if it was trapped in some futuristic prison, and it was accompanied by a rhyme.

Nine little figures
Lying in state.
One had a watercooler moment
And then there were eight.

Kit passed the phone to Archie, who groaned again. "This is terrible. Who's doing this to us?"

"Search me," said Lady Tabitha. "I haven't a clue, have you?"

"Not a one," sighed Archie.

Kit picked her moment. "I think I might. Does the name George Jamieson Pendragon mean anything to you?"

Tabitha stared at her. "Who?"

"While I was wandering around looking for Archie, I found this pen with George Jamieson Pendragon engraved on it."

She showed it to them. Tabitha took it and shrugged.

"Doesn't ring a bell. Archie?"

"Not me. We've got a lot of ancestors and I know the names of all of them. That's what one does when one is born into my position. One has to learn one's own family history. There *was* a great-great uncle called Gideon. But no, no George. Where did you find this?"

"In a room down the other end of that corridor."

Tabitha looked surprised. "The one at the end? The one that's locked with a great big padlock?"

"I'm sorry, I had an idea that the action figures had been stashed somewhere in the house, so I just thought I'd take a quick look around. I'm really sorry."

Archie gave an amiable grin. "Don't apologise, Kit, that's a perfectly reasonable conclusion to make. If you hadn't taken it upon yourself to search, I would have suggested it myself." His brow wrinkled. "I say... You didn't *find* the action figures, did you?"

"No."

"Oh well. Perhaps you could show us?"

* * *

They waited patiently as Kit grappled with the padlock and they both stepped inside. Archie walked around the room with wonder, gazing at the pictures, opening wardrobes and feeling the material of the clothes.

"Goodness me. I've lived in this place all my life and I've never seen anything like it."

Tabitha frowned. "I tried to open that padlock several times. How did you get in?"

Kit didn't know why but she decided on a white lie. "The... combination was only one number out. I just turned one reel and it clicked open."

"Well." Tabitha sniffed. "That was very lucky. Well done you."

Kit blushed again.

Archie's eyes flipped around the room. "Well, I confess I'm at a loss. This room is a completely new one on me."

Tabitha opened a desk drawer, took out a pen and held it up to her goggles. "George Jamieson Pendragon. Another one. Are you sure you don't know, little brother?"

"No. Haven't a clue."

Tabitha walked the perimeter of the room, her coat-tails flapping as she whirled from one corner to the other. Just as Archie had done, she opened the wardrobes, and looked behind the curtains. Then she grinned.

"Hey, do you know what, Archie? This room *could* be set aside for the concubines' sprogs."

"Oh, my heavens! Yes! It could be!"

Kit was confused. "Concubines' sprogs?"

"Our father called them that. It's just that... How can I phrase this?" Archie flashed a tight, embarrassed smile. "My father had a lot of what he called 'concubines' around the place. He had his little harem in the gamekeeper's lodge. Occasionally one of those young ladies would produce progeny. Children born on the wrong side of the blanket."

"Bastards," said Lady Tabitha flatly.

"Quite. My father was a very kind man..."

Tabitha harrumphed.

"... and would often indulge those ladies' fantasies that their children might inherit something, despite the fact they were born outside of wedlock. That was out of the question, of course."

Lady Tabitha gave a mock-bow. "Because, Kit, as you are no doubt aware, Archie is the firstborn son, and our mother managed to get the ring on our father's sweaty finger. There might be lots of *other* firstborn sons around, but as they didn't arrive after the purchase of bouquets and wedding cake, they're designated as filthy commoners."

Archie looked embarrassed. "Haha. Yes. Over the years, there have been quite a few 'sprogs' wandering about this place, assuming they would become a lord of the manor, before their mothers were let down gently by people who worked for my father, people whose job it was to do the unpleasant things my father didn't feel inclined to do. I would hazard a guess that one of those ladies ordered monogrammed pens for their children in preparation for their elevation to the aristocracy, and perhaps my father fashioned this room so they might create the *illusion* that they were going to stay?"

"I see. You've no idea where George Jamieson Pendragon would be now?"

Tabitha laughed. "Not a clue. Once they were gone, Daddy didn't worry about keeping records."

Archie sighed. "There have been so many lovely ladies drifting in and out of this estate over the years, some of them disappearing happily, with a large cheque in their pockets, some of them leaving in a rage, shouting and screaming and vandalising my father's Range Rover. They have all long disappeared into the mists of time."

"Right. That explains it."

Kit smiled. Archie smiled back. He clapped his hands together. "Well, we can't leave it like this, can we? I'll get Malcolm to clear it, give the suits to charity."

"This is nice stuff," muttered Lady Tabitha, opening a wardrobe door and fingering a sleeve. "Italian."

"Well, if you want to take a few for Nate?"

"Haha. No. Nate and I are like Furley House."

Archie looked perplexed.

"History."

"Ah. Sorry to hear that, old sis."

The two of them left the room. Kit hung back for a second and looked again at the jar in her pocket. The one with NATE printed on the side.

That's a bit of a coincidence.

She reapplied the padlock and hurried after them.

"Right," said Archie, giving a cub-scout salute. "I'll give Reverend Bell a call, to see what's going on."

Tabitha jogged ahead, calling over her shoulder, "You do that. I'm going to set up the clay-pigeon shoot in the lower field." She looked back at Kit. "Want to come?"

What an invitation, Kit! Go with her! You'd be mad to refuse. Utterly ma

"No, thank you. I'll wait for my friends if that's okay."

"Fine. Your loss. I'll be in the lower field if you get lonely, little one."

Kit was left alone in the corridor, her skin tingling from Tabitha's last sentence. She forced herself to focus on her discovery.

That would explain it, she thought. *Some lovestruck mistress of Roland Pendragon making plans for her son. But the wallet I found was brand new.*

EVERYTHING in that room was brand new.

Kit wondered if she'd stumbled on the hiding place of someone with a grudge, another motive to sabotage Furley House. Something that wasn't anything to do with the desire to own cult collectible action figures at all.

23

Kit googled 'George Jamieson Pendragon' on her phone but found nothing, just a few George Jamiesons (a long-dead diplomat, a roofer who was once a member of the masons, and someone with an impenetrable middle-management job on LinkedIn) but none of them were quite the right age to be a mysterious bastard son of a libidinous Marquess.

She went to the library and was leafing through a book that contained an extensive history of the Pendragon family tree when she heard a dull *crump* in the distance. It came from somewhere outside the house.

She dashed into the hallway and collided with Archie, running from upstairs.

"Did you hear that?" they both said as one.

They ran through the main entrance and saw a mushroom cloud slowly unfolding over the tops of the trees.

"Oh my goodness," muttered the Marquess. "What fresh hell is this?"

"Is that a bomb?" asked Kit.

"I'm not sure. We've discovered the odd left-over doodlebug, but none in the last thirty years."

Kit had her phone pressed to her ear, trying again to raise Binfire. No answer. Archie was also on his phone, talking to one of his staff. "Yes, I can see it too. Can you head over?"

Then came a distant roar of multiple engines.

A convoy of assorted cars and vans roared up the front drive in a cloud of dust, led by Binfire's colourful motorhome. They came to a grinding halt in a wide circle.

Reverend Bell, Matty, Fenton, Penny, Saskia and Vixy tumbled out, some of them looking bloodied, battered and much the worse for wear.

Freya was at the wheel of Binfire's motorhome. She wrenched open the door and screamed at Kit.

"It's Binfire," she shrieked. "He's been hurt!"

24

One hour ago

About twenty minutes before Kit opened her eyes and reached groggily for her watch, Binfire, Matty, Reverend Bell, Fenton, Saskia, Vixy and Freya were sitting around the table in the great hall, finishing breakfast. It was a self-service buffet, but a very nice one indeed, replete with slices of pheasant, scotch eggs the size of hedgehogs and jugs of milk that had been proudly labelled as 'locally sourced'.

Saskia leaned over to Freya. "I don't believe we've met. Where did you spring from?"

Binfire gestured at himself with a fork. "She's with me. She sleeps in the back of my van because the alarm doesn't work. If someone breaks in, she makes a *weow-weow-weow* noise."

"Binfire! Don't be silly!" Freya nudged him in the ribs. "That's not true. I'm sooo sorry about him. I hid in the back of his van so I could come and see the toy museum." She looked down at her tiny bowl of muesli and gave a guilty smile. "I hope I'm not taking anyone's breakfast."

Matty pointed his knife at Fenton and Reverend Bell. "*His* wife and *his* wife fucked off the moment they were able. Believe me when I say there's plenty of grub to go round."

Reverend Bell shot an angry look at Matty and turned to Freya. "I admire your dedication, my dear, travelling with this reprobate. Tell me, did he ever tell you how he came across his action figure? He seems awfully coy when I ask him about it."

Freya looked at Binfire, but Binfire was intent on dissecting a scotch egg. He had lost interest in listening to the conversation. She turned back to the Reverend and raised her incredibly black eyebrows. "No, he hasn't. Does it matter?"

The Reverend was about to answer when the air was suddenly filled with a cacophony of ringtones. Binfire, Fenton and Matty reached for their phones.

"Frokk," said Binfire, staring at the screen. "Has everyone else got this?"

"If what *you've* got is a doll in a plastic bottle, then yes," said Matty.

"Oh my god," said Fenton. "It's my action figure! It's Medula! The sicko took it out of its original packaging."

"Another nod to Agatha Christie!" exclaimed Bell, reading the rhyme. "Obviously this mysterious person is a fan."

"Oh my god," gasped Fenton again. "'One had a water-cooler moment'! He's going to do to my Medula what he did to Graham's Arkadia!"

The phones chimed again and again. More photos. They all scrolled through them with a frenzy. Each photo was taken at a slightly different angle. The refill bottle was attached to the top of a watercooler, and the watercooler seemed to be outside. Another photo showed it standing outside a field, next to a five-bar gate.

"It looks like it might be somewhere on the estate," said Matty. "We should ask Archie where it—"

"I know that gate!" yelled Bell. "I'm sure of it! I go past it when I drive home."

"You're sure?" whimpered Fenton.

"Oh yes. If you look really closely, there's an old sign, look." He pointed at the picture, at a dark wooden plank fixed to the top bar of the gate. "It's very faded, but you can see where the gamekeeper painted 'keep out pheasants' but he spelled 'pheasants' as 'peasants'. It's down the end of the estate, near where they raise the chicks."

There was one more chime. The final photo showed the bottom of the refill bottle. It was swimming in a pale green liquid.

"That's petrol," barked Binfire. "This muthafrokker isn't taking any prisoners. Come on! The game's a-frokking-foot!"

They dashed out of the main hall and scrambled towards the front entrance.

25

Fenton was without transport, thanks to his wife's angry departure, so he slipped into Reverend Bell's Morris Traveller. Vixy got in the back. Matty and Saskia rushed to Saskia's Tesla. Binfire climbed into his motorhome, and Freya scuttled around the front and scrambled into the passenger side.

Penny Lane dashed up from the stables, her phone in her hand.

"Wait! Mr Goldingay has had a message."

"We know," said Binfire. "We've all got a message." He pointed at Bell's car. "He knows where it is. Follow that chicken shed!"

Bell's car led the way, followed by Saskia's Tesla and Penny's transit van. Binfire's motorhome brought up the rear.

Binfire let go of the steering wheel and waved a fist out of the window. "Thunderbirds are GO!" He ejected the Guns N' Roses CD and pushed in the one poking out of the lower slot. Freya covered her ears as the motorhome shuddered with 'Oliver's Army' played at a decibel-mangling volume.

The vehicles careered down a poorly maintained track and lurched over potholes. Less than five minutes later, they bounced into a clearing that doubled as a car park. Doors flew open and everyone rushed out to the gate.

The watercooler was nowhere to be seen.

"That's the gate from the photo," said Bell. "No doubt about it."

"You're right," said Saskia.

"No watercooler," breathed Binfire.

"It's… Where is it?" said Bell.

"Fuck," said Matty.

Bell was scanning the horizon. He extended a trembling finger. "No. There it is. It's been moved."

They turned to follow the finger. There it was, by the far corner of a field, standing slightly drunkenly to one side. Fenton struggled to open the gate, but Bell rushed to stop him.

"Don't do that!"

Bell was stronger than he looked, and he managed to wrench the latch out of Fenton's fingers and relock the gate.

Fenton was quivering with frustration. He hopped from one foot to the other and yanked his dandruff-peppered hair in frustration.

"But she's there! My Medula is – right – there!"

"I know, but this particular field belongs to him." Reverend Bell pointed to the only occupant, a massive black bull, staring at them all with an expression of baleful contempt. "That's Rimbaud. Archie named him after the poet, but he might as well have named him after the Sylvester Stallone character. Believe me, Fenton, you cannot go in there. He'll go for you."

Saskia leaned over the wall. "Hey, if we all distracted it, led it to the other side of the field, then one of us could make a dash for it."

"Yes," yelled Fenton. "Good thought."

"I'll make a dash for it," said Matty.

"You can't go in there," retorted Penny. "It's crazy."

"Just as well I'm not married to you, so I don't have to do what you tell me. No offence."

Saskia said: "You go for it, Matty. I'll record it for the channel."

"Great idea."

Saskia brought her phone out and started to record. Matty looked directly into the lens. "This is me, Matty Kearney, about to launch himself into a field with a big fuck-off bull in it. I'm doing it of my own free will and I take full responsibility for my actions, and you can quote me on that. Just in case some woke snowflake health-and-safety lawyer decides to sue anyone after my death."

He leapt over the gate and hung off the top bar with one arm, flexing his legs by bouncing on the bottom bar. "You lot get over to the other side of the field and make a shit-ton of noise when I give the signal."

Saskia gave an 'okay' sign. Matty responded with an 'okay' sign of his own, let go of the gate and started edging into the field.

"Now!" he screamed.

Fenton, Bell, Vixy, Penny, Freya and Binfire ran to a part of the wall further along from the gate and started hollering and screaming their lungs out.

The bull flicked his ears in their direction but showed little interest in the noisy crowd of hysterical nerds.

"Wait a sec." Binfire ran for his motorhome. He hauled out a red blanket from the back and hurried back to the wall, whirling it over his head like a matador and making a *yi-yi-yi!* noise.

The bull's huge head swivelled in their direction. Then it took one step. Then it took another step. It started to trot closer. Encouraged, Binfire started dancing about on the wall, kicking his legs up and waggling the blanket. Then he hit a loose stone. He staggered and toppled into the field, disappearing from view.

Rimbaud was *definitely* interested now. Someone had entered his domain. The bull accelerated, broke into a gallop.

Matty, to his lack of credit, did not run to help Binfire. He stayed on course, sprinting towards the watercooler, his legs and arms pumping.

Vixy and Freya were already stretching over the wall, trying to find a way to reach over and pull Binfire to safety, but Binfire wasn't helping. The wall had shed some stones over the years, and it looked as though his head had hit one. He was lying there like a broken toy, dazed, on the ground, a red gash meandering across his forehead.

Vixy had one arm, and Freya tried to get him into a sitting position to loop the other over her shoulders.

"Count of three?" said Vixy.

"Frrah," Binfire muttered, spittle forming on his lips.

"Come on, Binfire," Freya hissed. "You need to get up."

"Pahr," he added.

They tried to drag him to the wall, but it was going far too slowly.

"He's coming!" yelled Fenton, pointing.

"We know he's coming. I can hear his hooves," Freya gasped, straining with the effort. "You might want to try and help us?"

"You all have to leave him!" said Fenton. "Vixy, just drop him!"

And then an explosion ripped through the air. A deafening thunderclap. The watercooler had just blown up with terrific force and a huge orange mushroom cloud was rising above the field. Black tendrils extended from it like plane contrails.

Matty had been blown about thirty feet, back towards the gate. His shirt was on fire and he was frantically rolling around on the grass to put the flames out.

The explosion had spooked Rimbaud, and the bull was charging around in small, panicked circles.

Freya and Vixy stared, stupefied, for just a few seconds, and then resumed manhandling Binfire over the wall. They dragged him over and collapsed, gasping, on the other side.

Saskia watched Matty stagger back to the gate. He grinned at her.

"You did keep filming, didn't you? You caught that?"

* * *

They draped Binfire in his red blanket and carried him above them like they were pallbearers. They got him to his motorhome and laid him gently into the back.

Reverend Bell smiled and said, "Shall I travel with Mr Binfire in the back? To make sure he's alright."

Freya looked. "Thank you. That's very thoughtful."

The Reverend Bell handed Fenton the keys to his Morris Traveller. "Drive it back for me, good sir. Make sure you don't prang it."

They ran to the vehicles, and Bell clambered into the back. Binfire was lying on the couch/bed, staring glassily at the light in the motorhome ceiling.

"Ooh looka ver light," he burbled.

The engine started and they lurched off. The Reverend sat at his side and looked down, a beatific smile on his face, a vision of a concerned vicar at the deathbed of a loved parishioner.

"I think now would be a good time to have a little chat, Binfire. Where exactly *did* you get hold of your action figure?"

Binfire gave him a woozy grin and attempted to tap the side of his nose.

Bell's voice stayed light and gentle. "You can be honest with me, Binfire. We're all friends here. You were at Braxtons factory that night, weren't you?"

"Fahrrr…"

"You were there, weren't you? You killed Jack Braxton, didn't you?"

"Hurrgh."

With a sigh, Bell gave up. There was silence for a minute. Then Binfire turned away, pulled the red blanket up over his head and mumbled: "He had to die. Had no choice."

26

Kit and Archie ran down the steps of Furley House and to the back of the motorhome. Freya was already opening the back door to reveal Reverend Bell sitting by Binfire.

Binfire's head was lolling violently back and forth, as if someone had just been shaking him. There was a vivid red streak across his forehead.

"He's had an accident," Freya said lamely.

"Binfire! Are you alright?"

At the sound of Kit's voice he jerked upright, looking around him as if he had no idea where he was.

"Ki? O' hiya, Ki!" He touched his bald head cautiously. "Got caught by incoming. Took some frenly fire. Don' worry. Ah'm finnne!"

She wanted to help him, but there was so much blood. So much *messiness*.

"I think he'll be alright," said Bell.

Kit looked annoyed. "Really? Are you a doctor?"

"I'm a doctor of divinity."

"So that's a no, then."

Vixy leaned into their conversation. "He's just got mild concussion."

"Are *you* a doctor?"

"No, but I've worked in enough nightclubs to know concussion when I see it."

"Let's get him into the library," snapped Archie. "There's a couch in there."

They carried him into the house and propped him up on a

low, leather-clad chaise longue. Archie bustled around the library and poured everyone a shot of whisky. Everyone gratefully took a glass, but rested it on their laps, unsure of how to consume it. Only Matty downed it in one, with a macho defiance bordering on madness.

Archie proffered a glass towards Binfire, but Kit neatly stepped in front of him. "Ex-alcoholic," she explained.

"Oh, sorry."

"It's fine. Normally he wouldn't take it, but as he's a bit groggy he might accidently take a sip."

"I'm *not* groggy!" thundered Binfire. "Iss the fresh countryside air. It's really giving me a buzzzzzzzzz." Binfire looked woozily around him. "Is there a bee in here?"

"No, it's you," explained Freya. "It's you that's making the buzzing noise."

"Ah!" He knocked the side of his nose with a finger. "Unnerstood." He focused on Bell. "Wha' were we talkin' abou'? In th' van?"

"Nothing," said Bell.

"What happened?" asked Kit.

"It was sooo awful!" said Freya.

They explained what happened with the watercooler and the bull.

Archie slammed his whisky glass angrily on the table. "This is *unacceptable*! Someone has trespassed on my estate, vandalised my museum, distressed my livestock and is destroying my guests' property! I'm going to call the police again and *demand* they do something."

"They won't do anything," Matty grunted. "They already think we're just playing some stupid game for rich twats."

"It *is* a bit like a game, though, in a way," mused Kit. "This mysterious person set a task and got everyone to work as a team to get hold of a prize. It's a lot like a reality gameshow, like *Survivor* or *The Traitors*."

Matty and Fenton looked at her in disgust.

"Hardly," said Fenton.

"It's not a fucking game, girlie," sneered Matty.

He walked over to a phone on the table, where Penny had propped it up on a pile of books. The screen was set on WhatsApp video, and the tiny head of Graham peered out.

"You hear this, Graham?" he said, pointing at Kit. "Your detective here thinks this is some kind of game. It's all just a bit of post-modern ironic nonsense to her. What did we tell you?"

"As I stated earlier, your opinion is irrelevant," Graham snapped. "I have stated why I have employed Kit Pelham. She has deductive capabilities."

Matty advanced on Kit. "Okay, girlie. You heard the man. You have 'deductive' capabilities. So, go on. Deduct. Tell us something about this mysterious fucking lunatic who's doing this. Better still, tell us who they are."

"I d-don't."

Damn. Her stammer had taken the opportunity to make an entrance.

"I d-d-d-d…"

"Oh dear!" Matty laughed. "Not impressed so far!"

Freya stepped in between Matty and Kit. "That's sooo not fair," she said. "That's like going up to a comedian when they're sitting having a drink in a pub and telling them to be funny. You're just heckling."

"That's my job, girlie. I'm a professional heckler," he sniffed.

"We have got an idea actually. We have a theory that the robbery was committed by a ghost."

Oh god no.

Something inside Kit withered and died. She slipped her head into her hands.

"What the fuck is she talking about?"

"It's true," said Freya. "Isn't it, Binfire?"

Binfire grinned woozily and put his thumbs up. "Yeah, ghosts. All the way." Then he looked at his thumbs and frowned. "I don't think these are my thumbs."

Matty looked around the group. "Will someone explain to me what the fuck this hippy is on about?"

Freya explained about what had happened to her last night, about the shattering of the window, and about the absence of anyone leaving or entering the museum through the window.

"So, I've been doing some research this morning, investigating all the ghosts that have appeared over the years." She ran across to a desk and held up a book. "There's a sad-looking maidservant, who appears from time to time. She was drowned in the fountain by the first Marquess in 1803. He took a dim view of female empowerment and resented the fact she claimed he'd got her pregnant."

She turned a page.

"And then there's the floating head of the third Marquess, who got extremely drunk and accidently hung himself on a curtain rope in his bedroom for some sordid reason. And there's a crying boy in rags who occasionally runs through the south passage before vanishing into the air. No one knows his story."

"Fuck's sake," groaned Matty.

Freya ploughed on. "Of course, this book was written before the death of Roland Pendragon, so it's possible it could be your father as a spirit, reclaiming his action figures."

Archie scratched his chin and smiled, humouring her. "I'm sorry, my dear. I'm not aware my father's ghost has made an appearance. I'd have certainly remembered if I'd seen him. We have had the odd ghost. But I expect if my father *has* become a poltergeist, the female staff would know about it before me."

He winked at the room.

Matty cast his eyes to the ceiling. "Jesus. This is crazy."

"Not quite," said Penny. "The ghost thing is ridiculous, obviously. But this is important. She's saying she didn't see anyone go in or out of the broken window. That's impossible."

"She didn't *notice* them go in or out, that's the more obvious reason." Matty pointed to Freya. "Just look at her! Bloody hippy is probably high on mushrooms or she's been sniffing Pritt Sticks."

Matty shot a contemptuous glance at Kit. "And that's it, Sherlock? Is this your big fucking theory? Fucking *ghosts*?"

"Stop it, Matty. This isn't fair," muttered Saskia.

Kit looked up at him. "Of c-course n-not." She bit her lip and concentrated on each word as they escaped from her lips.

"So, what is your big theory?"

"I don't have anything s-s-specific yet."

"Obviously."

"B-but this p-p-p…"

She narrowed her eyes in concentration.

"P-person or persons – I think it's pp-probably some kind of revenge mission. Either against Ff-urley House in general or the F-f-furley F-fff-fanboys."

"That's b-b-b-bloody obvious," said Matty mockingly.

Kit continued, "Th-this p-person or p-persons have thought out this n-narrative, they're determined, they've planned this out m… meticulously. They know where the c-cameras are on the grounds, and they can m-move around, confident they won't be detected."

"I c-c-c-could have told you all that," scoffed Matty.

"And there's also a p-pattern emerging. You've noticed the m-m-mmm…"

They waited for her.

"Mmmm… mmm…"

She scrunched her face up and forced out the word.

"M… mmm… Missing pieces?"

Reverend Bell raised his eyebrow. "What missing pieces?"

"Missing pieces?" echoed Fenton.

"Well, if you l-look at the photo of Graham's broken doll, there's only eight p-pieces. There are two mm-missing pieces. A b-bottom bit of the right leg, and the right upper arm."

Penny nodded. "Yes, we noticed that. We assumed they were lost when this madman tore the doll apart."

Kit was talking quickly now, with more authority. "That they were l-lost by accident? Yes, that's an easy assumption to make when you just have one body. But now we have two victims. If you zoom in on the photos of the doll inside the water-cooler, you can see that the lower left arm is missing, and the lower left leg."

Everyone scrambled for their phones and examined the picture.

"It's true," breathed Fenton, staring at his screen. "They dismembered my Medula before they blew her up!"

Kit continued, "So, it seems our m-mysterious antagonist is taking t-two pieces from each doll. I would conclude he's keeping those pieces back for a reason. Why?"

Reverend Bell was fighting to keep up. "Well, each doll is made of ten pieces, two arm pieces, two leg pieces, a head and a torso."

"Perhaps he's putting together his own doll?" said Penny.

"Exactly. That's my thought," agreed Kit.

"So what if he is?" said Matty. "It's not going to help catch this bastard."

Bell was energised. "No, but it tells us something. It's a

clue. A real clue. It gives us a psychological insight into this individual." He looked at Kit with glowing respect.

"Does it?" chirped Vixy. "I'm lost. What does it tell us?"

"It tells us that it's someone who likes to put dolls together," said Kit. She walked into the middle of the room; her stammer forgotten in the excitement. "Someone who *knows* what these dolls mean, their cultural value, but isn't bothered about *keeping* them, or even leaving them intact. Someone who doesn't like the dolls but has an appreciation about the way they're put together..."

She snapped her fingers. "Not a doll *collector*, a doll *maker*."

Once again, it didn't escape her attention that Fenton and Matty exchanged quick, worried glances.

"There's something else," said Kit. She looked at Archie. "P-perhaps you should explain about the concubines' sprogs?"

"Of course," said Archie. "My father had several illegitimate children. It's not beyond the bounds of possibility that one of them held a grudge against me and my inheritance."

"All very interesting," said Matty at last. "But I still don't see how this helps us find this nutter."

"Don't you?" said Saskia. "If we go from the assumption that this person *was* a child of Roland Pendragon, and we put it together with the assumption that this person *makes* models..."

"Lots of assumptions there, Saskia."

"Maybe. But if we built a profile, there's a chance we can stop him – or her!"

"No chance for me." Fenton shook his head sadly. "What difference does that make to me if we catch them? My Medula's gone. I'm done here. Why should I help?"

Matty wandered over to Fenton, leaned heavily on Fenton's shoulder and popped his bottom lip out. "Awww. Poor you! Well, if you're all done here, then I assume you're going to pack up and go back to the shop and your lovely wife?"

Fear sprinted across Fenton's face. "No... No, you're alright. I can see you need all the help you can get. I'll stick around and lend a hand."

Vixy came forward and put her arm around his shoulders.

"Has anyone seen Binfire?" said Freya.

They looked around. Binfire had disappeared.

"Where's he gone?"

Archie frowned. "No idea."

Kit went, "Oh."

They all looked at her.

"Oh?" said Penny. "What does that mean?"

"What's the time? Is it one o'clock yet?"

Kit fished in her pocket, but Penny was already looking at her wristwatch. "Yes, five minutes to one. Why?"

"It's clay-pigeon shooting time," sighed Kit.

27

Archie set the pace at a brisk walk, and the others had to trot to keep the rear of his tweed jacket in sight. Kit held the tails of her coat up, to avoid them getting damp from the wet grass.

They got to the south paddock, and everything had been set out: there was the big black square of a shotgun cabinet and a machine racked with piles of orange discs – the pigeon trap and thrower.

Lady Tabitha was there, still dressed as an intergalactic explorer, goggles planted on her face. She was handing a shotgun to Binfire.

"Wait! Sis! Hold on," yelled Archie.

Tabitha turned, her coat swishing around her knees. "What?"

"Mr Binfire should not handle a firearm at the moment."

"That's my call, isn't it, brother?"

"He's not well."

She glanced at Binfire, who had turned the shotgun around and was peering down the barrel. She gave a dismissive shrug. "He seems fine to me."

"Come on, big sis, be reasonable. He's had a knock on the noggin. There's been a bit of a fracas by the farm. Didn't you see the explosion?"

Another shrug. "I thought that was poachers bombing the lake."

"Tabby, see sense. It's obvious he's not fit to handle a firearm."

"Hey!" Binfire waggled the gun cheerfully in the direction of everyone, causing Fenton and Reverend Bell to duck. "I can handle guns, yeah? I'm experienced. I do Nerf wars all the time. I once shot a polystyrene projectile up the nostril of my friend Robbie at thirty yards."

Tabitha put her hands on her hips and glared at her brother. "Again, that's my call. This is my department. You do the fancy dinner, I do the shoot."

"*I'm* the Marquess here, Tabitha. I sign the cheques, and I pay the outrageous insurance bill, so it's my job to gauge the risk."

Tabitha was practically nose-to-nose with her little brother. She glared at him for what seemed like a minute before averting her eyes. She stomped over to Binfire and grabbed the shotgun from his grasp.

"Hey! What the frokk?" Binfire's voice was that of an eight-year-old cheated of a ride on a rollercoaster because the sign said he was too short. He looked appealingly at the group, inviting them to help him fight the injustice.

Freya stepped into his line of sight and looped her arm around his. "Come on, Binfire, let's go and see the lions."

"Okay." Binfire beamed. "Maybe we can see a lion roar like the MGM lion?"

"Maybe."

She took him by the hand and started to lead him back to the house.

Tabitha glared at the group assembled in front of her. She waggled the shotgun. "Okay. Fine. He's not doing it, apparently. Anyone else want a go?" she snapped.

"Fine, I'll have a bash," said Matty. He grabbed the shotgun and aimed it into the air.

"You should always aim it at the ground, when you're not actually shooting," snapped Tabitha.

"I know what to do, girlie, I've done all this before. Just let it fly and watch poetry."

She stamped on the pedal attached to the pigeon thrower, spitting an orange disc into the air. It wobbled slightly as it hurtled across the sky, like a UFO.

Matty brought the shotgun up to his cheek, brought it to bear on the saucer and pulled the trigger. There was a deafening crack which echoed around the paddock. The clay pigeon shattered, exploding into fragments that fluttered their way to earth.

A few seconds later, a familiar cacophony of ringtones blared out. Penny's phone – the one that belonged to Graham – had the fluting horn solo of 'Penny Lane'.

Matty, Fenton, Penny and Binfire scooped out their phones and stared at their messages. Kit sauntered over and looked over Binfire's shoulder.

It said:

Eight little figures
Flying up to heaven.
One flew a bit too high
And then there were seven.

And a photo. An action figure, minus head and upper left arm (the lower left arm was crudely sellotaped to the torso).

Binfire stared glassily at the picture. "That's mine!" he slurred. "That's my girl! Excelsior!"

It was stuck inside an orange object. An orange *circular* object.

They all realised at the same time, turning as one and running across to the paddock, where the fragments of clay pigeon were scattered. There were chunks of charred plastic. Bits of arm. Bits of leg. Fenton and Reverend Bell stared at the ground, unable to comprehend what had just happened.

"Damn," muttered Saskia.

Binfire picked up a bit of leg and stared at it. "Woah. My doll just got blown to pieces by a shotgun."

Freya put her hand on his arm. "I'm sorry, Binfire."

"Yeah. If anyone did that, it should have been me."

28

"Well don't look at *me*!" sniffed Tabitha. "I didn't put it in there. I didn't even put the pigeon thrower on the paddock. I thought Malcolm had set it up for me."

"He hadn't," said Archie. "We asked him."

"Well, I know that *now*."

They were back in the library. There was a row of hostile eyes pointing at Tabitha, who sat in the chair Reverend Bell had occupied last night. The chair Kit now considered to be the Interrogation Chair.

She was sitting, nonchalantly holding a cigarette, a bit like Sharon Stone (*Basic Instinct*, 1992), only this blonde seductress happened to be wearing goggles, a Nehru jacket, a pith helmet, and was holding a shooting stick.

Archie tried again. "You must see how this looks to all of us."

"I don't give a wet shit how it looks. He's the one who pulled the trigger."

Matty rolled his eyes. "Oh, fuck off. How was I to know?"

Fenton was still glaring at Tabitha. "It had to be you who put it in the clay pigeon."

Tabitha rolled her eyes at Fenton. "Yeah, I can see what you're getting at." She mimed out the actions in a suitably melodramatic manner. "I *put* the doll inside the clay pigeon and invited one of you to shoot it. And then when I *did* trick someone, I sent you all a crazy text by remote control, pointing out what I just did. That makes perfect sense. I must be a criminal mastermind!"

"Have you heard of a double bluff?" grated Graham, speaking from Penny's phone.

"Have you heard of a triple chin?" retorted Tabitha.

"I think what you're saying makes perfect sense," said Kit.

"Thank you! I'm glad someone's thinking! Well done you!"

"It could all be a double bluff, of course, but there was no way you could have been behind the watercooler explosion. Whoever detonated that had to know exactly when to do it. Not too late, or we'd have got the doll, but early enough so that Matty wouldn't have got badly injured when he tried to get it."

"Injured?" shrieked Matty. "I was on fucking fire!"

Kit continued as if Matty hadn't spoken. "You were in the opposite end of the estate when it went off. There was no way you could have known when to blow it up. The person responsible had to have had a clear view of the watercooler to detonate it at exactly the right point."

"Well done that detective." Tabitha winked at Kit. "You're good at this."

Kit did one of her blushes. "Thanks."

The room fell silent.

Archie patted his knees and stood up. "Well, if the police won't help, I'm not going to sit around and wait for another text from our mysterious antagonist or antagonists. I'm going to get my gamekeeper Cyril to arrange a search of the grounds to track this blighter to his lair tomorrow morning."

He pointed in the vague direction of Rimbaud's field.

"This blighter has to have a base somewhere in the grounds, somewhere to hide that watercooler, some kind of place to stow a vehicle, because transportation would have been needed to move it about. There are plenty of derelict buildings about the place, abandoned for years, and my hunch is he, or she, or they, are using one of them. Anyone want to help?"

There was a low murmur of agreement.

"Splendid. We'll assemble after breakfast tomorrow morning."

"Why not now?" Matty glowered. "He might fuck up my doll next. The clock's ticking."

"It's Saturday," said Archie simply. "A bit of a tall order for Cyril to assemble a group of men today, particularly at this short notice. He'll have to ring around this afternoon to see who's willing." He tapped his chin. "Of course, any one of you are welcome to search the estate yourselves. I give you leave to have the run of the place, as long as you don't agitate the pheasants."

"Great," thundered Matty. "That's exactly what I'm going to do."

He walked over to an umbrella stand in the corner and pulled out a cherrywood walking stick. He tapped it on his open palm menacingly, and strode out of the library, pausing only to yell, "Come on, everybody, let's give this bastard what for!"

29

Fenton, Reverend Bell, Saskia and Vixy ran out after Matty, and soon the roar of engines was heard again, slowly disappearing into the distance. Binfire started to follow them, but Freya grabbed his arm.

"Please don't go, Binfire. I don't think you're well enough to drive around the estate."

"Of course I am, pilgrim. I'm fine."

"We need you here," said Kit. "You, me and Freya have to go and put our heads together and make a list of suspects."

If Binfire knew he was being handled, he didn't show it. He frowned, then nodded. "You're right, guys. It's time to do some detective work."

"Splendid," said Archie. "I'll leave you three to do that. I'm going to go to my office and await news from our intrepid searchers." He turned to Penny. "What are you going to do, my dear?"

Penny stood up and waved her phone. "I've just had a text. Mr Goldingay's replacement automaton is being delivered by courier in a few minutes. I have to attend to that."

"Capital. And what are you...?" He had turned to speak to his big sister, but Lady Tabitha was nowhere to be seen. "Oh dear. She's gone off in a sulk. Do you know, I think she's still rather cross with me."

"I'm sure she'll come around," said Kit.

"I'm sure you're right. Blood is thicker than water, when all's said and done."

Kit, Freya and Binfire walked back to Kit's room. Kit kept looking at Binfire out of the corner of her eye. He seemed largely back to normal, but there was a glazed look in his gaze that was worrying. She knew he would refuse outright to go to a hospital, so the best they could do was keep a close eye on him and wait for him to recover.

The moment they arrived inside Kit's little room, her familiar 'Sweet Dreams (Are Made of This)' ringtone erupted into the air. She groped in her pocket but her phone wasn't there. Puzzled, she looked around, and saw Binfire was holding her phone, grinning.

"It's your girlfriend again, pilgrim!"

"Binfire, no!"

"Binfire!" echoed Freya.

Binfire pressed the speakerphone button.

"Hello," said Jackie.

Kit threw Binfire a murderous look. She put her finger to her lips. Both Freya and Binfire nodded.

"Hi," said Kit.

"Are you still up there in deepest Mummerset?"

Kit's pedant monster uncurled from its slumber and opened one eye.

"I think 'Mummerset' is a dialect, not a place, and it's a term used to describe exaggerated West Country accents used in the theatre, so I would be *down* in deepest Mummerset. I'm *up* in Lincolnshire at the moment."

"Whatever. You're still 'up' there."

Kit knew from the tone that she still hadn't been forgiven.

"Yes."

"Why are you doing this?"

Kit was thrown. "Why am I trying to do what?"

"You know. Play detective."

"I'm not playing."

"Yes, you are. It's all roleplay with you lot."

Kit felt her hand tightening on the phone, as if trying to crush it.

"My lot?"

"You. Binfire. That hippy girl…"

Freya made an *eek* shape with her mouth and pointed to herself in astonishment, as if she was in the audience of a televised rock festival and the camera had rested on her face.

"I'm serious," Jackie continued. "Is this something you have to prove? You know, that you can be a detective without messing it up?"

"Excuse me. I didn't mess it up. And I'm doing it because Graham asked me, and he's paying me a lot of money."

"Well, if you want to dance to the tune of that man."

"I work for a lot of people I don't like."

"You're used to bending the knee. You always do. And FYI, you did mess it up, because someone got murdered."

Kit *hated* FYI. And she *hated* people who said FYI. She knew that logic dictated she hated her girlfriend, but her brain didn't want to go there.

She looked at Freya and Binfire, both with enraged looks on their faces. She didn't want them to be there. Of course she didn't. But she knew that without them staring at her in sympathy, she wouldn't have had the courage to go where she was about to go next:

"I *am* a good detective."

"Says you."

Kit was seething. She'd been humiliated in front of her friends. Granted Jackie didn't know they were there, but the result was the same.

Jackie sighed. "It's very convenient that this new job takes you so far away from me. Any idea when you're coming home?"

"You mean 'home' to Tunbridge Wells?"

"To Brighton. To our 'home' with me. You remember? The home you never come to."

The pedant monster was now unstoppable. It poked Kit into a rage.

"Never come?" she squeaked, her voice cracking with emotion. "I make the journey to you *every* weekend! I spend over forty pounds a week on train fares going backwards and forwards to *you*! It's because of me going back and forth to *you* that I need to take Graham Goldingay's money and do this job!"

There was silence from the other end of the phone. Kit knew she'd gone too far, because she knew of all the times she *nearly* went too far, skated right to the edge and applied the brakes. This was new territory.

Eventually Jackie said: "Well, let me save you some money. We're over. The end. We're done. Hope you enjoy your new life with your new friends."

And she rang off.

30

Freya rushed forward and gripped Kit by the shoulder. "I'm sooo sorry, Kit."

Binfire folded his arms. "Good riddance."

"Binfire!" Freya squeaked. "Don't say things like that."

Kit started fiddling with her phone.

"Don't you dare phone her back, pilgrim," boomed Binfire.

"I'm not phoning her back. I'm turning off my *Life360* app, so she won't know where I am anymore. I've been wanting to do this for ages."

"Good for you. Let's crack open the minibar and celebrate with some Furley House traditional lemonade."

Freya sighed. "Just stop it, Binfire. Can't you see Kit is hurting?"

"I'm not hurting," Kit snapped.

"You look hurt."

"That's my impatient face. I want to get on with discussing the suspects."

Kit was telling the truth. She *wasn't* hurting, but it took a few moments to realise *what* she was feeling.

She had two emotions inside her, swinging at each other like Captain Kirk fighting the Gorn. The Gorn represented Kit's ever-present terror of uncertainty; a future without the comforting routine of going down to Brighton on a Friday, taking walks along the beach on a Saturday evening, making love on a Sunday morning (when Jackie wasn't working at the hotel) and the pleasant journey on the train alone on Sunday evening to reunite with her dog Milo felt very scary.

Captain Kirk represented a feeling of relief, and maybe a bit of exhilaration, that she no longer had to charge down to Brighton, take walks along the beach, etc., and could just stay in bed with her dog Milo and her laptop, catching up on episodes on her big telly without worrying if Jackie maybe wanted to watch the same show.

You know I wanted to watch it, so why did you start it without me? That's just selfish, Kit.

The Gorn took a few angry lunges at Kirk, but Captain Kirk dodged nimbly out of the way, gave it a well-placed elbow in its scaly stomach and won the day.

Kit pushed aside what had just happened and focused on the matter in hand. She got out her notebook, adjusted her cap and sat primly on the bed.

"Let's go," she said. "Let's look at what's happened in the last twenty-four hours."

Freya and Binfire looked at each other, unsure whether they should humour Kit or stage an intervention.

Kit held up her fist and unfurled a thumb. "Can I summarise? Point one: someone stole Graham's action figure. They got into his London house, took it and covered up the crime so it wouldn't be discovered straight away."

She brought out a finger. "Point two: they sent it back to him in bits."

She unfurled another finger. "Point three: this person steals all the other action figures right under the noses of the owners, and spirits them away without trace in seconds, trashing the museum into the bargain."

"Like a gho—" began Freya.

Kit charged through Freya's words. "*Point four*: this person destroys two more dolls and on both occasions a cryptic little poem is sent to the collectors, based on a rhyme that's best known for featuring in an old Agatha Christie book." She frowned, looking at her pinkie finger. "Do I have a point five?"

"I think you've finished," said Freya.

"Right. Now for my list of suspects."

Kit turned her notebook around and showed Binfire and Freya her list of suspects, neatly laid out in subcategories.

OWNERS OF CEREMONIAL RANGE ACTION
FIGURES
Graham Goldingay
Matty Kearney
Fenton Worth
Lady Tabitha Pendragon

CURATORS OF MUSEUM
Dr Jerome Bell
Archie Pendragon

FAMILY MEMBERS AND ASSOCIATES
Ruth Bell
Saskia Shapiro
Moni Worth
Penny Lane

OTHERS PRESENT
Miscellaneous staff of Furley House

"I'm assuming that whoever managed to steal the dolls was on-site, in Furley House. I want to go through everybody here. Let's start with Vixy. I'm not familiar with her."

Binfire snorted with laughter. "Vixy is very familiar with a *lot* of people."

"She seems a bit wacky. And by 'wacky' I mean borderline insane."

Binfire grinned. "Yeah, she is that. She's well known on the forums. She's one of *those* fans who always makes herself the centre of attention. She's got a habit of making a drunken spectacle of herself at conventions, always resorting to all-caps on Twitter and often posts near-naked photos of herself on Instagram. She's your typical internet drama queen."

"So, what's her story? Why is she here?"

"I can tell you that," said Freya. "I talked to her over breakfast. She ran away from home last year and put some photos on Facebook of her in a sleeping bag, sleeping rough. She got sooo many people volunteering to put her up, before she found a permanent spare room above The Battlestore Galactica."

"She *lives* with Fenton and his wife?"

"Yep. She works in the shop and lives in their spare room. Fenton took her in. Out of the goodness of his heart." Binfire grinned. "Well maybe not his heart." He flicked his hand down to his belly button. "But I'm sure one of his major blood-pumping muscles was responsible."

"Binfire! Don't be crude!"

Kit twirled the pen around her fingers. "All very interesting, but nothing that gives Vixy a motive. But what about Fenton? Didn't Robbie say Fenton was done for fraud?"

Binfire snapped his fingers. "He did. Let's ring him."

Before Kit had a chance to protest, Binfire brought out his phone and dialled the number. He propped it up by Kit's fancy coffee maker and Robbie answered it after one ring. He stared out of the screen, squinting suspiciously.

"Robbie, we need your help," said Binfire.

"What do you wa— is that Freya?"

Freya waved feebly at Robbie.

"What the hell are you doing there? You're meant to be here!"

"I'm sooo sorry. I hid in the back of Binfire's motorhome to see the museum."

Robbie looked hurt. "I see. So, everyone's there but me."

Binfire leaned in closer to the phone. "Robbie, concentrate, we need your help. You're the action-figure expert."

"I know! That's why I should be there with you!"

"Everyone's destroying the merchandise, man. Trust me, you don't wanna be here. You'd just get PTSD. I want to ask you a question. You said Fenton served time in prison for insurance fraud?"

"Yes. He staged a burglary in his old shop, claimed on several 'stolen' rare collectibles..." He brought up his fingers for air quotes. "But, in reality, he tried to sell them on the black market. He got rid of two of them, but he stupidly tried to sell one to a collector who turned out to be an online undercover policeman. He spent six months in prison!"

"You don't think he's doing the same here?" gasped Freya.

"It makes sense, doesn't it?" Binfire slapped his fist in his hand. "He *steals* the figures, plays the sad victim, gets money from the Furley House insurance, *pretends* to destroy the figures one by one, but in reality he's not destroying anything."

"What's that you're saying?" said Robbie. "He's doing what?"

"He's just destroying ordinary cheap figures you can pick up for a few quid on eBay. In reality, he's keeping the Ceremonial Range back. I bet he's got some rich buyer all lined up in the States! The yanks go mad for this kind of stuff."

"What's that?" said Robbie. "Is Fenton doing—"

"Thanks, Robbie!" chirped Binfire. "That was a great help, guy! Speak later!"

He ended the call, and Robbie's outraged face winked out of existence.

"That's a good steer," said Kit. "I'll make a note."

Binfire and Freya watched as Kit wrote slowly on a fresh page of her notebook.

"What about Matty?" Binfire said suddenly. "That sod could do something like this for clicks for his YouTube channel. He was getting Saskia to film him running into the field with the bull today."

Freya shook her head. "True. But it was *Saskia* who suggested filming it."

"What about Saskia? What's her story?"

Binfire flopped back on the bed. "I can tell you about her. She was a producer for one of those shock-jock radio shows in the US. She hooked up with Matty during an American convention and came over here to work as the producer of his YouTube channel."

"Doesn't sound like she has a motive."

"Maybe she has," Freya said. "I was talking to her over breakfast as well."

Freya's good at this, thought Kit. *She talks to people, unlike me and Binfire. Despite the nonsense about ghosts, I'm glad she's here to help us investigate.*

Freya continued, "And she was telling me she had a film script optioned by Fliptop."

"Wow. That's impressive."

"Uh-uh. I said 'had'. It's past tense now. They were just about to go into production when Matty *happened* to put a 'making of' feature on his YouTube channel, showing Saskia at a microphone doing the voice of an anti-woke cartoon character, saying icky stuff about minorities, and gays, and trans people. So Fliptop dropped her within the hour."

Binfire frowned. "But she was just doing the voice of a character. It was Matty who wrote the script, obviously."

"It makes no difference," said Kit. "Fliptop is like any global media company. One sniff of any controversy and you're out."

"Exactly," said Freya. "That's why Saskia and Matty aren't together anymore. Even though Matty thinks their break-up is just temporary, he's deluding himself. She wants to go back to the States and start again. She is sooo angry at Matty. I can easily see her planning some kind of revenge on him."

Kit scribbled on her list. "Okay, so 'maybe' to Fenton, Matty and Saskia. On to the Bell family. Can we see Reverend Bell re-enacting *And Then There Were None* because he's into Agatha Christie? That's a bit weak."

"But he's also crazy and icky," said Freya.

"That's true." Binfire nodded. "Look what he did that night, caressing my action figure's head." He shivered and twirled his finger against his head. "Cuckoo!" He gave a frown. "And there's something else about him. Something he said to me…" He shook his head. "Nah, it's gone. But the fact remains, he's as mad as a box of Gungans."

"It's true, but he did make a good point in his defence. Why trash the museum he's been working to put together for months? It doesn't seem worth it. The same goes for Archie Pendragon. There's no motive strong enough to warrant destroying the place. Now for Lady Tabitha. I'm definitely interested in her—"

"I'm sure you are." Binfire grinned.

Kit blushed, and so, ridiculously, did Freya.

She continued, "Lady Tabitha could be doing it to get back at her little brother for inheriting Furley House instead of her. And speaking of inheritance, we should talk about the concubines' sprogs."

"I've been thinking about that," said Binfire. "I think one of those bastards turned up out of the blue to claim his inheritance and Archie locked him in some tower to stop him escaping, and they put an iron mask on him, so no one would recognise the Pendragon family resemblance, so he looks like a robot! Then he goes mad thinking he's an action figure and one night he shimmies down the drainpipe and runs into the woods, vowing revenge on Furley House and all action figures that dare set foot on Furley property!"

Freya and Kit stared at him.

Binfire looked defensive. "It makes sense, if you don't think about it too hard."

"Or at all," said Kit.

Freya made an *ooh* sound. "I do like the idea of a long-lost illegitimate heir to the Furley fortune coming back to the ancestral seat to take revenge. It does sound sooo romantic."

Kit arched an eyebrow. "Better than a ghost?"

"Almost," said Freya. "I do like the ghost best. Can you put the ghost on your list? For me."

Kit sighed, obliged and showed them her addended suspect list.

OWNERS OF CEREMONIAL RANGE ACTION FIGURES
Graham Goldingay (no)
Matty Kearney (maybe)
Fenton Worth (strong maybe)
Lady Tabitha Pendragon (strong maybe)

CURATORS OF MUSEUM
Dr Jerome Bell (no)
Archie Pendragon (no)

FAMILY MEMBERS AND ASSOCIATES
Ruth Bell (no)
Saskia Shapiro (maybe)
Moni Worth (no)
Penny Lane (no)
Vixy (no)

OTHERS PRESENT
Miscellaneous staff of Furley House (?)

EXTERNAL SUSPECTS
George Jamieson Pendragon (maybe)
Ghost!!!! (maybe)

"As it stands at the moment, it's Lady Tabitha way at the top of the suspects, then Fenton, then Matty, Saskia and this George Jamieson Pendragon. Whoever he is. Then it's Reverend Bell, Ruth Bell, Moni Worth, Archie Pendragon, Graham Goldingay, Penny Lane, Vixy, and the mysterious ghost of Furley House way down at the bottom."

"So, one of those people is a murderer," said Binfire.

"We're not dealing with a murderer," retorted Kit. "These figures aren't living people."

Binfire winked and pointed in the vague direction of the other stables. "Are you going to tell *them* that?"

31

They left and Kit took herself to bed, listening to the odd screech of a fox and the gravelly call of a pheasant.

Then came a knock at the door.

"Just a minute!" She struggled back into her clothes.

Another knock.

"I'm coming!"

She opened it, and there was Graham Goldingay's new robot. Graham was glowering on the monitor, manipulating a remote control.

"Come in," Kit sighed.

It rumbled into the room easily. The new robot looked smaller, sleeker and more manoeuvrable, the metal framework looked as though it had been dipped in gold paint, and the panels were dark polished glass, like the latest iPhone.

"I am here for a progress report."

"Fine. Well, there's nothing to report. What do you think of my progress report?"

"I think you *have* made some progress. You deduced earlier that our antagonist could be a doll maker, rather than a doll collector."

"So?"

"That set me thinking."

"Okay…"

"I have other possible suspects for your list." The robot wobbled slightly as if shaking in embarrassment. "But, in doing so, I would reveal certain facts that could bring about serious repercussions for me."

"You're already in prison for ten years, Graham. I'm not sure repercussions could get more serious."

Graham blinked again.

Kit rolled her eyes and sighed. "I promise it will not go beyond these four walls."

Graham thought long and hard. Even through the speakers, his stentorian breathing was incredibly loud. "The suspects I have in mind are the Braxton family, the ones who made the dolls. I believe they might want revenge."

"On whom?"

"Me. Matty. Fenton. Perhaps even the whole Pendragon family."

"All of you?"

"Let me explain. It all started in the year 1995. *Vixens from the Void* had been cancelled two years previously. In the early part of that year, the BBC rescinded Braxtons' licence to make toys. They calculated that if they removed all the licences, then it would help to bury any residual enthusiasm for the programme and the fans would stop writing letters asking for its return."

"I know all that."

"Of course you do. At that time Braxtons had already announced the Ceremonial Range of dolls. There had even been photos of the range in the trade press. They looked incredible. The cloaks were made from real cloth, the breastplates made from die-cast metal, and they had ceremonial staff accessories. But now, with the news that they had lost the licence to make official *Vixens* merchandise, they were forbidden to release any new figures, so it looked like none of them would ever see the light of day."

Graham paused, reached off-screen and retrieved a huge bag of popcorn.

"I need to eat something. My doctor tells me it's vital to keep my strength up."

He opened the bag and stuffed huge handfuls of popcorn into his mouth, munching remorselessly.

Kit waited patiently until he finished the whole bag. It felt a little surreal and unnerving, watching a man on a screen staring at her while eating his popcorn. As if *she* was the main feature, and the movie was watching *her.*

Thankfully, the bag was soon emptied and Graham threw it to the floor, sucking the sugar off his fingers.

He continued, "Also at that time, my company was starting to turn a profit from our corporate videos and documentaries. I used my new-found wealth to hire out the *Vixens* museum at Furley House for private functions. Dinner parties for my clients, et cetera. It was through that arrangement I formed a friendship with Roland Pendragon, the seventh Marquess."

Kit struggled to imagine what kind of friendship there could have been between gregarious and charismatic Roland Pendragon and the black hole of personality that was Graham Goldingay.

Perhaps the Marquess kept him around as an adornment, like a living gargoyle.

Graham rumbled on, "The Marquess and I started to have monthly get-togethers with certain other like-minded fans who we judged were interesting company."

"You mean Matty and Fenton?"

"Precisely. The four of us used to get together and have video weekends, try on the costumes, play with the props and gossip about all things related to *Vixens from the Void.*"

His mouth twitched as it attempted an approximation of a smile. "The seventh Marquess called us the Furley Fanboys. We were all there, at Furley House, when we heard the terrible news that Braxtons had lost the licence. The seventh Marquess was most enraged at not being given the chance to own the Ceremonial Range. After consuming a bottle of sherry, he proposed that we break into the factory and steal the prototypes."

Kit's jaw dropped. "You are joking."

"This may sound drastic to you, but it seemed like the logical thing to do in the circumstances. They were probably going to end up in a landfill, so we thought it was our sacred duty to rescue them. The Marquess drew up a plan to go over to the factory and take them. Matty, Fenton and I were to stay outside in the van and keep watch..."

He stopped. His head fell back and his eyes swivelled up to the ceiling, staring at nothing, remembering that fateful night.

"The three of us were there, waiting in the van, when we saw the factory catch fire. The seventh Marquess ran from the flames, carrying the dolls. Later, the Marquess told us he set fire to some cardboard boxes in the delivery area to distract a security guard. He didn't expect it to get out of hand."

"My god! The police said it *could* have been arson."

"They were correct."

"But they didn't have enough evidence to be certain."

"An accident. That was the official verdict."

"The CEO of Braxtons died in that fire! Jack Braxton died!"

Graham huffed. "I am aware of that fact."

"You don't sound very concerned."

"At the time, we were very concerned. We organised a meeting at Furley House the following day. Tempers were high. Fenton and Matty wanted to go to the police. The Marquess convinced them not to. He said it would do no good." He levelled a piggy gaze at Kit. "And he was right. What good would it have done?"

"You mean what good would it have done *you*?"

"None of us intended for the factory to burn. We did not factor in the reckless behaviour of the seventh Marquess."

"Everyone knew what he was like. You only had to watch that BBC documentary to realise he was dangerously unhinged, to put it nicely. Everyone knew he was an inbred looney."

"In hindsight, all you say is true, but the fact remains, none of us wanted to go to prison for his actions. We would have been arrested and convicted as his accomplices. There was no incentive for us to go to the police."

"*Incentive*," Kit repeated disbelievingly. Not for the first time she boggled at the bland, transactional, matter-of-fact drone of Graham's voice. "So, you're saying that one of the Braxton family is now taking revenge?"

"Yes. On the Pendragons. On the Furley Fanboys – me, Fenton, Matty… and Binfire."

"Binfire?" Kit's head came up sharply. "What's he got to do with this?"

"You must have wondered why Binfire has the fifth doll in his possession."

"I hadn't really thought about it," Kit lied.

"We've all wondered about it. All of us. Ever since we saw it on Facebook last year."

Kit remembered the commotion of Binfire's doll. It was just over a year ago, after the case that Kit called 'The Fan Who Knew Too Much'. The occupants of 33 Hanover Parade had gone through some dramatic changes: one occupant had been murdered and another had been sent to prison.

Robbie and Freya couldn't cope with staying in the same rooms that they'd shared with their ex-partners, so they all agreed to swap. Robbie moved into the largest bedroom at the front of the house, previously occupied by Freya and Wolf. Freya moved into the small boxroom at the back (Binfire's old room) and Binfire moved into the room that used to be Robbie and Victor's.

Ever efficient, Freya had started to cart her stuff into her new room, which the less-efficient Binfire hadn't fully cleared out yet. She saw the doll, sitting in a half-open suitcase. She hadn't realised its significance – she just found it pretty. She took a photo of it with her phone, and put it on Facebook with the caption:

So many groovy toys in our house!

It went viral across the *Vixens* community. Binfire didn't have a social media presence (never take chances, pilgrim!), so Freya had to field the dozens of messages that ensued, offering money to buy it. The whole circus lasted for months. When a fan was actually caught trying to jemmy open a downstairs window of 33 Hanover Parade, Binfire decided to bury the action figure in the back garden.

"I still don't see the fact that Binfire has a doll has anything to do with—"

"Don't you?"

The robot lurched forward until Kit was nose-to-screen with Graham.

"As we arrived at the factory that night and watched the seventh Marquess creep inside, and we watched the fire start… Fenton said he could have sworn he saw flickers of flame in the factory *before* the Marquess got access to the building. He was almost certain the fire was already in motion, premeditated, planned by the Marquess to cover his tracks. There is a theory that Binfire was given the doll in return for starting that fire. The fire that killed Jack Braxton."

"That's ridiculous."

"It's what Reverend Bell thinks."

"God – what's he got to do with this?"

"Fenton is a fool with a big mouth. He got drunk at a convention one night and told Reverend Bell the whole story. As you know, Bell fancies himself a detective in the Agatha Christie tradition, and he's intent on proving his theory."

The robot waggled from side to side.

"Watch Reverend Bell, Kit. I don't want this to get out. Nor Matty. Nor Fenton. But the Reverend might be tempted to do something foolish and make a lot of trouble for all of us."

Without another word, the robot turned on its axis and whirred out of her room. Kit closed the door after it and watched from her little hobbit window as the tiny red lights on the robot winked and flickered as it lurched away, disappearing and reappearing from behind the trees and the ornamental lamp-posts. She didn't stop watching it until the lights had disappeared into the night.

Kit cast her mind back to last night in the toy museum. She remembered Binfire's words.

I activated its self-destruct sequence. It made a fantastic bang.

I regret nothing.

32

Kit lay on the bed, eyes open and staring vacantly into the gloom. She couldn't sleep. She was already regretting becoming a detective. What seemed like a reasonable spur-of-the-moment decision became less attractive with every passing hour.

I don't want to find out these new facts about my friend, she thought. *It's like Binfire is a character in a series who is in the process of being rebooted, and I don't like the direction the writers are taking him.*

Wait.

What was that?

There had been the tiniest of noises. Practically nothing, but it was *there*, just by the desk. It was a faint rustle of paper, but there was no window open to invite a breeze.

So, what had made the papers rustle?

"Hello?" she croaked.

No answer.

"I heard you. There's no point pretending you're not there."

No answer.

"I have to let you know," she called in a voice she hoped was strident, but knew wasn't. "I've scheduled a Dungeons and Dragons game here for ten o'clock. They'll all be turning up in five minutes."

Nothing.

As Kit reached up to flick on the bedside light, a hand grasped her wrist. "Don't put the light on."

It was Lady Tabitha's voice.

Kit started to say something, but a hand clamped over her mouth. "Don't."

"Mmph,' Kit said.

"I'm going to remove my hand now. Don't shout, don't scream. I'm not going to hurt you."

The hand stayed clamped to Kit's mouth for a few more seconds, and then the pressure was gone.

"What do you want?" Kit whispered.

"It's not a question of what *I* want. It's a question of what *you* want."

"I don't understand."

"I hear you want to interrogate me as your chief suspect."

The duvet was lifted and Lady Tabitha's body slid beneath and pressed against hers. Kit realised she was naked.

"What would you like to ask me? I have to tell you, I'm a tough nut to crack. You'll have to break me first."

There was hot breath on Kit's ear, and then it was engulfed in something warm and wet. A mouth. She felt a hand gliding down her body, ducking under the elastic of her pyjama bottoms and resting on her abdomen.

"I… I'm not… I have a girlfriend."

"No, you don't. You don't have anyone," hissed Tabitha's disembodied voice. "I have my sources. A madman wearing an ear necklace just told me you've been dumped."

The warmth returned, and a tongue slithered inside Kit's ear.

She spoke, and her voice was low, but incredibly loud. "You're alone now. Like me. Just enjoy your freedom."

"Um."

"Okay?"

"Can't we just… Cuddle?"

A long silence.

"Sure we can."

33

Kit was still awake, still staring into the gloom.

She wanted to explain to the woman lying beside her that her relationships were not that passionate and not that frequent. They didn't occur every other month, like Marvel movies. They were more like the *Star Wars* franchise: one major event every couple of years and a couple of disappointing straight-to-streaming efforts that were best forgotten.

In short, she wanted to tell Tabitha that she wasn't That Kind of Girl.

She had a sudden impulse to click on the bedside lamp, to break the spell. Her hand was poised on the button when Tabitha spoke. Her voice was loud in the darkness.

"Don't turn on the light."

"Okay."

"Keep the lights off. If we can't see each other, then none of this is real. That way there's no guilt."

"I don't feel guilty. I just—"

"Wait until the morning. If you don't feel guilty, then perhaps we'll put the lights on tomorrow night."

Tomorrow night?

"But maybe we won't. I like that we can't see each other. It makes things more exciting."

Kit wondered how she could cope with things being *more* exciting, but she did as she was told. The light stayed off.

"Archie said you were seeing someone called Nate."

"That's all in the past. History. He doesn't matter."

"He?"

"I can experiment, can't I?" The tongue slipped into Kit's ear again. "I wear lots of costumes. Can't I try *you* on for size?"

"Please, not yet. I'm not ready."

The tongue left her ear. "I understand. I've been hiding in the shadows for a long time too. I know how it feels."

34

When the light touched Kit's eyelids and her eyes flicked open, she knew instantly that Tabitha was gone. The only evidence she'd been there was the faint smell of expensive fruity soap.

She got up, got dressed, and attended to her hair and make-up. When she looked in the mirror she realised it wasn't just the fragrance of oranges and lemons that Tabitha had left behind. There was a semi-circle of dark red marks on her neck.

Teeth marks.

Fortunately, Kit habitually wore a healthy layer of make-up, so she could disguise the marks without it looking odd. Once she finished, she performed a quick self-diagnostic. Her dissociative disorder had once again done its work. There was not a trace of guilt about spooning with another woman. After all, it was Jackie who had ended it. Whether Jackie meant what she said or not was immaterial. Words have meaning.

It is what it is.

She decided that the next logical step was to head to Braxton Hall and investigate Graham's accusations. She strode down the drive, out of the gates and was met with a road running parallel to the walls of Furley Park. A road sign pointed two ways. One arrow pointed to FURLEY 2 MILES; the other direction read PETERBOROUGH 11 MILES.

She hesitated. She was hoping for a nearby bus stop or a train station but remembered there wasn't one. It was going to be a stiff walk in her boots.

Then she had a thought. She walked back to Furley House and knocked on Penny's door.

Penny answered.

"Hello, Kit, what can I do for you?"

"Can you take me to Braxton Hall? I want to question the Braxton family. Your boss has given me a lead."

"Okay… But… Didn't you want to have Binfire take you?"

Not now. Not today. I can't deal with him today. If what Graham says is true, then he's a murderer and our friendship is at an end.

"No. Let's make this official. We're both employed by Graham Goldingay. We should go together."

"Okay, that makes sense. Meet me in the car park in twenty minutes?"

35

Penny waved cheerfully at Kit from the driver's side as she approached the shiny transit van. She was still in her stylish lavender suit but had replaced her blouse with a white T-shirt.

"Fancy a lift?"

"Thanks."

Kit climbed in and they roared off down the drive. Kit glanced behind her, into the back of the van, where Graham's automaton lay dormant, fastened to the floor with thick straps.

"Is Graham coming with us?"

Penny smiled. "Not today. He had an argument with a fellow inmate last night, about which was the best series of *Star Trek*. He's currently in solitary for twenty-four hours. Probably just as well, really. I'm not sure the Braxton family would take kindly to being interrogated by a robot."

"No. Being interrogated by a robot never works out well in sci-fi."

The van chugged around the outskirts of Furley until the arrows pointed to the motorway.

"You do know why we're going to Braxton Hall?" said Kit cautiously. "I mean, the reason why I might want to interview them?"

"You mean the fire at the factory, and who was behind it?" Penny's voice was very casual. "Yes, of course. Mr Goldingay told me a few years ago. I pride myself on having his full trust and confidence."

She glanced at Kit. "If you want to do some research about it, read the wiki pages. We've got about half an hour. It's about ten miles to Braxton Hall. Everywhere is always ten miles to somewhere else around here." She gestured out of the passenger side window, at the horizon that rolled out into nothingness. "Everything's all spread out in Lincolnshire."

"You know the area?"

"I was born… ohh…" She grinned again. "About ten miles away." She nodded out of the window. "Thattaway."

Kit looked surprised. "You were born around here? That's a bit of a coincidence."

Penny shrugged. "Not really. My mother worked for Braxtons as an accountant. A lot of people around here end up working for the same companies. There's not that much work to be found."

She flashed Kit a quick smile. "My mum watched Roland Pendragon rock up in his Range Rover almost every month, visiting Jack Braxton and looking at the toys being made, so when the factory burned down and she was out of work, she wrote to the Marquess about a job. He already had an accountant, but he passed her C V on to Mr Goldingay. She worked for him for ages, doing the books for his production company."

She smiled. "Knowing what I know now, I guess it was all guilt on their part. Mum retired last year. After I graduated from Loughborough five years ago, she put in a word for me with Graham and here I am."

"Here you are."

Penny continued, "There's no such thing as a coincidence. I mean, there are a lot of things that *seem* like coincidences but which aren't really coincidences. I mean, take who we're going to see? Nate Braxton, son of Sylvia, nephew of Jack, and grandson of Albert and Vera. Did you know he dated Lady Tabitha until recently?"

"No!"

"Yes! Spooky huh?"

NATE Braxton??!!!

"Sylvia Braxton and the seventh Marquess stayed in touch after Jack's death. Call it a guilty conscience if you like. Nate and Tabitha knew each other as kids, and they both went to adjoining posh schools. I think Roland Pendragon hoped they'd get married, the old romantic. I mean, she didn't have to marry into the nobility, because she wasn't going to inherit the estate… You've gone quiet," said Penny. "Don't you believe me?"

"You say they split up?"

"Yes, about three months ago. They put out a break-up video on Instagram. It's all the rage with dysfunctional celebrity couples."

Her mind still swirling with the implications, Kit took out her phone and went to Instagram. There it was, clearly labelled 'our final message'. It looked like it was in Lady Tabitha's bedroom. Tabitha was sitting in a chair. A man loomed over her, young, handsome, late twenties, with a smooth round face and angry eyebrows. He was wearing a blazer and tie. It looked a bit like a hostage video.

Before clicking on the video, she studied Tabitha first, mouthing silently at the camera. Kit guessed the video had been made in high summer, because Tabitha was dressed in a tight red sleeveless T-shirt with the Wonder Woman logo on it.

Kit was particularly impressed by Tabitha's arms; she hadn't seen them properly before. They were long and toned and completely covered in tattoos from wrist to shoulder. She could just see one bicep, upon which was an open grave with a circle with a cross underneath as a headstone – the female symbol – and below it was a copy of the famous World War II poster of a woman in dungarees showing a bicep and saying WE CAN DO IT!, only, in this case, the woman was sporting a huge handlebar moustache.

Tabitha turned to look up at Nate, and Kit could see her other bicep, upon which there was a lot of writing in tiny copperplate font. She could make out an elaborate 'I' at the beginning of the text, but everything else was a forest of lines and squiggles.

Kit pressed play and the video restarted, this time with sound.

"Hi, everyone," said Tabitha. "We've got something to tell you guys."

Tabitha's voice was surprisingly low and gravelly. Kit wondered if she and Nate had spent the day shouting at each other before deciding to make the video.

"You, that is my YouTube family, have followed Nate and I through our ups and downs over the last few years. It's been quite a ride, hasn't it, Nate?"

Nate grunted.

"All the big things that happened to us. Nate getting arrested for being drunk outside the Groucho and shouting at a traffic warden. Me getting my tattoos… You've been there for us. So, I think it's only right to tell you first. We've decided to call it a day on our relationship…"

She glanced at Nate Braxton.

"… haven't we?"

He gave a grudging nod. He looked as though he was just about keeping a lid on a boiling mass of rage.

Obviously the 'we' in that sentence is doing a lot of heavy lifting.

Tabitha continued, "We both agree that we've been wanting different things for some time now, so we've concluded that, sadly, we, that is us, is not working. So, we're consciously uncoupling. But we'll still be friends, won't we, Nate?"

Nate made another non-committal grunt.

"He might pop up in future videos, but platonically, and probably not straight away. I know this is just as upsetting for all of you as it is to us, but we will get through this together. Okay? Remember to keep going to my YouTube channel and keep liking and subscribing. Ciao."

Tabitha reached forward to switch the camera off. The screen went black.

"When they split up it was a real shock. Instagram went mad," said Penny. "They looked really happy in the other videos."

Kit was lost in thought.

Did Tabitha and Nate split up because of Tabitha's... other interests?

Wait.

That room she discovered in Furley House. The torn label on the jar said NATE. A tiny thought occurred to her, which quickly bloomed into a larger thought. She turned the sound off on her phone and watched the video again. She looked at Nate's face closely.

Is it my imagination, or does Nate look a bit like Roland Pendragon?

There was certainly some similarity, particularly those angry, bushy eyebrows. That round face. Kit's thought was so big it bloomed into a theory.

I'm sure Roland Pendragon must have felt pretty guilty over Jack Braxton's death. I bet he visited the Braxton family to give his condolences. Perhaps his roving eye rested on Sylvia Braxton, Jack's sister?

Have I found the mysterious bastard son of Roland? The occupant of that room? I read somewhere that Sylvia brought Nate up on her own. Strong woman making it in business despite being a single mum...

Maybe there was a far more substantial reason for Tabitha and Nate's break-up than irreconcilable differences? The fact that they discovered they were half-brother and sister?

Or...

Perhaps Nate found out who his dad was, and ONLY dated Tabitha to gain access to Furley House, in order to get his revenge on the Pendragons? And Tabitha discovered Nate was her half-brother and then dumped him, but he'd already been told of a secret passageway and hidden in the house in—

Hold on a second!

Kit realised her brain was getting silly. It had a habit of throwing absurd and fanciful narratives in the air, because, as the brain of a Cult TV fan, it was stuffed full of absurd and fanciful narratives. It was a fun notion, but it didn't even begin to address the mystery. Why the rack of new clothes? Why the pens with 'George Jamieson Pendragon' on them?

"I'm worse than Freya. I might as well blame it all on ghosts."

"What?" said Penny.

Kit realised she'd muttered her last thought out loud.

"Nothing. I was just—"

Thankfully they were interrupted by Kit's phone. It was Jackie. But Kit did not want to speak to Jackie. That was the last thing she wanted to do. She let it ring and go to voicemail.

Then as soon as that call stopped, another one arrived, this time from Binfire. Someone else who she didn't want to talk to. Again, she let it ring.

Let them go away. Let them all leave me alone.

Penny glanced quizzically across at her but said nothing.

36

Kit's little room in the Furley stables was still, quiet and empty. Then the silence was broken by a tiny click and the front door swung open.

"Never fails," said Binfire, stuffing his credit card back into his pocket and peering into the gloom.

"Where has she got to?" said Freya, poking her head around Binfire's shoulder. "I thought she'd want to help with searching the grounds."

"I told you, pilgrim. She's gone off on a little *Thelma and Louise* jaunt with the Cosplay Countess."

He winked. Freya's face crumped into a disapproving glare. "That's slander, Binfire. You could get into trouble for that."

"It's true, Frey, scout's honour." He held up his three fingers in a salute. "I passed Lady Tabitha yesterday and told her Kit had been dumped. And I just happened to be on manoeuvres about three hundred hours this morning, crawling through the undergrowth, and hey presto! I spy Lady Tabitha leaving this very room."

"That's not evidence. Perhaps they'd been out badger-watching."

Binfire waggled his huge eyebrows. "Perhaps they stayed *in* badger-watching."

"Binfire!"

"Well, she's not here, is she?" He pulled his phone out, dialled and waited. "No answer. Nope, she's definitely out on the pull. Let's go grab a pitchfork and join the mob."

They were leaving when the room phone started ringing.

Binfire dived across the bed and flicked the switch on the bottom that said 'speaker'.

"Kit's room, can I take a message?"

"Hello? Who is this?"

Binfire and Freya looked at each other in alarm.

Jackie Hillier's voice.

"Hello, is that Binfire?"

Binfire shrugged. "Yep. It's me."

"What are you doing in Kit's room?"

"Oh, just hanging out, you know, being detectives. 'Cos that's what we do, me and Kit. Holmes and Watson, that's us."

He grinned at Freya, who was shaking her head furiously and flapping her hands, as if trying to stop Binfire by the power of telekinesis.

"Where's Kit? I tried to ring her but she's not answering."

"Really? That's a surprise."

A pause from Jackie. When she replied there was menace in her voice.

"Where is Kit?"

"Oh, around. Who wants to know?"

"Me."

"Right."

"So put her on now. *Please.*"

"Sorry, pilgrim, as I understand it, phone access is reserved only for *current* girlfriends. It says here in my database that you're only an *ex*-girlfriend." He made a computer-says-no noise.

"God's sake, you bald twat, put her on the phone!"

"No can do. She's out with her sexy new girlfriend having a whale of a time, doing all that stuff lesbians do. You know. Holding hands. Going to Pilates. Making sweet love to the sounds of k.d. lang… Perhaps you should call back later? How about never? Does never sound good?"

He slammed his hand on the top of the phone, cutting off the call. He looked up at Freya, who was frozen in horror.

"Eek," she squeaked.

"Well, that's one problem solved." He beamed.

37

Penny Lane cleared her throat.

"We're here."

Kit looked up in surprise. She'd been so deep in thought that the half-hour drive had passed without her noticing.

Braxton Hall was like Furley House, from a mirror universe. Furley was old money, Braxton was new. Furley had crumbling brickwork and teetering gargoyles. Braxton had lightweight Doric columns made from duropolymer and a tinkling fountain composed of geometric shapes.

The transit van trundled up to the massive gates, which glided open of their own accord. As Kit got out of the van and her boots came into contact with the gravel of the driveway (coloured bright purple), she allowed herself a few moments to stare up at the facade. She wondered how big the brown envelope had been to get planning permission to construct this place – a gleaming carbuncle that looked like an American's idea of a stately home – in the depths of the English countryside.

They walked up to the massive door, which had *Braxtons* written over the top. Penny stepped forward and rang the bell. She grinned at Kit.

"This is your show now. I'm just here to be nice."

After a few seconds, a ghostly shape metamorphosed in the stained glass of the door.

A woman's voice said, "Hello?"

"We'd like to see Mrs Vera Braxton?"

"Who wants to know?"

"My name is Kit Pelham. I'm with *Vixmag* magazine."

"So what?"

"There's a new toy museum in Furley House, and they're featuring an exhibition of Braxtons' *Vixens from the Void* toys. I wonder if Mrs Braxton would like to be interviewed about her husband, if that's alright?"

"Wait a moment."

The door opened and a woman appeared. She was incredibly beautiful, tall and willowy, with toned arms and long legs. Her blonde hair cascaded around her slender neck, bouncing around her shoulders with the merest hint of a curl, as if she had just stepped out of a salon.

"Hi," she said. "I'm Sylvia Braxton, I'm her daughter."

Oh yes, thought Kit. *Definitely a woman that would catch Roland Pendragon's eye. Hell, she'd catch anyone's eye, man or woman.*

She was in her late fifties, but if Kit hadn't known that she would have sworn that Sylvia was twenty years younger. The only hint of her true age was a slight crimping around her Adam's apple.

"I'll take you to see her, but I don't think you'll be very welcome," Sylvia said. "Mother isn't a fan of those dolls. I wouldn't mention them if I were you." She shrugged. "Still, it's your funeral. I'll take you to her."

She turned without another word and went into the house. They followed.

Sylvia Braxton was dressed casually, but not what an ordinary human being would call casual. She was clad in black jeans and a baggy navy-blue sweater made from merino wool. A pear-drop pendant hung around her neck and white-gold bracelets slid up and down her arms. Kit immediately thought of a sculpture made flesh but realised what she really looked like: a living, breathing Barbie doll.

Sylvia took them into a library/sitting room. It was a huge round room with a circular table, half-a-dozen chairs arranged around an iron fireplace, a globe suspended in a Perspex holder and a wall of books. The edges were clean and modern, but in a nod to older, more traditional libraries the predominant colour was dark mahogany.

Covering the ceiling was a blue stained-glass window, with images representing all the toy ranges made by Braxtons. There was a steam-train, a tractor, a World War II tank... They were all rendered beautifully in stained glass as if they had all carried Jesus Christ across the desert.

The far side of the room was dominated by a train set that was bigger than any Kit had seen. It looked as though someone had recreated the whole of Lincolnshire just for the pleasure of watching a train scoot across it. As she watched, one train emerged from a tunnel, parked at a station for a few seconds and then scooted off. It looked completely automatic.

"Make yourself at home," Sylvia said.

"So why aren't the *Vixens from the Void* figures popular with your mother?"

Sylvia sat down in a chair, took a huge breath and allowed air to sigh through her nostrils. "She blames them – not unfairly – for the collapse of Braxtons Models."

"Oh."

"When Father died in '91, the business passed down to my brother Jack. He was my younger brother by a few years, but he was more enthusiastic about running the company than me. I wasn't keen at the time."

She gave a sour smile. "And to be brutally honest, that might have been because Jack was already the apple of my father and mother's eye. I was never 'encouraged' to take on a role, let's leave it at that. Jack took over Braxtons when he was only in his twenties, and he was hopelessly out of his depth from the get-go. Everyone knew it. He tried to differentiate himself from Father, so he got this idea in his head about the company getting into space toys."

She gestured upwards, to the last picture in the stained-glass ceiling, right next to the tractor. It was a stylised version of the *Vixens from the Void* spaceship, the *Hydra*, just like the one in Archie's toy museum.

"All the other model companies had done it and he saw it as an absolute no-brainer to do the same. And he embarked on a huge commitment to making *Vixens from the Void* toys just when the BBC decided to cancel the bloody show. It was a financial disaster."

She gestured them to sit, and, when they did, she leaned forward and whispered into their ears.

"I know I shouldn't say this, but the factory fire was the best thing that ever happened to Braxtons. It helped us to start again. But I wouldn't *dare* say that in front of Mother. Mother is of a generation that expects the men to go out to work of a Tuesday with their briefcases, bowler hats and with a pipe firmly clenched between their teeth, and the women to stay at home, strap on a pinny and bake apple tarts."

She shrugged, and her blonde fringe shimmied around her forehead. "She didn't want me to take over the business, but at the time I was the only option. Mother still doesn't like it and she *certainly* doesn't approve of my... innovations." She raised her voice. "Mother! We've got company! Some journalists are here! They want to talk about Dad!"

At that moment, Vera Braxton entered, a welcoming smile on her face.

Vera was in her eighties, but just as well preserved as her daughter. She was extremely thin but had an oddly bountiful décolletage that Kit suspected wasn't completely natural. She had a pyramid of shocking white hair, and her body was tanned until golden brown and covered in a brown linen dress. She looked a bit like an ice-cream cone.

"Albert? They want to talk about Albert? Is that what they want to do?"

"They do," cooed Sylvia. "They want to know all about him."

Vera smiled with delight, and her face exploded into a mass of wrinkles. "We'd better have some tea then."

She stepped forward and shook Penny's hand. "So, you want to chat to me about Albert?"

"Not me." Penny smiled, pointing at Kit. "She's the journalist."

Vera shook Kit's hand in turn. Vera's hand was so soft and warm, Kit didn't even feel the need to flinch.

"You don't look like a journalist, dear," Vera creaked. "More like a pearly queen who's lost her pearls."

Kit explained, "I'm not a journalist. I mean, not really. I'm a writer. I write for magazines. I'm writing a piece about the toy museum at Furley House…"

"Shall I stick around, Mum?"

"I don't think that will be necessary," sniffed her mother.

"Are you able to lift up the teapot?" Sylvia's question sounded extremely rhetorical.

"You know I can't. But these ladies look sturdy enough to pour their own tea, don't you?"

"Oh yes," said Penny.

"It's hardly polite to make guests serve their own tea, Mother," Sylvia said. "I think I'll do it if it's all the same to you."

Sylvia sat down with them. Kit got the impression that she was determined to chaperone her mother.

Vera knew she had lost and changed the subject. She pointed at the miniature landscape of the railway.

"So, what do you think of our train set?"

"Incredible," gushed Penny.

Vera purred, "That's Albert's doing of course. He was obsessed with model trains from when he was a little boy. He thought it would be amazing if someone made custom train sets of different areas of the country, so children could actually have model trains chuffing past landmarks they recognised, and within ten years he'd created his factory to do just that. And, from that point on, there was no stopping him. Farm models, zoo models, models from the Second World War, the First World War, the Boer War... Probably every international conflict that's happened in the last thousand years."

She thought for a second, tapping an exquisitely manicured fingernail on her chin. "And he did Roman legions too, so even further back than that. You name it, he miniaturised it."

"The company was your husband's, wasn't it?" asked Kit. "It belonged to him."

"Of course, dear. Braxtons was all his."

"I just wondered why there isn't a possessive apostrophe in the Braxtons name."

Vera sniffed. "Albert wouldn't have anything to do with apostrophes. Wouldn't have them in the house. 'Look at them up there, hanging above the other letters,' he used to say. 'Hanging up there, looking down all snooty, like they think they're better than everyone else.' You can see his point of view, can't you? He wasn't keen on umlauts either."

She picked up a biscuit and nibbled it.

"Now, what would you like from me? I do know about the museum, of course. Archie asked me if I wanted to come along to the opening. Sadly, we had a prior engagement."

"No, we didn't, Mother," said Sylvia, sighing. "We spent Saturday evening playing bridge."

"So we did." Vera glared at her daughter, then smiled beatifically at Kit and Penny.

"You see, my dears… Those space toys… I wasn't a fan, to be brutally honest. They weren't part of my Albert's vision for the company. They were a bold but misguided attempt to bring Braxtons up to date. Not a success."

"A disaster. Jack's folly," snapped Sylvia.

Sylvia got another glare from her mother. "Jack meant well. He was so enthusiastic."

"And stupid."

"His heart was in the right place, Sylvia. At least he wanted to carry on my husband's work, unlike *some*."

"It's thanks to *my* work that you're still sitting pretty in this huge centrally heated monstrosity, and not rotting in some council estate, or in some rest home."

Kit and Penny exchanged awkward glances. This was obviously a well-rehearsed argument between mother and daughter.

Thankfully, a young woman in a smart trouser suit interrupted the shadow boxing, arriving with a tray piled high with cups, saucers and a large teapot decorated with daisies. She placed it down on the table and left without a word.

Sylvia leaned forward, swished the pot in the air, and poured tea into the cups.

"I love the sound of tea flowing into a cup," twittered Vera. "It's probably the best part of tea, even more than drinking it."

"You could be right," said Kit.

"You have a lovely house, Mrs Braxton." Penny smiled.

"Call me Vera."

"Well, you have a lovely house, Vera. Very distinctive."

"Very expensive to run," muttered Sylvia. "Cream?"

"Yes, please," said Penny.

"No thanks," said Kit.

Sylvia poured cream into Penny's cup.

Vera continued, "A lot of people in the company never understood why he wanted to make space action figures. Our Managing Director thought it was very distasteful, selling dollies with big bosoms to twelve-year-old boys, but Jack was absolutely adamant. And, as you know, it didn't end well. The poor workers—"

"Half of them got their jobs back, Mum. I made sure of it. You *know* that."

"But hardly job satisfaction, dear."

"My mum actually worked for Braxtons," said Penny.

"Oh really!" Vera hooted with delight. "What a small world! That's what my husband used to say: 'When Braxtons is involved, it's always a small world.' He used to say that a lot. Did your mother work on the shop floor?"

"No, as an accountant."

"Ah, one of the office people. Albert would have known her name."

"He did."

"He knew everybody's name in the company. And their birthdays. And their children's names. He was special like that. If you want a bit of backstory, there's a fair bit in the library. Follow me."

She stood up and walked over to a far wall with framed panels of writing and more models under glass.

"This is the history of Braxtons all laid out on these walls. As you can see it starts right here, far left, just by the fire alarm, and you follow the line all the way to the present day."

Sylvia gave a hollow laugh. "Not quite the *present* day, Mother."

"Well, obviously not! If you ever put those things on display, I'd just die of heart failure."

"Now *there's* an idea."

Vera ignored her daughter. "Would you like a closer look at the train set? It's a perfect reconstruction of the railway line by the factory."

She pressed a button and the train gave a tiny toot.

"It's incredibly accurate. Albert used to update it every year. When they pulled down the nightclub and replaced it with a Sainsbury's, he made a tiny supermarket and installed it within the week."

Kit peered, and sure enough, there was a Sainsbury's nestling at the top of the high street. "When was this last updated?"

Vera sighed. "Oh, let me think. Albert used to go up and photograph the landscape every month and note the changes. Jack continued the tradition of updating the railway. So, I would guess, thinking about it, it was last altered about a fortnight before he... Before the fire. That's why, if you look, the factory is still there, instead of the warehouse that was built on the site."

Kit took a closer look, down the high street, past the tiny figures shopping, sweeping the pavement, waiting to cross the road, over a little bridge stretching over a ribbon of wavy blue plastic, past the little pub and over to the factory—

Wait! Back up!

Her eyes went back to the pub. The pub was perched on the side of a hill, and the car park was a huge ledge that looked down into the village, the river and the factory. In amongst the multi-coloured swarm of cars was a Range Rover. It was definitely—

"You can use this if you like."

She jumped. Vera was holding out a magnifying glass. Kit took it and aimed it at the model railway, trying not to look as if she was looking directly at the pub car park.

The Range Rover ballooned through the lens of the magnifying glass. To her shock, the detail extended to the number plate. She could clearly read it, so there was no room for doubt. Four tiny figures were standing by the vehicle. A short man with a shabby jacket leaning on the wall. Fenton Worth. Right beside him, pointing a pair of binoculars directly at the factory, was a man wearing a multi-coloured shirt and what looked like loon pants. Kit didn't need to consult a Debrett's to know she was staring at a tiny figurine of Roland Pendragon, the seventh Marquess of Furley.

Sitting just a little apart from them on a pub garden table – well it had to be Matty Kearney. And leaning on the side of the Land Rover was the portly figure of Graham Goldingay.

"What are you looking at?" Penny was suddenly at her elbow.

"I'm looking at that."

Penny took the magnifying glass and looked. "My god," she whispered. "Oh my god, look! Look at the Braxtons factory!"

Kit looked. It was also beautifully rendered, and very accurate. She looked closer. There was a tiny figure dressed in black clothes and balaclava climbing over one of the walls, as if someone were leaving the scene of a crime.

"Holy moly," she whispered. "It's like *Thomas the Tank Engine* had a *Crimewatch* reconstruction."

"It's wonderful, isn't it? Such detail."

They both turned and looked at Vera, but she was oblivious to their panic. She was looking at the tiny model factory with wistful eyes.

"When the factory burned down and we lost Jack, I didn't have the energy to rebuild."

"Luckily you had *me*." Sylvia had joined them.

"We just put a warehouse on the site, to occasionally store stock. We don't use it that much anymore, do we?"

"No, Mother," said Sylvia. "Everything gets sent straight from the factory these days."

Kit and Penny edged away from the models and dragged Vera's attention back to the tea set. "Can I ask you about the last range of models you were going to make?" asked Kit. "The Ceremonial Range? The ones Jack was going to release just before the fire?"

Vera looked blank. "I wouldn't know about them. I chose not to interfere with my son's running of the company."

"Oh lucky, *lucky* Jack," whispered Sylvia, rolling her eyes. She turned to Kit and Penny. "You're talking about the swanky versions of the Vixen toys. Yeah, my brother was extremely excited by them. When I came back home, he would talk of little else."

She mimicked a man's voice, presumably her brother's. "So, Sylvia, you know Dad, he started off doing little metal trains, cars and buses, yeah? So, I want to do something for him, like a dedication, go back to the toys having a heavy, solid feel. I'm gonna make special little metal breastplates and metal staffs for the toys to carry. Even though they're basically the same dolls, they're gonna be heavier and chunkier, man. It's going to be fr—"

"*Don't talk to them, Mother!*"

Standing in the doorway was a young man with angry eyebrows and immaculate hair wearing a polo shirt.

Nate Braxton.

"Don't talk to them!"

Sylvia frowned. "They're only here to talk about Braxtons, Nate. They've been putting your Uncle Jack's space toys in a museum in Furley House and they want to talk about how—"

"Is that what they told you?" He advanced towards his mother. "Did they tell you that the museum got *vandalised* the night before last?"

"What?" exclaimed Vera. "They didn't say."

"Of course they didn't, Gran. And I bet they didn't tell you that some nutcase is tearing apart the toys one by one and sending them back in bits?"

Vera glanced at Penny and Kit with suspicion. "No, they didn't."

"Well, that's what's happened. I've had that *bitch* texting me this morning, accusing me of having something to do with it."

Sylvia sighed. "Don't use the 'b' word, Nate. Not for Tabitha. She's a lady."

"She's no lady, Mother. You don't know her like I do. She's sending me all-caps accusations and she won't even talk to me about it on the phone. Well, her texts are evidence of defamation. I'm going to sue the cow."

He ran his fingers through his thick dark curls, his face a picture of anguish. "Why the hell would I want to vandalise a bloody toy museum? I know we didn't part on the best of terms, but why would I want to do something like that?"

He whirled to face Kit and Penny, glaring at them murderously. "Bit of a bloody coincidence that you turn up here, asking questions, isn't it?"

Kit opened her mouth but no words came out, just a croak. Penny realised Kit was having trouble and said, "Yes, it's a complete coincidence."

"Really?" he said sharply. He glared at Kit. "What newspaper are you working for again?"

"I w-work for V-v-*Vixmag*. It's a m-magazine that c-covers *Vixens from the V-void*." She produced a card from her pocket. "Th-that's m-my editor's phone n-number. He'll c-confirm why I'm here."

Nate Braxton didn't even look at it. He just slipped the card into his pocket. "Well, okay, fair enough. But I'm going to have to ask you to leave anyway. I've been accused of a crime.

Anything I have to say regarding that will be through my solicitors. That goes for my mother and grandmother too."

"Nate!" Vera was indignant. "Don't be so rude!"

"It's fine," said Penny. "I think we've taken up enough of your time. We should be getting back to Furley House."

"Thanks for your hospitality," added Kit.

"You're welcome, dear," simpered Vera. "Perhaps we can talk anon, when Nate has calmed down."

"I'll see you out," said Sylvia.

38

Sylvia led them out, but not directly to the main door. She turned to them and gave a conspiratorial wink.

"Before you go, I thought you might want to see what Braxtons is up to now. And why my mother always looks at me like I've just farted in her face."

She led them down a flight of steps, opened a shiny white door and beckoned them to follow her inside. They found themselves in a gleaming minimalist office, with a black desk and a black leather desk chair in the middle, framed with modern art. A huge window bestowed a stunning view of the Lincolnshire countryside. But it wasn't the stylish furniture, the artworks or the view that immediately caught the eye.

What dominated the office was a wall of glass shelves. Or, to be specific, what dominated the office were the *objects* arranged on the glass shelves. A collection of interesting shapes, pointing upright like multi-coloured stalagmites. Alongside the shelves, gripped on the neck by a stand, was an inflatable naked blonde lady who looked quite surprised at Kit and Penny's arrival.

"Oh," said Kit.

"Oh, right! *Sylvia!*" Penny grinned. "I hadn't made the connection."

"You're not meant to, dear, that's the point. I'd hardly call it *Braxtons Sex Toys*, would I? Mother would have had the vapours and keeled over on the spot."

Above the objects was the logo of the company: Sylvia's name rendered like an autograph, as if she had personally signed every item.

"When we rebuilt the factory, I repurposed our production line, which was surprisingly easy. The Braxtons workers had years of experience of designing shapes out of a few inches of plastic."

Sylvia gestured at a collection of scary-looking pink truncheons. She picked one up and slapped it into her palm. "Those are our bestsellers – the wobbler, the buzzer, the throbber and the squirter… My little friends here are what keep the smiles on the faces of the shareholders. Mum might not like it, but nothing else makes any money around here. They'll keep her in tea and biccies and holidays in Bora Bora until she pegs it."

She waggled the blow-up doll's hand, waving at them in greeting. "Say hello to this little lady. She's also called Sylvia. Can you see the family resemblance?"

Sylvia pursed her lips and widened her eyes to ape the doll's shocked expression. Then she cackled.

"She's the only doll we make anymore. In my quieter moments, I like to imagine the twelve-year-old boys who got their *Vixens from the Void* action figures in the 90s are still buying their toys from Braxtons."

She gazed at them, a smile twitching on the corners of her mouth. Then she went to the desk, opened a drawer, pulled out a couple of plastic bags with 'Sylvia' printed on them and thrust them into the arms of Kit and Penny.

"Here you go, girls." She chuckled. "Have a goodie bag on me." She winked at Kit. "You look like you need it."

"Thanks!" said Penny, looking inside.

Kit looked at the bag, contemplated opening it, thought better of it and held it limply by her side. "Thanks," she said, in a less enthusiastic tone.

"I'll take you out now. I just wanted to show you Braxtons' dark secret." A frown flitted across her unnaturally smooth forehead. "One of them, anyway."

As she walked towards the door, Kit made sure she was at Sylvia's shoulder, keeping up with the older woman's long strides.

"What you've done for Braxtons is amazing," said Kit.

"Thanks. I like to think so."

"Rebuilding a company from practically nothing, making a name for yourself in business. And as a woman, too. It can't have been easy."

"It's easier than it looks, to be honest. All you've got to do is think like a man, and if you look at the average man, it's not hard to think like them." She grinned. "That's what I said to Tabitha, when she used to come here moping about being cut out of the Furley inheritance. I really felt for her situation. The law of primogeniture is an absolute bastard, isn't it?"

"The law of what?"

"You know. Knob law. Firstborn son inherits. Firstborn daughter gets sweet Fanny Adams."

Penny frowned. "I thought the law of primogeniture had been rescinded? I read something about that."

"Only for the royals. The House of Lords prevented it from being extended to the rest of the British nobility." Sylvia barked with laughter. "Huh. I wonder why! But there's no point moping about being stuck in this medieval monstrosity of a country. 'You don't need everything dropped in your lap, Tabitha,' I said. 'That's the worst thing that can happen to you. That won't build character. Do your own thing. Think like a man and you'll make it in a man's world.'"

"Good advice."

Let's push my luck.

"I'm amazed you've done so much; it couldn't have been easy for a single mother."

Kit found herself on the receiving end of Sylvia's side-eye.

"It's not that hard. As I said, once you decide to think like a man, everything else falls into place. Having a kid's no bother when you rid yourself of that fantasy of motherhood that you have to be with them every step of the way."

They reached the door. Sylvia opened it with a smile.

"Why do you have to be there for their first steps? He won't remember, will he? Kids raise themselves – they find a way to survive. That's just nature."

At the front entrance, she shook hands warmly with both of them. Kit noticed that her handshake was firm and masculine, and as smooth and warm as Vera Braxton's hand.

"Say hi to Tabitha for me. I really feel for that girl. Younger brother inheriting the family business, just like me. But I was able to rescue mine. She's stuck with Archie, sadly. That's English feudalism for you."

* * *

They were back in the transit van, speeding away from Braxton Hall.

"What did you get?" Penny grinned. "I got a squirter."

"I haven't looked."

"Oh, go on. Have a peek."

Kit's hand snaked inside the bag, as if it contained a live tarantula. She turned the box, still inside the bag, so she could read it. "It says here that I've got a hen-night survival kit."

Kit flipped open the lid.

"It contains some lollipops shaped like penises. Some deely boppers with antennae shaped like penises. A silver balloon shaped like a penis. A sash with 'Bride to Be' on it decorated with penises… I think I'm detecting a theme."

Penny snorted with laughter.

Kit hurriedly changed the subject. "Did you see what was on the model railway?"

"Yes. God. I couldn't believe it, and I saw it with my own eyes."

"That was odd," muttered Kit.

"Are you not a bit spooked?"

"I was, but I'm not now."

"Why aren't you spooked? They've got *actual evidence*."

"Tiny toy figures are not *evidence*," snapped Kit. "Otherwise they'd have used *The Hobbit* Lego set as evidence to arrest Martin Freeman for stealing Gollum's ring."

She wrinkled her nose in thought. "If they still had the photos they used as reference, then perhaps there's cause to worry, I suppose."

Not that I care about most of the Furley Fanboys getting a taste of justice. But I don't want Binfire to go to prison. Does that make me a hypocrite? I don't really care if it does.

"Well, apart from us getting our goody bags, that visit was a whole heap of a waste of time."

"Was it?" said Kit.

"I thought it was. Do you think it wasn't?"

"I suppose." Kit frowned.

"Tell me it wasn't a waste of time. I could do with cheering up."

"I don't know."

"Do you think any one of them could be behind it? Nate? Sylvia? Vera? Or all of them?"

"I don't know."

"So, it *was* a waste of time."

"Maybe not. I think I learned something important, but I'm not sure what it was."

"Right."

"That's the annoying thing. I know when I've missed something important, but whenever I miss it, I don't realise what it is until something else turns up to tell me what I've missed."

"Great." Penny pulled a face. "I'll just call Mr Goldingay and tell him to wait until something turns up."

"Wait," said Kit. "I've got it. Those figures on that model railway? They prove that Jack Braxton knew what Roland Pendragon was planning. He knew in advance."

"Oh yes! It does! You're right! Do you think Jack Braxton was lying in wait for them, ready to defend his factory? And Roland killed him in a struggle?"

"I don't know."

"I don't know" is getting to be my catchphrase, thought Kit. *In recent days I've definitely said it more than "criminy".*

She glanced back at the immobile robot strapped to the floor of the van.

"I've just had another thought," said Kit.

"Is it about Braxton Hall?"

"No, it's about your boss Mr Goldingay, and his robot. He uses a computer monitor to look around him, doesn't he?"

"Yes."

"Well doesn't a computer monitor have a camera in it? Like a video feed for Zoom calls and things like that?"

"Erm. Does it?"

"Of course it does. Wouldn't that monitor have footage of what happened in the museum that night?"

"It was destroyed."

"Of course it was, but isn't everything in the cloud these days?"

"I don't know." Penny's eyes were fixed to the road.

"I'm surprised it didn't occur to Graham. He does run a media company."

"He gets all the computer stuff done for him by people on his payroll. Oddly enough, he's not very technically minded."

But you are, thought Kit. *I saw you put together a whole robot from scratch. You're very technically minded. So why did it not occur to you?*

Perhaps it did.

Then there was the familiar parping sound of the 'Penny Lane' horn solo. Penny's phone. Or to be more precise, Graham's phone.

The phone was attached to the dashboard, and Penny snaked out a fingernail to see what the message was.

"Shit. It's another poem."

She pulled the phone free of its clasp and tossed it into Kit's lap.

Kit picked it up and read:

Seven little figures
Roasting on a spit.
One had a meltdown
And then there were six.

Included was a gloomy photo of Lady Tabitha's action figure, strapped to a skewer. The figure was missing its lower right arm, and her lower leg was sticky-taped to her body because her upper right thigh was missing.

"Oh no," said Kit. "Here we go again."

Kit's phone trilled. It was an unknown number and a WhatsApp call. She accepted it and was surprised to see Lady Tabitha on her screen. She was dressed in her steampunk pirate costume, but without the coat. Just the mask with the eye patch, the big pirate shirt, waistcoat, baggy trousers and boots.

She looks amazing.

"Hi," said Kit.

"Hi, sexpot."

Once again, Kit could feel her face blooming into a delicate shade of pink.

"Um. Yes."

Lady Tabitha got tired of toying with her. "Are you with the others?"

"I'm with Penny Lane."

"I presume she got a WhatsApp too? A little rhyme and a photo of my doll attached to a skewer?"

"Yes."

"Well don't start dashing to its rescue. It's far too bloody late."

Lady Tabitha pivoted her phone to show her surroundings. She was in Furley House, in a large high-ceilinged room with black wooden beams. Shiny copper pots and pans hung from a rack above a heavy wooden table, at least twelve feet long, running through the centre of the kitchen.

She pointed her camera down to show Kit what was in front of her. On the big table was a baking tray with what, at first glance, looked like a giant fried egg. It was a flattened orangey-yellowy-white splodge. A skewer was lying across it, half-embedded in the ooze.

"We found it in one of the kitchen ovens. It had been put in at two hundred degrees. It didn't last very long, obviously. The whole kitchen stinks of melted plastic. We're probably doing our lungs a mischief just being here."

Reverend Bell wandered into the picture, breathing in sharply, as if inhaling the scent of a bouquet of flowers.

"Ah," he sighed wistfully, "the heady odour. Nothing like it. Acrylonitrile butadiene styrene with a hint of polyvinyl chloride... I always think I can smell strawberries."

Tabitha lowered her voice. "Reverend Bell has gone a bit weird. I think he's high on the fumes."

He giggled, off-screen. "Such a fruit basket of delight we have here…"

He wandered off.

"There's only one fruit basket around here," muttered Tabitha. "And it's not me."

39

They convened in the library: Matty, Kit, Binfire, Freya, Fenton, Vixy, Archie, Penny, Saskia, Reverend Bell and Lady Tabitha, who was once again lounging in the upper gallery like a rebellious cat.

"So, *no one* saw anybody go into the kitchen?" asked Kit, pacing around the perimeter of the room.

"I'm afraid not," sighed Archie. "The kitchen staff all have their lunch at two p.m. in the pantry, which is when, presumably, the perpetrator sneaked in. The oven was put on a timer, to activate at four p.m. And alas…"

Matty finished his sentence for him. "… and you don't have cameras inside the house."

"No, we don't. Damn shame."

"Oh yes, *damn shame*," repeated Matty mockingly. "What a *damn* shame!"

Archie looked hurt. "Are you making an insinuation?"

"Well, it's pretty obvious that whoever did this knew Furley House." He pointed at Archie and Tabitha. "Ergo, you."

Archie stood up. "I resent that insinuation!"

"Resent all you want, your lordship. I've got you bang to rights." He nodded to Penny. "Contact your boss, ginger, you can sack the lesbian. I've got this."

Penny groaned and rolled her eyes. So did Saskia.

"Utter poppycock," hooted Archie. "Why on earth would I want to ruin my own museum?"

"I dunno. Some kind of publicity stunt? You get in all the newspapers and this little place becomes more famous than Chessington World of Adventures?"

Archie was shaking his head. "I'm not sure publicity like this would prove to be very positive."

"I'd do it," Matty said. "Can you imagine it going viral?"

"That may be the case, Mr Kearney," sighed Archie. "But I'm not you. I'm not a 'shock jock', and I have no wish to go 'viral' as you would put it. This will not encourage anyone to come here, and it will probably put our insurance premiums up."

"Insurance! That's it!" Fenton snapped his fingers. "I bet you're in deep financial doo-doo. All stately homes haemorrhage money. Proven fact. You've done this to pull yourself out of a financial hole. Pretend the figures are destroyed, take the insurance money, and sell them on the dark web. It's perfect."

"You're even more stupid than you look," snapped Lady Tabitha from her perch. "Do you have any idea how ridiculous you sound. It makes no sense."

Fenton said: "It makes perfect sense."

Tabitha laughed. "Fraud always makes sense to a fraudster."

"You come down here and say that."

"Don't let her goad you, Fenton," said Vixy.

"Don't try and dodge the accusation, Dickless Turpin," said Matty. "Fenton's bang on the money. He's right, isn't he? Don't try to deny it."

Tabitha's eyes were still obscured by her steampunk goggles but her mouth was visible, and it twisted into a sneer. She aimed it down at Matty. "Tell me, little bro, what's the average running cost of this place?"

Archie frowned. "Um… About two hundred and fifty thousand a year."

"And how much income do we get from visitors?"

"Since the pandemic? Oh, we're back to about seven hundred thousand paying customers, fiver each for the house tour, thirty quid for the premium tour, that's about two million…"

"Plus revenue from the concerts, weddings…"

"Um. Oh. Well. That would put another ten million on top of that…"

"And from the estate? Forestry, livestock, hunting, fishing?"

"Another ten million."

"Exactly," she sneered. "And yes, Mr Kearney, I do know how much those figures are worth. As do all of us. Thanks to you. Would you like to tell us how much you auctioned your dolly for?"

Matty was stung. "I didn't sell it."

Saskia piped up. "But you did *try* to sell it, Matty. To fund your horror movie."

Matty looked daggers in Saskia's direction.

Saskia waved her hands in exasperation. "Well you *did*, Matty! It's not a secret!"

"But I didn't *sell* it, did I?"

"I know you didn't. But you *did* put it up for auction last month. Because I was *there*. You put it up for sale in Sotheby's last sci-fi memorabilia auction. You put a reserve price on it for ten thousand pounds?"

"Saskia, just… shut the fuck up!"

"Don't tell me to shut up." She held her hands up in frustration. "It doesn't matter whether I say it or not. It's obvious she knows. It didn't make the reserve price. The highest bid was one thousand pounds. So, going by that, the current market value of all those figures put together is five thousand pounds."

"Yep, five thousand pounds," repeated Tabitha. "Well done. I can see we ladies are the ones with maths skills here. So, we've got a possible insurance claim of a massive FIVE THOUSAND POUNDS, plus, perhaps, maybe, the chance of reselling them on the black market for another FIVE THOUSAND POUNDS. That's a whopping TEN THOUSAND POUNDS, which I'm sure you'll all agree, makes all the difference to a stately home with an annual revenue of twenty-two million pounds."

There was no response from Matty.

"Yes, me and my brother would certainly take the trouble to invite you all here, wine and dine you, go to the insane trouble of putting this museum together, and do all that to steal your stuff under your noses for the chance of making TEN THOUSAND POUNDS. I think you'll find it would be far less effort on our part if we just torched the whole museum for the insurance."

Matty glared up at her, then, defeated, he turned away.

There was a knock at the door.

"Come," said Archie.

Malcolm entered, holding a package on a silver tray. "This just arrived for you, sir, brought by courier."

"For me?"

"Yes?"

"Gosh." He took the padded envelope with childish wonder and read the label. "Archie Pendragon. Goodness. I don't get a lot of post for 'Archie', it's always 'The Marquess of Furley' or variations on that theme."

He ripped it open and slid out the contents. It was a shiny disc in a plastic case. PLAY ME was written with marker pen on the case, in fat, lazy capitals.

"Shit." Matty backed away and flattened himself against the wall. "It's from the nutter!"

Archie peered at the package. "Is this a CD or a DVD?"

Tabitha looked down at them. "It's a DVD. There's a DVD player in the museum. It's used to play that ghastly advert."

Archie plopped the DVD case into the hands of Reverend Bell, who looked at it uncomprehendingly.

"That's right, Reverend? It can play DVDs, right?"

Bell shook his head, as if waking up from a dream. "Yes. Of course. We need to go to the museum."

* * *

The museum had been thoroughly tidied up. Apart from the ruined pyramid in the centre, there was little sign of the break-in and burglary.

Everyone gathered around as Bell pulled the cover off a cabinet painted like a *Vixens from the Void* computer control panel, to reveal a box made from plywood and a DVD player nestling within. He ejected the DVD of the television advertisement, slotted in the mystery disc and pushed a button on the remote.

The screen flared into life, stuttering and wobbling – and showed exactly the same advert that had been playing on a loop.

"You just put in the same DVD, you arse," snapped Matty.

"I haven't!" protested Bell, waggling the disc. "I've got it in my hand! That's my handwriting right here, in marker pen!"

The picture went into a split screen with a man sliding onto the right-hand side, a moon-faced man in his forties, wearing a red long-sleeved T-shirt. He had a crewcut, which was his only distinguishing feature as his face was bland to the point of annoyance.

"My name is Kenneth Willoughby. I thought I'd introduce myself. Though some of you might know my name already."

They all looked at each other, mystified. "Any clue?" said Archie.

"Nope," said Fenton.

"Not one," said Matty.

Kenneth Willoughby continued, "You're probably all discussing whether you know me, and most of you are shrugging now. I hate that! I can just imagine you in my mind's eye, shrugging at one another with your blank looks. It drives me mad! I hate you all!"

He stopped and rammed an inhaler into his mouth, sucking deeply on it.

"Just who the fuck *is* this guy?" said Matty.

"Don't say that," said Binfire. "You'll just make him angry again."

"It's a recording on a DVD, you twat!"

On the screen, Kenneth Willoughby had finally calmed himself. He put his inhaler in his top pocket.

"I destroyed your dolls because of this – thing – playing beside me. You see this advert? You see the boy! The one who says, 'Not so fast, Medula! We have our laser cannon ready, and it can pulse with a death ray!'? That was *me*! I was that boy! I may have lost my hair and my rosy cheeks but that's me! That happy smiling child with the full head of blond hair. That advert – that was the last time I was *happy*!"

His face crumpled with rage. "That advert was my introduction to showbiz. It encouraged me to become an actor. And guess what? Spoilers! My life has been miserable ever since! I've spent my whole life working in pubs and doing terrible magic tricks at children's birthday parties, and the only acting jobs..."

He threw air quotes into the sky.

"... the only 'acting jobs' I've ever got in all those years have been Murder Mystery weekends, corporate training videos and 'ironic' re-enactments of that bloody *Vixens from the Void* advert!"

He lunged for his asthma inhaler again, moved it to his mouth but thought better of it. Instead, he used it to jab at the advert playing on the other half of the screen.

"You see that girl who's playing with me? You see her? She got a part on *Byker Grove* and she never looked back! She spent eight years on *EastEnders*! I bet no one ever looks puzzled in restaurants when she says, 'Don't you know who I am?' But it happens to me *all the time*!"

"He does go on, doesn't he?" muttered Tabitha.

"That's why I've done this. I've made it my ambition to

destroy all the dolls that made my life a misery. And I started with the most important ones of all. The rarest ones!"

He leaned into the camera until his face was a blur. "But I'm not without compassion. I'm going to give you a fighting chance to save the last doll. I'm going to send you instructions later. A place to go to, tomorrow. You'd better be there, or the last doll gets it, and the Ceremonial Range will be no more. Gone forever. You hear me? Gone! And I will finally be famous!"

The screen went dark.

"Oh my goodness," said Archie softly.

"Bloody hell," said Matty. "Is that who we're up against? An out-of-work actor? Is that it?"

The phones pinged again, delivering another message:

These are your instructions. You will go to the location I have just sent to you on Google maps. You will arrive at midday exactly, no earlier, no later. You will bring a suitcase containing five thousand pounds, in used notes.

The owners of all five dolls must be present. Matty Kearney, Fenton Worth, Lady Tabitha Pendragon and Ben Ferry. Penny Lane may stand in for Graham Goldingay. No one else is allowed to attend, except for Kit Pelham.

When the figure is delivered, one person will be allowed to approach and one person only. That person will be Kit Pelham. Only she will be allowed to check the merchandise. Once the merchandise is confirmed, another of your number will bring the money across and give it to me.

Do not deviate from these instructions or the deal is off.

Kit peered over Binfire's shoulder, reading the message.

"Me?" She was shocked. "Why does he want me to be there?"

"You tell us, Kitty Kat." Matty looked at her suspiciously. "What are you to this crazy thespian?"

A thought struck Kit. "Oh."

"Oh?"

"I *did* interview him once."

Everyone looked at her.

"You interviewed him?" spluttered Saskia.

"I interviewed *everyone* involved in the making of the Braxtons adverts for my podcast, *The First Cult is the Deepest*."

"Really?" Tabitha sounded amused. "You interviewed *child actors* who appeared in a thirty-second advert, because...?"

"I'm a bit of a completist," said Kit simply.

"Understatement of the millennium," said Binfire.

"They appeared in a terrestrial television broadcast related to the programme, ergo, they're in the extended universe of *Vixens from the Void*." She frowned. "Though, as far as I remember, Kenneth talked very fondly about recording the advert. He didn't seem angry about doing it."

"So, when did you interview him?" asked Saskia.

"It was via Zoom, so it was definitely during COVID. So, four years ago. July 2020 at a guess. Which isn't really a guess, because I know."

"Well, there's your explanation." Saskia flipped a murderous expression in the direction of Matty. "Four years is quite long enough to go from incredibly happy to incredibly bitter."

Reverend Bell struggled to his feet. He drew himself up to his full height and tapped his cane against his boot. In the last few hours, Bell had become something of a caricature of himself, tutting and fussing and adjusting his spectacles like an Edwardian patriarch. Kit eyed him warily.

I think he's heading towards a nervous breakdown.

"None of this is relevant, is it?" he retorted. "I think the most important matter to address is how to get hold of five thousand pounds by midday tomorrow."

Matty scowled. "We don't need the money, do we? We just go there with a suitcase full of shredded newspaper, and when he arrives – *if* he arrives – we kick the living shit out of him."

"I don't want to be a bore," muttered Saskia. "But he's just confessed and told us who he is. The police can track him down. We don't have to do anything."

Reverend Bell had the shining eyes of a fanatic. "Nevertheless, there is a chance to get this doll back intact and to apprehend this… this… *murderer* by our own hand and bring him to justice. I think we should go."

"You're not going anywhere, mate," snapped Matty. "Just the *owners* of the figures and the lesbian. Them's the rules."

Reverend Bell glared at Matty.

Saskia shook her head. "But you can't go with a suitcase full of shredded newspaper. Too risky."

"Why the fuck not?"

"Matty, no! It's obvious this guy has ways of finding things out. He seems to have eyes and ears everywhere. I'm sure if we try anything stupid, he'll know. There's no telling what he might do."

Penny was thinking. "Okay. How about this? I'll contact Mr Goldingay and see if he wants to put up the collateral. He can get the money transferred to my account, and I can go to the bank tomorrow morning."

"You'll do no such thing, my dear," retorted Archie. "As

I have said, I feel responsible for this mess. It was my notion to create a toy museum here and, thanks to me, you agreed to put your prized possessions here in my care. I will provide the money. I have the amount in my office. There is no need for you to fiddle around with bank transfers."

Binfire slapped his palms together. "Great. Now we're cooking with napalm."

* * *

Kit was about to close the door on her room when Freya poked her head around the door.

"Um. I don't suppose you've seen Matty's YouTube channel in the last few minutes?"

"No."

"Oh. Well, there's been an upload."

She held her phone out and Kit could immediately see the problem. There was a list of clickbait thumbnails, and the one at the top featured Kit's face, comically stretched into an expression of idiocy. The name of the video was WOKE-ATHA CHRISTIE HASN'T A CLUE!!!

Without asking, Freya pressed play, and there was a collection of screens arranged like a Zoom call. Matty was in one screen, a number of other men of similar age and similar unwise choices of facial hair were in the others.

"So, she's clumping around this old house, and all these dolls are showing up mangled to bits, and she's just stuttering and guessing and getting nowhere. It just goes to show that reputations are built on nothing."

One of the other men nodded. "What did she actually do in Brighton?"

"Solve that murder apparently. I don't know how. I guess she was just in the right place at the right time."

Another man chuckled. "Well she's a gay woman. If they just stand there and don't fuck up, the media just holds them up like they're some kind of goddess genius."

"Yeah." Matty chuckled. "And, in the meantime, yours truly is here, getting his hands dirty, putting the work in, being the hero."

There was a short burst of Saskia's footage. Matty dashing to the watercooler, only to have it blow up in his face.

"Woah," said a third. "That was some serious stuff. You're doing the business."

"I know. I'm doing a bit more than Kit fucking Pelham, I can tell you that for nothing."

The second one nodded. "Kit fucking Pelham. What is she even dressed as? Is that her image? I'm not getting it."

The third said, "She's doing the 1980s, right?"

"Yeah." The second one laughed. "Like there was so many great detectives in the 80s!"

They all laughed.

"I was gonna tell her." Matty chuckled. "I was gonna say, the thing is, lady, no offence, it's a nice effort but you look *nothing* like a typical 80s woman. If you ask the great British male and tell him to 'name an 80s woman', they wouldn't say Annie Lennox, or Princess Di, or even Wincey bloody Willis. You know what they'd say? They'd say Samantha Fox or Linda Lusardi. *They* were the 80s women. So, my advice to you is ditch the hat and coat, buy yourself a nice lacy teddy and get yourself a pair of tits."

"I don't see it happening," said the third one.

"No." Matty shook his head. "Let's be honest, she's a pretty difficult wank. No offence."

They all laughed.

40

Kit lay in her little room that night, duvet tucked under her chin, eyes open, staring at the blackness. She started off being furious about Matty's video, but then she was able to compartmentalise it, thrust it into the back of her mind. That was what she was good at. It was just a stupid piece of nonsense. The only people who would click on it were saddoes like him. Forget about it.

But she *still* wasn't able to sleep. And she knew why. She knew she was waiting for the click of the door, and the soft breath on her ear, and the warmth of Lady Tabitha's body against hers.

But she couldn't be *certain*.

Uncertainty usually irritated her, but this, this was a new feeling. The tension of not knowing what was going to happen sent her heart skittering in her chest. It reminded her of Milo's paws when he charged across her kitchen floor.

She hated herself for it, but she couldn't help comparing the smoothness of Tabitha's skin with Jackie's wrinkly edges. Kit never hid from the facts, and it was a fact that her recently estranged girlfriend had been nearly twenty years older than her, and she was facing up to the truth that maybe – just maybe – she'd got together with Jackie because she was subconsciously seeking a mother figure.

Then came the creak of the door, and the familiar silhouette of the woman who'd crept into her bed the night before.

"Hi," Tabitha whispered.

"Back again?"

"Can't keep away, can I?"

The bed lurched and Kit felt warm arms around her waist, exploring her hips and her belly button.

Kit flinched. She couldn't help herself.

"Are you okay?"

"Yes. No. I suppose I'm nervous about tomorrow."

"Why?"

"Kenneth Willoughby asked for me to be there. I didn't own a doll. Why does he want me there?"

"I don't know."

"It makes me nervous."

"You don't have to worry. I hear you faced off against a murderer once."

"Huh. I still get the sweats thinking about that."

"You don't smell sweaty. You smell lovely."

"It's just soap."

"Well, your soap smells lovely."

"Your soap smells nice too. I like the oranges."

"Thanks. He's just an angry dickhead. If he turns nasty, I'll be there to protect you."

"I feel better knowing that."

"I'm sure none of those other losers will. It's up to me to be the man."

Kit remembered Sylvia Braxton's words.

Think like a man and you'll make it in a man's world.

They fell silent, and the silence made Kit nervous, as it felt that something was supposed to happen, and she still wasn't ready.

Tabitha's hand advanced another centimetre. Now it was fiddling with the knot on Kit's pyjama elastic.

"Can I ask you a question?"

"If you want."

"Why did you and Nate Braxton split up?"

The hand froze, retreated to Kit's hip. Tabitha didn't speak for a while.

"I watched your Instagram video. I just wondered."

"Is this why you don't want to?"

"No."

"Because of me and him?"

"Not at all," Kit lied. "I really am quite nervous about tomorrow."

Silence. And then:

"I split up with Nate because he bored me. That's it. That's all. I got bored with him. I was looking for something different."

"Am I different?"

"I should say so."

"Different enough not to get bored with me?"

The arm around Kit's waist pulled her tight. "I think so."

"I like your arms," she said stupidly.

"Thank you."

"They're very strong."

"Thanks."

"In the videos, I saw you had lots of tattoos. The gravestone. The woman with the moustache. And there was lots of writing."

"I know. They're my tattoos. I know what they are."

"They looked very interesting. Do they mean anything?"

"No, Kit." There was a flavour of irritation in her voice. "They don't mean anything. Nothing about me means anything."

"Okay. But can I see them?"

"No. I told you. The light stays off."

"You said you'd think about putting the light on."

"I did. I thought about it. The light stays off. You're not ready. I'm not ready."

Kit felt things had suddenly got a bit sinister. Lady Tabitha obviously thought so too, because she said, in a softer voice, "I like you, Kit. I hope, whatever happens tomorrow, we see each other again."

"Yes, I'd like that too."

"Good."

"Maybe we can have a drink in daylight, and you don't have to wear your goggles, or the highwayman mask. I have a very swanky coffee machine here in my room we can use to drink coffee. They have pods of every kind for—"

Lady Tabitha kissed her.

"Shut up about your coffee pods."

"I'll shut up."

"Are you sure you don't want to do more than cuddle?"

"If you switch the lights on, then maybe."

There was a *hiss* from Tabitha, as she pushed breath through her teeth.

Stalemate.

"No can do."

"Okay."

"I'll go."

"Okay. Perhaps next time."

But Lady Tabitha didn't answer.

41

They held each other for about fifteen minutes, then Tabitha slipped out from under the duvet and went searching for her clothes. The moon was full and it bathed the room in a pale blue light, so Kit was able to watch as the Tabitha-shaped silhouette padded around the room, picking up items and putting them on.

Finally, she shrugged on her coat, pushed her feet into her boots, then walked back to the bed. Kit had no time for awkward goodbyes, so she feigned sleep, watching Tabitha advance through half-closed eyes. Kit could see Tabitha's goggle-clad head loom into her line of view, filling her eyeline. She was staring at Kit's face searchingly. Then she kissed Kit gently on the forehead.

"Good night," she whispered.

Kit fought the urge to pretend to wake up.

Tabitha clumped gently to the door, and there was the clatter of the latch as she left. Kit waited quietly, listening for the clump of her boots on the path, but instead she heard voices.

"You have to stop this." That was Saskia's voice.

"Stop what?"

"You *know* what I'm talking about."

"No, I really don't. Tell me what I've got to stop."

"Fine. If you want to play dumb, then I can't stop you. I'm just saying. Read your WhatsApp messages."

Kit struggled to her feet, but by the time she got to her little round hobbit window, the two women had walked their separate ways, swallowed by the night.

42

It was 11.30 a.m. when they assembled outside Penny's transit van. Penny, Matty, Fenton and Binfire were waiting to board. Archie, Reverend Bell, Vixy and Freya were there to wave them off.

"Is Graham accompanying us today?" asked Kit.

"Alas, no." A smile twitched on Penny's face. "He's still got his privileges revoked. Twenty-four hours. He'll get his phone – and his remote control – back tonight."

She reached into the van and pressed the satnav on the dashboard. "It says this windmill isn't far…"

"About ten miles away?"

"Ha. Yes."

"So, this place is a derelict windmill on the edge of Spalding." Kit frowned. "Perhaps it's some kind of joke at our expense. How he keeps making us tilt at windmills like Don Quixote."

"He can joke all he likes," muttered Matty. "When I get hold of him, I'm going to get the last fucking laugh." He nudged Kit. "Hey, have you seen my YouTube channel this morning?"

"No," snapped Kit. "I told you. I don't watch it."

"Oh. Well, you might have a look when you've got a minute. It might interest you."

"I don't have a minute. I'm too busy solving this mystery."

Matty laughed. "Sure you are."

Lady Tabitha was, as usual, standing a little apart from the group. Today, she was wearing old-style aviator goggles, a World War II German soldier's greatcoat, SS cap, boots, gloves and leather trousers. She was holding a tiny leather suitcase, filled with Archie's money, which seemed to fit right in with her outfit.

She looks... stunning, thought Kit. *A woman who seems to have sprung from my dreams. So, what is my problem? Is it Nate? Is it Jackie? Is it just me? That I can't cope with something nice happening?*

In an unspoken deference to Lady Tabitha's status, the others waited and watched as she climbed into the passenger seat and then they clambered into the back.

Vixy hugged Fenton tightly. "Good luck," she cooed. "I'll be here when you get back."

Fenton didn't look overjoyed at that prospect. He gave a tight smile and disappeared into the van.

"Good luck, everyone," cried Freya. Archie gave a half-wave, half-salute, and Reverend Bell pulled a handkerchief out of his pocket and waved it as the van made a three-point turn and headed for the front gates.

Penny drove out of the gates, around the Furley ring road, and soon they were on the road to Spalding.

The landscape was terrifyingly flat, untroubled by the tiniest hills. Just looking out of the window of the van, Kit could see the spires from the churches of five different villages. There were trees that were so far away they were tiny twigs on the horizon. Agoraphobia crept up behind her, but fortunately she was able to see it coming, as there was nowhere for it to hide.

The van continued along an endless ribbon of road, their journey only punctuated by the odd passing car or tractor. Penny abruptly yanked the wheel and they veered onto a pot-hole strewn track.

"Watch it!" yelled Matty.

"Sorry," Penny shouted into the back of the van. "You get lulled into a trance by these roads. It's easy to miss the turnings."

They bumped along for about a mile until the track dwindled to nothing. There was emptiness, apart from an empty car parked untidily by a ditch. It looked abandoned.

The windmill loomed up in front of them, surrounded by ploughed fields. Penny stayed in the van while Binfire, Matty, Lady Tabitha, Fenton and Kit got out and tottered like tightrope walkers along the muddy verge until they reached the huge, half-ruined structure. It had no sails or doors or windows, just cavernous holes in the surface, like a sandcastle eroded by the oncoming tide.

They waited.

Fenton shivered in his thin cagoule. "This is a waste of time. Look around us. Nobody's going to come here. There's no one within miles of this place." He pushed his hands deep into his pockets. "It's cold. Really cold. I never thought it could get this cold."

"It's the wind-chill factor," explained Kit. "There's no hills and valleys to slow down the wind."

"Thanks," he huffed. "Now I know why I'm cold, I feel a lot better."

"What's the time?" asked Tabitha.

Binfire looked at his chunky watch. "Five minutes to twelve hundred hours."

"Just say five to twelve, you freak," snapped Matty.

They looked out at the unending flatness. Not a flicker of movement.

Fenton sighed. "Let's give it ten minutes and then go."

"We'll give it as long as it takes!" snapped Matty.

Kit walked around the perimeter of the windmill, peering through the gaping blackened holes that used to be windows. She reached a point where the holes aligned and she could see right through the structure – and saw a faint cloud of dust in the distance. She ran around the rest of the windmill to where the men were mooching, vaping and scrolling on their phones.

"Someone's coming."

She pointed. The cloud of dust was larger, the size of a fifty pence piece.

They scrambled for a better look. Binfire looked at his watch again. "Twelve hundred hours precisely."

They watched intently as the cloud of dust metamorphosed into a vehicle – a white Ford van bumping along the dirt track. It was taking an age to get to them.

"Is that him?" Binfire frowned, staring through his binoculars. "It doesn't look like him."

"You'd think if he was the mastermind behind this, he'd be driving a flashier vehicle," said Fenton.

"That's probably what he wants the five grand for," muttered Matty. "A van that doesn't have 'clean me' written on the back."

The silence was broken by the familiar cacophony of chimes and noises, as everyone received another text. This time Kit got a message too.

Everybody stay back except Kit Pelham.

"What?"

"Looks like you're up, Kitty Kat." Matty tittered. "Every Hollywood movie ends up sidelining the men in favour of a Strong Female Character. Let's see how it works out in real life."

The van reached the end of the track and stopped.

A young man got out. Short dark hair, a trace of a moustache. He was wearing jeans, a polo shirt and trainers.

"Let's get him," said Matty.

Lady Tabitha held up a gloved hand. "That's not Kenneth Willoughby."

"So what?"

"So he's not here. Until he turns up, we do as we're told." Tabitha held up the suitcase. "Or no one gets anything."

The man cast an incurious eye at Penny, watching from her transit van. Then he went around to the back of his vehicle and opened the doors. He brought out a big cardboard box and held it carefully in both hands. He looked around the fields, slightly bemused, and walked to the end of the track.

He placed the box gently down on the ground, looked at his watch, and stood there, his hands in his pockets. He pulled out a vape and started puffing.

Lady Tabitha cocked an eye in Kit's direction. "Okay, you're up."

"Oh, yes. I suppose I am. Off I go."

Tabitha leaned over and hissed in her ear, "Don't worry, sexpot. I'm here."

Kit staggered out in the open, legs wobbling like a new-born fawn.

The man realised he wasn't alone and he turned and stared in her direction, shielding his eyes with his hand pressed against his thick eyebrows.

She reached him and they stood there, looking at each other.

"Hi there," he said.

"Hi," said Kit.

"I've got a package."

"Yes."

"Are you Kit Pelham?"

"Yes."

"I've got instructions to give this to you."

"Okay…"

"It's yours."

"Right."

"So then. There you go."

"Okay."

"Okay then."

Kit tried to find the right question to ask. "Do... you know *why* you're here?"

"Of course I do. I run a delivery service." He pointed to a cotton badge stitched to his polo shirt. It said DEL'S DELIVERIES. "I'm Del." He pointed again at the box. "So, this is for you."

"Yes."

"I've had instructions to wait until you've got it in your hands. So, there it is. If you want to put it in your hands, I can go."

Kit picked it up. "It's light."

He grinned. "It's a big box, but it feels like there's nothing in it, like one of your Amazon packages. I worked for them once. Never again."

He took a step back and gestured to her. "You can do the honours. Do you want a knife?"

Kit put it back on the ground and tugged at the packing tape. It peeled off in her hand. "No, I'm fine. There, look, I've opened it."

"Okay, great," said Del. "That's me done." He put a leaflet on the ground. "This is instructions for how to get to our website. If you leave some nice feedback and a five-star review that would be really cool."

He got in his van, and Kit watched it disappear down the dirt track in a cloud of dust.

"What do we do now?" said Fenton.

"Open it!" shouted Matty.

"It could be a bomb!" yelled Kit.

"Well, you wanted to be the hero of this particular story, Kitty Kat." He laughed. "Them's the breaks."

"Whoever told you you were funny," snapped Kit. "They have a lot to answer for."

"Hi there!" someone shouted.

Kit sprang to her feet and turned to see who it was.

Walking towards her over the field was Kenneth Willoughby, looking exactly like Kevin Spacey in *Seven* (1995). He was wearing red trousers, a red T-shirt and a red collarless jacket.

"Where did you come from, Kenneth? Have you been hiding all this time?"

"That's not important."

Kenneth's voice was calm, unnaturally so. So languid it was unnerving.

He's definitely doing a Kevin Spacey. This is getting ridiculous.

"We've met before," said Kit. "I interviewed you."

"What?"

"For my podcast."

"I— don't remember. So what?"

"Well, I just don't remember you being that bitter about doing the advert."

Kenneth looked stunned. His mouth opened and closed several times. "Well… Things change."

The collectors dashed out of hiding and charged towards Kit and the man. Penny had also left the van and was running across the ploughed field as quickly as she was able.

"Keep your distance!" Kenneth's hands were deep inside his pockets, and he waggled the corner of his jacket at them. "I'm armed. I've got a gun."

They stopped. He waggled his pocket at Kit.

"I suggest you open the box."

Kit flipped open the box flaps. It was full of dense packing paper.

She reached inside. There was nothing.

She rooted around inside the box. Still nothing.

Wait.

There was something tiny and hard in the bottom. It felt like a stone, or a top of a shampoo bottle. She pulled it to the top to look at it – and recoiled.

"What?" Matty shouted. "What?"

She looked back at him.

"What's in the box?" he yelled.

"What do you think's in the box?" retorted Kit. "Given we seem to be standing in a cosplay reconstruction of *Seven*?"

Kit held up the tiny object. It was the head of Velhellan, Matty's action figure.

"You bastard!"

Kit noted Matty's expression of outrage with some satisfaction. She couldn't help feeling good hearing his pain, after his shitty YouTube video. Then she rummaged around and felt more body parts at the bottom of the box. "There's more of her here. All in little bits." She tried to keep the smile out of her voice.

There was a strip of paper stuck to the inside flap of the box lid.

"And there's another rhyme." She read it out:

Six little figures
All newly arrived.
One got unboxed
And then there were five.

"You brought it on yourself. All of you," said Kenneth. "I want all your lives ruined by action figures, just as mine was."

"You bastard," said Matty. "You utter bastard. I'm going to tear your arms and legs off and stick *you* in a fucking oven."

"That advert was my introduction to showbiz. It encouraged me to become an actor. And guess what? Spoilers! My life has been miserable ever since! I've spent my whole life working in pubs and doing terrible magic tricks at children's birthday parties, and the only acting jobs…"

He threw air quotes into the sky.

"The only 'acting jobs' I've ever got in all those years have been Murder Mystery weekends, corporate training videos and 'ironic' re-enactments of that bloody *Vixens from the Void* advert!"

He waggled his pocket wildly in the direction of the collectors. "That's why I did all this. I've made it my ambition to destroy all the dolls that made my life a misery. And I'm starting with the most important ones of all. The rarest ones!"

"Oh frokk this, man," said Binfire, and he charged Kenneth, diving at his legs and performing a perfect rugby tackle. They crashed onto the ground, throwing up a cloud of dirt.

"Well done, Binfire, you crazy bastard!" yelled Matty. "Baggsy I get to kick him in the bollocks!"

"Arrgh! No!" screamed Kenneth. "Don't hurt me!"

"You should have thought of that before you blew up my Medula!" spat Fenton. "After you're done with him, I want a piece!"

"Wait!" shouted Kit. She stepped in front of Binfire and Kenneth, both still sprawled on the ground. Binfire had put his knees on Kenneth's legs and was pressing his hands onto his shoulders.

"You're hurting me!" wailed Kenneth.

"Good!" muttered Matty.

"Wait!" shouted Kit again. "This is wrong! It doesn't fit. I don't think he's behind this."

Kenneth seemed to agree, but he was only capable of going *hmmph*. Binfire had adjusted his posture so he could press a hand over Kenneth's mouth.

"I'm sorry, call me slow on the uptake, but I'm pretty positive he just admitted it," said Fenton.

"Exactly," said Matty, glaring at Kit. "Stop doing the Sherlock Holmes shtick, girlie! It's over! And you made absolutely fuck all difference to the result, 'cos he confessed anyway!"

"I know he did," said Kit. "He just confessed using *exactly* the same words as he did on his recording. *Exactly* the same. Word for word."

Fenton frowned. "So what?"

Binfire looked up from the dirt. "Are you saying he's a robot?"

"I'm saying he's an actor."

"He *is* an actor," said Fenton. "We know that."

"I *know* he's an actor. That's the point. Don't you see?"

"No."

"It's a performance. That's what I'm saying. He's saying lines. And when I confronted him about the interview he did with me, he didn't know what to say. Like he was trying to improvise but couldn't."

There was an empty silence, broken by Penny. "Shall we see what he has to say for himself? That seems the logical thing to do."

Binfire rolled off Kenneth, and Kenneth scrambled to his feet, coughing and spluttering and rubbing his thighs.

Matty advanced on him. "Okay, freako. Talk! And be quick about it. Did you destroy our action figures?"

"I don't know what's going on here," Kenneth said miserably. "I'm really confused!"

"Join the club."

Kenneth peered up at them, looking wildly from face to face. "Are you serious? Are you telling me that someone r*eally* ruined your *Vixens from the Void* action figures?"

Matty crossed his arms. "As you've just fucking admitted it, then you would know, wouldn't you?"

"But I was told to say all that stuff. It's part of the job!"

Kit frowned. "Told? By whom."

Kenneth held his hands up as a gesture of surrender. "Look, first off, cards on the table, most of what I said was true. I *am* Kenneth Willoughby, the actor." He looked at Kit. "You're right. I *was* in that advert for *Vixens from the Void* toys, but I'm not bitter..." He pulled a face. "Well, all actors are bitter, but I'm not *that* bitter... And I *can* do improv, as a matter of fact. I'm really good at it. You just caught me on a bad day. When you interviewed me, I told you the truth; I enjoyed doing the toy advert when I was a kid, and it did inspire me to go into acting. But I *like* being an actor. I don't regret it. Yeah, it's tough, and I don't get much work, but I wouldn't swap it for anything else. It's got such a variety, you see—"

"Cut the actor chit-chat bollocks," snapped Matty. "Do I look like I'm Graham fucking Norton?"

"Why are you out here in the middle of nowhere doing a Kevin Spacey?" asked Fenton.

Kenneth shrugged. "Well, as I said, I do a lot of Murder Mystery weekends. You know, taking on a role, guiding guests through a story. I got contacted via my website by someone who got me to record a video—"

"Yes, we saw your video," said Fenton acidly.

"Oh, did you? Did you like it?"

"Not really."

Kenneth frowned. "Damn. I knew I should have toned it down. Perhaps the asthma inhaler was a bit much. You don't strictly use them that way. I know. I researched it, but I did it anyway."

"Get to the point," snapped Fenton.

"Anyway, I got paid a hundred quid to do a self-tape and say those lines. Then I got another message which offered me two hundred quid to drive up here for a day's roleplay. I was even asked to shave my head, and I did, because when I get into a part, I really think myself into it, even when the part I'm asked to play is myself, but bonkers…"

He rummaged in his pocket and pulled out three crumpled sheets of paper. Kit took them and skimmed the contents. Sure enough, the script was very precise, and Kenneth had followed it to the letter.

DRIVE UP TO WEST DROVE.

MAKE SURE YOU ARE IN PLACE AT 11.00 A.M. AND PARK WITHIN SIGHT OF THE OLD WINDMILL.

1. PUT ON THE COSTUME IN THE SUITBAG.

2. THERE IS ALSO A TOY GUN IN THE FRONT POCKET OF THE SUITBAG. STICK IT IN YOUR POCKET AND USE IT TO THREATEN THE PLAYERS. DO NOT TAKE IT OUT OF YOUR POCKET AS IT LOOKS LIKE A TOY!

3. HIDE IN THE BACK OF YOUR CAR. **DO NOT BE SEEN!**

4. A DELIVERY MAN WILL ARRIVE AT THE OLD WINDMILL AT **MIDDAY** PRECISELY. WAIT UNTIL HE DRIVES AWAY, AND THEN APPROACH THE INDIVIDUALS OUTSIDE THE WINDMILL.

5. **REMEMBER!** YOU ARE PLAYING A BITTER VERSION OF **YOURSELF!** A VERSION OF KENNETH WILLOUGHBY, DRIVEN BITTER AND INSANE BY

YOUR FIRST JOB AS A CHILD ACTOR, ON THE
'VIXENS FROM THE VOID' TOY ADVERT. YOU BLAME
IT FOR RUINING YOUR LIFE.

6.   BECAUSE OF THIS, YOU HAVE STOLEN PRICELESS
ACTION FIGURES FROM THESE PEOPLE, AND YOU
HAVE DESTROYED THEM ONE BY ONE, AND NOW
YOU ARE GOING TO EXPLAIN EVERYTHING!!

KENNETH

I expect you're wondering why I did all this.

The second page was full of dialogue – exactly the words
Kenneth had spoken.

Kit passed them around to the others, who snatched impa-
tiently at the sheets.

Kenneth watched them warily as they perused the papers.
"I didn't know I was party to anything illegal. Honest. That's
all I got, a few messages to my website, and that document was
emailed to me, and three hundred quid paid directly into my
business account."

He nodded at the bits of paper. "The email address at the
top? That's where the correspondence came from. It's just a
jumble of letters and numbers. It's pretty generic."

"So I can see," said Kit. "I'm willing to bet that the bank
account that paid your fee was very recently set up, and I'm sure
it's now been closed."

Kenneth shrugged. "I don't know, but, yeah, thinking about
it, I wouldn't put it past her."

"Her?"

"Yes, I was hired by a woman. She called me on the phone

before we exchanged emails. She had a bit of a northern accent, but I think she was putting it on." He tapped the side of his nose with his finger. "Actors can detect these things."

"Did you get a name?"

"Of course!" Kenneth looked indignant. "All my accounts are above board. No telling when the taxman will come sniffing around. Let me see…" He looked at his phone. "I put all my VAT receipts on an app. It's the modern thing to do."

After sweeping his finger across the screen, he found the relevant document. "Yes, it was Sue Denham."

"Sue Denham?" muttered Fenton.

"Pseudonym," said Kit. "Sue Denham is a Pseu-donym."

"When did this Sue Denham last call you?" asked Penny.

Kenneth frowned. "The last time? Only a few hours ago. She called to make sure I got the instructions through the post. I told her that I had, and it was fine."

"What's the number this Sue Denham called you on?" asked Kit.

Kenneth handed over his phone and pointed at the screen. "That one. I labelled it 'Client'."

"You're wasting your time," huffed Matty. "You know that we were all sent texts from a phone that didn't take incoming messages. We tried to call the number, remember?"

Fenton's eyes widened. "Perhaps this number takes incoming calls?"

Kit didn't answer. She was already calling the number on Kenneth's phone. She held it to her ear. "It's ringing."

"Frokk!"

They were all frozen in a tableau, on a muddy track by a ditch and a burnt-out windmill. Everyone was focused on Kit with Kenneth's phone pressed against her ear.

"It's still ringing."

She activated the speaker to prove her point. The *brrrr-brrrr* crackled out of the phone and kept on going.

Kit looked at Kenneth. "Does she take a lot of time to answer?"

"I don't know." Kenneth shrugged. "She only rang me. And even then she only called me twice."

The *brrrr-brrrr* continued.

Fenton sighed. "It was a nice try. But I don't think she'd be stupid enough to answer her phone now. She must know that we've—"

"*Brrrr*-Yes?"

It was a male voice. Slightly out of breath.

Kit nearly dropped the phone.

"Hello?" she said cautiously.

"Yes? Hello?"

The voice sounded familiar.

"Um…" said Kit.

"Who is this?" The voice sounded annoyed.

Matty lunged forward and grabbed the phone out of Kit's hand. "Never mind who we are! You're not the one asking the questions! We're asking the questions! Who the fuck are *you*?"

"I beg your pardon?"

"You heard me, you sick fuck. Tell me who the fuck you are or I'll find you and I'll pull your head off, just like you did to my Velhellan."

There was a long pause.

Finally, the voice said: "Well really! That's not the way to talk to *anyone*. Let alone the Marquess of Furley!"

43

"We heard this phone ringing, and we went to find it," said the Reverend.

They were back at Furley House. Back in the library.

They had all taken their positions; Reverend Bell was by the mantelpiece, Fenton in the high-backed leather chair in front of the fire. Vixy was leaning on the back, nuzzling the top of his head. Matty was pacing the floor. Binfire was lounging on the chair by the side of Archie's desk.

Kit had found a new place to perch; she was on the library steps, flicking delicately through the first edition of the Agatha Christie mystery with the naughty title. Freya was just above her head in the gallery, looking down like Tabitha had before.

Lady Tabitha had not joined them; she had disappeared into the bowels of Furley House the moment Penny's transit van had parked in the drive. Kit wondered what was so urgent, particularly as they were on the verge of making a major breakthrough in the case.

Penny had also rushed out to make some phone calls, which did seem rather suspicious in the circumstances. Kit told herself not to be silly: this wasn't an Agatha Christie play, despite their mysterious antagonist's efforts to make it so. People had lives outside of the investigation; there was no law that said everyone had to assemble neatly in the same room for every development in the case.

They had, however, been joined by Graham's robot, squatting in the corner of the room. He had finally been given back his privileges, and his scowling face was once more on the computer screen.

Archie was sitting behind the desk, frowning at a mobile phone. He had propped it up against a pile of old books.

"We had to dash all over the house to find it, up and down the corridors," explained Reverend Bell to the others.

"We were sure it was going to stop ringing before we got to it," added Freya.

Archie continued the story. "Then I found it in a room upstairs, in an empty office that we don't use anymore because of the damp. I answered it, and lo and behold, I was talking to you."

Matty was trying to control his rage, with little success. He punched his hand with his fist. "It was an inside job the whole fucking time!"

"Logically, it always had to be an inside job," said Kit.

"'Logically, it always had to be an inside job.'" Matty mocked Kit's intonation. "Thanks for that lesbian intuition. Boy, she's really earned her detective fee, hasn't she, Graham?"

The robot whirred angrily in the corner. "Your observation is irrelevant, Matty Kearney. The most important thing is to find out who the phone belongs to."

"Exactly." Fenton nodded. "But it's locked and we don't have the code."

Kit carefully put the book down, got off the steps, picked the phone up and examined it. "There might be a way to open it."

"Oho!" Matty rolled his eyes. "Here comes more lesbian intuition from our genius lady detective. How are we going to open it?"

Kit didn't look up. She kept staring at the phone. "This has a facial recognition option. It unlocks when it recognises its owner's face." She pointed it straight at Matty. "Would you like to eliminate yourself from suspicion?"

Matty took several steps back, palms out, as if Kit had suddenly drawn a gun on him. He recovered his composure and took the phone. "No problem," he said, trying to sound casual. He held the phone up to his face, like he was taking a selfie. "See? Nothing happened. It's not mine."

"Don't pull any stupid expressions," said Fenton. "We all know that trick."

"I'm not pulling any expressions," retorted Matty. "See?" He put the phone up to his face again. "Definitely not me."

He passed it to Binfire, who grinned. "This is like *The Deer Hunter* with iPhones." He held the phone up to his face and struck a pose. "Not me."

One by one, they went around the room. Freya came down from the gallery to show her face. Nothing happened. Binfire helpfully pressed the phone against the robot's computer monitor, so that Graham could lean forward and allow his face to register on the screen. Nothing happened.

The phone stayed stubbornly locked.

"So, it doesn't belong to any of us," mused Reverend Bell, scratching his beard.

"Then we're fucked," growled Matty. "Unless our ace detective can rub her little grey cells together and find a way to open it."

Kit sighed. "I do have an idea. Give it to me."

Binfire handed the phone to Kit, who left the room. They could hear her boots clumping down the corridor and up the stairs.

"What the fuck? What the fuck is she doing?"

"She knows what she's doing," sighed Freya. "She *always* knows what she's doing."

After a few minutes, they could hear her boots clumping down the stairs, back along the corridor, getting slowly louder until she stood in the doorway. Her face was even paler than usual, and she looked close to tears. The phone was in her hand and she stretched her arm out as far as it would go, as if it was contagious.

"It's open," she said, in a very tiny voice.

"Well done, old girl!" said Archie.

"But how?" said Bell.

"Are you okay, pilgrim?" asked Binfire.

Kit didn't answer.

Matty snatched the phone out of her hand. "Good work, Kitty Kat. How do we find out who it belongs to?"

"I've opened the WhatsApp. Just look at the messages."

"Of course, yeah." He scrolled through the messages, outrage spreading across his face. "What the actual fuck?"

44

It was four hours later, and the sky behind Furley House was softening into a dark purple when the cars arrived. Moni, Ruth and Saskia had been summoned.

They were just about to enter when Penny met them at the door. Her face was deathly pale.

"What are you lot doing here?" she hissed. "I just rang each and every one of you and told you what they'd found out… and you've come *here*?"

"Saskia persuaded us it was time to face the music," Ruth said simply. "And I agree.'

"I'm actually looking forward to it." Moni grinned.

The women entered the library and were greeted by a wall of stern faces. Fenton, Matty, Reverend Bell and Archie had assumed their usual positions. Freya was still up in the gallery. Vixy was sitting at Fenton's feet. Graham's robot was back in the corner. Graham's head was close to the camera, his scowl was in extreme close-up.

"Kit, the floor is yours," said Archie.

"Thank you. So, I guess you're wondering why I called you here," said Kit. "We know who stole the dolls."

"We know. Penny rang us and warned us." Saskia sighed. She offered Matty a watery grin. "Sorry."

Matty glared at them. "What the actual fucking hell. What a bunch of fucking—"

"Be quiet, Mr Kearney!" snapped Archie, with a sudden surprising burst of anger. "You will be quiet! We're under my roof, and these are my rules. I decide how this goes. If you can't control your temper, I will get Malcolm to eject you from the premises."

Matty didn't respond. He threw himself into one of the leather chairs and folded his arms on his chest.

Archie waved his hand. "Kit, the floor is yours, as I said previously."

Kit held up the mobile. "As you probably know, we encountered an actor who was employed by our mysterious antagonist. We phoned the number on the actor's phone, and imagine our surprise when Archie answered it."

Archie raised his eyebrows. "Imagine *my* surprise, when I heard the phone ringing in the house. I found it hidden in a pot plant upstairs."

"We managed to open it, accessed the WhatsApp and we found a chat group labelled 'Babes in Toyland'."

"Look," sighed Saskia. "We didn't do anything."

"Don't make excuses," snapped Moni. "We have nothing to apologise for."

"Allow me to read some posts from the group." Kit cleared her throat. "'Hey, girls. You know that bloody toy museum thing coming up? I've got an idea for an amazing joke to play. It's going to really put the wind up the men'… And then there are the responses. 'Ruth B' says 'Oh wow, tell me more' and 'M.W.' says 'Anything to stave off the boredom' and then another from 'M.W.': 'If it makes Fenton shit his filthy pants, I'm up for it, exclamation mark, exclamation mark.'"

"His pants are *not* filthy!" said Vixy.

"They are. And you should know!" snarled Moni. "It's only the skid marks that hold his filthy pants together!"

"Be quiet, both of you!" retorted Archie.

Kit scrolled down. "Then it says, 'I reckon I can steal those bloody dolls from under their noses and hold them to ransom.

What do you think?' and 'M.W.' says 'WTF question mark, exclamation mark', and 'Ruth B' says: 'That sounds like the best thing ever. If you can do that you will never have to buy a drink again.' And then Penny joins the conversation and says: 'I'm in. I've been waiting for a chance to do something like this for years.'"

"Moni!" groaned Fenton. "How could you do this to me?"

"How could I not?" snarled Moni. "You deserved it, you fat loser!"

"I am very disappointed in you," muttered Reverend Bell.

"Now wait a second," said Ruth.

Matty erupted. "Well, if we're all chipping in… Saskia, you are a fucking *Judas*!"

"What do you expect, Matty? You ruined my scriptwriting career!"

"What? That was an accident!"

"The fuck it was! It's the way you always do things. Your masculine ego couldn't stand the fact that I was going to make it in Hollywood, and you were going to stay behind doing your pathetic YouTube videos!"

"No way!"

"Yes way! You're a misogynistic bigot!"

"Typical woman, always making generalisations. Not every white man happens to be a misogynist bigot!"

"I am not making generalisations! You *are* a misogynist bigot. You are the definition of a misogynistic bigot!"

"I'm only a misogynistic bigot because I'm reacting to the woke mob."

There was a whirring sound as Graham's robot lurched forward, gliding up to Penny.

"Did you help them?" he grated.

"Of course I did! Who did you think stole your doll in the first place? Of course I helped her!"

"You are fired, Penny Lane."

"Do you think I care?"

"I want to know why."

"Why? Don't you know?"

"No."

"Of course you don't. It was your Furley Fanboys who helped burn down the Braxtons factory and made my mum lose her job! She never recovered from it. Yes, she got another job, but she *loved* working there."

"The fire was an accident."

Penny spat, "As Saskia just said, 'The fuck it was.' It was the same as it ever was: boys with their toys playing stupid games. And it's always the girls that get hurt."

"You are extremely fired, Penny Lane."

Penny gave a harsh cackle. "Good luck getting your robot home."

She flicked a switch on the neck of the robot and it went dark.

"I've wanted to do that for ages."

There was a terrific *thud* which echoed around the room. Archie had pulled out a baseball bat from the umbrella stand and brought it down on his desk with incredible force, embedding it in the leather top and splintering the mahogany frame.

"Be QUIET!" he roared. "I order you all to BE QUIET! I want to know how this escapade transpired, and we will get nowhere by arguing like this!"

"Let me speak," said Ruth. "Please. I want to say something."

Archie nodded. "You have the floor."

Ruth stepped forward, putting her hands behind her back, marshalling her arguments like the experienced lawyer she was.

"If you read those messages, you will see who it was who suggested kidnapping the dolls and holding them to ransom. Not Penny, not me, not Moni, not Saskia. We all thought it was a fun idea, yes. We've been sick and tired of the waste of time and expense…" She directed an icy glare at her husband. "And yes, darling, I know you've done all the work on the toy museum without pay. Do you *really* think I don't know when you're lying?"

"I did…" Reverend Bell gave up mid-sentence. He was bang to rights.

Ruth continued, "So, when she told us what she was planning, we thought it was a great wheeze, but we did *nothing* to help her."

"Except me," snapped Penny.

Ruth grimaced. "Except Penny. And when the toys started getting broken, we were assured *on her life* that they weren't the originals. You can see that on the WhatsApp messages."

"But the museum was *vandalised*!" said Freya from her perch. "That's more than just theft. That's a crime. You should have told the police who was responsible when you had the chance."

This time it was Saskia who spoke. "It was her home too. We didn't want to get involved in this feud with her brother."

"And when the dolls started getting destroyed?"

"Ruth's telling the truth. We convinced ourselves that she was destroying fakes. We knew it was getting out of hand. I asked her to stop it."

"You know all this," Ruth said. "You've *seen* our WhatsApp conversations. You can see what we said. We *all* told her to stop. We did nothing to help her. She *said* they were fakes. She said they *looked* like ordinary *Vixens from the Void* dolls to us, just with bits added."

Reverend Bell's face was chalk white. "I don't believe it," he spluttered, his voice shaking with rage. "After all I've told you about the importance of these figures. The *uniqueness* of them. The book I wrote about *Vixens from the Void* merchandise…

You couldn't even tell the difference between ordinary action figures and the Ceremonial Range?"

"Not really," said Ruth.

"But the capes! The die-cast metal breastplates! They were completely different to the standard line. I told you!"

"Sorry, darling. I try to listen to you. But you're just too boring."

Reverend Bell clutched his heart and sank back in his chair. He groped for the whisky decanter and poured himself a stiff drink.

"You…" hissed Fenton with cold fury. He pointed at his wife. "You… You could have prevented the murder of my Medula!"

"Yes, I could have, couldn't I?" Moni smiled. "And now I know it was the real thing, that gives me a *warm* feeling inside. Sitting back and watching someone else murder the *REAL* woman in your life, and not to have to lift a finger. God must have been smiling down on me this week."

"Fenton, I *told* you you should have left her ages ago," squeaked Vixy. "I told you. She's just a very nasty person."

"Yes, you should have left me." Moni pouted, mocking Vixy's voice. "Do as she says, Fenton. Leave me, divorce me!" She laughed. "Don't you see? Divorce me, he gets nothing, you little tramp! The shop's in a prenup! The only way he gets anything is if I die, and I'm changing my will as soon as I possibly can – you can count on it!"

Fenton snapped. He lunged for her; arms outstretched. Fortunately, Binfire was next to him and dived for his legs, wrestling him to the ground.

While Binfire struggled with a flailing and wailing Fenton, Reverend Bell started laughing hysterically and propelled himself out of his chair. He went to the umbrella stand and grabbed a hockey stick. He advanced on his wife, waving the stick wildly in front of him like he was scything wheat. He managed to give Ruth a hefty blow on her shoulder before Binfire let go of Fenton and launched himself at the Reverend. He grabbed his waist, holding him up so his legs whirled helplessly in mid-air.

"Jesus, guys, have some respect," muttered Binfire.

Binfire dragged Bell back to his chair and threw him on it, pressing a hand on each shoulder. Fenton started to lever himself off the floor, but Binfire planted a boot on his back, pressing him down so his whimpers were muffled by the fireplace rug.

"Wait! WAIT!"

Archie was at the door, his baseball bat raised.

"I will not let this descend into fighting. We're not done here yet!"

As if on cue, the door clicked and slid open. Lady Tabitha was in the doorway, back in her space highwayman outfit.

45

"What's going on?" she said. "Malcolm said you wanted to talk to me."

"Ah, here she is!" Matty gave a savage grin. "The dandy highwayman behind the robbery. The mastermind behind it all."

"What?"

"Don't play dumb, girlie. We found your phone, there's no point denying it."

Tabitha looked confused. "What are you talking about? What phone?"

"This is your phone," Kit said, holding it up. "The one from which you texted Penny and told her to steal Graham's doll from his collection and mail it to a PO Box."

"Woah! Back up! That is NOT my phone! You are *not* pinning this on me!"

"It *is* your phone," sighed Kit. "I opened it using the facial recognition system. I opened it using the big photo of you hanging in your bedroom."

Archie sighed. "Oh, big sis. I can take almost anything from you, but not this…"

"I didn't DO anything, Archie!"

"The game's up, Tabitha," said Saskia. "They found our WhatsApp messages."

"There's no point playing dumb. We've all admitted it," added Ruth. "Now it's your turn."

Moni rolled her eyes. "Come on, lady."

"I swear. I don't know what you're talking about."

"You sent us all WhatsApp messages," said Penny. "Telling me to steal Graham's doll."

"I didn't send ANY WhatsApp messages. Can't you see I'm being framed?"

"By who? Who would want to frame you?"

"Lots of people!" She angrily pointed at nothing in particular. "Nate! Nate Braxton! He's still hurting from when I dumped him! It could be him!"

Archie shook his head sadly. "You're not pushing the blame onto someone else. Not this time. If it was just between us, I might be able to keep the police out of this, but sadly, no one else here is quite as forgiving."

Matty folded his arms. "Too bloody right, I want the police to throw the book at you." He spun a murderous glance around the room at Penny, Saskia, Moni and Ruth. "At *all* of you fuckers."

Tabitha started to run, but not away, not to the door.

Towards them.

They didn't know what she was doing until she sprinted past them, jumping into the air and planting her boots firmly on the library ladder. The momentum sent it skittering along the shelf and, as it glided to the rear of the library, Tabitha was already clambering up the steps and she vaulted herself onto the gallery, landing on her feet like a cat.

She elbowed Freya to one side, who slammed into a book-shelf with a cry, then she started running again, arms and legs pumping, boots thudding above their heads and straight towards the arch of the pretty stained-glass window.

"No! Please, *no*, not *another* window," groaned Archie.

Tabitha held her hands in front of her face and launched herself through. The image was frozen in Kit's mind. Tabitha spread her arms wide as she floated up into the night, looking like Adam Ant in his 'Prince Charming' video.

No. Not like that.

No, floating in the air, in her antiquated highwayman clothing, she looked more like a *ghost*.

And then she was gone.

PART TWO:

TEN LITTLE FIGURES

46

Binfire looked up at the ruined window.

"I bet she must have half-climbed down from that tree, dropped the rest of the way, and used that bush to cushion her fall."

Archie, Fenton, Matty, Reverend Bell, Binfire, Kit and Freya had rushed outside to intercept her, but Lady Tabitha was nowhere to be seen. There was only a crushed bit of hedge and a crazy-paving pattern of glass fragments on the terrace, twinkling in the moonlight.

They were staring at each other, bathed in the faint glow that shone through the gaping hole in the library window, when they heard the sound of a powerful motorbike roaring into the distance.

Matty's voice was first to be heard. "Whatever she did, she's gone. That posh bitch. It was her all along."

Archie's face looked as shattered as the window. "I can't believe it. I know she resented me. I didn't know how much."

"Yeah, you can't pick your family, can you?" That was Binfire.

Kit was only half-listening to them. It all seemed a bit surreal.

Tabitha's the obvious suspect. She did it and it's as simple as that. No ghost of Furley House. Nothing to do with the mysterious room full of freshly bought suits and the unused toothbrush and the jar labelled NATE. Nothing to do with Jack Braxton's death.

Every piece of evidence pointed right to her and I didn't want to know. Perhaps because it was TOO obvious.

Or perhaps it's simpler than that. I just didn't want it to be her.

"Oh well, Kitty Kat. Looks like you failed." After this final jibe, Matty trudged back into Furley House. The others followed, leaving Kit with her two Doctor Watsons.

Binfire came over and clapped her heartily on the shoulder. "You didn't fail, pilgrim. You found out whodunnit."

"Exactly," added Freya. "That's a win in any detective's book, isn't it?"

"But that wasn't my job, was it? I was hired to stop a maniac before all the dolls got broken, and she broke them all. So I failed."

Binfire shrugged. "Hey, if you want to be *pedantic*."

Kit gave him a look.

"Hey, what am I saying? You *always* want to be pedantic."

They trudged back inside the house. Kit followed but someone grabbed her arm.

She flinched, wriggled out of the unseen person's grip, turned, and found the crazed eyeballs of Reverend Bell boring into hers.

"They're not just action figures, you know?"

"No?"

"No."

"What are they?"

"They're alive."

"Alive?"

"Alive with dark magic. They're cursed."

"Is that something a man of the cloth should be saying?"

"You don't work in my profession without acknowledging the presence of evil. And they *are* evil. Don't you see?"

"Not really," said Kit gently. "Why don't you explain it to me?"

"Isn't it obvious? I broke the first rule of toy collection: I touched the mint-in-box figures. You're not supposed to do that. I opened their boxes and I ran the tip of my finger along their little plastic heads. I disturbed their slumber, like Howard Carter did when he entered Tutankhamun's tomb. And now they visit retribution on the sinners. Graham, Matty, Fenton… And now the daughter of Roland Pendragon. His sins are passed down to her. That's how it works."

"That's ridiculous."

"They all covered up a murder. Jack Braxton. *I know.* They all stood by and let the guilty men go free. And now look at them. Their loved ones are in pieces. And I found the truth and I did nothing. And now I'm affected…"

His eyes glittered with joy and madness.

"… and the retribution won't end there. Worse things are to come. They will lose more of their loved ones…" He gave a sly grin. "And Binfire. He will be the worst affected. He killed Jack Braxton. He confessed to me, in the back of his van, when he was concussed. He said Jack Braxton deserved to die."

Kit felt a stone plunge into the bottom of her stomach.

"He'll lose everything now. Watch yourself. Watch out, Kit. Watch out for yourself. It's coming. Retribution is coming…"

Kit almost ran back into the house.

* * *

It was late in the evening. Everyone had left apart from Kit's friends, Archie and Penny. Penny switched the robot on. Lights flickered into life but the screen remained blank, showing that Graham was not at home.

She sighed. "Archie, I don't suppose… that I can stay one more night? I've agreed to take the robot back to London. It's my last act as Mr Goldingay's employee."

"Do as you wish, Penny," said Archie, not unkindly. "After all, you're doing me a favour by taking that machine away. I have no wish for it to be left on the premises."

"Thanks." She gave an embarrassed smile and pulled out the remote. She wiggled a toggle and guided it slowly out of the library and down to the stables.

Archie turned to Kit and gave a slight bow. "Thank you, Kit, for getting to the bottom of this mystery for us. I can't claim to be overjoyed at what you've uncovered, but I'm indebted to you for resolving it."

Kit didn't argue. She was still thinking about Reverend Bell's words.

"Thanks."

"Naturally, you're all welcome to stay for another night."

47

Kit was in bed when her phone rang. No caller ID. Her first thought was that it might be Jackie, trying to fool her into picking up. She had left a dozen messages since they'd broken up, and Kit refused to listen to any of them.

The cringing mouse part of her that craved familiarity urged her to respond. *Your new love hasn't turned out to be a good long-term prospect*, it hissed. *You might as well go back to the old one. She might be controlling, petty and almost two decades older than you, but at least you'll have SOMEONE.*

She answered it.

"Hi, sexpot, it's me."

It was Tabitha.

"Oh…"

"Look, I know I'm probably not your favourite person right now, but I just want you to listen to me."

There was silence down the phone.

"Kit, are you still there?"

"Yes."

"You weren't saying anything."

"I know. That was me listening to you."

"Oh. Look. I'm just telling you that phone you had in your hand? That wasn't my phone. I'd never seen that phone before. I've been framed."

"You said."

"You do believe me, don't you?"

Kit hesitated.

"Don't you?"

Kit felt like she was in a time loop, but not an exciting one with a cliffhanger in which the hero's spaceship exploded over and over again. This was a time loop in which a domineering girlfriend forced her to take a loyalty test.

"I'd like to believe you," Kit said slowly. "But, to be honest, I feel betrayed right now. I feel you've made a fool of me."

"Those are feelings…"

"But I also have to look at the *facts*. And I don't know you well enough to say, hand on heart, that I believe you."

"Kit…"

"You have to agree the evidence is overwhelming. You had the motive – you were bitter about not inheriting the estate and you wanted to hurt your brother – and you had all the opportunities. You had everyone's phone numbers because Reverend Bell gave you and your brother a contacts list of all the guests. You knew the layout of the grounds. You were already living in the house, so you could prepare everything beforehand. There's no one else it could be."

There was a sigh.

"I know I'm in the shit. Which is why I need your help."

"I don't know what I can do."

"I'm going over to Braxton Hall *now* to have it out with Nate. I'm sure the little turd's behind it. I bet he's got someone working at Furley House who passed the phone numbers on to him."

"It's the middle of the night."

"Exactly. The best time to catch him off guard. Come with me."

"I don't think I should. I was asked to leave the last time."

"So? You'll be with me. I'll deal with him."

"He can still make a complaint to my boss. I can't lose the *Vixmag* job. That's ninety per cent of my income."

Kit heard a very long, very elegant sigh. "You are a little mouse, Kit Pelham."

"I know."

"Okay, I'll go alone. I'll prove to you I'm innocent. Okay?"

"I would like that."

The last four words just tumbled out of Kit's mouth before she could stop them.

"Good. Then I'll try not to let you down. Promise you'll stay until I give you the evidence. Do you promise?"

The phone went dead.

48

"Come on, pilgrim, wake up!"

Kit struggled into her Furley House monogrammed dressing gown and opened the door. Binfire and Freya were there, wearing identical dressing gowns.

"Sorry to wake you," Freya trilled helplessly. "But…"

"But I just got a WhatsApp message," Binfire said grimly. "You'd better look at it, Kit."

Kit. He never calls me Kit. It's always pilgrim or Captain Kit, or something like that.

Has Reverend Bell gone to the police? Is Binfire getting arrested?

He held up his phone. The photo was of an unconscious woman in a steampunk space highwayman costume. She'd been gagged and tied up. Her knees had been pulled up to her chin as she had been stuffed inside a cramped space; from what little Kit could see it was probably the boot of a car.

And there was a rhyme.

Five little figures
Knocking on my door.
One knocked herself cold
And then there were four.

Someone bustled across the courtyard towards them, also clad in an expensive dressing gown. As the figure got closer, it was bathed in the pool of light cast by Kit's doorway. It was Penny. She was holding her phone.

"You got the same message as Mr Goldingay?"

Binfire nodded. "Yep."

"I guess all the collectors got a message. Same as before." She held up a phone. "Is it her? Is it Lady Tabitha?"

"Who can be certain with those goggles on her face?" said Kit. "But, yes, it could be her."

"It's sooo her," said Freya. "I know it. She's in danger."

Binfire stuck his chin out and slapped his fist into his palm. "We'd better go and debrief Archie. He's not a collector. He might not have got a WhatsApp."

"No need," came a voice. "I'm fully appraised of the situation."

Archie strode towards them, fully clothed in his tweeds and plus fours. His sensible shoes echoed around the courtyard. "I was working in my office when I got phone calls from Mr Worth and Mr Kearney. They sent me the photo in question. I thought I would pop down here to see if my guests were getting agitated." He smiled. "Looks like I was right."

"Shouldn't we phone the police or something?" said Freya.

"I don't think so, my dear." Archie sounded grim. "I'm sorry, but this photo is obviously posed. My dear sister is playing silly buggers again."

Kit frowned. "Are you sure?"

"How can it possibly be anything else? Thanks to you we know for a fact that she was behind it all. Ergo, she was the one sending the photos and the ridiculous rhymes. No, this is yet another stunt to get attention and remind us how she fooled us all good and proper. I'm sure this is not sufficient to concern the police, certainly not after the last few times we've troubled them. I doubt they'd take this as anything other than a waste of time."

"Perhaps you're right," muttered Kit.

Archie shook his head ruefully. "I'm starting to regret persuading the others not to press charges. It seems Tabitha will never learn her lesson." He held up his hand and waggled his fingers. "Anyway, goodnight, everyone. I trust you'll be on your way after breakfast."

"Yes," said Penny.

"Yes," said Binfire.

"Yes," said Freya.

"No," said Kit.

They all looked at her. She felt very uncomfortable.

"I'm s-sorry. But… Tabitha phoned me this evening before I went to bed."

Penny looked shocked. "What?"

"Really." Archie's expression was inscrutable.

"She said she was innocent."

Archie raised his eyebrow.

"I know, I know, weight of evidence and all that. But she was adamant and she wanted me to believe her. Anyway, she made me promise that I wouldn't leave until she cleared her name."

"Woah," said Binfire.

Freya sighed. "That's sooo romantic."

"So, I'm staying for a bit longer. You two don't have to stay here. You can go back to Brighton. I made the promise, not you."

"All for one and one for all, pilgrim."

"As I just said, that's just sooo romantic. I'm definitely staying."

"Fair enough." She turned to Archie. "If you know of any good B&Bs around here, then can you point us in the right direction?"

Archie shook his head, smiling. "Alas, I think you're on a fool's errand. If you're committed to staying until my big sister proves her innocence, I fear you'll be here when Furley House

270

crumbles to dust. But, if you wish to stay for her sake, I wouldn't dream of letting you stay anywhere else but here as long as you like, gratis. And that goes for any time you wish to come to Furley House. As I say, I am indebted to you and your friends."

He held his arms out, as if expecting a hug. Kit froze to the spot. Thankfully Freya was used to these awkward moments, and she smoothly stepped between Kit and the Marquess, intercepting Archie's hug with enthusiasm.

"Thank you sooo much."

49

Saskia nosed her little Tesla into the parking space and pulled her bags of groceries from the passenger seat. She walked up the path, wrestled the key out of her jeans pocket and almost fell over the threshold of the door in relief.

It was Saskia's habit not to do long motorway drives. She was a nervous driver, so she used A roads and made frequent stops along the way. Their 'Babes in Toyland' WhatsApp discussion group had proved ultimately embarrassing, but before that it had proved invaluable. Saskia couldn't remember who recommended the Airbnb in Oundle when she'd asked the group about good places to stay, but it had been a real find. Just a few miles from Furley, it was clean and dry, with a cosy wood burner and a dinky little garden. A perfect place to hide out for a few nights before the long drive home.

She was glad to be out of Furley House. If she was honest, the events of the last few days had severely rattled her.

It was only meant to be a prank! That's what Lady Tabitha had said!

As soon as she'd surveyed the wrecked toy museum that first night, she knew Lady Tabitha was taking things too far. She should have said something right then, pointed the finger, but, hey, it was Lady Tabitha's family home. She was entitled to do a bit of self-vandalism, right? But she'd said nothing, and she'd been happy to train her camera phone on the watercooler, so Tabitha knew when to set off the explosives. And, after that, she'd been a willing accomplice after the fact.

No going back.

And the worst thing? It had given Matty the moral high ground.

The drive to Furley railway station hadn't been pleasant. Matty had sat sullenly in the passenger seat, emitting the occasional, "Fuck."

When they'd arrived at the station, he had glared at her. "So, this is it, yeah? You cook up this plan to humiliate me, destroy my property…"

"It wasn't my plan—"

Matty had shouted over her. "*You cook up this plan to destroy my property…* And now you've had your fun, you just dump me in the middle of nowhere? Wham, bam, thank you, mister?"

"There's a train to London in fifteen minutes. I can see the platform sign from here."

"You dump me on a train, can't even drive me home, after all that you've done?"

"I don't want to be in this car with you for two hours. You get that, don't you?"

"Oh, I get that. Guilt is a terrible thing."

"Get out."

He'd sighed and shaken his head. "Look, I've hurt you, you've hurt me. All's fair in love and war. Let's call it quits and start again. You don't have to go back to America. We can just reboot and carry on."

"You don't get it, do you? God, I wish it *had* been me that vandalised your dolly. Perhaps then you'd have got the message."

"You don't mean that."

"I don't mean it? This. This is what I mean."

She'd opened the car door and stalked angrily around to the rear, pulling open the boot and dragging out Matty's holdall and his rucksack, then she'd hauled them onto her shoulder and carted them to the middle of the car park. Then she'd come back to the car and wrenched the passenger side door open.

"Out."

"Hey."

"Out, or I drive my car right over your shit. I know you've got your laptop in there, and don't think I won't do it."

"Fuck you!" Matty had scrambled out of the car and dashed to rescue his things.

She hadn't looked back when she'd roared out of the car park, but she had caught a glimpse of Matty furiously giving her the finger in the rear-view mirror.

Perhaps, if she hadn't been in so much of a rush to get out of there, she might have seen Matty dash to the taxi rank and throw his stuff in the back of a cab, pointing at Saskia's Tesla in an obvious 'follow that car' gesture.

But she hadn't, and when she emptied her groceries into the kitchen cupboards, she thought she was completely alone.

But…

Was there a flash of movement in the garden?

She slid open the screen door and poked her head out, but there was nothing to see. But there *had* been someone watching her.

She was sure of it.

* * *

Furley was a very charming market town. From the waist up. The upper floors were a charming collection of dark timber frames, leaded windows and ornamental clocks. Underneath, there was a less charming assortment of betting shops, charity shops, pound shops, coffee shops and mobile phone repair shops.

It was a fine summer morning as Kit wandered along the high street, looking for a Marks & Spencer. She had only packed for the weekend and she was becoming dangerously short of underwear. Embarrassment prevented her from presenting her knickers to the Marquess of Furley and asking him if he had a washing machine – and she had a suspicion it was only a fifty-fifty chance that Archie knew what a washing machine was. So, buying more pairs seemed the only option.

She found a branch at the bottom of the street, and having bought several packs of three, wondered what she could do now. Binfire had given her a lift into town and gone off in search of a fabled second-hand record shop that, legend had it, had an unrivalled collection of The Velvet Underground bootlegs.

They'd arranged to meet in an hour and it had only taken her less than ten minutes to get her pants.

What to do? Perhaps wander down the high street, pop into all the charity shops and arrange all the books in release order? Or buy a cup of coffee in Costa and stare at it until it grows cold? The possibilities were endless.

She stared in the windows of an art gallery that specialised in local artists. She looked at her shadowy reflection, peeking between the insipid watercolours – and she saw another face, superimposed on her own.

Staring at her. A face wearing a protective COVID mask.

She turned. There was no one behind her. She looked around. The street was very quiet, as were most high streets these days. Just a few buskers howling into the abyss, and a multi-coloured stall selling artisanal cheeses.

Who was it?

Lady Tabitha of course.

Archie's right. That photo was staged. Lady Tabitha is playing silly buggers. She's using me and abusing my trust. Now she's stalking me, so she can laugh at me. Revel in my confusion.

She was walking back down the high street, looking for the lane to cut across to the car park and Binfire's motorhome when she looked back and realised why she hadn't seen the watcher behind her. The watcher had just emerged from *inside* the shop. The watcher must have been staring *out* at Kit through a pane of smoked glass.

Kit dodged into a doorway and peered around the corner.

The watcher walked further down the high street and Kit pressed herself further back into the doorway. Then she became aware of a sickly, pungent stench in her nostrils. And she started to gag.

"What are you doing?"

There was someone behind her. She jumped. It was Binfire.

"Why are you skulking in the doorway of Lush, pilgrim?"

Kit realised that she was indeed standing outside a branch of Lush, and the smell was the choking aroma of ten thousand smelly soaps. She'd often wondered how the staff coped without gas marks.

Binfire continued, "It's nothing to be ashamed of, buying soap. I've done it once or twice myself."

"I'm hiding because someone's following me."

"What? Where?"

Binfire was instantly alert. He adopted a crouch position and peered out into the high street.

Kit peered too. "They seem to have gone."

Binfire walked into the middle of the street and put his binoculars to his eyes. "What did they look like?"

"Shapeless grey sweatshirt with hoodie, COVID mask, sweatpants. Trainers…"

"Like they were trying to hide their identity?"

"Exactly."

"Man or woman?"

"Couldn't be sure."

"Could it be Lady Tabitha?"

"Again, couldn't be sure."

He surveyed the street. "Well, they're gone now."

Kit sighed. "If it is Tabitha, then she's probably just amusing herself."

"Perhaps, pilgrim. Let's be on our guard, just in case."

50

Kit and Binfire walked back to the motorhome, looking suspiciously around them as they went.

Freya was standing outside the motorhome, looking agitated. When she caught sight of them, she rushed to meet them, her fairy skirt rippling as she ran.

"I just got a call from Vixy!" she wailed. "We have to go to Peterborough *right now*!"

Binfire's phone chimed. On it was a picture of an unconscious Moni, trussed up and lying on the floor of Fenton's shop, The Battlestore Galactica.

And, of course, there was a rhyme.

Four little figures
With a lifetime guarantee.
One got shop-soiled
And then there were three.

* * *

They were too late.

As they drove into the little street that contained The Battlestore Galactica, they could see fire engulfing the shop with an uncontrolled rage. Full-size cardboard figures of Boba Fett, Gandalf and Captain Picard were curling and blackening in the shop window. Fingers of flame tickled the sign. A little plastic spaceship dropped out of the 'o' in 'Battlestore' and plummeted into oblivion.

Fire engines were at the scene, their hoses snaking along the kerb and throwing clouds of water everywhere, chasing the inferno as it danced and devoured everything it could touch. A new tongue of orange flame roared into the sky as it discovered the graphic-novel section.

A small cluster of people stood outside their homes, watching the spectacle like it was a fireworks display.

Fenton was sitting on the kerb, arms cuddling his knees, staring at the flames as if hypnotised. He had made no secret of the fact he'd started the fire; he was surrounded with three empty petrol cans. A police car had pulled up near the fire engines, and two police officers walked towards him. It was PCs Kelly and Howard.

Vixy saw the motorhome arrive and ran over, pushing her face through the open driver's side window. Her cheeks were Rorschach blobs of tears and eyeliner.

"I tried to stop him! I really tried."

"Frokk," said Binfire, staring at the curtain of flame. "Is Moni in there?"

"He just kept talking about teaching his wife a lesson," Vixy babbled. "How she'd now know how it feels to lose something precious to her. He kept saying it over and over again. I rang Freya, and then I rang the police, but it was too late."

They left the motorhome and ran over to Fenton, but the two police officers had got to him first.

"I think you'd better come with us, Mr Worth," said PC Kelly gently. "Clean yourself up."

"It's for the best," added PC Howard.

A shiny black Volvo roared up behind them, screeching to a halt in the middle of the street. Two men got out, all long coats and grim faces. They walked towards Fenton, flipping their badges at the police officers.

"Hi, I'm DI Stephen Mendelson," said the senior one. "This is DS Banks. And you are?"

Kelly looked at them uncertainly. "I'm Constable Rona Kelly. This is Constable Mike Howard."

"Nice to meet you both. Sorry to butt in, but we need to talk to Fenton Worth. I believe that's him?"

"Yes. Can't it wait?" said Kelly. "As you can see, he's just committed rather a lot of arson."

"Sorry it can't. We've just found his dead wife in the boot of her car. Well, bits of her."

"Oh my god," breathed Kelly. She looked down at Fenton with a horror bordering on awe. Fenton stared glassily up at her and grinned.

As the 'police – do not cross' tapes were yet to be stretched across the area, Kit, Vixy, Binfire and Freya were free to hover on the edges of their conversation. The four officers were too intent on their little territorial discussion to notice that their voices were carrying.

Vixy's eyes grew wide and she crammed the knuckles of her hand into her mouth to stifle a scream.

"What did they just say?" said Freya in a faint voice.

"They just said that Fenton killed his wife and chopped her up," Binfire whispered helpfully.

"Yes, I heard what they said!" Freya clamped her hands to her ears.

They watched as the two constables gently lifted Fenton to his feet. The officers tried to disengage, but Fenton gripped PC Kelly's arm with sudden intensity.

"Did you just say that Moni was... dead? My wife is dead?"

"Yes, I'm afraid so."

Several expressions crossed Fenton's face: shock, disbelief, anger and wonderment. He stared at PC Kelly, then he stared at the blackened remains of The Battlestore Galactica. Then he struggled with his jacket and produced his phone. He stared at the WhatsApp messages: the photo of his wife on the floor, the rhyme, then he showed it to PC Kelly.

"My phone was off. I didn't see this. If I'd only seen this. Then I wouldn't…"

"Wouldn't what, sir?"

"Don't you see? I did this to hurt her for what she did to me. The shop is my wife's. It's in the prenup. He killed her, and now the shop comes to me. I didn't have to… I burned my own shop! That shop's mine!" He started to giggle. "She's dead, so it all comes to me. It's mine."

He started laughing hysterically, interspersing his giggles with coughing and retching until he was bent double and his head was pointing at the floor.

"I just burned down my own shop!"

Another even shinier black Volvo roared into view, parking aggressively across the street next to the previous shiny black Volvo.

Two more policemen got out, with even longer coats and grimmer faces. They strode towards the four police officers.

"Good morning," said the one in front. "I'm DCI Smallgreen and this is DC Butcher." He pointed at Fenton. "Is that Mr Worth?"

"Yes it is," said DI Mendelson. "We were just about to take him in to ask him a few questions about his wife's murder."

"Uh-uh, nope." DCI Smallgreen shook his head. "No, you're not."

"Can I ask why, sir?"

"We're with Northamptonshire MIT. Lady Tabitha Pendragon went missing yesterday. A jogger found her motorbike in the River Welland."

Mendelson looked sympathetic, but suspicious. "That's terrible. Sorry to hear that. These country roads can be dangerous. What's that got to do with Fenton Worth?"

"A *lot*. When the jogger waded into the river to examine it, he didn't find her. He just found a severed hand."

Mendelson's jaw dropped open. "A severed hand?"

"Yep."

Smallgreen strode over to Fenton and spoke in a bright, friendly voice normally reserved for small children. "Mr Worth, can I see your phone please? Can I see the messages you've been getting from that person who sends you all the little rhymes?"

Fenton nodded dumbly and opened his WhatsApp. Smallgreen took it gently off him and scrolled through the messages.

He held the phone, screen-out, and showed them the photos of Lady Tabitha and Moni, both trussed up and unconscious.

"Two women. One definitely dead. One almost certainly dead. Both photographed in the same way, and photos sent with four lines of doggerel by persons unknown," said Smallgreen evenly to the assembled police officers. "This is now officially a serial-killer investigation. And that happens to be our department."

51

They led Fenton away. Vixy trotted after them and made a beeline for DC Butcher, who, of the six police officers, looked the youngest and most approachable.

"Excuse me, sir! Excuse me!"

The young DC turned his head.

"Hi. It was me who phoned the police, you know, to try and stop Fenton setting fire to the shop."

"Oh right. And what's your relationship to Mr Worth?"

"I'm a lodger. My room was up there." She pointed to a patch of empty sky where the upper floor of The Battlestore Galactica used to be.

"Oh. I'm sorry."

"That's not important. I can find a place to stay. I usually manage, you know. But I just want to tell you that I've been with Fenton all last night and this morning – I didn't let him out of my sight."

"All through last night?"

She blushed. "Yes. His wife left him after a thing that had happened, in Furley House? So I've been comforting him. So, I know for definite he didn't kill his wife."

"Oh. Are you prepared to make a statement to that effect?"

"Yes."

"Would you like to come with us?"

"Absolutely, yeah. I better tell my friends I'm going to the station."

She turned, but there was no one there. Kit, Binfire and Freya had all slipped away.

* * *

"Frokk. Shit just got frokking real."

Binfire was frowning extremely hard. His wild eyebrows were knitted together. His knuckles were pure white, hands clamped tightly on the steering wheel.

"You said it," agreed Kit, looking out of the window at the endless flat fields. She didn't feel like saying anything at that point, so she settled on the bare minimum.

"This is sooo awful. I can't believe this is happening," said Freya, sitting between them.

"Me neither," said Kit.

Freya made a decision. "We should go back to Furley House, say a quick 'Hi' to Archie, see if he's okay, then we should go straight back to Brighton." She flicked Binfire's (purely ornamental) dashboard switch. "Warp nine, okay?"

"No," said Kit.

"Kit, we've got to go!"

"I made a promise."

"To a dead woman!"

"We don't know for certain she's dead."

Freya shook her head disbelievingly. "Kit, they found a *hand*."

"Lots of people live quite happily with only one hand."

Binfire chipped in, "She's got a point, Frey. Bucky Barnes. Captain Hook. Luke Skywalker lost a hand and he still beat the Empire single-handed. Literally."

Freya slapped Binfire's knee, and the motorhome wobbled. "Be sensible. You can't talk like *daft* Binfire now. You have to be *sensible* Binfire. You have to convince Kit to leave."

"Yeah, right. Okay." He glanced at Kit. "We should all scarper. This insane person is turning people into Lego sets. He's killing people we *know*."

"More than that," snapped Kit. "This insane person is targeting *women*. A woman who owned a doll, and a woman married to someone who owned a doll."

"Exactly."

"Therefore, you should leave now, Freya. Binfire owned a doll, and you're Binfire's friend..."

"But so are you! You're Binfire's friend too!"

"But there's a difference."

"What difference?"

"The difference is I'm staying."

And that was that.

52

Kit went into the library to find Archie slumped in a chair, brooding, staring at a glass of whisky.

"Hi."

Archie jumped. "Oh hello, Kit. I didn't know you were back."

"We've just got in."

"Right. And where are your friends?"

"Freya is leaving. Binfire's agreed to drive her to the station. He's helping her pack."

"I don't blame her." He placed his hand wearily on his forehead. "This is a terrible business. Terrible business. I called the police this morning because I thought, on reflection, I'd still do my duty and report Tabitha as a missing person. Maybe if she was just playing silly buggers it would teach her a lesson."

"I understand."

"Then, while they were here, they got a call. They found my sister's bike in the River Welland. Horrible."

"I'm so sorry."

Archie rubbed his left eye, stopping a tear from travelling down his cheek. "I can't believe this is happening. Who would play such an evil game? I don't think the police have a clue."

"Do you think Tabitha is still alive?"

"I'd love to think so, Kit. But I'm sorry. She's very dead."

"It's just a hand. People can live without a hand."

"Yes, well. It's not just the hand. There were other parts found downstream." He shuddered. "Her legs too. They're looking for her torso, and her arms. The police told me that the body parts showed signs of having been frozen. As were Mrs Worth's parts—"

"Frozen?"

"Yes, they think some of the remains of both women are being stored somewhere, in a refrigerated container." He shuddered. "For what ghastly purpose, I shudder to think…"

Archie's words slammed into her chest.

She's dead.

It affected Kit far more than she expected. She was usually excellent at compartmentalising shocking events. *Talking* about them was tough on her stammer but actually *feeling* something. That was someone else's problem.

Tabitha is dead. Why do I feel so awful? All I did was cuddle her for a few nights. That was all. Why do I feel so blindsided by these emotions?

You know why. It's because you saw her as a way out from Jackie. A soft landing. And now she's gone.

A comical *parp-parp* came from outside, shredding her gloomy thoughts.

She and Archie looked out of the window and saw a tiny green Fiat 500 chugging up the drive, veering from one verge to the other like a rocket-powered tortoise.

It wobbled to a halt outside Furley House and a woman in a shapeless red sweater, glasses and bob-cut emerged, carrying a suitcase and a rucksack.

"Angelina!" exclaimed Archie.

Archie hurried out to meet his fiancée. Angelina ran up the steps and surged towards him, wrapping her arms around his chest, compressing his ribcage and knocking the air out of his lungs.

"Oh, *Archie*! Archie! I'm so sorry!"

"I know, darling."

"Your poor sister!"

"I know."

"How could this be happening, munchkin? I don't believe it!"

She gave him one last extra-vigorous hug, disengaged and looked earnestly up at her fiancé. "I know Tabitha never liked me, but I hoped in time, after the wedding, we would become friends."

"Yes. I hoped that too, Angel."

Angelina noticed Kit standing by the entrance and rushed towards her, the huge collar of her jumper concertinaing around her neck. She stopped short of hugging Kit, much to Kit's relief, and gave her a sunny wave.

"Hey, Miss Sleuth! So, we meet in person at last!"

"So we do."

"But not in the best of circumstances, hey?"

"No."

"Do you have any idea about who's doing these awful things?"

"I have a few ideas."

"Fab! I'd love to hear them. And I'd love to see more pictures of your dog. But later. I'm going to look after Archipoos – he's had a terrible shock."

Archie looked embarrassed. "I'm just fine, button."

"No, you're not, big bear. You need me to give you lashings of T L C on toast."

She threaded her arm through his and marched him through the entrance to Furley House.

53

Penny was packing to leave, hurling her clothes into a bag, when Kit knocked on her door.

"I'm going to go back to Braxton Hall," said Kit.

Penny looked at her, incredulous. "Why?"

"Because that's where Lady Tabitha was going just before she disappeared. She was going to have it out with Nate Braxton. She blamed him for framing her. So, I'm going to talk to Nate."

"Do you realise what you're saying?"

"Yes."

"Two women are dead. Tabitha and Moni. And from the way the poem is going, they're not going to be the last. Three little figures to go, right?"

"I understand all that."

Penny reached into her jacket pocket and pulled out a lighter and a pack of cigarettes. She flipped it open, pulled one out and lit it with trembling fingers. "We could be next. Any of us. And you're proposing to go alone to the house that contains the whole Braxton family? They could be behind the murders. Any one of them. Or all of them."

"I'm not proposing I go alone at all. I'm proposing that you come with me."

"No way."

"I don't have anyone to take me."

"Get Binfire to drive you."

"Binfire is driving Freya away from here, as far away as possible."

"Sounds like a brilliant plan. That's my plan too."

"Look, you don't have to come inside. Just wait for me. If I don't come out because I've been murdered, you can ring the police and catch him right there, stop him killing anyone else, while you're safely locked inside your van."

Penny grinned. "Like the bear?"

"What bear?"

"You know, that old joke. Or saying, or whatever it is. 'You don't have to run faster than the bear, you just have to run faster than the person next to you.' You want to get eaten by the bear, and you want me to watch you?"

Kit was getting impatient. "Come on, Penny. Let's do this."

* * *

On the way to Braxton Hall, Kit made sure Penny's eyes were on the road before slipping out her phone, turning it to 'mute' and texting Binfire.

MAKE YOURSELF SCARCE.

A long pause. Then a message came back.

Why?

Kit typed some more.

The police will start to investigate what happened the night the Braxtons factory burned down.

There was a very long pause.

A little pulsing speech bubble popped up, the sign that someone was typing. Then it disappeared. Then it appeared again. Then, finally, something appeared. One word.

Okay.

No denial, no 'What are you frokking talking about pilgrim?'.
Just 'okay'.

Binfire knew what Kit's texts meant – and for Kit that was
devastating.

54

Braxton Hall looked as though it was playing host to a massive garden party, sponsored by the local constabulary.

The drive was full of cars. Bright yellow BMWs with POLICE written over them jostled for parking spaces with civilian BMWs. Officers with luminous bibs with POLICE written on their backs were standing around the house with their hands in their pockets. Just in case any passers-by were in any doubt that it was a police operation, two big tents were erected on the front lawn with POLICE written on the canvas, and yellow ribbons were draped around the house with POLICE – DO NOT CROSS written on them.

"This is not what I was expecting," muttered Penny.

They tucked the transit van just inside the gates, far enough away not to attract any attention.

Kit looked into the sky and pointed. "Is that a helicopter?"

Penny followed her finger. "Bloody hell, I think it is! It's a bloody police helicopter! I thought they'd just interview them in the house. Perhaps take them down to the station and give them the third degree. I didn't expect this."

"What are they doing?"

"They're digging up Jack Braxton's grave," came a sepulchral voice.

Penny and Kit both screamed in shock. Reverend Bell was right outside Kit's passenger window, leering in at them with a mad glint in his eyes.

Penny slammed her hands against the steering wheel, gasping for air. "FUCK! Reverend! You scared the shit out of me!"

Kit wound down her window. "Digging up his grave? Why are they doing that?"

Reverend Bell pouted. "I don't know. How should I know? I came over here to tell the family I know who murdered Jack Braxton. I thought if I assembled them all in a drawing room, I could recount the events of that night and reveal the murderer to be Ben 'Binfire' Ferry. I'm sure they'd appreciate that. Perhaps that would bring closure and break the curse."

"And have you told them?" said Kit in a tiny voice.

"I can't get near the dratted house, can I? And when I go up to the police cordon with my information, they just send me away and tell me to ring the hotline, like I'm some kind of... *timewaster*."

Reverend Bell looked like he'd been sleeping under a hedge. His grey coat was smeared with grass stains and there were things living in his beard and moustache. He reminded Kit of Ben Gunn in the Robert Newton version of *Treasure Island* (1950). He looked just like the kind of mad conspiracy theorist that came out of the woodwork when there was a major murder investigation. It wasn't a surprise he'd been ignored.

Thank heavens.

"And how do you know they're digging up his grave?" Penny asked.

"I walked around the perimeter, silly! Where the trees are. No one can see you in the trees. I watched them, in the distance, putting a tent up around it. I watched them go in with shovels."

"I wonder why?" said Kit.

Penny sighed. "Well, I'm sure they're not going to tell us if we ask. And you can hardly waltz in and tell them you're the great amateur detective."

Kit fell silent. The only sound was Reverend Bell's tuneless humming.

Finally, she said, "No. I can't waltz in. But perhaps we can disguise ourselves as part of the investigating team."

"We hardly look like coppers, Kit."

"No, we don't. But we don't have to." She turned to Reverend Bell. "Could you steal a few metres of that POLICE – DO NOT CROSS tape for us?"

Bell gave a loopy grin. "Simplicity itself, my lady."

* * *

PC Howard and PC Kelly were standing by the big tent erected around Jack Braxton's grave. They were on their fourteenth round of I spy when the robot chugged around the side of the house and lurched towards them.

"Not seen one of those before," said Howard, scratching his sideburns.

"Haven't you?" Kelly grinned.

"Well, on the telly, obviously. Not in real life."

"Right."

"There was one in last night's episode of *Wistful* on ITV. Terrorist bomb blew it to pieces."

Howard watched as it chugged past, noting the POLICE – DO NOT CROSS ribbons threaded across its carapace.

"I didn't know we were getting one of those things."

"Why should the SOCOs tell us anything? We're just the doormen."

"You don't think the coffin's dangerous, do you? You don't think they put a bomb in it?"

"Belts and braces, Mike. Belts and braces. We're dealing with a grade-one psycho. No telling what he's capable of."

"Yeah."

They watched as the robot disappeared inside the tent.

55

Kit, Penny and Reverend Bell were sitting in the transit van, watching the visuals on Penny's laptop. The screen showed them the robot's eye view as it wobbled inside the tent. It revealed an elaborate gravestone, a pile of soil, a body-shaped hole, a dirt-encrusted coffin that had been disgorged from the hole, and two police officers covered head-to-toe in protective clothing. One officer was rather portly, one slender.

The officers looked at each other and then directly at the camera.

"What?" said the portly one.

The slender one shrugged.

"Ooooh dear," muttered Penny.

The portly one walked right up to the robot until his masked face filled the screen.

"Is that you in there, Larry?"

Kit and Penny exchanged panicked glances.

"What do I do?" hissed Penny.

"Give him the thumbs up," said Kit.

Penny leaned across and put her hands on the keyboard. "This isn't as easy doing it on the laptop," she muttered. "If I'd known I was operating the robot, I'd have brought the remote from my room."

One of the robot's claw-like hands hovered into view at the bottom of the screen. The digits twitched and gave a thumbs up.

On the screen, the policeman's facemask jiggled up and down as he spoke again.

"I didn't know you were…" He shrugged. "Do you want us to go while you do the honours?"

Penny jiggled the claw again.

"Okay." The portly one gestured to the slender one, who leapt out of the hole. They both left the tent.

Kit glanced at Penny. "I don't think we'll have a lot of time before they work out we're not with the investigating team. Can you…?"

But Penny was well ahead of her. She moved the robot over to the coffin.

Reverend Bell gave another insane grin. "Ladies, we are about to have the unboxing video to end all unboxing videos."

Penny extended one claw until two of its appendages slid beneath the lid.

"Here we have the traditional premium casket with brass accessories, handle and nameplate," Reverend Bell intoned in a sing-song voice. "Note the design detailing on the lid which gives extra definition to the top of the box. The packaging is surprisingly intact. So, the figure inside should be mint, with any luck."

"Shut up," snapped Kit. "She's concentrating."

Penny opened the claw, levering the lid slightly open, popping the nails out of their resting places. Then, with excruciating slowness, she moved it to the next corner, performing the same operation. And then the next.

"I can hear voices," said Penny nervously. "I think the police are starting to realise the robot doesn't belong to them."

Penny concentrated on popping the last few nails. Finally, the last corner was free, and the lid wobbled in place. She manoeuvred one of the arms lower and got it to push the lid aside. It slid off and landed in the hole with a sickening crash.

"Quicklyquicklyquickly," muttered Penny under her breath.

She extended the robot's viewscreen, so they could see inside the coffin.

There was no body.

But it wasn't empty.

There was an action figure inside.

It was six feet tall, with a beard, and it was dressed in the remains of Jack Braxton's clothes, but it was definitely an action figure.

56

Incredibly, when Penny manoeuvred the robot to leave the tent and head back, it was *still* allowed to carry on unimpeded. Obviously, the police were still of the opinion the robot was probably another department's responsibility.

Apart from a few heart-squeezing moments when one of its caterpillar tracks got stuck in a herbaceous border, the robot managed to trundle all the way back to them. They bundled it into the transit van and drove to a pub car park.

Penny's phone rang.

"It's Graham," she said to Kit. "He's finished his lunch and he's now back in his cell. He wants to join our meeting. If that's okay with you."

"If that's okay with *you*," corrected Kit. "He fired you for stealing his action figure and passing it to a maniac."

Penny sighed. "Yeah, well, me and Graham, we've talked a bit. We've come to the conclusion that whoever's behind all this is *not* Lady Tabitha Pendragon, what with her being in little bits now." She grimaced. "I think we both have a common aim to find out who's doing this. Obviously, *he* wants to find out who broke his doll, and *I* want to not get murdered and cut into little pieces." She shrugged. "But essentially we're on the same side."

"Then that's fine with me," said Kit.

Penny activated the robot's screen and up popped Graham's huge face.

"Report," he growled.

"We're just looking at some footage. You might find it interesting."

They clustered around the robot and Penny held her laptop up so Graham could see the recording they'd made.

"It looks like a mannequin," said Penny.

"No." Graham shook his huge head. "That isn't just any mannequin."

"I agree," said Kit. "It's one of those giant-sized versions of the dolls Braxtons made to promote the first range. There's a bunch of them in the toy museum."

Reverend Bell clicked his fingers and let loose a squeal. "Of course! That's right. They made them for a trade fair, didn't they? And they all got loaned out to vendors? Didn't Fenton get one?"

"Yes," said Kit. "I remember that one very well. It was outside the door of his shop for ages. I'd have loved to have one in my flat."

Graham continued, "They were recalled after the promotion had finished and Braxtons auctioned them for a new charity called Reach for children who'd lost limbs in accidents. They went for a great deal of money. I bought nearly all of them. That particular mannequin never came up at auction. It's the mannequin of Professor Daxatar, which I was not overly concerned about."

The mannequin had the vague look of Professor Daxatar, played by actor Brian Crowbridge, but a beard and wig had been added, and the body had been clad in a three-piece suit. It was an interesting attempt to make the figure look like Jack Braxton.

Penny's phone pinged. "News alert," she explained. She looked at her phone. "Woah… Oh my…"

"What?" Kit had a creeping feeling of dread.

"They've taken Sylvia and Vera Braxton in for questioning. Let me get it on the BBC news channel."

She turned her phone on its side to get a bigger picture and propped it up on the dashboard.

There was a collage of film clips on a loop. Firstly, there was footage of Sylvia and Vera Braxton being escorted into a police station by a phalanx of coppers. Sylvia looked exquisite in a figure-hugging camel coat and sunglasses. She was holding her mother's arm. Vera was still in her brown linen dress, but had added an elegant three-quarter-length white cardigan over the top, which flapped against her knees.

They were pursued by a ragged crowd of reporters and photographers.

This was succeeded by an archive clip of a young Jack Braxton doing a publicity event, holding an action figure and standing in front of a chorus line of scantily dressed models dressed as Vixens. Lastly, there was footage of the fire at Braxtons Models, great gobbets of flame surging into the night while firemen threw jets of water impotently onto the blaze. It was accompanied by a pre-recorded voice that had that half-serious, half-sardonic tone beloved of BBC reporters everywhere.

"It's been twenty-eight years since toy baron Jack Braxton apparently died during a fire at his factory in Lincolnshire. Jack, son of the founder of Braxtons Models, Albert Braxton, had only been in control of the company for three years before it all ended in tragedy.

"There has been a lot of speculation through the years about the incident, but that was usually about whether the fire was an accident or arson. There was rather less speculation as to whether Jack Braxton died in the fire, as a body was found in the remains of the factory and an inquest pronounced him dead at the scene.

"But now, following a series of murders in the area, the investigation has apparently led the police to Braxton Hall and his final resting place in the grounds. An exhumation of Braxton's grave has found no body present, leading to many questions. Has he been alive all this time? What does the lack of a body have to do with the ongoing investigation into the deaths of Moni Worth and Lady Tabitha Pendragon? And, if Jack Braxton is alive, where is he now? Does Vera Braxton know where her son is? Does Sylvia know what happened to her brother?"

The film clips ended and the channel went back to the news anchor. Penny switched off the phone.

"There was no murder?" said Bell, with a tiny voice.

Graham rumbled like a volcano about to erupt. "We have all been duped. I've been duped. For twenty-eight years I was led to believe that I was a participant in the death of Jack Braxton."

"There was no murder?" croaked Bell again.

"There have been *lots* of murders, you idiot," snapped Penny. "They're happening *now*! Get your head out of the past, you two!"

"We need to find out some more *facts*," said Kit.

"How do you want to do that?"

"Nate Braxton wasn't on the news. He might still be home. We go back to Braxton Hall."

"Braxton Hall is full of policemen!"

"It soon won't be. They've found what they were looking for. Now they have two people to interview. If there are any policemen there, we wait until they leave, and then we talk to Nate Braxton."

Kit adjusted her cap and put on a determined expression.

"We go back."

57

There were policemen still at Braxton Hall, but Kit was right. They were packing up their tents and getting ready to leave.

Penny parked the van outside the gate and they waited. Graham fumed inside his prison of metal. Reverend Bell sat on the floor, his head hung low, muttering, "There was no murder." Penny kept popping out to smoke endless cigarettes.

Kit took a moment to ring Binfire. No answer. She rang Freya. Again, no answer. She hoped Freya was on her way to safety. She wondered if Binfire had gone with her. But mostly the same ten words were going through her mind like a Buddhist incantation.

If Jack Braxton is alive, then Binfire isn't a murderer.

Kit's phone rang. A WhatsApp video call. At first Kit thought the picture feed wasn't working, as the screen was black, but then Matty's face loomed into view. He was sitting in a tiny, dark room.

"Hi there, Kitty Kat."

"Hello." Kit's voice was wary.

"Guess what I'm doing," leered Matty. His voice was low and sinister, and his face, caught in the half-light of a single electric bulb, hung there in the darkness like a Halloween decoration. "Actually, fuck guessing. I'll tell you anyway. I'm doing the thing you were supposed to do, sweetheart. I'm solving this case. I'm catching this murderer. I'm using *this*."

He tapped the side of his head with a finger.

"Much better than your lesbian's intuition I think you'll—"

Matty stopped as he heard a thud from outside.

"Is that?" He shook his head. "No, it's Saskia. I think she's taking a shower. Anyway, I've worked out a pattern. Two supposed murders. Both women, female, like the dolls. And both connected to these dolls. Tabitha owned one. Moni was married to someone who owned one."

"Yes."

"The obvious conclusion is that there's *another* woman who's next."

"We guessed that."

"I bet you a fiver it's gonna be Saskia. She's a woman. I owned a doll. We've been... connected in the past..."

The door of the van slid open as Penny returned from her fag-break. "Who's that on the phone?" she asked.

"It's Matty," explained Kit. "He seems to be hiding in a closet."

"Don't belittle my masculinity," snarled Matty. "I'm the hero of this narrative, not you."

"So, explain your narrative."

"Saskia dropped me off at the train station, but I didn't get on a train. I hailed a cab and followed her." He tapped his forehead again. "I know her. She always stops off for a few days before she starts a long drive. She checked in to an Airbnb in Oundle, and I checked in to a pub down the road."

"You've been stalking her," said Penny.

Matty rolled his eyes disdainfully, as if to say *Don't worry about the details*.

"Then I got the WhatsApp message about Lady Tabitha. Unlike you lot, I took it seriously. And when I got the picture message of Moni, I knew I had to do something. I waited until Saskia popped out to get some breakfast, then I broke in, and now I'm hiding in the linen cupboard in her bedroom."

He held up a baseball bat. "When the murderer comes for her, I'll be ready."

Kit frowned. "You're hiding in her bedroom cupboard with a baseball bat?"

"Yes. Something that you would never think of."

"No, I would definitely never think of that. That's bizarre."

"Typical. Normalise the abnormal and slut-shame the heteronormative."

"I think the *heteronormative* thing would be to just protect Saskia, make sure she's safe, and *not* use her as bait."

But Matty was no longer listening. He gripped the baseball bat, propped the phone up on the floor and pressed his eye against the crack of light that bled around the edge of the cupboard door.

"Wait... I think... I can see..."

The door was wrenched open. The screen on Kit's phone went white as light streamed into the cupboard. Matty blinked furiously, trying to adjust to the glare. Then he frowned. "Of course," he sighed. "It had to be you. How fucking clichéd. How fucking predict—"

Someone grabbed the end of the baseball bat and wrenched it out of Matty's hand, turning it on him. Trapped in a tiny space, Matty was helpless as the baseball bat hurtled down on his head with terrific force.

He screamed, but not for long. The cupboard door was shut and everything turned black once more.

"Oh – my – god! Oh my god!" whimpered Penny.

"He said Saskia was at an Airbnb in Oundle. We need to phone the police now!"

"Oh my god!"

"Penny, we have to focus."

The phone in Penny's pocket went off. Graham's phone. Penny's face as she looked at Graham's phone told Kit all she needed to know. She wasn't surprised when she turned it around to show an image of Saskia tied up and lying unconscious on the floor of a bedroom.

The poem said:

Three little figures
Hiding in plain view.
One checked out early
And then there were two.

Penny's face drained of what little colour was left. "Saskia too! I can't cope with this! This is insane!"

"We phone the police right now," said Kit calmly. "And then we go into Braxton Hall and talk to Nate Braxton."

Kit rang the police and got the front desk. After playing a game of tag with the switchboard she was finally put through to Constable Kelly.

"Hello, Ms Pelham?"

"Kit Pelham, yes. We have met. I was at Furley House when the toy museum got vandalised."

Kelly was instantly on the alert. "I see."

"We've – well a friend of mine – she's received another picture message on her phone. This one's of Saskia Shapiro. And there's a poem—"

"Yes, we're aware. We have Mr Worth's phone. We can see all the messages. We've just seen the photo of Miss Shapiro."

"Oh." Kit hadn't thought of that. "Is Fenton still with you?"

"No. He's been released. He's no longer a person of interest. He gave permission for us to keep his phone."

"Right. Okay. But do you know where the photo of Saskia was taken?"

"Not at this moment. Do you?"

"Not quite. But just before we got the photo, I was rung by

Matty Kearney – he's one of the owners of the action figures. He was at the address where Saskia Shapiro was staying. He said Saskia was staying at an Airbnb in Oundle."

"Okay, that's good to know. You don't have a full address?"

"Sorry, no."

"Well, I'm sure we can narrow it down."

"While Matty was on the phone to me, he was attacked. I think it was this maniac. He could be hurt or dead. I don't know."

"Thanks for that information. You've been very helpful. We'll track them both down. Don't worry. Where are you at the moment?"

"I'm in a van with Reverend Jerome Bell – he's the organiser of the toy museum – and Penny Lane, an ex-employee of the owner of one of the dolls. You interviewed them both when you came to Furley House."

"Yes, I remember them. Listen to me, Kit. For your own safety and theirs, get to somewhere secure, a locked room or a car, and when you're able, come into the police station. Will you do that for me, Kit?"

"Yes, I will."

"Good. Thank you."

* * *

Kit ended the call and looked out of the passenger side window. The last police van was just ambling out of the drive of Braxton Hall.

"Let's get going."

"Are you mad?" Penny's voice was trembling. "You told the police lady…"

"I told her I'd go when I'm able. We're in the best position to find this killer. We know far more about what's happening than they do. They're still playing catch-up. And we need *answers*.

And that place is the only place where we might get them."

"There's a murderer out there."

"Exactly. He's *out there*, isn't he? Near Oundle? He can't be in two places at once."

"It could be the whole Braxton family – nieces and cousins and all. They could be lying in wait for us in there with chain-saws and meat hooks. No, Kit, I'm not going in. As I said, you don't have to be faster than the bear, you just have to be faster than your friend. I'm staying here, safe in this van, with the doors locked, just like we agreed. And at the slightest hint of trouble, I'm driving to the police station."

"Fair enough."

"I'd like to come with you," said Bell suddenly. "I would like to be present at the denouement of this particular mystery."

Kit wasn't entirely happy about Reverend Bell accompanying her – he was obviously going through some sort of mental crisis – but the alternative was going in alone, and she knew she was sounding braver than she felt.

"Fine. Come on then."

They left the van. Penny immediately locked the doors.

* * *

It took a long time before Nate Braxton poked his head around the door. He was pale and unshaven, and his usual immaculate hair was scattered around his head, as if he'd just been disturbed from his slumber. The fact he was still wearing his dressing gown confirmed it. Kit was irresistibly reminded of Arthur Dent (*The Hitchhiker's Guide to the Galaxy*, 1981).

"Hi," said Kit. "It's me."

"Oh. It's you again. What the hell do you want?"

"We would like to ask you some questions, sir," trumpeted Reverend Bell.

"Who the hell are you?" Nate glared at the Reverend. "Wait. You've been here before. You're the organiser of the toy museum at Furley? You came here asking for exhibits."

"Indeed. I am the curator. I have that honour." Bell gave a tight bow.

"Well, I'm telling you what I told her. I had nothing to do with the trashing of your museum. You can't pin that one on me."

"It's all gone a bit past vandalism, Nate," said Kit. "I want to ask you about your Uncle Jack."

Nate's bloodshot eyes narrowed. "You're quite a presumptuous woman, aren't you?" He glared at Kit. "I thought you wrote for a toy magazine or something? Isn't it a bit out of your remit?"

"A bit."

"And why do you want to talk about Uncle Jack?"

"We saw the news. We know he's not dead."

"I'm not talking to journalists at this time."

The door was closing on her when Kit said, "Don't you care about what happened to Tabitha?"

The door stopped closing.

"I do," continued Kit. "I thought you might too."

He turned and glared at them. Then sighed.

"Oh well, come on in then, if you're coming. Mum and Granny would probably go spare if they knew you were here. But they're not here, are they? And quite frankly I don't care what they think anymore. Come on then."

He beckoned for them to follow. Kit trotted alongside him, while the Reverend hung back, examining the fixtures with a pocket magnifying glass and stroking his lapels.

Kit got straight to the point. "Tabitha said she was coming here to have it out with you, just before she was found dead."

Nate threw an angry look at her. "Oh really? And you think I did her in, is that it?"

"Not really. I'm just saying what she told me."

"Well, I didn't see her. I haven't seen her. I haven't seen her face to face in *three whole months*, and that's the absolute truth. If she did come here, I have no knowledge of it. Because I did *not see her.*"

* * *

When they reached the library, he half-sat, half-dropped into a chair and gestured for them to sit. Kit sat primly on a chair, but the Reverend stayed standing, his eyes flipping around the room.

Despite his dishevelled appearance, Nate was a brutally attractive young man, with a well-fed arrogance. Even his resting face had a faint curl about the lips and nostrils, which conveyed an impression that, even in his dressing gown and slippers, he was slightly too grand to be bothered to speak to her.

"Well," he sighed. "It's not going to be a secret for much longer, so there's no harm in telling you."

"Go on."

"The police were just here, digging up Uncle Jack's grave. They heard from an anonymous source that he's still alive. And guess what? He actually is. And it's as much of a surprise to me as it is to you. And before you start to get any ideas, Mother's certain he's not behind these murders."

"So where is your uncle?" asked Kit.

"Not a bloody clue."

"Right, are you seriously telling me—?"

"It's true. Look, let me explain. Mum's only just told me the whole story. When the toy business got in the shit in the 90s, it hit Uncle Jack very hard. He got it into his head that he'd failed the Braxton name. His behaviour got more and more erratic until… Well, he had this crazy idea to torch the place for the insurance, and he asked his friend Roland Pendragon to help him."

"You're saying the seventh Marquess of Furley agreed to commit arson?" said Kit.

"Mum says the Marquess was a complete lunatic. He'd do anything for a laugh, if it appealed to him. Anyway, while they were planning it, Uncle Jack made a discovery that changed everything."

He paused for dramatic effect. "He found the body of a tramp in the factory grounds. He'd fallen in one of the skips, behind the loading bay, covered in boxes and bubble wrap. A dead tramp. Can you believe it?"

"A dead tramp?" mused Kit. "How did he die?"

He shrugged. "I dunno. Why would I know that?"

"I thought you might."

"Well I don't. Why would I care about a tramp that's been dead for thirty-odd years? Do you want to hear the story or not?"

"I do. Please continue."

"Anyway, Uncle Jack saw finding the body as a sign. His brain took hold of this notion that, if he was still around after the fire, then it would be obvious the factory had been torched for the insurance and he would be chief suspect. No payout. But if he could set fire to the place and put the tramp's body in his office and everyone would think it was him, it would look more like an accident."

Kit was following Nate's story with only one half of her brain. The other half was twitching with relief. Her best friend was not a murderer after all.

An arsonist perhaps, a lunatic maybe, a wanton destroyer of other people's property, definitely, but he's NOT a murderer!

Nate carried on his story in an exhausted, hollowed-out drone. "Roland Pendragon knew a friendly doctor, and by friendly, I mean *corrupt* – a doctor he used to pay to arrange abortions when one of his concubines ended up the duff – to identify the burned body as Uncle Jack's."

The Reverend suddenly spoke, making Kit and Nate jump. "Excuse me, Mr Braxton. Do you know why the Marquess involved the Furley Fanboys in the events of that night?"

Nate blinked at him. "I don't know what those words mean."

Kit told them who the Furley Fanboys were, and how they'd been present at the scene of the crime, waiting in a car for Roland Pendragon to emerge when the factory exploded. Nate listened with a grin on his face, and then emitted a chuckle when she finished.

"Ha. I dunno anything about that either, but from the way Mum describes Roland Pendragon, it sounds like something he would have done. It sounds like he never missed an opportunity to screw with people's heads."

"I think it was a loyalty test," said Kit. "I think Roland Pendragon wanted to know how much his friends would do to get hold of a rare action figure. Like keep quiet about arson and manslaughter."

Nate shrugged. "Maybe. I don't really care either way. Do you want me to tell the story?"

Kit nodded.

"Actually." He struggled to his feet. "Come on. There's a room I want to show you. It's over in the other part of the house, away from prying eyes."

58

Penny waited nervously in the van. She watched as Nate appeared at the door, and Kit and the Reverend were ushered inside. Now she was alone, listening to the gentle ticking of the engine as it cooled down. It all seemed a bit anti-climactic.

She looked around at the countryside, the patchwork of fields, punctuated by the lollipop shapes of trees in the distance.

Perhaps Kit was right, she thought uneasily. *The killer isn't in Braxton Hall. He's out there somewhere. Perhaps I was safer going with them into the house.*

Nevertheless, she stayed put, resting her finger on the door locks, making sure they were firmly shut. She sat listening to the silence, complete save for the tiny whirring sound.

Whirring sound?

Penny looked in her driver's rear-view mirror and saw that one of the robot's claws was moving slightly, opening and closing, like the feeble spasms of a dying creature.

"Graham?" she hissed. "Mr Goldingay?"

The screen didn't boot up. No image of Graham. No grating voice demanding "Report!" The claw just kept opening and closing feebly.

Penny tried calling Graham. No answer. It just kept ringing. She gave up and clambered into the back of the van. She peered at the claw.

Probably a dodgy servo. It happens. Well, that's Goldingay's problem now, not mine. I'll just take the arm off. Let him know it's knackered.

She was about to unclip the arm when the whole top half of

the body revolved away from her, smashing brutally into the side of the van with a deafening clang.

"What the fu—"

Then it swivelled back again, with massive force, scything into her knees and sweeping her legs from under her. She tumbled backwards, hitting her head on the other side of the van. She yelled in pain and started to scramble to her feet, only for the top half to swivel back again. The claw came into contact with her chin with tremendous force, knocking her out cold.

And then everything went quiet again. The claw stopped moving. The only sound that broke the silence was the quiet pop of the door locks on the van as they released.

* * *

"Well done for coming with me. You're very brave. I look like shit. I look like everyone's idea of a serial killer."

Nate took them further into the interior of Braxton Hall, this time along windowless corridors. Electric lights flared into life when they passed, creating an eerie impression that someone was watching over them and lighting their way.

Nate talked as they walked. "So, the factory was burned to the ground, and everyone thought Uncle Jack was dead. His plan was to get on a ferry to Calais, and drive to Benidorm so he could wear straw hats and drink sangrias for the rest of his days."

They went up a narrow flight of stairs and were faced with an even longer, darker corridor with a door at the far end.

"Unfortunately, the sight of his beloved factory as a charred hole in the ground caused Uncle Jack to have a complete mental breakdown."

He offered up a weak smile. "That was when Mum came in. She found her little brother hiding under his bed, practically catatonic, which was a bit of a shock to her, as you can imagine, because by that time he'd already been pronounced dead. She was in a bit of a dilemma. She didn't feel she could reveal to the world what had actually happened, because of all the hoo-ha and the media circus, and that wouldn't have helped Uncle Jack's mental state one bit. Not to mention – no insurance payout."

They'd reached the door. A sturdy, dark rectangle. Nate grabbed the silver door handle, yanked it down and ushered them inside.

"This was her solution."

The room was as anonymous as the door. No windows. A bed covered in a single blanket. A desk. A bucket in the corner. Each of the four walls was dominated by an unassuming water-colour painting of a landscape. The only thing that was unusual about the room was the transparent cubicle that jutted out of the far wall, like a shower with no door.

"She stuck him in this room and hoped he'd recover his wits. No luck. Mum said he was completely gone. He'd retreated into his own dreamworld and there was no getting him out of it."

The Reverend walked up to the cubicle. It was decorated with paintings of stars and planets. "My goodness! This looks like a giant version of *Vixens from the Void* action figures boxes. An exact replica!"

"Yep. That's no accident. It's got a door at the back where you can access it from the outside."

Nate gave it a hefty slap. The Perspex shuddered and the room hummed with a dull booming sound.

"Toughened Perspex. No one can get through that."

He turned and looked at their puzzled faces. "Mum found out that Uncle Jack would only listen to her if she dressed up in a sparkly costume with a cloak, stand in that cubicle and pretend to be a walking, talking, living doll." He grinned and shook his head. "I don't know *how* she found that out. I shudder to think.

Can you imagine being witness to her standing in there and talking to Uncle Jack? I can't decide if I'd find it horrifying or hilarious."

Kit sat on the bed and looked around her. "So, Jack Braxton was kept here, in this room?"

"Yes, I just told you."

"But he's not here now."

Nate looked uncomfortable. "No. He isn't."

"So where—?"

"He was kept in here about six months before Mum realised she couldn't go on with the charade indefinitely. She asked for help from Roland Pendragon. He got Jack put into a very discreet sanatorium way out in the wilds of Dartmoor, usually reserved for inbred nobility. He went in under a fake name, of course. He seemed very happy there." He drew a quick breath. "So, when he made a break for it and climbed the wall, no one expected it. He disappeared and we never saw him again."

Bell was shocked. "Never?"

"Never. I don't even have any memories of him. He disappeared before I was born."

"When did this happen?"

Nate frowned. "The fire was in '95. So, it must have been in '96."

"He's been missing for nearly thirty years? And no one found out about it until now?"

"Roland Pendragon knew, of course. And he told his best girl, Lady Tabitha. But she didn't tell me, of course. I was only her *boyfriend*. I only know all this because Mum literally told me everything in the half-hour before the police turned up. This has been quite a day for me."

Kit's phone rang. An unknown number.

"Hello?"

"Hello, Kit? It's Constable Kelly here. We just talked on the phone."

"Hello, Constable."

"Kit, did you just say you were with Penny Lane?"

"That's right."

"Are you still with Penny Lane?"

"No." Kit decided to be evasive. "She just gave us a lift. She dropped us off in her van."

"I see. Was Penny planning to come to the police station?"

"Is there a problem?"

"As you know, we kept Mr Worth's phone as evidence, and to stay abreast of this murderer's intentions. We've just had a message come through, similar to the others."

"Oh."

"I'm just forwarding it to you now."

Kit's phone chimed. The picture was of Penny, lying on the floor of her van next to the robot, unconscious, gagged and trussed up like a turkey. There was a halo of blood around her head.

The accompanying rhyme said:

Two little figures
Cashing in for fun.
One spent a Penny
And then there was one.

"Oh criminy," sighed Kit.

"Do you know what that means?" asked Kelly.

"Yes."

"What does it mean?"

"I think it means that there are only two people who are actually making money out of this terrible business. Penny Lane and me. Penny is taking a salary from Graham Goldingay…

and I was hired by Graham to investigate the disappearance of the action figures, so…" She looked grim. "That would seem to suggest I'm the one who's next. I'm the last little figure."

"Okay, Kit. This is very important. You need to tell me where you think Penny Lane went. And you really need to tell me where you are *right now*."

Kit was about to tell her, when there was a dry click next to her ear.

She turned.

Reverend Bell was pointing a revolver right at her head.

* * *

"Do not say another word."

Kit froze, staring at the barrel of the revolver.

"End the call please, Ms Pelham," said Bell.

Kit ended the call and slowly removed the phone from her ear. Bell snatched the phone off her and turned the gun on Nate.

"Do you have a phone about your person?"

"What the hell?"

"I'll not ask again, Mr Braxton."

"I'm in my bloody dressing gown!"

"Dressing gowns have pockets. I'm not a fool."

Reluctantly, Nate fished out his phone and held it up.

"Slide it over to me."

He did so.

Kit tried to keep her voice steady. "What are you d-doing, Reverend Bell?"

Bell gave a cracked smile. "All will become clear. Very soon."

He backed out of the room and the door swung shut with a *ker-chunk*.

Nate said, "Shit!" and ran to it, his fingers scrabbling ineffectively at the crack.

Kit knew it was hopeless because she'd already noticed there was no door handle on their side. She knew it could only be opened from the outside.

"What the hell is he playing at?"

"It's very simple," said a voice behind them.

Both Kit and Nate yelled and turned. Reverend Bell was standing in the Perspex cubicle.

"Look at me!" He chortled. "I'm a collectible. One-of-a-kind!"

"Could you please let us out?" said Kit.

"Not going to do that. I'm sorry, Kit."

"Why not?"

Nate advanced on the cubicle. "Let us out of here, you sick bastard!"

"Sorry. No can do."

"What the hell are you playing at?"

"It's very simple, Mr Braxton," sniffed Bell. "In all my years studying Agatha Christie, I've always had a hankering to catch a killer. That's why I helped with the toy museum." He grinned. "One of the reasons, anyway. I thought I'd be able to persuade Archie to invite all the collectors to Furley House personally, for a gala dinner. To my delight, I didn't have to try to persuade him! He was thinking along the exact same lines. I thought it would be a wonderful opportunity to meet Mr Binfire in person and ascertain if he murdered Jack Braxton."

Nate slammed his fist on the Perspex, making Bell jump back.

"You mad bastard! Who the hell is Binfire?"

"It doesn't matter now. *He* doesn't matter. Binfire didn't murder anyone. Jack Braxton wasn't a victim, as it turns out. He's the hidden killer. And now I'm able to flush him out into the open."

Kit realised what Bell was saying.

"Me, you mean?"

"You said yourself, Kit. You are the last one to die. The tenth little figure. Jack Braxton has proved incredibly inventive in gaining access to his victims. I'm sure he'll have a way of finding your location and seeking you out. We just have to wait. And I'll be waiting with my trusty service revolver."

He sat cross-legged on the floor of the cubicle and rested his gun in his lap.

Nate launched himself at the cubicle, banging his fist on the wall and making it shudder. This time Bell ignored him.

Realising threats were useless, Kit tried to logic her way out of the situation.

"This is not a good plan, Jerome."

"I think it's an excellent plan. Worthy of Poirot himself."

"Listen to me. Right now, Nate's mother and grandmother are in a police station, telling them about Jack, and about this very room. They're going to come in here to check it out and they'll find you holding us against our will, *and* in possession of a firearm."

"She's right," said Nate, nodding furiously. "Mum and Gran will be back here soon, and so will the cops."

Bell's smile flickered. "We still have time."

"So has Jack Braxton. If he's as clever as we think he is, he'll realise I'm going to be released from here soon anyway. I'll be free, and you'll be sitting in a cell for what you're doing here. You won't be in any position to stop him."

Bell's smile faded. "I'll take my chances."

Kit had a brainwave. She walked up to the Perspex wall and spoke in a low, confidential whisper.

"I didn't tell you that I found his lair, did I?"

Bell's eyes narrowed. "I beg your pardon?"

"Jack Braxton's secret base. He has a hidden room in Furley House."

"I don't believe you."

"It's true. True as I'm standing here."

"I see. And you conveniently just raised this now? Didn't think to tell anyone about it before?"

"I thought the murderer was my best friend until about half an hour ago. Why would I say anything?"

"That makes a certain logic. But you're still lying."

"You've got my phone. Look at the last photos on my camera roll. I searched the house while you were fighting Archie's bull in the field. I found a padlocked room. I got in and there were loads of clothes and ablutions. Archie didn't know who it belonged to, but logic dictates it must have been where Jack was hiding out."

"Fine, show me," muttered Bell. "What's your passcode?"

Kit told him, and he flicked through her camera roll. He frowned at the pictures. Then he stood up.

"I'm going to investigate this place," he retorted. "It could have some bearing on my investigation."

"We can come too," said Kit. "All investigators together, right, Nate?"

"Bloody right." Nate nodded. "If my uncle is doing all these horrible things, then I have a right to know."

"Do you take me for a fool?" Bell laughed. "You're staying here. I'll be back presently."

Bell flashed a brief, cracked smile at them and disappeared into the back of the cubicle.

"Hey!" Nate yelled into the cubicle and hammered on the wall. "HEY!"

No answer. He rested his head against the Perspex and his shoulders slumped. "Hell. He's gone. What a crazy fucker. Well, I'm not waiting for that lunatic to come back."

"You'll get no argument from me," sighed Kit. "He's right. There is still a murderer on the loose. He could get here before your mum and your gran."

Nate ran back to the door and had another go at trying to find a purchase on the frame. Again, no luck. Then he lay on his belly and dug his fingers under the tiny gap. "Mum said they used to push Uncle Jack's meals through a slot at the bottom. It's been blocked up since, but it should be weaker than the rest of the door."

He dug his fingers into the bottom and tugged, bracing his feet against the wall. Suddenly, a fat chunk of wood came away with an explosion of sawdust, leaving a narrow two-inch chink of daylight at the bottom. He thrust his arm into the gap and scrabbled at the other side of the door.

He gasped in frustration. "I can only go as far as my wrist. I can't reach the door handle. Can you?"

"I'll try."

"By the looks of you, you can probably slip your whole body through."

Kit chose not to respond to Nate's thin-shaming. She slipped off her Mandalorian backpack and put it on the bed. Then she took off her coat and folded it neatly by her backpack. Then she slipped off her waistcoat and folded it neatly onto her coat.

"Get a move on!" Nate was growing impatient.

She tentatively lowered herself onto the hard wooden floor, grimacing at the motes of dust that had already been sent floating by Nate's efforts. She pushed her arm through, squirmed into position so her elbow was resting on the floor and stretched up as far as she could go, her fingers sliding against the outside of the door.

"It's no good," she gasped. "I'm nowhere near."

She wriggled back out.

Nate got back down and pressed his mouth into the gap. "Hey! HEYYYYY!" he bellowed. "HEEEELP!"

Kit withdrew to the bed and sat down, nursing her scraped elbow and trying to cover both ears with one hand. Thankfully, Nate gave up yelling. He grunted with frustration and scrambled to his feet. "Not a chance. There's a reason why Mum picked this room to hold Uncle Jack."

He paced back and forth across the tiny room. "This is a nightmare," he moaned. "How can everything suddenly turn to shit like this? Tabitha's been murdered, my long-disappeared uncle seems to be responsible for her death, and my mum and gran are being interviewed by the police as accessories after the fact. How the *hell* is this all happening to me?"

Kit's pedant monster opened one eye and decided to intervene. "It's not just happening to you."

"It bloody feels like it."

"*Two* people are dead, Tabitha and Moni, and that's just for definite. Saskia and Penny are missing, presumed dead."

"Yeah, you're right." Nate sounded almost irritated. "We've got to focus."

Kit unzipped her backpack, spilling the contents on the mattress. "Perhaps there's something in here that can help us get out."

It was a sad collection of objects. Her laptop was still in the safe in her room in Furley House, so there was just a Walkman, a few cassette tapes, a pencil case, her sonic screwdriver penknife and Sylvia's hen-night survival kit.

"I've got a penknife," she said hopefully.

"That's no good. There's no handle on this side, and we can't get at the hinge screws."

She shook the goodie bag and the contents spilled out on her coat. "Your mother gave this to me. Free samples."

"She does that a lot. She's got this brassy, up-front persona she likes to cultivate for the press. She loves making people embarrassed by bringing out her products – including me. But she's very nice, on the quiet."

Kit looked at the multi-coloured pile of tat. A tiny bottle of champagne, complete with plastic champagne flute. Lollipop penises, a deflated penis-shaped balloon with helium pump, a disposable camera, a hand-mirror with 'who is the most fuckable of them all?' written on the back in barely legible italics, a sparkly vibrator with a cardboard 'L' tied to the bottom, a sash and a packet of Love Hearts.

She picked up the Love Hearts. "At least we won't go hungry. Do you want one?"

"No thanks."

Her fingernails absent-mindedly tore at the clear plastic wrapper. She was almost going to flip one out and pop it in her mouth before realising she didn't know the calorie count. She hurriedly put them down.

Perhaps when we really start to starve, I might eat a few in ignorance. But, even then, I doubt it.

She picked up the vibrator and twisted the base. It hummed in her hand.

Nate looked at it with obvious distaste. "Please don't tell me you've got an itch you need to scratch. I can't cope with that on top of everything else."

Kit blushed. "I was thinking, perhaps if we roll this as far as we can, it might just jiggle off down the corridor and down the stairwell? Maybe your lady butler might find it?"

Nate looked aghast, then wrestled a hopeful expression onto his face. "It's worth a try."

Kit pulled a top off one of her pens. "Where would you describe this place? I mean, our location in relation to the rest of the house?"

"If you write 'East wing, inner rooms', they'd know what you meant."

Kit wrote HELP! WE ARE TRAPPED IN THE EAST WING – INNER ROOMS on the tiny L-plate and knelt down by the door. Nate joined her.

"Let me do this," he insisted. "I used to bowl for the school First XI."

She gratefully slapped the vibrator into his palm. He drew his arm back, then forth, then back again, then hurled it with as much force as he could muster. They watched as it bounced and rolled along the corridor.

Ten yards. Twelve yards. Fifteen yards...

It slid to a halt, jumping and spasming across the corridor. It almost looked like it would topple off the top step, but then it started juddering around in a wide circle, going nowhere.

"Dammit," Nate hissed. "And we were so close."

Kit went back to her disgorged backpack, looking through the motley collection of objects. She rooted through them in a desultory fashion. Nate sat on the bed by her, keeping a respectful distance.

When he's not shaking his metaphorical fist at the world, Nate seems like a nice young man, she thought. *I'm not surprised that Tabitha had a relationship with him. The bigger mystery is why she dumped him.*

Nestling in the bottom of her pocket was the jar with NATE written on it. She held it up.

"Would you know anything about this?"

He looked at it. His eyes bulged in recognition. "Where did you get that?"

"I found it in Furley House. On a shelf in that mysterious room I just told Reverend Bell about. The one full of unused toothbrushes, a brand-new watch and brand-new clothes."

He grabbed it off her. "Yeah, I certainly recognise this. This little jar is the reason why me and Tabitha split up."

He nestled it in his fingers and lay it on his lap. He gave a long sigh.

"What did you do?" Kit said gently.

"What do you mean?"

"I mean, what did you do with this jar, to make her dump you?"

Nate gave a crooked smile. "She didn't dump me! I dumped *her*!"

"You?"

"Yes!"

"Huh. You didn't give that impression. I saw the break-up YouTube video. You looked pretty mad."

"I *was* pretty mad. I was furious. I practically frogmarched Tabitha into that room and forced her to record it. I wanted the world to know I didn't want anything more to do with her."

"Why?"

"To sum it up in a single word – drugs." He got up and leaned against the wall, his arms folded tightly in front of him. "This isn't easy for me to talk about."

"I understand."

"I didn't want to talk about it up till now, because I did still love her, and didn't want to embarrass her. I hoped she'd get some help. But now she's gone, I guess none of that matters." He sighed. "We'd been together a few years and everything was just fine. And then, just a couple of months ago, Tabitha started getting evasive about stuff, and really *really* erratic into the bargain. Sometimes she disappeared without a word and lied about where she was going. I caught her out several times. It wasn't hard. One time she said she was with her mates at some wine bar, and one of them called me, and asked me where she'd got to. Another time she said she was out filming her cosplay videos, and I went into her room and found all of her costumes were still in their boxes. She was really snappy when I called her out about it. I thought she was having an affair."

Kit shifted uncomfortably on the bed.

"Then, about four months ago, I walked in on her in the bathroom at Furley House. Most of those damn bathrooms don't have any locks on the doors, courtesy of that mad bastard Roland Pendragon. Anyway, she was sitting on the loo, injecting herself in the leg with some noxious substance. I don't exactly know what it was, but the details don't matter, do they? She was doing drugs. It was the only explanation."

Kit's pedant monster interjected. "Not the only explanation. People inject themselves with insulin."

"Hey. I *knew* her. We'd been together a while. If she had a medical thing, if she needed to do something like that on a daily basis, I would *know*. Anyway, it's moot, because she didn't deny it. She begged me not to tell anyone and to give her some time so she could go cold turkey. Like a fool, I agreed."

He started pacing now, anger rising in his voice.

"Then, the next thing I know, I started getting grief from her girlfriends. They were ringing me up and calling me a drug-dealer! They called me scum!"

Nate shook his head in disbelief.

"They were at a club and her friend Amber did exactly the same as me – she went to the loo and walked in on Tabitha injecting herself in the leg. Amber was shocked, left the toilets, told the other girls what she'd seen, and they went back in there right away to stage an intervention. They demanded to know what it was she was using. Tabitha told them it was liquid heroin, and she showed them the jar. And *this* time Tabitha blamed *me* for being her supplier!"

He pointed a shaking finger at the little jar in Kit's hand.

"You see on there? My name? I have *no* idea why that's on there. She must have thought fast and scraped most of the label off and left my name on it! Well, that was the last straw. No way was I going to get a reputation for that crap. I'm not one of your landed gentry types that can get away with snorting stuff up my nose and injecting it into my veins. I need to live in the real world, apply for jobs and shit. After I got all the grief and accusations from her friends, I split up with Tabitha that day, and told her I didn't want anything more to do with her. That was just a few months ago. Now she's gone." He suddenly blinked back tears. "Oh my god, she's gone. I can't believe she's gone."

"Me neither."

"You knew her, didn't you?"

"A little bit."

"You must have seen that… she was such a force of nature."

"Oh definitely."

He slumped back on the bed and rubbed his eyes with the palms of his hands.

Kit felt she should give him a comforting hug, but what she *should* do and what she *wanted* to do were two very different things. She hoped he was so distraught that he just assumed she'd already done that.

"It's so very sad," she said at last.

"Yes."

"And surprising. I never imagined that was why you two split up."

"That's the reason."

"I did have a theory. Huh. You're going to laugh at me."

He raised his head and looked at her with red-rimmed eyes. "What?"

"Well, Archie and Tabitha filled my head with stories about armies of their father's bastard children wanting a piece of the estate, and I thought one of them was taking revenge by destroying the museum."

"Yes, well, old Roland Pendragon was a bit of a boy. Everyone knew that."

"I got it in my head that *you* might have been one of them."

"Me?"

"That when Roland came around to comfort your mum over Jack's 'death', I thought she might have been a bit more than a shoulder to cry on."

Nate frowned and then sniggered. "That's funny. That's really funny."

"I thought you and Tabitha might have split up because you discovered you were half-siblings."

This time Nate spluttered with laughter. "Haha! My mum used Roland a lot, for help, but she never *liked* him. No way is he my dad!"

"Okay. I was just floating some theories." She picked up a piece of flattened plastic with a string attached and a small plastic tube.

"Floating..." she muttered. "Huh. Wait a second..."

A thought. Definitely a thought. It slowly unfolded in her head, like a speeded-up recording of a flower blooming and greeting the morning.

"Yes. That could work."

"What?"

"Balloon," she said, holding up the plastic. "And helium," she added, holding up the tube. She went to the door, knelt down and unrolled the balloon along the bottom. Then she fixed the helium injector to the neck of the balloon.

"Are you trying to blow up the door with a balloon? Bit optimistic."

"Nothing like that. Whenever I can't get to sleep, I spend the night surfing YouTube and looking up 'how to' videos. I know how to crochet, use chopsticks and bleed a radiator, should I ever find the need, and I also found this really interesting way of opening doors…"

She pressed a button on the helium injector, slowly filling up the balloon until it was half-full. Then she pushed it all the way through the gap in the door and pumped the balloon until it was full. She removed the injector, tied the neck of the balloon and let it bob out of view. Kit kept the string wrapped around her fingers, and slowly paid it out. She could hear the balloon thudding gently against the outside of the door.

Kit grinned up at him. "Are you any good at those crane machines you get at funfairs? The ones where you have to try and grab the cuddly toy and guide it to the hole?"

"Not really. But then who is? Why?"

"Because your job is to get this balloon over the top of the door handle, so you can pull it down."

Nate leapt to his feet. "That's bloody brilliant! I'm game."

He wriggled to the floor, grabbed the string and paid it out further.

"This might help." Kit slid the tiny hand-mirror with 'who is the most fuckable of them all?' on the back through the bottom of the door until they could see the handle. Nate started to drag it up and down, up and down, over the handle. He must have tried it two dozen times before he felt the string grow taut.

"I think I've trapped one of the testicles over the handle!" He grinned. "I never thought I'd ever say a sentence like that, let alone be excited about it."

He tugged the string, very gently, until they felt the door free itself from the doorframe.

"Success!" gasped Nate.

They pulled the door open and ran into the corridor.

59

They ran downstairs to the reassuringly familiar fixtures and fittings of Braxton Hall, Nate's slippers flapping on the stairs and Kit's big boots clumping after.

Sylvia was in the library when Kit and Nate blundered in. She stood up in alarm, allowing the *Tatler* she was reading to fall from her lap and topple onto the floor.

"Where the bloody hell have you been?" she hooted. "Me and your gran have just been stuck inside a particularly tedious episode of *Line of Duty* for the past three hours and you're not even dressed!"

"It's a long story, Mother..."

"Well, we've got all day. The bloody house is surrounded by bloody reporters, so we're going bloody nowhere."

"Where's Gran?"

"She's having a lie down from the stress of it all, and don't change the subject." She pointed a beautifully manicured fingernail at Kit. "And what's *she* doing here?"

Nate sighed and recounted the events of the last three hours. Multiple expressions meandered across Sylvia's face as she listened: outrage, shock, horror and finally amusement as she learned of their ingenious escape from the room using Sylvia's hen-night survival kit.

"That's good." She chuckled. "Clever. I like that. Perhaps I should put you in my latest social media video, Kit. We're doing an adult version of *The Shawshank Redemption*, called *The Sore Wank Resumption*, set in a women's prison. You could be the one who tunnels out using a strap-on."

"Mother, shut up," sighed Nate.

"Sorry. It's all been a bit much today." Sylvia reached across and grabbed a glass on the table. Her hand was shaking so much the whisky nearly sloshed over the sides. "We're in a shit-ton of trouble," she snapped. "Insurance fraud is the least of it. Have you seen the news?"

"Mother – there have been deaths…"

"Don't you think I know that? They're calling this madman the Braxtons Butcher. That's the BBC. ITV are calling him the Doll Dismemberer, which I don't think is quite as catchy. Thank god I didn't put the Braxtons name on my products, or we'd be looking at another bankruptcy."

Kit's phone rang. She answered it and heard the stentorian growl of Graham Goldingay.

"Report."

"Penny Lane is gone."

"I know. My automaton is being held as a possible murder weapon. I'm being interviewed by the police."

"I think I'm his last victim. I need to get out of here and get to the police station. Can you help me?"

Goldingay said nothing. Amplified by the phone's speakers, Graham's breathing sounded like the rushing of a terrible wind.

"My van has been released by the police," he said at last. "Archie is sending one of his men over to drive it back to London. He can drive to Braxton Hall. The man can drop you off at Furley House, or the police station if you need protection. Or you can accompany him back to London and get a train to Tunbridge Wells from there. Whatever you want."

"Fine. Thanks."

60

This was the ultimate test for Kit. To get past the cordon of journalists and photographers. They surged forward when the gate glided open, almost pushing it shut with the weight of their bodies.

I can see why they're called 'press', she thought. *They're very good at pressing against people.*

The noise was unbearable. Everyone was shouting questions at her, but they weren't nice questions, like *What's your favourite episode?* or *How do you get your ideas?* or *Would you return to the series if asked?* They were questions like *Do you know where Jack Braxton is? Are you hiding him? Did you help him commit the murders?*

Her hand instinctively reached for the panic badge on her lapel, ready to turn it upside down and send a message to…

Who? Who is here to rescue me? Binfire is long gone.

She took several steps backwards, stumbling over the stones that separated the lawn from the bright purple driveway.

But then, a miracle. Like a startled shoal of fish, the journalists and photographers all swerved away from her and moved in another direction, towards Nate Braxton, who was dressed and standing in the driveway, making a big show of climbing into a beautiful silver-blue E-Type Jaguar. They converged on him, only to part like the Red Sea as the car roared through them, out of the gates and onto the open road.

As he passed her, he slowed down and gave Kit a friendly wink.

This is your chance, Kit!

Kit took her opportunity and ran down the road towards the transit van. A moustachioed man wearing thick tweeds and driving gloves was standing outside the van, and he doffed his cap at her as she approached. He gestured to the side door.

Kit hopped into the back seat and sighed with relief.

"Where to, miss?" said the man.

"The police station, please."

61

They were in a small office at the police station. DCI Smallgreen and DC Butcher had decided to conduct the interview.

DCI Smallgreen asked the same question again. "So can you describe the man who was driving the van?"

Binfire frowned. "I've told you. I'm not sure. I was quite far away. My motorhome was parked way across the other side of the crossroads, and my night-vision binoculars don't work as well in the day."

"Okay, well… If we brought in a sketch artist, do you think it would help?"

"Yeah, I'll have a go."

"Good. Thank you for your assistance, Mr Ferry."

Binfire looked worried. "Are you sure he wasn't the man who was sent to drive Kit?"

"The Marquess of Furley didn't send anyone to drive Kit. He got delayed."

62

Kit was awake, but she wasn't ready to open her eyes yet. She lay there, safe in the dark, listening to the gentle *tick-tock* of her pocket watch. There was something wrong, she could feel it, but she wasn't ready for that either.

You can't just lie here forever. You're in danger. You know you're in danger.

She forced herself to open her eyes, which wasn't easy as goo had stuck her eyelashes together, but she managed it.

There was more darkness, and then there was grey, and then there were fuzzy shapes. She could feel a cool breeze and assumed she was lying on a table. She moved her arm slightly and the plastic sheeting beneath her body popped and crackled with terrifying volume.

She craned her head up and could see medical machines, hospital beds and the kind of overhead light you found in operating theatres.

A mad scientist's laboratory, she thought madly. *I'm in a mad scientist's laboratory.*

"Hello, Kit."

The voice was distorted because it was behind a blank unsmiling mask, but it was also artificial, machine-like. It crackled.

She tried to speak but didn't have the muscles in her face to respond. She just made a low gurgling noise.

"I'm so glad you could join us, Kit," the voice grated. "I've been waiting for you. You're the last."

The masked figure dipped its head low.

"One little Kit. Left all alone. Then they lost the instructions. And then there were none."

63

The sketch artist wasn't doing as well as the police had hoped. It didn't help that Binfire was offering vague and contradictory opinions.

"He had a moustache, a bit like that guy in that film. You know, the one with the cowboys and the time-travelling car."

The sketch artist frowned. "You mean *Back to the Future Part Three*?"

"Not that one, the other one."

The sketch artist forced a smile on his face. "Can you pick a movie that I *have* seen?"

They struggled to the end of the task, and the sketch artist showed Binfire the face he'd drawn.

Binfire frowned. "Nah, I don't think that's it. It's a bit… wrong. Well, it's just frokking *bad*, man. This is hopeless."

He threw his arm up over his head, showing his hairy pits.

"We're never gonna find Kit at this rate. Frokk it."

64

Kit woke again, swimming towards consciousness. She could feel leather straps holding her in place. The buckles were fastened as tight as they would go, but they weren't pressing on her wrists and she found she could slip out of them easily. She stretched her arms, rubbed her wrists and gave silent thanks to her extreme dieting habits. Now all she had to do was to unfasten her legs.

She unbuckled the right one, just the right, and she was suddenly free. She collapsed bonelessly onto the floor.

I wasn't expecting that.

She pulled herself up, but something was wrong. She plunged back onto the floor. *It's the anaesthetic. It must be the anaesthetic in my system.* She lay there, her cheek pressed against the cool floor, extremely tempted to go back to sleep. But no. She had to leave.

Slowly and clumsily, she crept from under the table, pulling herself up and leaning heavily on the sheet of plastic – and came face to face with a nightmare.

She gasped in horror.

On the far wall was a piece of moulded plastic in the shape of a person, the kind of blister pack used to keep action figures held in place. Pushed inside the plastic form were body parts. Arms, legs and a torso. The only piece missing, Kit noted with a shudder, was a head. She moved a little closer. There was no blood; each chunk of person had been neatly severed, cauterised and covered in a stretchy fabric that approximated the costume of a *Vixens from the Void* character.

This is not just a pile of limbs stacked in the charnel house of a butcher, she thought. *This is a sculpture lovingly erected in the home of an utter maniac.*

The limbs had obviously come from Moni, Saskia and Penny. The torso? Was that *really* Lady Tabitha?

The area around the monstrosity was shiny, smooth metal. She could see her reflection in the mirror. Her make-up was smashed across her face. Her hair was a tousled mess. She recoiled from her reflection like Frankenstein's monster.

Then she saw what was on her neck. A dotted line drawn in marker pen.

Cut here.

By this collage of horror was a tiny little figure, fixed to a stand, made up of parts of dismembered Ceremonial Range *Vixens from the Void* dolls.

So, I was right. He was making his own Vixens from the Void *doll. But his ambitions went far beyond that.*

She knew that every second she spent in this place the chances grew that she would end up back on the table where a mysterious *someone* would start hacking at her neck to liberate her head from her shoulders.

In the middle of the gloom there was a golden thread of daylight stretching up from floor to ceiling, like a Tesseract beam (*Avengers Assemble*, 2012). She rolled herself along the floor towards it, over and over until her stomach lurched, until she came into contact with the wall with a dull clang.

Her hands felt like they belonged to someone else, and she mushed them against the light. It felt as though she was trying to crack open a safe by throwing sausages at it, but eventually she realised it was a door, a heavy sliding square of metal, and her efforts were slowly nudging it open, widening the shaft of daylight until it became a glaring furnace of brilliance.

She rolled out into the sunshine and sprawled into a car park. Then there were voices.

"Are you alright?"

"Is she drunk?"

Her eyes tried to open, but saw there were lots of people, black silhouettes against the sky. She wanted to tell them to go away. Leave her alone. Normally, she wouldn't have the strength to say anything, but the drugs in her system emboldened her.

"G'wuugh."

"She's definitely drunk," said a woman.

"What was she doing in the warehouse, do you think?" said a man.

"Sleeping it off, most likely," said the woman.

"Where's her leg gone?"

Another voice further away was shouting.

"Holy shit! Don't look in there! Shit! It's the Braxtons Butcher!"

"Don't you mean the Doll Dismemberer?"

"Whatever! Someone call the police!"

And then there was an ear-piercing scream.

65

"Hi there, pilgrim."

The last person she expected to see when she opened her eyes was Binfire, but there he was, looming over her.

"Hello. What are you doing here?"

"I thought I'd pop in and see the local celebrity."

"Celebrity?"

"Yeah, pilgrim. You're famous. The only one of the Braxtons Butcher victims who got out in one piece." He frowned. "Unfortunate choice of words, but you know what I mean."

"Where am I?"

"Hospital of course," grunted Binfire. "Where else smells like this?"

Kit flipped her gaze around the room. It was indeed a hospital room. Pale blue, with a window looking out onto the countryside. There was a bedside table straining under the weight of a huge fruit basket and flowers on the windowsill.

"This is nice. Is this a private room? Am I on BUPA?"

"You are," said Binfire. "Don't worry about it. Archie took care of it. You've been unconscious for two days."

"Wow. How long have you been here?"

"All day and night," said Binfire. "That murdering frokker is still at large. I'm on bodyguard duty. That's why I'm here. He could strike again at any time and take your other leg."

Kit looked down at her legs. *Leg.* Her left one was missing. There was her thigh, her knee… But below that, nothing.

"My leg's gone," she said stupidly.

"I know, pilgrim. I'm sure it's a shock, but you were lucky. It looked like he was after your head as well."

She allowed her head to fall back on her pillow. "This is bad. My boots won't fit now." She gave a high-pitched woozy laugh. "Hey. This is funny. Did I tell you why my parents called me Kit?"

"No."

"Go on, guess. It's not short for Katherine, or anything like that."

"Sorry."

"No, I won't let you guess. I don't know why I'm asking you to guess. I hate it when people ask you to guess. My parents were huge *Vixens from the Void* fans. I got born during the broadcast of the last episode of the series and those buggers *still* blame me for missing it."

She cackled again, her head wobbling like it was attached to a spring.

"Mum was passing the time being heavily pregnant by making kit forms of *Vixens from the Void* spaceships. She'd just finished one of the *Hydra* when she went into labour. I say 'just finished'. She *couldn't* finish it because there was a piece missing. My grandparents on my mother's side really wanted a grandson. They weren't subtle about it, so when I came out, my parents joked that I'd come out with a piece missing, just like the kit. So that's what I ended up being called. Kit. It was either that or Arkadia, so I think I dodged a raygun there." She grinned and pointed down. "Looks like I've got another piece missing."

"This will end with blood," growled Binfire. "I'm going to get the frokker who did this to you."

Kit laughed again. "It's funny."

"What's funny?"

"I thought you were the one who was a murderer."

"Me?"

"Well, Reverend Bell certainly did. He thought that's why you had that action figure. He thought you burned the factory down and killed Jack Braxton. Now it's Jack Braxton who's the murderer. It's all turned upside down. That's funny."

Binfire looked queasy. "Can we change the subject?"

Kit waved her hand imperiously. "Of course we can. What's been happening while I've been here? Have they caught him? Obviously not, as you're guarding me. Stupid question. So, the others? Penny? Saskia? Are they all dead?"

"Afraid so," said Binfire. "Moni, Saskia, Penny, Tabitha. All gone. Carved into little pieces.

"They're all definitely gone?"

"Definitely. They've been finding body parts all over Lincolnshire."

"They're sure it's their bits?"

"Why do you ask?"

"I don't know. I thought... Maybe..."

"The victims are definitely them. They've checked the DNA of every victim. Looks like you were very lucky. Apart from that *thing*, the place was empty."

There was a knock on the door. Binfire sprang into a combat-ready position. Then he yanked it open. It was Angelina, Archie's fiancée. She was laden down with boxes and bags.

"Hail to the conquering hero! Oh my gosh you look so brave!"

"She is," said Binfire proudly. "The bravest."

Angelina crash-landed into the room, hurling parcels onto a spare chair. "We've come bearing gifts. We've brought fruit. And chocolates."

"She'll take the fruit." Binfire winked. "I'll have the chocolates."

342

"I can't take the sugar spike," said Kit. "You should have the fruit as well."

"I'm sorry." Angelina looked scared. "Have I done something wrong?"

"Not at all." Kit gave a serene smile. "It's lovely to see you. Come on in."

"Thank you so much. Archie's just parking the car."

She scuttled inside and perched on the end of the bed. Then she noticed the mound under the blankets.

"Oh goodness, is that? Is that?"

"Yes. It's my lack of leg."

"Oh my. How does it feel? Oh my, what a silly question. It doesn't feel like anything, does it? Because it's not there."

"Huh." Binfire nodded like a man in the know. "You haven't heard of phantom-limb syndrome. You can still feel a leg that's not there."

Angelina looked at Kit with wide eyes. "Do you? Can you? Can you feel it?"

"Not really." Kit beamed. "But they've pumped me so full of drugs I can't feel anything, and I don't care if I do."

"They've got cases, pilgrim. Long-dead limbs just coming to life and feeling like they're still around."

Kit giggled. "Like ghosts."

"Yep, like ghosts. Freya sometimes has a point. Not often. But she does."

"Hail to the wounded soldier!"

Archie had appeared in the door. "How are you, Kit?"

"I'm good."

He looked around. "Is this really a private room? Doesn't look very swanky to me. Should I have a word with the administrators?"

"No," said Kit. "It's lovely. Thank you."

"Don't mention it. Anyway, we just thought we'd bring you a few things. Don't forget, once you're ready to leave, come to Furley House. You don't have to take that long drive down south. Not in your condition. Stay in the stables as long as you like and enjoy your coffee machine."

"Thanks," said Kit. "I appreciate that."

66

Kit didn't feel any grief about her missing leg. Not yet. She was compartmentalising. She pushed herself around the hospital on crutches, not looking down; allowing the fantastical part of her brain to construct a scenario in which it would grow back, like a lizard's tail.

She kept abreast of developments. Binfire told her that Matty Kearney was in a coma in another part of the same hospital. She had thought about Matty a lot, mainly his angry words about her, directed at Graham:

"She's a woman and *a lesbian. She only has to be black and disabled and you've ticked all the boxes."*

Well, I'm disabled now too. I'm really ticking all the woke boxes.

* * *

The recovery of the grisly body parts from the warehouse was the main item on all the news channels, and Kit watched the coverage endlessly. Occasionally, a photo flashed up of her, a screengrab from a Blu-Ray extra in which Kit was being a talking head. Binfire said the screengrab showed her looking rather thoughtful. Kit thought the picture made her look fat.

Better start upping my game when it comes to counting those calories.

Reverend Bell had completely disappeared, along with her phone, so Binfire had brought her a new one. She wiled away a few long minutes googling 'George Jamieson Pendragon' again, with exactly the same results. On a whim, she knocked off 'Pendragon' and just googled 'George Jamieson'.

Now, that's interesting.

There were a few George Jamiesons: lawyers, estate agents… But the George Jamieson that caught her eye happened to be the deadname of April Ashley, a supermodel from the 1960s, who had been born a boy and had married into aristocracy. She'd been one of the first people in Britain to undertake gender-reassignment surgery – in secret – and became the wife of the third Baron Rowellan. When her secret was discovered, the baron was granted permission from the courts to annul the marriage – even though he knew her secret when he married her. It was indeed a fascinating and tragic story.

And the photos accompanying the Wikipedia article were identical to that glamour pic above Tabitha's bed.

But why would an illegitimate son of Roland have that name? And why would Tabitha be interested in a woman who used to have that same name?

Too many questions. I'm too tired to think about it.

She called her parents. Binfire had already phoned them to keep them updated, and they'd followed the lurid coverage on the news channels ever since. Obviously, they were shocked at the news of their only daughter being held by a serial killer and losing a limb, but it was nothing compared to the shock of finding out how much the train fare was from Devon to Lincolnshire. Kit assured them she was fine, and she didn't need visitors rushing up to stare at her and eat her grapes, and after a few parent-daughter Zoom calls, during which Kit showed them how she was happily hobbling around on her crutches, they relaxed.

There really is nothing wrong with me, she thought. *But the hospital doesn't seem in any hurry to let me go. If I was on the NHS, I'd have been outside in the car park waiting for a taxi long before now.*

In fact, they wouldn't let her alone. A lady came in and introduced herself as Kit's physical therapist. That was when Kit realised she really needed to get out of the hospital.

And so the day came when Binfire arrived pushing a wheelchair.

* * *

"This is a good wheelchair, pilgrim," he said approvingly, for about the eighth time. "I could put switches in the armrest. You could pretend you're launching missiles."

"No, we have to return it. I don't think the hospital would approve of missile launchers."

"When you get your false leg, can I customise it?"

"Sure," she said wearily.

"Brilliant," he chirped. "I can put a gun inside it, like Robocop."

Kit was waiting, leaning against a stone lion while Binfire was wrestling the wheelchair out of his motorhome. She moved slowly around the lion to see the reassuring figure of Archie in his plus fours in front of the Furley House entrance, waiting for her. This time he was with Angelina, still wearing her big, chunky sweater. They both waved in unison and pointed to the ramp that had been laid over the steps to the house.

Was it just nine days since she'd arrived here to witness the opening of the toy museum? It felt like nine years.

So much had happened. So many had died. Of course, she felt for all the victims, but one face kept appearing in her mind, both when asleep and in those half-dozing moments when she was waiting for the painkillers to take her away.

Tabitha. What might have been.

Marking Kit's relationships on a curve, that had been quite a rollercoaster. The excitement. The apparent betrayal. And then the shocking loss. Kit wanted to believe her, when Tabitha protested that she wasn't behind the destruction of the action figures, but she knew she hadn't quite managed it. And now Tabitha was dead, and Kit had been wrong about her. She wasn't good at mourning, but perhaps Nate Braxton was able to weep for the both of them.

Binfire snapped the wheelchair open with one hand, popped it down in front of Kit and she sank gratefully into the padded seat.

"Thanks."

Angelina ran over to them. "Welcome, welcome! You are a hero, Kit, no bones about it. You're a hero and no mistake!"

"I'm not a hero," sighed Kit. "I'm just *not* a victim."

"Please, let me push her! I have to push her!" Angelina grabbed one of the handles.

Binfire wrestled the chair away from her fingers. "Sorry, no can do. I'm designated driver, ma'am. If anything happens to her, my superiors will have my head."

"Please don't fuss, button!" called Archie. "Let Mr Binfire do it. We don't want to tip her out on the gravel, do we?"

"We do not, Archiepops! Point taken!"

Angelina obediently hopped aside and let Binfire launch Kit up the ramp.

* * *

They had a meal in the great hall, just like before. But, as it was just the four of them, it felt incredibly creepy. Their voices were almost lost in the gigantic, wood-panelled echo chamber.

Binfire upended a huge scoop of mashed potato on a plate, threw in a few sausages and a pile of broccoli, drowned it all in gravy and placed it in front of Kit.

"Are you not counting calories, Kit?" asked Archie.

"No, she's not. Not at the moment," said Binfire, before Kit had a chance to speak. "The doctor says she needs to eat plenty to keep her strength up."

"You're not the boss of me," grumbled Kit.

"Oh yes I am, Captain Kit." Binfire grinned. "Until your ass is out of that wheelchair, your ass is mine."

"I promise never to complain about being stuck in a van with you for two and a half hours. This is far worse."

Archie and Angelina tittered, assuming Kit was making a joke. She wasn't.

Archie stood up, holding his glass of wine until it was level with his nose. "I want to make a toast. To absent friends. To all those we've sadly lost."

The others raised their glasses: Angelina her glass of wine, Kit her orange juice and Binfire his glass of water.

"To Moni Worth, to Saskia Shapiro, to Penny Lane…"

"To Kit's departed leg," added Binfire.

"Indeed. And, of course, to my dear sister, Tabitha."

"To Tabitha," they echoed.

"A great sister. A feisty individual. A great personal loss to me and, of course, to all her fans."

"Gosh, yes, she had so many, didn't she? Fans I mean," twittered Angelina.

Binfire aimed his fork at Kit. "Kit was a massive fan."

"Really?" gasped Angelina.

Kit stared at her food. "Yes, I was," she said quietly.

"Did you watch all her YouTube video thingies?"

"Oh yes," Kit said sadly. She turned to Archie. "I didn't like to say, but I knew all about your sister before I even met her. I knew her favourite flavour was salted caramel. I knew she was allergic to citrus fruits. I knew her favourite song was 'In the Year 2525' by Zager and Evans. I knew she liked tidy men who buff their nails."

Archie nodded. "That's all true, actually. Nate was very well turned out."

"Oh gosh! Nate must be feeling awful," added Angelina. "Knowing his own uncle did the terrible deed."

Kit wasn't listening. She was slowly moving her fork through her mashed potato, making a viaduct for the gravy to flow through.

"So, that was odd," she said at last.

Binfire peered at her. "What was?"

"That room upstairs with all the new clothes in it."

"Agreed, it was an odd room." Archie nodded. "Thankfully, the Salvation Army agreed to take all the suits."

"Not the suits. That was odd, but I wasn't thinking about that. When I went in there... I thought it was Lady Tabitha's room for a moment."

Angelina looked sharply at her. "Why do you say that?"

"Because I opened the padlock using the number 2525. I tried it because it was her favourite song, so when it opened, I thought that padlock – and the room – belonged to her. But when she came into the room, she looked like she'd never seen it before. And she said she'd been trying to open it for a while, trying different combinations... But she didn't try 2525. That was odd."

"A coincidence, I expect. It wasn't her padlock, I'm sure. It was just a coincidence the combination was 2525."

"Yes, that's probably it. A coincidence. Sorry. These things pop into my head."

The room fell silent, save for the odd scrape of cutlery on china.

Kit put her cutlery down.

"But these things pop into my head for a reason. And I don't know why."

"I know what we can do!" Angelina piped up excitedly. "We can go and have a look at the toy museum. It's all been patched up and Graham Goldingay has sent us some exhibits from his own collection to replace the ones that got broken!"

Despite herself, Kit was intrigued. She couldn't imagine Graham as a reformed Ebenezer Scrooge, so a visit to the museum might not be such a bad idea.

I could even finish my Vixmag *article.*

"Okay, I'm game," she said.

Angelina practically jumped for joy. "Splendid! Let's go off on an adventure. I'll get my pac-a-mac from the hallway and we can embark!"

* * *

It was getting dark as Archie, Binfire, Angelina and Kit approached the chapel, and it was starting to spit with rain. Angelina insisted on pushing Kit's wheelchair and she raced it to the door of the chapel with terrifying speed.

Angelina pulled open the heavy door, dived inside, and, a few seconds later, the lights flickered on. She returned to push Kit inside.

"In we go, chuff chuff."

They were standing in the atrium, the small antechamber in which hymn books used to be collected, when Binfire stopped and turned to face them. "Okay, I can't put this off any longer. I've got to leave you lot."

"Leave?" said Kit. "Go where?"

"To the police. To face up to my responsibilities."

"I'm not following."

"All those women died. Matty's in a coma, Reverend Bell's gone mad, Fenton's burned his livelihood to the ground and, to cap it all, you lost your frokking *leg*. I couldn't protect you."

"It wasn't your fault."

"I wouldn't beat yourself up about it," said Archie soothingly. "There's nothing you could have done. This chap is an absolute maniac."

"Frokk it. There was plenty I could have done, but I didn't take it seriously."

"Beg pardon?"

"I'm just a coward. I could have done more."

"I don't see how..."

"Explain yourself," said Kit.

"At least you saved her from the fate shared by others," said Archie. "This Jack Braxton seems to be on a murderous mission – and you thwarted him at the climax, so to speak."

There was a sudden thunderclap. The storm outside was gathering strength. Lightning shone through the tall windows and illuminated Binfire's shiny head.

"But here's the thing," said Binfire. "I *am* Jack Braxton."

* * *

"Of course," said Kit softly. "Of course you are."

Kit was gripped by shock, but also recognition, because in that instant it made so much sense. Her erratic friend with very little past. Her crazy companion whose hobbies included *Vixens from the Void* and blowing up things.

Archie spoke and his voice was steady, calming. His words dripped with honey. "I don't understand, old man. I don't see how you could be?"

"I had this breakdown when everything went to shit," muttered Binfire. "And I set fire to my factory. My big sister looked after me, but then she put me in a nuthouse. I escaped and ran away from everything that I did, all my stupid mistakes. I ran and ran, and I never looked back."

He gave a long, shuddering sigh. "The action figure was the only souvenir I kept. That and my alias Ben Ferry. The name came from my planned escape route. Ferry to Calais. Then drive to Benidorm. Benidorm Ferry. I wasn't in a good place at the time and my memory was incredibly frokked. I needed a mnemonic. Turns out I didn't get to Benidorm. Hey ho. Brighton's a close second, right?"

Kit pushed her wheelchair forward. "But... Why didn't you tell me? I'm your best friend?"

"C'mon, pilgrim. How could I tell *anyone* I used to be the CEO of a major toy company that made *Vixens from the Void* action figures? All my fan friends would go *mental*. I turned my life upside down trying to get away from all the shit that sent me crazy. Why would I just blurt it out and bring it all back? Bit frokking stupid, Captain Kit."

"But you came back home to here! You're here! We're just ten miles from Braxton Hall!"

"Jerome Bell called me. They *needed* my action figure for their museum to make it work. Roland Pendragon helped me out when I needed him, so I *had* to help Furley House, didn't I? I owed the silly old dead sod. That's why I risked it all to come back home."

He turned his red-rimmed eyes to Archie. "I owed a lot to your dad. I had to come back and help. It was a matter of honour."

Kit got straight to the point. "But you're not behind all this? The break-in? The thefts? The kidnappings? The *murders*?"

Binfire didn't answer. He pressed his knuckle on his chin and closed his eyes.

"I thought at one point I might have been. Right back when the museum was broken into. You see, I *wanted* something like that to happen. I really did, man. I was fantasising about it in my head, so me and you could do some more investigating. When it actually happened and Goldingay gave you the job... Well, I've never been in complete control of my actions, not since the breakdown. I thought I might have done it while my brain was looking the other way."

He sighed. "But then things got serious and I realised that I couldn't have done those murders. Could I? But just in case, I have to turn myself in. Go to the police."

"Binfire, you didn't do anything. I'm your best friend, and I know in my heart you haven't done anything. Let's just go back to the hall and talk about—"

There was a sudden *clink* behind the internal door. As if someone had put something large and heavy on one of the display cabinets.

They fell silent. Kit noticed there was light shining under the door.

"There's someone inside," hissed Archie. "There's someone inside my museum."

Binfire edged to the door.

"No, don't."

"I'll be fine," hissed Binfire. "And, even if I'm not, I'm expendable."

"No, you're not!"

But it was too late. Binfire pushed his boot against the door and heaved. Light spilled in on them, blinding them, and Kit could dimly see a figure amidst the glow.

"You BITCH!" came a scream.

Kit felt something scuttle across her skin. Fear.

I know that voice.

After a few seconds, Kit's eyes adjusted and she could see a sturdy woman in her fifties, dressed in a trench coat. She was holding a shotgun and pointing it in their direction.

"You utter BITCH!" screamed Jackie Hillier.

67

Jackie was quivering with fury. She pointed the shotgun at Kit.

"I did everything for you!" she screamed at Kit. "I loved you and I protected you! You have no idea what I've done for you. The sacrifices I made. And this is how you repay me?"

"What have I done?"

"What have you done? WHAT – HAVE – YOU – DONE? How dare you say that! Don't act all innocent! I've been following you!"

Kit realised.

That figure in Furley high street with the mask and hoodie.

"You have, haven't you! You *have* been following me!"

"Yes, I bloody have! I've seen everything you've been up to!" She gestured to Angelina. "You swan around with your new fancy girlfriend before we've had a chance to break up properly. You spend the *night* with her. How could you do this to me?"

Kit didn't know how to respond. Fear gave way to embarrassment. She turned to Angelina, who was stunned, rooted to the spot. "I'm sorry."

"Don't apologise to your *lover*, Kit, it's me you should be apologising to! Me! You just dump me for her, and drop me like a fucking hot potato? You don't even *call* me after you lose a fucking *leg*. You're all over the telly after being kidnapped by a maniac…"

She prodded herself in the chest.

"You don't think I would empathise with you after I got kidnapped by a maniac as *well*? And you don't even *call* me?"

"What are you *talking* about, Jackie? You split up with *me*!" yelled Kit.

"That wasn't a splitting up! That was a lovers' spat!"

"A lovers' spat in which you just happened to split up with me!"

"That's not how it works!"

"Oh *god*!" screamed Angelina. She pointed a finger at Jackie. "Listen, chunky. It doesn't matter how you think it works! You broke up with Kit and now you have to face the consequences – just like the time you last went into a hairdresser and asked for a cockapoo cut!"

"What? Fuck you!"

"Just go, you chav! You lost! So, get over it, suck it up and piss off back to Brighton!"

Angelina was going through an astonishing metamorphosis. Gone was the golly-gosh wet flannel. She was morphing into a snarling, take-no-prisoners hardcore bitch before their eyes.

Jackie's face twisted in hatred and the gun turned towards Angelina. "You think you've got her? Well, you're welcome to her! She's got all the passion of a pebble and the conversational skills of a speak-your-weight machine!"

Angelina sneered. "Perhaps Kit is just like that with *you*?"

Kit had had enough. She rolled up to Jackie and slammed the brake on, glaring at her ex.

She won't shoot someone in a wheelchair, Kit thought. *I hope.*

"Please don't shout at Angelina. If you have a problem, say it to me, not her. Angelina is nothing to do with me. She happens to be Archie's fiancée. I barely know her."

Jackie glared down at her. Kit could see her flared nostrils and her double chin. She felt guilty about thinking it, but *It's not Jackie's best angle. No one looks good in an up-the-nostril shot. No one in their fifties anyway.*

"Oh yeah! Pull the other one!" She tapped her nose with

her finger. "You always underestimated *my* detective skills, Kit Pelham. I'm better at this than you. I've got a nose for sin. Thirty-odd years in the hotel business and I can *smell* affairs. I know the stench of infidelity."

Jackie looked triumphant. "And I can do the credit card trick just as well as Binfire. I've been inside your *room*, Kit. I smelled that soap in the air, just as I can smell it on her now! Orange and nectarine! That poncy stuff doesn't grow on trees, funnily enough."

"You're wrong, Jackie."

"Don't insult me with lies."

"I'm not lying." Kit took a breath. "Yes, I did meet someone."

"I know you did."

"I'm not denying it."

"Good! Because I know she's standing *right there*!"

"No she's not... She's... not...?"

Kit's voice slowed to a crawl. Realisation was setting in.

She turned and looked at Angelina.

Kit then did something that was very unlike Kit. She disengaged the brake and pirouetted back to Angelina, stood up and pushed her head close, breathing deeply through her nose.

"She's right," said Kit. "You smell of oranges. You smell of Lady Tabitha Pendragon. Well, you don't *actually* smell of Lady Tabitha Pendragon because she would never smell of oranges as she was allergic to citrus fruit. But you *smell* like the woman who crept into my room two nights running..." Kit's voice hardened. "Who are you?"

Angelina didn't get a chance to answer, because Binfire took his chance. While Jackie was staring with hatred at Angelina, he slid across the room, pushing Jackie's legs from under her and wrenching the shotgun out of her hands.

"Here," he gasped, tossing the gun to Archie.

"Thank you," breathed Archie in relief. "One should never leave one's firearms in an unlocked cabinet." He broke open the gun and checked it. "Fully loaded. That was foolish." He snapped the gun shut and aimed it at Binfire.

"Up you get please, Mr Binfire. Over there with the others."

Binfire looked stunned.

"Archie, you don't have to point the gun at him. He's not the murderer," said Kit. "I know he isn't."

"I know he's not the murderer," snapped Archie. "I am. I killed them all. Can't you tell?"

68

"Mr Binfire cannot go to the police and tell them he's Jack Braxton."

He waved the gun.

"Shuffle over there and join your friends. I've seen you do several handy rugby tackles this past week. I have no desire to become a victim of another one."

Binfire reluctantly got to his feet and stood near Kit, Jackie and Angelina.

Archie smiled. "It was I who 'tipped off' the police – as the criminal fraternity put it – to the fact that Jack Braxton had not died in the fire, that his coffin was empty and that he was at large. My father knew that Jack was alive, of course. And, of course, he didn't feel obliged to tell *me*. He told his beloved eldest, and it was only many years later, in a moment of weakness, that Tabitha told me of Father's scheme. I kept it filed in the back of my noggin. It seemed an opportunity too good to miss – to use a vanished escaped lunatic as a very handy fall guy. Very Agatha Christie."

"You murdered all of them? Saskia? Penny? Moni?"

"With a little help, yes."

"And Lady Tabitha? You killed her too?"

"My dear Kit, of course I did. That's the reason why we're all here."

"He's mad," gasped Jackie. "He's a freaking headcase."

"Don't get his back up, Jax," said Binfire. "He's the one with the gun."

"Don't call me Jax, you weirdo," Jackie said automatically.

"Ha!" Archie was amused. "She doesn't like you very much. Perhaps I should give her back the shotgun."

"But... Why?" said Kit. "Why did you do all this?"

"I think my dear Angelina was almost ready to tell you the truth." He moved the shotgun away and turned it towards Angelina. "You seem ready to unburden yourself. Why don't you tell them?"

Angelina shook her head, afraid. "No."

"Fine. If one wants something doing, one has to do it oneself. It was quite amusing when your goth friend had her theory about a ghost being responsible for everything. She wasn't far wrong. My wonderful sister, Lady Tabitha Pendragon, died three months ago. What you have been interacting with is an echo of her. She's only been here in spirit, if not the flesh."

He waggled the shotgun at Angelina.

"I met the lovely Angelina at the George Club last year. A friend of a friend of a friend. The moment I saw her, I could see she was amazing. Poise. Breeding. Blistering intelligence. The only drawback was the lesbian thing. After meeting a few more times, at the parties of mutual friends, we decided it wasn't a drawback after all. Didn't we?"

Angelina didn't respond.

"We were very fond of each other, don't get me wrong, but it was, when all's said and done, a truly transactional arrangement. For my part, I'd get the perfect wife, a woman who was able to carry herself in the social circles in which I operate, a woman who would not panic about 'love' or 'compatibility' or other such nonsense, and who was more than capable of running the estate. For her part, she would get a very comfortable lifestyle and give me issue. That was part of the deal. I don't like children, myself. Horrible little snotty things, running about knocking over the Meissen vases and leaving jammy fingerprints on the

Gainsboroughs. But when one is in my position, one is expected to have offspring."

He sighed and rolled his eyes to the ceiling.

"Big sister was absolutely livid. Oh, I did everything I could to placate her: fund her little whims, plane tickets across the world so she could attend her conventions, money to set herself up as her own company, with her own studio in the grounds. I was willing to do anything to make her happy. But to no avail. She felt that, as she was Father's favourite, she was being robbed of her birthright – having being, through no fault of her own, born a woman."

"Of course," said Kit.

"What do you mean, 'of course'?"

"That's when Lady Tabitha Pendragon decided to change her gender, wasn't it?"

Archie grinned and winked. "Finally she realises."

"It all makes sense. The room full of men's clothes. The injections in her leg. Her weirdly low voice in that break-up video with Nate... And George Jamieson Pendragon! That was the new name she'd chosen for herself. She was preparing for her new life."

"Now she's thinking. Finally, she gets it!"

"She was going to transition from being the eldest daughter of the seventh Marquess of Furley and become his eldest son."

What was it that Sylvia Braxton said? "I told Tabitha to think like a man. That's what you do in a man's world."

Archie narrowed his eyes at her. "It's all the fashion these days, isn't it? Big sis was very thorough. She'd done all her research. She'd combed through that wretched gender-recognition act, the one the government – in their infinite wisdom – had passed in the early 2000s, and she reasoned that if she became a man, not only would she be a male in the eyes of the law, it would also be illegal to discriminate against her. She reasoned that if she went to court and made it a test case, asserting her legal right to be the elder son, then it was even-stevens they'd rule in her favour."

Archie laughed, a short hysterical bark.

"Hah! Who knows how it would have played out? Perhaps a jury might have, quite sensibly, thrown it out, favouring centuries of tradition over some passing social fad. But the pressures involved these days, the pressure exhibited on *anyone* who is perceived to be not waving from a float at the gender-fluid carnival... Who could possibly know what that verdict would be?"

"And you couldn't take that chance. So you murdered her."

Archie pouted. "Only by accident. There was an argument, a confrontation. Harsh words were spoken. Tabitha had taken the opportunity to come up to the house and gloat about her scheme. She'd started taking – what was it? – testosterone cypi... cypi... Ah, yes. Testosterone *cypionate* to change her body to prepare for her surgery."

Testosterone cypioNATE.

"Tabitha showed me what she'd done to her arms. She'd covered them in tattoos telling the world what she intended. Copies of application forms she'd had to fill in to apply for a gender reassignment. An entire document tattooed on her bicep that said, 'In the event of my death I was probably killed to prevent me going through with my plan', et cetera, et cetera, et cetera. She was very thorough, but that was my big sis. Thorough. Things turned very unpleasant. Before I knew it, I was rolling around on the floor of the great hall with Tabby's hands around my neck, getting my head bashed against the oak floor. And then, all of a sudden, she was lying beside me, and her head had gone, and Angelina was standing there with my father's shotgun."

"That's not true!" blurted Angelina. "It was *my* head that was getting banged against the floor, and it was *you* standing there with a smoking double-barrelled shotgun!"

"Oh, who cares who did what? I don't know if there's any way you can disprove my story as that particular shotgun is currently lying at the bottom of the moat. Anyway, that's neither here nor there."

The man is completely barking, Kit thought. *As mad as his father. The regressive genes certainly run strong in these old families.*

Archie put his shotgun in one hand and held his arms wide. They trembled.

"Picture the scene if you will: Angelina and I, standing over the bloodied headless body of my sister; a sister who had been openly antagonistic towards us for months, railing against me for robbing her of her birthright. Plenty of motivation on my part for revenge. I think I would be the obvious suspect, given the circumstances. The old self-defence argument was looking pretty ropey. I needed time to think about what to do next. We stashed her body in the fridge freezer, the one in the cellar, where we keep the venison."

There was a long pause, as everyone thought about the image of Lady Tabitha stuffed inside a chest freezer, and let the horror of it sink in.

"I had three problems. The first problem, naturally, was the absence of my sister. She was a social animal, and if she disappeared from her social media outlets, people would notice. Then Angelina had this stroke of genius. She pointed out that she was a similar height and build to Tabitha, and, furthermore, a lot of the time my sister covered herself in all manner of costumes, most of them with masks. She volunteered to substitute herself for Tabitha, so we could move her time of death and thus create an alibi for ourselves."

He gave Angelina an appreciative wink.

"She was very good. She got the voice just right, and as long as she didn't come too near to anyone, she was able to convincingly pass for my sister. It was not a long-term solution, but it would do for the moment."

Kit looked at Angelina. "All those masks and goggles you wore, those times when you refused to turn on the light. You didn't want me to see that you hadn't any tattoos on your arms."

Angelina smiled sadly. "I wanted to turn on the light, Kit. I really did."

"Oh, for fuck's sake," muttered Jackie. "Get a room."

"I quite agree," said Archie. "Can I continue? The second and third problems dovetailed. Secondly, Tabitha no longer had a head to speak of, and thirdly, her arms were covered in her 'j'accuse' tattoos, pointing the finger at me from beyond the grave. It was not enough to create an alibi. We had to allow the body to be plausibly discovered without the head and without the arms. It took us a long time to work out what to do."

He closed his eyes wearily. "Eventually, it was Angelina who came up with the plan, didn't you?"

Angelina erupted, "It wasn't a plan! I just said..."

"What?" asked Kit.

"I studied biology in university. I specialised in forensics. All I said was, if a body was kept at a freezing temperature, it would prevent the police from determining the exact time of death—"

Archie interrupted her. "So, if Tabitha's dismembered torso was discovered, hidden alongside dismembered parts of other bodies that had also been frozen, the police would assume she'd been killed alongside the others. It certainly helped that Angelina was able to run into the night, burst through a window and meet her doom, thus securing my sister's time of death as shortly after that evening."

He sighed. "It was a marvellous plan, devilish in its intricacy. Employing that wretched actor to play himself! Hilarious! Leading everyone to view Tabitha as the chief suspect, before removing her from the chessboard, so to speak. It was an act of genius to programme that phone to unlock to Tabitha's face. We used the same picture on the wall, ironically. I knew the great detective Kit Pelham wouldn't disappoint. We had fun, didn't we, Angelina?"

Angelina looked sick. "It's been a nightmare. I had to stand back and watch this ghastly dream unfold. All those deaths. I didn't think he'd... I thought once I stopped being Tabitha, he'd just end there, pretend the murderer had just killed his sister. But he *carried on*... He said he'd kill me too if I went to the police."

"Now, now." Archie chortled. "You're an accomplice. Can't pretend to be the innocent victim in all of this, just because you're female. Equality. That's how this works, don't you know?"

"Okay, I want to pause here." Binfire held his hand up. "Let me sum up. You, you mad frokker, you murdered and dismembered four innocent people. JUST so you could reveal the parts of Tabitha's body that didn't incriminate you?"

"For the record, yes, I murdered them. Suffocated them with my chap Malcolm's help. But I DIDN'T dismember them. It was my gamekeeper Cyril who did the honours with the bonesaw. He's had the practice with our livestock. Done it all his life."

"Livestock? You got your gamekeeper to cut off my leg?" said Kit faintly.

"I did. It was Angelina's idea to keep you alive."

"It was the best I could do," sobbed Angelina. "He wanted to kill you like the others, and get Cyril to cut you up, but I persuaded him not to. I said a victim who looked like she'd escaped would help to convince the police it was the work of some insane loner." She pointed at Archie. "He agreed, but he said it had to look like Jack Braxton had started the job of hacking you to bits and been interrupted. It was either just your leg, or your head as well."

"Enough of this." Archie was losing patience. "Mr Binfire's shock reveal of his true identity has sent my plan awry and we need to set it back on track. Never let it be said that I don't think on my feet."

He levelled the shotgun at Jackie. "I've heard tell that a spurned lover has been stalking the woman who broke her heart across the Lincolnshire countryside. I hear that tonight she will track down the object of her love…"

The shotgun barrel moved to Kit. "… and corner her in the stately home in which she has been staying. The lover will grab a shotgun from the house and blast her estranged love into kingdom come…"

The shotgun moved to Binfire. "… taking in her loyal best friend…"

The shotgun muzzle wandered across to Angelina. "… and, tragically, a passing observer, the Marquess's own fiancée, visiting for a short stay. The spurned lover is spotted by the Marquess himself, as she emerges from the house. He is concerned about intruders in the middle of the night, and he shoots *her* when she tries to make a run for it. How tragic. The bereaved Marquess will of course put up a memorial plaque to those fallen. What do you think?"

"Complete rubbish," sneered Binfire.

"Ah, the undiscerning naivety of the unsophisticated plebian mind."

"I agree with him, it *is* rubbish," said Kit.

"Of course you would."

"It's a pretty rubbish plan which relies on you pointing a gun at four people, and shooting all four people before any of them can rush you, when you've only got two barrels."

For the first time, an expression of uncertainty crossed Archie's face. "Hmm. Well, Angelina? Here's a proposal. Would you like to cross the floor and return to my side?"

Angelina wiped her eyes and pulled a disbelieving face. "Why should I? Won't you just kill me later?"

"I swear on the Pendragon name, I won't kill you. And you know how important that name is to me."

Angelina hesitated. Then she walked over to Kit's wheelchair, bent down and gave Kit the biggest, deepest French kiss Kit had ever had in her life. "Goodbye," said Angelina. And she walked across the chamber to stand by Archie.

"Don't do this, Angelina."

"Sorry, Kit. I'm in this too far. I stood by and didn't do anything. I can't get past that."

"I think you'll recall it was for *money*, dear," mocked Archie.

"Hey, genius! There are still three of us, and only two barrels," sneered Binfire.

"Easily remedied." Archie turned to Angelina. "Would you like to get my spare shotgun, my dear? You know where it is."

Angelina left.

"Don't get your hopes up. She won't save you. Angelina knows I'm her only hope to escape justice. Though I confess she grew into an increasingly unwilling accomplice as the plan unfolded. I did sense she had an ulterior motive when she suggested *you*, Kit, could be a last, living witness, but I did agree with the logic – it *would* be the icing on the cake to persuade the police there was a madman at large."

"There *was* a madman at large," said Binfire. "I'm frokking looking at him."

"You sound like you disapprove," sniffed Archie.

"Do you think? Gods, you posh types are so perceptive."

"I can tell from the expression on your idiotic face that you think what I did was disproportionate in some way. I can tell you're not understanding what's at stake. There are hundreds of years of tradition locked up in Furley House and the nine thousand acres that surround it. Generations took arms and fought and died to make Furley what it is. When you think of the enormity of all that disappearing, the lives of a mere handful of people are nothing. They are just fleeting impressions of history, whereas Furley House IS history."

Archie walked to the door and peered outside, waiting for Angelina's return.

"We can still rush them," whispered Binfire. "They can shoot one of us, maybe two, but not all of us."

"We're not doing that," Jackie hissed.

"We've got no frokking choice."

"You are such a mad bastard."

Kit shook her head. "We should wait and see what Angelina is going to do."

"Oh, of course we should listen to *her*." Jackie glowered. "We should all trust her, because the girl who makes *The Texas Chainsaw Massacre* look like *Love Actually* happens to be your *girlfriend*."

Archie returned with Angelina. She was brandishing a shotgun in her right hand.

"Well, well," said Archie. "Alas, we have reached our final act."

Angelina also had something in her left hand. A chunky metal device with a large dial.

Kit recognised it instantly. She'd seen one used on her long nights of watching 'how to' YouTube videos. It had been featured in one about electromagnets.

"Of course," said Kit, when she saw it. She looked up. "Obvious. Magnetism. It's so simple. Is there a false compartment in the ceiling? I bet there is. How can you steal four rare action figures and leave the others behind? There's a perfect way, when the rare set of figures all happen to be wearing die-cast metal armour."

Archie's face wrinkled in confusion. "What are you...?"

Then he noticed the device in Angelina's hand.

"No! You little—" Archie swung his shotgun to give her both barrels, but it was too late. She pressed the button and the gun was plucked out of his hand. Angelina's gun did likewise. Jackie gave a sudden piercing scream, as her earrings were ripped from her ears by the powerful electromagnet secreted in the chapel roof.

Kit was suddenly flying above everyone's heads, hurtling upwards. Her wheelchair fastened itself to the top of the chapel and Kit found herself dangling by the seat belt. Something whizzed past her and she saw that Binfire's belt-buckle had embedded itself into the ceiling, just inches from her nose.

She was nose-to-nose with the repaired window. It had stayed intact. *That was how they got it to smash inwards so spontaneously, with no one else around*, she thought madly. *They attached a lump of metal to it and let the magnet pull it into the room.*

Binfire didn't miss his chance. The moment the shotgun was plucked from Archie's hand, he hurtled towards the Marquess and performed his classic rugby tackle. He threw himself on top of Archie, who struggled and twisted, but the Queensbury Rules were useless when his arms were pinioned, and he had a raging ex-CEO of a bankrupt toy company on top of him, turning his face to pulp with his fists.

Intent on venting his rage, Binfire wasn't aware that Kit was in peril. The wheelchair was folding in on itself, crumpling like Graham's robot. Kit had no choice but to release the seat belt, pull herself out from the seat and dangle from one of the chair's armrests. It was an incredibly long way down, and the newly reconstructed glass pyramid was right below her, jutting up like a knife.

Kit dropped.

But Angelina was ready. She rushed forward, kicking the pyramid over and standing foursquare on the dais. She caught Kit smoothly with two hands.

"Wow, you're strong," was all Kit could say, before Angelina kissed her again, and put her gently down on the floor.

Binfire got to his feet, holding his cargo pants up with his left hand and blowing on the bloody knuckles of his right. "We'd better call for an ambulance," he said. "I think, after nine hundred odd years, I might have accidently ended the Pendragon family tree."

* * *

"I need some air," gasped Kit.

Binfire supported her as they hobbled outside into the night to ring for the emergency services.

As soon as they had finished the call, they heard the bang of a shotgun inside the chapel. They rushed back inside to find the magnet had been turned off, and bits and pieces of metal had dropped from the ceiling and scattered across the floor. The wheelchair was a crumpled mess, resembling Graham's robot from that first night.

Angelina was gone. Jackie was on the floor, the shotgun lying beside her.

"Oh my god," sobbed Jackie. "She turned the magnet off and the gun fell. She picked it up and fired it at me. She nearly killed me."

"Oh dear," gurgled Archie, lying in his own crimson pool. "What a tragic accident."

And then he half-laughed, half-choked on his own blood, until the ambulance crew arrived.

EPILOGUE

"Turn right towards Lewes at the next junction, you must."

Kit and Binfire were back in Binfire's van. This time they were travelling from Tunbridge Wells to Brighton, and the rear of his motorhome was chock-full of Kit's stuff. Kit's dachshund Milo was sitting between them, secure in his little seat belt, staring out of the window on constant guard, protecting his mistress from the countryside.

Binfire tried to break the tension that had filled the cabin like a choking fog. "What do you think of the new paint job, pilgrim?"

"Very nice."

When Binfire had arrived to pick her up, the first thing Kit noticed was the extra murals on the side of the motorhome. The space figures had been joined by a machine-gun-wielding, muscle-bound hunk who looked about seventy per cent Arnold Schwarzenegger, thirty per cent Jean-Claude Van Damme.

"Turns out the sketch artist for the Lincolnshire police also used to paint murals for fairground rides. He did this one for free."

"Well, it looks great."

They hadn't seen each other for three months, not since Archie had been arrested, but Kit had followed what had been happening at Furley House in the newspapers. She'd even subscribed to the *Tatler* to find out how the story was reported in the World of Posh. With Tabitha gone and Archie in prison, along with Malcolm and Cyril the gamekeeper, Furley House had been left with no one at the helm. Fortunately, Roland Pendragon's younger brother, Oliver Pendragon, was on hand. He was happy to drop everything and bring his family over from Canada to take over the estate. Oliver Pendragon was an incredibly boring bald man who worked in private equity, but Kit guessed the remaining staff who worked on the estate would think Oliver a great change for the better.

"I heard you went to Fenton and Vixy's wedding," said Kit.

"Yeah, me and Freya took a trip up to London. They got married inside a *Star Trek*-themed Escape Room, and they had to find their way out in one hour, or the taxi would leave and they'd miss their honeymoon."

"Nice concept."

"Yeah, I thought so. They were dressed as a Klingon and an Orion slave girl. Vixy was the Klingon and Fenton was the slave girl."

"Ugh. Is Fenton still running his shop in Peterborough?"

"Nah. He couldn't be bothered. He sold off the charred remains of The Battlestore Galactica to property developers and used the money to open the tiniest cupboard of a comic store in Catford, called And So to Dredd. He's running an internet mail-order service."

Binfire cackled. "Fenton doesn't know this, but Vixy has also set up her own internet business, an OnlyFans account on which she charges viewers money to watch her play with objects, some of them made by my sister."

"Have you *seen* your sister?"

"On the telly? Yeah, she's good. In fact, she's more than good. She's amazing. I'm very proud."

The Braxton family had managed to load the blame for Jack Braxton's life-insurance fraud onto Vera Braxton, who was too old and baffled to go to jail. Nevertheless, the family did have to pay a historically massive fine, and Sylvia had to close half her stores to pay for it. Her solution to resuscitating the business was to become a regular on the BBC show *The Bearpit*, where she took great delight at sneering at young entrepreneurs in a Lincolnshire accent and placing her products in strategic places by her chair.

"No, I meant have you *seen* your sister? *Seen* her? Like, told her you're alive?"

A pained expression slipped over Binfire's features. "I haven't. No. Sometimes I think I should. But then I think, it's probably best to leave it. The past is past, right? She's better off without me."

"I can't believe *anyone* would be better off without a Binfire."

His pained expression slid off as quickly as it slid on, and he grinned at Kit.

"Thanks. I'm really looking forward to sharing digs with you, pilgrim."

Kit smiled but didn't respond.

Kit had heard on the grapevine from a few of her journalist friends that Archie Pendragon *had* tried to tell the world of Binfire's identity, but the world of journalism was not interested. Not surprisingly, the world of journalism was more interested in analysing Archie's sociopathy in the hope of producing best-selling books about upper-class serial killers.

"How's Matty Kearney?"

"Out of his coma."

"I heard. But is he okay?"

"Yes, right as rain. Just the same as he was before."

"Oh dear."

"Yeah. Oh dear. You not heard his latest podcast?"

"I try to avoid them."

"He told his posse why he said those words 'It had to be you.

How fucking clichéd. How fucking predictable' before he was bludgeoned into a coma."

"Why?"

"He'd seen Archie Pendragon's face at the door of the cupboard when it was wrenched open and was disgusted to see that the villain of the story was, once again, a rich, cis het white male with an English accent."

Despite herself, Kit smiled.

"And Reverend Bell? Did we ever find out where he went after he locked Nate and me up in Braxton Hall? He never did get to Furley House."

"That's because he got knocked over by a tractor."

"What?"

"Don't worry. He was okay. Just a broken collarbone. But he should have known – those Lincolnshire roads are treacherous. You can't walk along them like that. Anyway, he recovered and had a kind of reverse-epiphany. He's left the church and now devotes his life to peddling disinformation on the web. He got his own show on a tiny cable channel and calls himself the Conspiracy Cleric."

"Hah."

"So…"

"So?"

"So have you heard from Jackie?"

The reason why she was in the motorhome travelling to Brighton.

"Not yet."

No one had pressed charges against Jackie for holding a loaded shotgun on them. That minor transgression had been swallowed up by Archie's appalling crimes and the subsequent manhunt for Angelina.

Perhaps that was a missed opportunity.

As soon as Kit struggled back to her little flat in Tunbridge Wells, Jackie was ringing her doorbell like nothing had happened. She conceded that harsh words had been spoken in the heat of the moment, and there was *much* to regret, but she reasoned that had only made their relationship *stronger*. Don't you *think*?

She proposed to move in and nurse Kit back to health, and Kit, because she was exhausted and shell-shocked from the whole experience of losing her leg, let Jackie in. To her regret. During the long process of learning to use her swanky new carbon-fibre leg, practising weight transfer and living with the phantom pain of the missing limb, she truly needed someone who was really prepared to mother her to infinity and back again.

During the long nights, with Jackie's huge arms wrapped around her shoulders, Kit often lay awake suffering from phantom-limb syndrome, but not just in her missing leg. She also felt an ache deep in her ribcage for another phantom: she knew her heart was still aching for Lady Tabitha Pendragon, a woman she'd never actually met, and who had died before Kit had even known her.

After a while, Kit recovered her energy and was able to master her new leg. She also wanted to be master of her own life again and was ashamed that she'd allowed Jackie in her flat to cook her meals and feed her pills. This was a woman who she knew she didn't love anymore, and was, frankly, a little frightened by.

But Jackie was too terrifying for Kit to even start that conversation.

So they carried on.

Until one morning, when Kit got a call.

"Hello, sexpot."

"Hello."

"Are you alone?" asked Tabitha.

No. Not Tabitha. Angelina.

But Angelina was putting on the Tabitha voice.

For me.

She poked her head into the tiny sitting room. Jackie had just popped to the shops for some milk. It was just her and Milo.

"Yes, I'm alone."

"I'm on the run again. For real this time. I've been finding all my cosplay practice useful. Lots of disguises. No one's recognised me. Yet."

"Huh."

"I'd like to see you. I know that would be difficult. Perhaps one day we might have a drink in daylight, and I won't have to wear a disguise. You must have bought a very swanky coffee machine by now. Perhaps we could share a coffee."

Kit didn't respond.

"Perhaps when you're at a convention, I can slip into your bed in the middle of the night. We wouldn't have to put the light on, so you don't have to lie to the police when they ask you if you've seen me."

Kit still didn't reply.

"Look. I'm only calling because I couldn't leave it like this. You needed to hear what I'm going to say. That night? When all that shit went down? I don't know what Jackie told you, but *she* knocked my control box out of my hands and *she* switched off the magnet, and *she* grabbed the shotgun when it fell, and *she* fired at me. That's why I ran."

"That's why you ran."

"Fine. I *ran* from your mad girlfriend. I *kept running* from the police. Okay?"

"Why would I believe you? You've done nothing but lie to me since we met."

"I don't think I'm the only one. Perhaps the other woman in

376

your life has a few skeletons in her closet?" Angelina sighed, a slow hopeless sigh. "Fine. Believe me or don't believe. It's up to you. You've got two women in your life who lie to you. You have to decide which one is lying now. Use your gut, Kit. Use your famous detecting skills to work out which one you can trust."

* * *

Two weeks later, Kit waited for Jackie to go back home for the weekend – to where Kit had addressed a 'Dear Jackie' letter. It would have been waiting for her, on the mat. Waiting for her arrival.

The minute Jackie left for her train, Binfire roared up and stripped the flat of everything Kit owned, hurling it into the back of his motorhome. Then, at midday, Kit handed the keys to a nice young couple who had emailed her the moment she advertised the flat through a rental agency.

And then they were off.

Perhaps it *was* perverse to move to Brighton, which was much *much* closer to Jackie, but Kit felt alone and vulnerable in Tunbridge Wells. At least in 33 Hanover Parade she was surrounded by friends all of the time: Robbie, Freya and Binfire. There was always someone to look after little Milo, and always someone to open the front door on her behalf.

And there was no one there who wanted to control her.

Like a doll.

"Arrived at your destination, you have."

And there they were at 33 Hanover Parade, nosing into a parking space. Robbie and Freya were at the door, smiling and waving. Binfire must have quietly texted them an ETA.

Kit felt a huge feeling of relief.

"Welcome home, pilgrim," said Binfire.

ACKNOWLEDGEMENTS

This book has languished in a box in a pile of bits for over a decade, until I worked out a way to screw it all together and provide some articulation. The people below are the ones who handed me the ball joints.

Thanks to my grandfather Alfrey Cyril Fountain, gamekeeper of Burghley House. Thanks for those first five years of my life playing in the grounds of that amazing place. Living at the Roundhouse in Burghley Park really gave me a feel for life around a stately home. Actually, thanks to his brother Pete, and Pete's son John. Gamekeepers all.

Props to Adrienne 'The black' Knight (Barrister at Law) for her legal advice.

Thanks to Toby Fountain, who I should have thanked in the last book, for his assistance in testing the flammability of vodka mixed with mouthwash. Good work, son!

A nod to David A. McIntee, *Doctor Who* author who sadly died in 2024. It was his *Babylon 5*-themed wedding at the Gallifrey One convention that inspired Fenton and Vixy's nuptials.

I conducted a lot of research on collectible action figures. My two main sources are books, specifically *Action Figures of the 1980s* by John Marshall, and YouTube channels, particularly 'Analog Toys' presented by Tony Roberts.

Applause is given to Agatha Christie. This book would not have existed without her, but of course you all know that.

ABOUT THE AUTHOR

Nev Fountain is an award-winning comedy writer and journalist for *Private Eye*, chiefly known for his work on the radio and television show *Dead Ringers*. He has also contributed to programmes such as *Have I Got News For You*, *2DTV* and the children's sitcom *Scoop*. A huge *Doctor Who* fan, Nev has written several audio plays based on the series, and occasionally appears as a host or MC at *Doctor Who* conventions. His three Mervyn Stone Mysteries novels – *Geek Tragedy*, *DVD Extras Include: Murder* and *Cursed Among Sequels* – follow the exploits of an ex-*Vixens from the Void* script editor as he investigates crimes. He is also the author of the thriller *Painkiller*. His first novel in the Kit Pelham Mysteries series, *The Fan Who Knew Too Much*, was published by Titan Books in 2024. Follow him on Twitter/X at @Nevfountain.

For more fantastic fiction, author events,
exclusive excerpts, competitions, limited editions and more

VISIT OUR WEBSITE
titanbooks.com

LIKE US ON FACEBOOK
facebook.com/titanbooks

FOLLOW US ON TWITTER AND INSTAGRAM
@TitanBooks

EMAIL US
readerfeedback@titanemail.com